PHANTOM PAINS

ALSO BY MISHELL BAKER

Borderline

MISHELL BAKER

PHANTOM PAINS

THE ARCADIA PROJECT 2

SAGA PRESS

LONDON SYDNEY **NEW YORK** TORONTO NEW DELHI

SAGA PRESS
AN IMPRINT OF SIMON & SCHUSTER, INC.

1230 AVENUE OF THE AMERICAS, NEW YORK, NEW YORK 10020

SAGA PRESS and colophon are trademarks of Simon & Schuster, Inc.

For information about special discounts for bulk purchases, please contact Simon & Schuster Special Sales at 1-866-506-1949 or business@simonandschuster.com.

The Simon & Schuster Speakers Bureau can bring authors to your live event. For more information or to book an event, contact the Simon & Schuster Speakers Bureau at 1-866-248-3049 or visit our website at www.simonspeakers.com.

Also available in a Saga Press paperback edition

The text for this book was set in Chapparal Pro.

Manufactured in the United States of America

First Saga Press hardcover edition March 2017

2 4 6 8 10 9 7 5 3 1

Library of Congress Cataloging-in-Publication Data
Names: Baker, Mishell, author. Title: Phantom pains / Mishell Baker. Description: First Edition. | New York : Saga Press, [2017] | Series: Arcadia project ; 2 Identifiers: LCCN 2016020852 | ISBN 9781481451925 (trade pbk.) | ISBN 9781481480178 (hardcover) | ISBN 9781481451932 (eBook) Classification: LCC PS3602.A58665 P48 2017 | DDC 813/.6—dc23
LC record available at https://lccn.loc.gov/2016020852

For Navah
Not just contractually—with all my heart.

1

Here's the thing about PTSD: it doesn't understand the rules. When I was seven, for example, I stepped in a nest of fire ants and ran screaming for two blocks, so crazed with pain and panic I didn't notice I'd run over a broken bottle until I saw the smears of red on my front steps. And still I spent every summer barefoot after that, at least until I got drunk at twenty-five and lost both feet in a seven-story fall.

Then there was that time I choked the life out of a bloodsucking mantis-woman who'd just killed two of my friends. I slept like a baby afterward. And yet somehow, four months later, when I picked up the office phone at Valiant Studios and heard the voice of a nineteen-year-old warlock, I turned into a sweating iceberg at my desk.

"Millie? Are you there?" Caryl Vallo said. That voice, that impossible middle-aged rasp that made you forget she couldn't buy beer. She sounded calm, so she must have had her familiar out. He was probably perched on her shoulder, tail wrapped amiably around her neck as she cradled the phone to her ear with a gloved hand.

"I'm here," I said.

"You seem to be settling in well at Valiant," she said in a tone that implied she couldn't have cared less, but four months ago I'd held her bloodstained hand on a nearby soundstage while she waited to die, so I knew differently.

"Well enough, I guess." I pushed back from the massive U-shaped desk Araceli and I shared, glancing over my shoulder at Inaya's closed office door. Araceli was out running an errand, but Inaya's door wasn't exactly soundproof, so honesty wasn't wise here. "I wasn't expecting to hear from you, Caryl. I've left how many messages now?"

"Twenty-eight, all told."

"Well, here you are, so let's not waste time on why you've been dodging my calls. Dare I hope you're actually going to come down to the studio?"

"I should like to come tomorrow, if that's agreeable." She always had the strangest way of talking.

"Can I ask what brought on this sudden change of heart?"

"I've just been informed that the head of the United States Arcadia Project and one of his senior agents are flying out from New Orleans for a visit. It would be helpful if Inaya could give them a glowing review of my performance as regional manager."

"Ah." I noted my disappointment without judging myself for it, as my shrink had taught me. "Would you like me to put you through to Inaya, then?"

"I don't need to disturb her," she said. "Just let me know when you'd be free to open up the soundstage. I can give her my report directly afterward."

I scooted my chair closer to my desk and lowered my voice. "I can go in there with you, if it will help."

There was a long silence on the other end of the line, and

I knew that even if she'd been in the room I would have had difficulty interpreting it.

"Yes," she said then. "I think that would be best. I'll have my familiar with me of course, so you don't need to worry that I'll— cause trouble."

"Caryl, the only person your feelings are any trouble to is you."

Another silence.

"Around two p.m. tomorrow would work," I said when I got tired of waiting for her reply. I tried to remember what her face looked like and found I couldn't. That was partly the fault of lingering brain damage, but mostly it was due to the extraordinary efforts she went to not to be memorable. "I've kind of missed you," I said.

"I've missed you too, Millie," she surprised me by saying. Then she ended the call, probably afraid she'd overload her familiar with all the feelings she was refusing to feel. That was the whole point of him: a miniature dragon-shaped carry-on bag for the traumatized mess that Dr. Davis would have called her Emotion Mind. I could have used a trick like that myself, but not being a warlock or a wizard, I had to deal with my mental health issues the old-fashioned way: by paying a lot of money to talk to people about them.

I put the phone back in its cradle and glanced at Inaya's door again, then at the assortment of Post-it notes that littered the fringes of my monitor. I reached for the pad to tear off yet another, scrawled CARYL WED OCT 14 2P.M. on it, and found an open spot to stick it.

My computer, of course, was installed with all manner of productivity software, but digital information had a stubborn way of slithering out of my consciousness. Something about the physical placement of paper helped me to remember, or at the very least to remember that I'd forgotten something and check the paper to see what it was.

Even with Araceli to handle most of the complicated stuff, if Inaya hadn't owed me a massive debt and needed someone on her team who knew about the Arcadia Project, I'd have been fired in the first week. I was pretty good at mobilizing people and getting answers from them, but the rest of my job was tailor-made to remind me hourly of my weaknesses: low stress tolerance, faulty memory, general misanthropy. I sometimes fantasized about quitting, but this job beat scrubbing deep fryers, and Dr. Davis said I needed to push myself, especially when it came to memory. Even a damaged brain has a remarkable ability to pave neurological detours around the rubble.

Still, getting a phone call from the woman who had fired me from far more interesting work wasn't helping endear this job to me.

I was under no circumstances allowed to bother Inaya if her door was closed, so I rose carefully from my desk chair and came out from behind the semi-oval shared workspace to get the blood flowing back down what remained of my left thigh. My AK prosthesis was designed for walking, not sitting. Inaya had offered to convert my half of the workstation into a standing desk, but I'd refused; my mind balked at that gesture of commitment.

When I felt a long, slow buzz in my pocket, I cringed; the only person who used my cell for voice calls was Parisa Naderi, showrunner of *Maneaters* and human wrecking ball. I considered just letting it go to voice mail, but then I worried she'd call Inaya directly, and I'd have to mop up the carnage. So I answered.

"I need to see Inaya," she said shortly. "Ten minutes should do it, as soon as you can get me in."

"You'll want to talk to Araceli about scheduling," I said, glancing over at her empty chair out of habit.

"Araceli said Inaya wasn't available today. So I'm calling you. Make it happen."

I suppressed the first five responses that came to mind, breathing in deeply through my nose. "As Inaya doesn't keep her own schedule, I'm afraid all I could do would be to call Araceli myself, and she would tell me the same thing. I do have some good news for you, though."

"Tell me it's about stage 13."

"It is."

"*Ya Bahá'u'l-Abhá!*" I had no idea what that meant, but it was unmistakably joyful, and it made me smile. I wasn't used to joy from Naderi.

"We've got an inspector coming tomorrow," I said. "She should be able to tell us what steps need to be taken to get the soundstage into usable condition."

"What time is she coming?"

There was no way I was telling her that. "She didn't say," I extemporized, which was technically true, since I'd been the one to set the time.

"I need you to call me the minute she gets here," Naderi said.

"If I do that, you'll stop working on that script and come meet us there, and not only will that put you further behind, but we can't afford the liability."

"Okay, first, I don't like this tone you're taking. Second, if it's safe enough for an inspector to go in, it's safe enough for me to go in too. Need me to sign a waiver or something? Just send it over."

Lady, there are no waivers that cover what you might find in there. "I'm sorry," I said. "I'm under very specific instructions. I know how frustrating this must be for you, but it's—"

"How old are you, twenty-five? Don't talk to me like I'm a child. Telling me how I feel, when you've never had something like this under you. Who did you sleep with to get a job here, if you don't understand this? Stage 8 is a closet. I'm making your biggest show in a *closet*. Valiant is a wobbly little fawn surrounded by lions, and right now I'm your only rifle. You really want to keep blowing me off when I ask for ammo?"

My skin was hot; my heart hammered in my chest. Inaya's office door opened just as Naderi's voice was reaching a crescendo. Inaya took one look at me and, from the expression on her face, must have guessed who was on the other end of my call. She ducked behind her door again as though Naderi might somehow sense her presence.

"I promise I will let you know the moment stage 13 is clear for you to enter," I said. "That's honestly all I can offer."

"You have to know how insulting this is. What a *personal* insult this is."

I really wasn't cut out for this job. I was a suicide survivor with an emotional-regulation disorder; what the hell had I been thinking, that this place would be calming?

"The safety of your cast and crew comes first," I said as evenly as I could, but my voice betrayed me by shaking. "I know stage 8 is slowing you down, but if something were to happen to one of your people in 13, it would set you back far worse. Please trust that Inaya isn't making some sort of—"

She'd hung up already. Damn it! I resisted the urge to pelt my phone across the room.

Inaya slowly peeked her head around the edge of the door. She'd been wearing her shoulder-length hair in twists lately to hide the break between relaxed ends and new growth; the style made her look even younger than she was. She could easily have given A-list starlets competition for romantic leads for another half-dozen years. For Inaya West, of all people, to completely retire from acting at thirty-eight to run a studio bordered on absurd. Then again, it hadn't exactly been Plan A.

"Is it safe?" she said. I couldn't tell how much of her cowed demeanor was for comic effect.

"For all I know she could be on her way over here," I said, heart still racing. "But probably not, since she hasn't turned in a script yet. I think she just needed to let off some steam."

Inaya's face softened a little. "I hate that you're stuck in the middle of this," she said. "I've tried to put her onto Araceli as much as I can, because of your . . ." She trailed off politely.

My borderline personality disorder. My brain damage. My amputated legs. Pick a card, any card. I was a controversial candidate to work a drive-thru, let alone provide meaningful assistance to one of the most powerful women in Hollywood. But I was the only one at Valiant besides Inaya who knew about her Echo: her muse, the source of her inspiration. I was also the only one who knew what was really wrong with stage 13. My job was a facade, but I needed to make it look real, and I was on the verge of failing even at that.

"Naderi would never bother with Araceli," I said. "She can't make Araceli cry."

"Oh, honey." Inaya shifted in the doorway. "You're seeing your—doctor tonight?"

"Yes." I had individual therapy on Tuesday nights, group on Thursdays; I'd been in formal dialectical behavior therapy more or less consistently for nine months, barring that crazy week in June I'd spent helping the Arcadia Project hunt down a fey viscount. "It's helping. It is. It's just going to take time. Anyway, the good news is that Caryl finally called me back."

"Caryl?" Inaya's tone was shocked. She came all the way out of the office and perched on the edge of my desk. "Caryl Vallo, from the fairyland people?"

"The Arcadia Project. Yes."

"Praise Jesus. I was starting to worry she was dead or something."

A flash: Caryl lying cold and gray on the floor, blood drying around her mouth, silver-haired David doing chest compressions. Oh wonderful. So *that* memory I could hold on to just fine.

"Nope, Caryl's very much alive. Just understandably reluctant to go back to that place."

"But I need to talk to her too," she said. "When are they going to let my angel come back?"

She meant her Echo, Baroness Foxfeather of the Seelie Court. I sighed and raked my hands through my hair, messing up the cute layered cut Inaya had paid for. She frowned and rose to ruffle it back into place as though she were straightening a stack of papers.

"Stop that," she said. "Every time I come out here you look like you just rolled out of bed."

"Sorry. Look, I got an e-mail two months ago that said there was some trouble processing her for reentry, something about hazardous conditions on their side? It's not like I have influence with them. I don't even work there anymore."

Inaya sighed and threw up her hands. "It would just make things a hell of a lot easier if I had an angel to come home to at the end of the day. Naderi knows exactly how to eat away at my sanity."

For sixteen years, it had been understood that Inaya was Naderi's subordinate, as one might expect when a starlet forms a friendship with a film auteur seven years her senior. When Inaya had become a studio head overnight and told her old pal over too many cocktails that "our lives would make a great HBO drama," what could she say when Naderi pitched an expanded, polished version of that idea right back to her a week later?

Inaya had figured *Maneaters* would be a brave failure. And although Naderi hadn't been shocked when the pilot eventually got a late pickup, even she hadn't expected it to carry every single demographic in its time slot. The two women had created a beautiful monster together, and now it was rampaging all over their friendship.

"Caryl will handle this," I said. "Once Naderi gets stage 13, you'll be best pals again. I promise."

"But Caryl hasn't been handling it," said Inaya. "I've been counting on you to answer all my Arcadia questions, and you're not exactly an expert. You were with them how long?"

"Technically they never officially hired me."

"And yet you're all I have. They've thrown me to the wolves."

"Be patient," I said, aware of the irony of this advice coming from me. "Caryl will be here tomorrow; she'll make sure there's no bad juju lingering on the stage, and if there is, she'll walk me through getting rid of it. We'll fill in the hole in the floor and voilà."

"I hope you're right," she said. "I'm about to lose it. I did not expect to be doing this on my own."

I winced; that part was my fault. She'd originally had two partners; I'd killed one of them and driven the other into retirement. Inaya West was one of the strongest people I'd ever met, but I was pretty sure no one was strong enough for this mess.

"You're not on your own," I said. "Remember, even when your Echo isn't here, she's still watching out for you."

She smiled, the tension on her face easing a little.

I had an Echo too, technically. Somewhere on the other side of that invisible barrier that separated our worlds was my fey soul mate, a faun named Claybriar that I'd rescued from the between-worlds void that still yawned darkly at the heart of stage 13. But all the steel hardware holding my shattered ribs and skull and limbs together acted as an arcane signal scrambler; his magic couldn't get to me no matter how close we were. Unlike Inaya, I really was on my own.

"Just hang in there," I said. "Things are about to get a lot easier for everyone."

It's pretty hilarious how wrong I can be sometimes.

2

It had only been four months, but I almost didn't recognize her. She wore gloves, of course, but also jeans—*jeans*—and a loose, light sweater, tawny and rust, dangerously close to actual colors. She'd cut off all her hair just before Gloria's funeral, some archaic mourning gesture maybe, and there was something very 1920s about the way its dark ripples lay close against her head.

I was half paralyzed by the enviable *elegance* of her, even in jeans, a poise I'd have found impossible at nineteen. Suddenly my pantsuit felt shabby.

"Millie," she said with her usual flat expression, holding out her silk-sheathed hand when I finally managed to rise and come out from behind my desk. Caryl always wore gloves, because skin-to-skin contact drove her a little batty. As I shook her hand, her hazel-gray eyes wandered off somewhere over my shoulder. "It would appear that I am overwhelmed with joy at seeing you again."

She must have been watching her familiar. I couldn't see him, but apparently six formative years in an alternate universe had done things to Caryl's eyes that let her see spellwork without fey lenses.

"Hey, Elliott," I said in the general direction Caryl was looking. I'd always enjoyed annoying her by treating the mostly imaginary dragon as though it were sentient. I felt a faint tingling sensation pass by my left ear—he'd flown by.

"Shall we?" Caryl said with a tilt of her head toward the door.

I patted the heavy key ring clipped to my belt, giving it a jingle. "Let's."

As we took the stairs down to the lobby, she watched the way I descended step over step at a relatively normal pace and gave me a raised eyebrow. "You're hardly touching the rail," she said.

"I'm a lot slower going up," I said, taking a compliment with my usual lack of grace.

Outside, perfectly parallel to and equidistant from the white lines in the parking lot, was Caryl's midnight-blue SUV. I smiled a little wistfully as we walked past it, remembering the day she'd made it disappear.

"How are things?" I said to fill the silence. We didn't need to confer about where we were headed; it loomed like an event horizon.

"Which things?"

"Arcadia Project things."

"Every day is full of things, Millie. I wouldn't know where to start."

"How is everyone at Residence Four?"

Caryl paused. "Residence Four is a problem," she said.

"Still shorthanded? I thought by now you'd have replaced Gloria and everyone."

Her eyes flicked toward me; aside from me there were two people missing, and the name I hadn't said hung between us. Teo. My partner that week, and Caryl's best friend.

To my relief, she didn't say the name either, and her eyes slid away. "I have not found suitable replacements. Hiring is always difficult. And Tjuan has been too ill to work, meaning that Phil and Stevie—"

"Tjuan's sick? What's wrong with him?"

She glanced at me again and said nothing.

"Right, I'm sorry, none of my business. I'm just—it's not serious, is it? Do you mean physically ill or—?"

Caryl shook her head. "A relapse of sorts, brought on by the events here."

Tjuan had been there when they'd died too. Gloria had been his partner. "I'm so sorry," I said. "Tell him I send my sympathies."

Not that he'd care; we hadn't been close. I had no idea what his diagnosis was. Everyone at the Arcadia Project had some sort of sketchy mental health history, but we weren't supposed to talk about it unless people felt like sharing. Tjuan had not.

The soundstage blocked the sun as we approached, throwing us into its shadow. I shivered and wished I hadn't left my jacket hanging over the back of my chair.

"So it's just Phil and Stevie then," I said, unclipping my key ring from my belt and sorting through it.

"And Song," Caryl reminded me.

I flinched a little at the Residence manager's name; I'd treated her pretty badly and for no good reason. "Agents, I mean. Two people to manage everyone coming through that Gate."

"We've diverted some of the travelers to LA5 in Burbank, but it's still not going well. Phil has risen to the occasion fairly well, but Stevie isn't suited for some of her new responsibilities, and there is only so much one man can do."

"I don't suppose National is coming to help?"

"Certainly not. They only appointed me in the first place because they had no other options, and they've been looking for an excuse to replace me ever since. This visit is clearly part of the twice-yearly lockdown the Project does before the—" She hesitated. "As you're not an employee, suffice it to say that at this time of year, any potential security weaknesses are shored up or eliminated. It seems I have been identified as such a weakness."

"Is there anything I can do?"

"No."

We were standing at the bottom of a short flight of steps now, looking up at the door that had nearly killed her. It wasn't cursed anymore; the excess iron in my body had ruptured the lethal spellwork when I'd touched it back in June. But the memory was fresh.

"You saved my life by killing her," Caryl said, sounding bored. She always sounded bored. "I never thanked you."

"You were a little busy," I said. "Plus, you'd specifically ordered me *not* to kill her. I don't think you were in a thanking mood." I climbed the steps, leading with my only remaining knee, and Caryl followed.

I unlocked the door and pushed it open, then switched on the floodlights. Rather than build an entirely new studio, Valiant had moved into a derelict one in Manhattan Beach, tearing down only those buildings that were beyond repair. Stage 13 was one of the oldest remaining structures; its lights flickered fitfully for a full three minutes before settling into a dull, steady glow.

"The paintings are still here," Caryl observed, looking around. The walls of the soundstage were covered with a gorgeous mural that made it look like a desert landscape. It had been painted by iconic, now-retired director David Berenbaum and was probably worth a fortune; Inaya and I had gone several rounds about whether or not it would all have to go.

"According to Inaya," I said, "no one's come in here since David heard some weird whispers during cleanup. We've been waiting for you to give the all clear."

"I have been seeing Dr. Davis again," said Caryl, not a direct response but a sort of oblique apology. "For post-traumatic stress."

I was stunned. "She never said anything."

"Of course she wouldn't."

"We have the same therapist? That's kind of awesome."

Caryl tugged on the cuff of one of her gloves, then looked around. "The good news is, I see absolutely no traces of lingering spellwork. All the same, I'd like to take a look at the Gate. Has anyone damaged it on this end to prevent further attempts at transit?"

"No, we haven't touched it."

"I'd be alarmed by its remaining open, but the census hasn't shown any activity, and it's fairly well locked down on the Arcadian side due to—recent unrest on that side of the border."

"No one can get in the building on this side," I reassured her. "Only I have the key." I shuddered and followed her deeper in.

When we'd been here before, the Gate had been disguised as a well in the center of an 1850s-style ghost town. Now it was a large, perfectly circular hole in the floor of a cavernous empty room. The buildings, the sand, the decaying bell tower; all of it had been in our minds, suggested by the murals and a few painted cardboard flats long since taken down. Real Hollywood magic.

Caryl and I approached the hole. The crates that had been stacked around it to keep people from stumbling in, as well as the crank used for lowering a platform into it, were gone; David had apparently disposed of them before pissing off to an emu ranch. The floodlights penetrated only about ten feet down into the darkness.

"I can't figure out how we'd disassemble it," I said. "Is there even a bottom?"

"Certainly," said Caryl. "The trapped fey were sitting on it, remember? The shaft is a perfectly normal cylindrical shape; the illusion of infinite depth comes from the fact that the space bounded by the circumference is interdimensional, and the visual cortex cannot process the paradox. Removing a single piece would create enough difference between the two structures to keep them from merging along the v-axis and transform it into an ordinary hole in the ground."

"Right, of course."

If she noticed my sarcasm, she paid no attention to it, circling the well and looking down it meditatively.

I was about to ask her another question when the floodlights flickered and the muscles along my spine tightened. I had the sudden dismaying thought that Naderi had followed us in, and I turned.

Teo stood there, half in shadow.

You hear, sometimes, about being "frozen" with fear. I'd had no idea what it meant until that moment. My skin went icy; I was paralyzed; speaking was impossible.

There was no moment where I mistook him for living; I could see the mural behind him through the slouch of his shoulders. He held his pocketknife clutched in his right hand, its blade dark and dripping. His left wrist spurted erratic pulses of blood. Stringy hair and shadow veiled his eyes; his lips were gray and pressed thin.

I tried to say his name, but my muscles still weren't working. I managed to feebly move the arm nearest to Caryl, to clutch the edge of her sweater and tug a little.

She turned to look at me and instantly stepped back. "Millie, what's happening?"

I weakly pointed toward the apparition; he was about fifteen feet away, still motionless.

"What is it?" asked Caryl, looking where I was looking. "Millie, whatever you're seeing, it isn't real. Something must have—"

"Teo," I said. "It's Teo's ghost."

"There are no such things as ghosts, Millie. The Arcadia Project has thoroughly investigated all reports of—"

"I'm looking right at him!"

Teo dropped his knife. I heard it clatter to the floor, almost felt the vibration in the floorboards. He swayed slightly, as though about to fall, and my fear was replaced with a sudden rush of pained tenderness. I started toward him but felt Caryl's gloved hand close around my elbow.

"There is a spell cast upon you," she said, releasing me as soon as I'd stopped. "Psychic spellwork; I can see its fabric. What I cannot see, however, is a caster. Another of Vivian's metaspells?"

Vivian was the mantis-woman I'd killed. She could do some crazy fractal shit with magic, as I had unfortunate cause to know.

"But no," Caryl continued. "There was no fabric here before, not anywhere. Unless it's somehow hidden in the well."

"It's *Teo!*"

"Close your eyes," she said.

I did and instantly saw what she meant. *Teo was still there.* As though painted on the back of my fucking eyelids. I started to cry. "Make it stop, Caryl."

"I can't," she said. "You can't either, as there is no physical anchor point for the fabric, nothing for you to touch. Perhaps if you leave the area—"

She didn't have to say that twice; I bolted for the door.

"Millie!"

Not Caryl's voice calling after me, but Teo's. It stopped me in my tracks. It sounded just like him, reverberated the way his voice would have in the empty space.

Somehow he was still fifteen feet in front of me, head bowed, arms slack.

I stared through him at the soundstage door, and then my gaze moved to the posse of mounted cowboys painted on the wall beside it, the ones a spell had made me think were riding me down four months ago. *It's just like that,* I tried to tell my panicked self. *It's not real.*

"Don't leave," said Teo softly toward the floor.

"I'm sorry," I said aloud, weak and hoarse.

"It's not Teo," said Caryl's voice behind me. "Teo is gone."

My sadness had now completely overwhelmed my fear, not that it was a vast improvement.

Teo slowly lifted his head, and the light showed me his eyes, the sleepless shadows under them. "Everyone always leaves," he said.

"They fired me," I choked out. "I had no choice."

"Not then," he said. "Here. You left me here, bleeding out."

I sucked in a breath like I'd plunged my arm into ice water.

"Remember that day in the car?" he said. "You told me you were different. That you weren't going anywhere."

"Oh God," I whispered, squeezing my eyes shut, for all the good that did. "Teo, I meant it. I did. I wanted—"

Words abandoned me. I felt the way I imagined Elliott feeling when Caryl's emotions started to overload him. There were a thousand tiny cracks in me about to give way, and when the pressure broke, it would end me.

"It's too late," I finally said. "I can't do anything for you now."

"Let me in," he said.

My eyes opened. That wasn't a very Teo thing to say at all. My skepticism was like a breeze dispersing a fog.

Then I felt a hand on the back of my neck, and I screamed.

3

Even as I whirled around, I realized the hand on my neck had been warm, and that it was Caryl's.

She'd taken off one of her gloves, and she stood there with tears streaming down her cheeks, her eyeliner smudged, her face as open as a child's. She'd dismissed Elliott, or he'd broken.

She reached for me again, put her bare hand to my cheek, on the good side with all the unscarred nerve endings. It wasn't magic, but it may as well have been. I could still see Teo fifteen feet in front of me, but the warmth of her palm against my skin made me feel I was listening to two songs at once.

It was enough. As though the phantom had been feeding on my undivided misery, it vanished.

"Thank God," I said. "It's gone. How did you do that?"

Her eyes slid away from me, but she left her hand on my cheek. "I didn't expect that it would end the spell; I just—skin contact is calming."

"It doesn't seem to be calming you," I said, looking down at her.

"It's difficult for me," she said, her voice even rougher than usual. "Everything is difficult for me."

"I know," I said, taking her hand from my cheek and holding it. "I know, sweetie. Did Elliott break?"

"I dismissed him so that he would not."

"That means you can get him right back. It's okay. Let's go outside." I reached out with my free hand to wipe the tears from her cheeks, and she closed her eyes.

"I love you," she said.

I resisted the instinctive shock of warmth that tried to wipe out my higher thought and looked away, blowing hair from my face. "You're going to be so embarrassed when you sober up." I tugged at her hand, leading her to the door.

"I do, though," she persisted as we left the soundstage. "I didn't say it when I had the chance. If I had, would you have come back?"

"Caryl, don't," I said. "You are nineteen fucking years old, if that, and I am a really poor choice for a first crush."

The fresh air was more than welcome; it was a gorgeous crisp day. Even though the seasons don't change in L.A. quite the same way they do back east, there's still a palpable shift in the atmosphere in October; a subtle autumnal clarity. I didn't want to sit down, but I wanted her to sit down, so we sat. She fell against me, but when I put my arms around her, she tensed and pulled away.

"Sorry," I said. "Your claustrophobia thing."

"Don't be sorry," she said, sliding her hands into her hair as though her head were about to burst. "I'm such a mess, I can't—"

"I know, sweetie. Call Elliott back."

"I don't want to."

"What? Caryl, you have to. You can't figure out what to do about the soundstage if you're freaking out."

"You have to listen to me," she said with the kind of profound urgency only teenagers and Borderlines can feel. "I really do love you." She searched my eyes, and then hers brimmed over again. "But you don't. I thought maybe you did."

Please let this be a really surreal, awful dream. "Caryl, I've got borderline personality disorder. Even if I did return your feelings, this would not be some sunset happy ending. It's going to take years of therapy, probably, before I can trust myself not to abuse you."

"You're evading the question," she said, sounding a little more like her adult self despite the wobble in her voice.

"I can't think about you like that," I said. "You're a child."

"I'll be twenty in January."

"That's exactly the sort of thing a child would say."

"If I were older? If I weren't—broken?"

I shrank against the stair railing. "God, Caryl, don't do this! You're going to force the issue right here? *Now?* After *that?*"

That silenced her for a moment, but then she set her jaw. "Just say it. Don't treat me like a child. Say you don't love me."

Before I even quite knew what I was doing I seized her head between my hands, holding her at arm's length.

"I will *never* say that," I said. "I killed someone for hurting you. So *shut up.* If you pushed me, I'd probably sleep with you. But then I'd treat you like shit and leave you, because that's what I do. So don't put your fragile little eggs in my fucked-up basket, all right?"

She tried to draw away, looking frightened, and I released her.

"I'm sorry," I said, putting my hands in my lap. I was suddenly acutely aware of how awkwardly my prosthetic legs were sprawled on the steps.

Caryl began to murmur unsteadily under her breath in a language I didn't understand: the dark, nauseating cadence of the Unseelie tongue. A breath of foul air swept over us, and then her face became expressionless. She wiped the last traces of moisture carefully from her cheeks and lashes.

"I apologize for that," she said. "I've been having trouble with the Elliott construct recently. It may be a side effect of the trauma in June."

It could give a girl whiplash, watching Caryl switch back and forth from child to adult. Now she was all elegance again, except for the smudged eyeliner. As irony would have it, I found her suddenly and devastatingly sexy.

"What kind of trouble?" I asked.

"My emotions seem almost to be rebelling against constraint. The construct has begun to display behavior that makes no sense."

Normally the little illusory dragon served as a visual indicator of what she was feeling. If she was sad, he drooped. If she was happy, he flew in exuberant loops.

"What kind of things is he doing?"

"He gets agitated around Tjuan, for example. Or sometimes goes completely haywire and attacks me."

"That's disturbing."

"To say the least."

"Is there some kind of expert in familiars, someone who could help you sort it out?"

"I consulted with Mr. Spielberg, but—"

"Mr. Spielberg. Steven."

"Yes, Steven; it was the very devil to get a meeting with him, but he's the only other practitioner on this side of the country.

He said the problem likely isn't with the spellwork; it's with my emotions. He's the one who suggested I seek therapy."

"How very . . ." I couldn't think of an adjective.

"Indeed," she said dryly. "Now, about the soundstage."

"Right, that."

"What just happened is, as far as I can tell, impossible. The fabric of psychic spellwork is unmistakable; it shows in the eyes of the person being enchanted."

"If I was enchanted, who did the enchanting?"

"That is the puzzle. We were alone in the soundstage, and there were no wards left upon it. No fabric in which Vivian or anyone else might have hidden a metaspell."

"We were standing by the well, though, and couldn't see all the way down. Could someone have been down there?"

"You remember what it was like down there for the fey we rescued. You've touched a Gate yourself. I can't imagine that anything would be capable of casting a spell while in contact with it. I suppose it's possible that there could be a ward hidden *inside* the Gate that is casting metaspells. But I have never heard of anyone anchoring a spell to a Gate. I suppose of all the theories it's the most plausible."

"In any case," I said, "it looks like Naderi's stuck in stage 8 for the foreseeable future."

Caryl gave me a look. "Is that truly your priority?"

"It's the job I haven't been fired from yet."

She gave a little sigh of concession. "Once we destroy the Gate, it should take care of the problem, but that will require approval from London. Could you get free of work tomorrow to come and meet Lamb? His plane gets in at around eleven a.m., so he should be ready to meet with you by the afternoon."

"Who's Lamb exactly?"

"Alvin Lamb; he runs National Headquarters in New Orleans. My boss, I suppose you'd say. He's bringing one of his senior agents, Tamika Durand by name. I don't know her. I imagine they are mostly coming to look for excuses to fire me, but I hope they will see stage 13 as the more pressing issue if you can explain to them what you experienced."

"This could be a good chance to show them how capable you are," I said.

Caryl looked at me flatly. "That is precisely what I am afraid of."

I didn't get home until after eight, thanks to some idiot who T-boned some other idiot right on the bus route. When I finally got back, my next-door neighbor Zach must have recognized my lopsided rhythm on the stairs that zigzagged up the outside of the apartment building, because his front door opened as I passed it on the way to mine.

"Hey," he said.

The smell of pot smoke wafted from his apartment, and I wrinkled my nose. That was how we'd met, actually; I'd come over to tell him to knock that shit off before I puked up my actual guts.

"Sorry," he said when he saw my face. "I thought maybe you weren't coming home tonight. Don't worry—it's already put out."

"Put out?" I echoed with a smirk. He grinned sheepishly, smoothing his thinning hair in an almost endearing display of false shyness.

"You must be tired," he said, still lingering in his open door-way. I couldn't help but think how weirdly domestic it was that he'd hurried to snuff out his evening's indulgence at the sound of my footsteps.

"Shut up and come on," I said. "If a girl ever needed her mind off a day's work it's today."

"You want to talk?"

"Not even a little."

Zach didn't say *good* out loud, but I inferred it heavily. Our relationship, such as it was, revolved around convenience and giving a complete mutual lack of shits.

It had been going on since two weeks after I moved in, and over the last few months it had settled into an absurdly comfortable routine. Lights off, clothes off, minds elsewhere. He'd do the kind of fabulous tongue tricks a guy learns when girls aren't likely to stick around on account of his charm, and then I'd zone out sleepily while he slipped on a condom and knocked himself out. Literally—the man was comatose afterward every time, so sending him home was never an option until the next morning. I was lucky he lived next door, or I'd have had to feed him breakfast, and then conversations would have been needed.

I normally go off like a 1911 pistol at the least opportunity, but that night something just wasn't working right. Teo would keep popping into my head and killing the moment, or I'd think of Caryl and feel sick about it.

It went on so long Zach actually stopped to ask what was up, and I told him my mind was wandering. He told me to fucking focus, which made me laugh, and then I solved the problem by remembering the way Inaya had touched my hair at work and imagining it escalating into a hot make-out session on my desk. Off I went, and then Zach was on top of me thinking about whatever he thought about while he finished up. About a minute and a half later I was drifting off to the gentle, oceanic sound of his snores.

I still didn't know his last name.

"I need to take off after lunch," I told Inaya the next morning as she swept by my desk on the way to her office.

"I beg your pardon?" Inaya wasn't wearing sunglasses, but she looked at me as though she were peering over the top of a pair. "You did not just say that. You know Araceli and I are in meetings from two thirty straight through four. Who's going to take Mason's call?"

I felt a hint of shame, not for staring into the eyes of the person I'd fantasized about the night before—I was used to that—but for the swooping thrill of relief I felt when I realized I would not have to pretend cordiality toward Australia's most misogynistic talent agent. It occurred to me yet again that I was terrible at my job.

"I'll figure it out," I said. "But I'm not asking leave to get my teeth cleaned or something; I have to go to an urgent meeting at Residence Four."

Inaya hesitated, from what I presumed was unease. She'd been to Residence Four once—the time she'd let us onto this very lot in the dead of night to free the captive fey from sound-stage 13—and she had not left with the best impression of the Arcadia Project's operations. Residence Four was basically a loony bin-slash-interdimensional portal disguised as a crumbling Victorian house in the North University Park district near USC. Inaya was staunchly Christian, and despite her love for her Echo, the whole magical-parallel-world thing still gave her the screaming creeps.

"Some people are flying in from National Headquarters," I explained. "Residence Four had bedrooms open for them to stay in, what with two of the residents dying and one getting fired. So that's where they're headed once they fly in. I'm supposed to meet them there."

"You don't think it'll—mess you up?"

I stared at her for a second. That was not what I'd thought her hesitation was about. "I'm pretty sure the worst is over," I said. "If I were going to fall apart, I'd have fallen apart after seeing my ex-partner's ghost."

"Do you really think it was his ghost?" Her voice was hushed, her eyes soft. I didn't like playing the pity card, but pity looked good on her.

"Caryl says ghosts aren't real," I said. "Given the amount of stuff she insists *is* real, I find it hard to believe she'd be needlessly skeptical. She said it was a spell that made me think I was seeing him. We just couldn't figure out where it was coming from."

"And that's what this meeting's about. It'll lead to us getting the soundstage back?"

"That's right."

"But it also means you're not here when Mason calls, and that contract is already on thin ice."

"Look. Javier owes me one; I'll have him take the call." Javier was Parisa Naderi's assistant, and Inaya had cheerfully forced me to become buddies with him over the past couple months. "There's no guarantee Mason will even call this afternoon, and if he does, he'll be happier talking to a man anyway."

"Javier doesn't know the whole situation."

"I'll fill him in. It'll be fine."

Inaya made a sound of frustrated acquiescence. "On one condition," she said. "You're going to treat Javier to lunch today, and while you're over there picking him up you're going to figure out what to tell Parisa about the soundstage. In person."

4

When I was finally released for lunch, I made my way down the stairs and out of the gleaming glass-fronted office building, grumbling curses under my breath. There was a golf cart parked waiting for me at the curb, one of the few concessions I'd allowed for my disability. I didn't have the money or the guts to have a regular car altered so I could drive it, but I was pretty handy with a golf cart. I started it up and waved at security guards as I passed them heading west; it served me well to be on friendly terms with security, since I knew I might have to ask them to overlook some weird-ass stuff.

Valiant Studios was a constant work in progress; the idea was eventually to replace all the old 1940s and '50s buildings with sleek new construction like the building I'd just left, all glass and open courtyards to take advantage of the climate in Manhattan Beach. But for the time being, people like Naderi were working out of cramped little bungalows with prisonlike windows and touchy plumbing. It didn't do a lot to improve anyone's mood.

There were, thankfully, no stairs. The sidewalk led right up to the dun-colored door, and behind that was the cramped reception area and Javier, the wry thirtysomething I was here to see.

"Hey, Millie," he said when I entered. "You're early." I couldn't blame him for looking a little disconcerted; since I represented Inaya, I usually brought drama.

"I'm supposed to talk to Naderi before we go," I said, confirming his suspicions.

Javier gave me a stern look, narrowing his kohl-rimmed eyes. "She's writing."

"The sooner I'm done with her, the sooner we can go to lunch."

Javier arched a brow at me, then sat back at his desk with an exaggerated show of ignoring my presence. I just stood there checking my text messages, because I knew it would drive him crazy.

One from Caryl: *3pm please* was all it said.

I texted her back *Can CB visit* and fourteen smiley faces. If I was going to be getting mixed up in Arcadia Project stuff again, Caryl might as well allow my Echo to see me while I was at the Residence. It didn't do me any good in the arcane sense, but he was a good guy and cared about me, and I hadn't seen him since I'd pulled him out of that pit in stage 13 four months ago. I needed to know he was okay.

Javier let out a stormy exhale and picked up his desk phone, stabbing some buttons. "Parisa, Millie wants to talk to you," he said. Then, "I have *no* idea. But she's not taking me to lunch until you do. She's just standing here."

A door to his left opened and Parisa Naderi appeared. Her wildly curly mane of lead-and-sable hair was piled atop her head in a sort of exploded ponytail, and a pair of red cat's-eye glasses sat perched atop her regal nose. She looked pissed off, but I'd never seen her look any other way.

"Hi," I said. "Let's talk about stage 13."

"Not unless you're about to hand me the keys," she said. She'd learned English at age ten; her speech had a flavor too subtle to be associated with her native Farsi unless you knew what you were listening for.

"There's nothing I'd love more, believe me," I said. "Does 'progress' count as good news?"

"Come back to my office," she said. "Javier gets cranky when I yell at people in front of him."

Fantastic. I followed her to her office, which was at the far end of the bungalow. It was littered with pillows and stained-glass baubles and weird lion-themed art that showed a peculiar lack of taste for a two-time Oscar nominee. The tablet she wrote the show on had been left sitting facedown on a pile of pillows; apparently she'd sent it to the corner to think about what it had done.

"Just exactly how successful does this show need to become," she said to me between clenched teeth, "before Inaya stops treating it like Fredo fucking Corleone?"

I lifted my hands in the universal gesture of surrender and declined to remind Naderi that a month ago she had made everyone at the studio promise to enforce her vow to avoid foul language. Like Inaya, Naderi was religious; she just wasn't very good at it.

"This situation sucks," I agreed. "I know it does. But what do you expect Inaya to do, exactly? She can't get the stage up to code herself, and it's taken us this long just to get an inspector to come and look at the place. There's a problem."

"What problem?"

"A huge hole in the floor, for one."

"So fix it."

"It's not that simple," I improvised. "There's all kinds of crap stored in the basement that has to be sorted through, and now we think there might be something living down there."

"*What?*" Naderi made a sound that might have been a laugh. "Like what? Rats? The Loch Ness Monster?"

"I didn't hang around to make friends."

"So call an exterminator."

The word made me cringe a little, because it made me think of Vivian, the woman I'd killed. Among other things, her human alter ego had apparently left behind an international pest control empire, and what little I knew about the Arcadia Project's recent activities seemed to involve fruitless attempts to sniff out her conspirators at the company.

"I'm going to meet with some specialists this afternoon," I told Naderi, "to find out the safest way to go about getting down there and cleaning it all out."

"Ugh!" Naderi paced the floor, scratching viciously at the back of her hair and pulling loose a few more ringleted strands. "Can you please keep this out of the press? If my actors hear about this—"

"There is nothing I want less."

"PR aside, if we can't get in there within about two weeks, I'm going to have to pull the show off the air."

"Wait, what?" Now she had my attention.

"I can't keep making the show in 8. I'm carrying this whole damned studio, and I'm in the smallest stage on the lot."

"That's not Inaya's fault. The pickup came so late—"

"It's not a threat; it's a fact. Every week we have to tear down old standing sets to make room for new ones, then tear down the new ones to put the old ones back up. We're losing time.

Directors aren't making their days; everything gets pushed back and back and back. We're going to have to take a hiatus just to catch back up."

"I know you don't like green screens, but at this point—"

"If I'd known from the beginning I'd be stuck in 8, maybe that would be an option, but she kept promising 13, and now it's too late. There are no effects people available."

"Maybe I can swing something. McGarry's already got a meeting coming up with MDE about *Quantum 8*, and MDE's in the process of buying Wendigo. Maybe I can waylay them, talk them into sending someone from Wendigo about *Maneaters*."

"I don't want Wendigo; I want stage 13."

"Then I'll get it for you. Just please, not another word about hiatus. Inaya will fire me and burn down the studio. Trust me when I say there is nothing I want more than a cleaned-up stage 13. I will make it happen."

"See that you do," said Naderi. Her tone was frosty, but some of the murder had gone out of her eyes, so I counted it as a win.

With that visit out of the way, my dread of it was replaced by dread of returning to Residence Four.

I had only lived there for a week, but like summer camp, the time had a strange, dilated quality that made it feel like its own era. I'd made friends and enemies, and then made enemies of my friends, and then I'd seen three people die.

Mostly I'd buried the trauma in some kind of mental tar pit, but thinking about the house I'd stayed in during that time brought it bubbling back up. At lunch I could hardly summon an appetite, and the way I picked at my chicken Caesar salad started Javier on a rant about body issues that I mostly tuned out. As soon as I'd gotten him prepared to handle Mason's call, I excused myself, called a cab, and had a security guy drop me off at the studio entrance.

At this time of day it was a forty-five-minute drive from Manhattan Beach to the North University Park historic district, and I ended up feeling a little carsick in the back of the cab. I leaned my forehead against the window, letting the cool glass soothe me, and closed my eyes.

When we arrived, I paid and got out but waited until the cab had driven away to actually turn and look at the place.

It was pretty much as I remembered it, though I could swear that the deep bluish-green of its paint had faded half a shade. Something about the autumn air and the leaves that choked the rain gutters made it look even more as though the huge Queen Anne–style house might be haunted. I knew now what I hadn't known the first time I'd seen it: that at the very top of that peculiar tower on the right side was a portal to another world.

Teo's battered bronze Honda Civic was still parked in the driveway; it looked clean, and there were only a few leaves resting on the roof. Someone had been driving it, caring for it. I averted my eyes.

There was no easy way across the weed-infested lawn, but I'd gotten pretty good with my prosthetic legs in the last four months, and I had only the briefest fleeting wish for the cane I'd used in the summer. I hoped Caryl would answer the door, because Tjuan and I weren't exactly the best of friends, the Residence manager was (perhaps justifiably) afraid of me, and I didn't know the other two residents at all. I knocked on the door and waited.

When it opened, I found myself looking down ever so slightly at a man with a silver goatee and mischievous peaked eyebrows. I'd never seen him before in my life.

"You must be Millie," he said. "I'm Alvin Lamb, head of the United States Arcadia Project."

"Caryl mentioned that you were coming," I said a bit numbly as Alvin stepped aside to let me enter the house. "This must be serious business."

The battered grand piano was in the same spot in the two-story living room, but someone had rearranged the couches, and I didn't recognize any of the other stuff littering the room other than Manager Song's hydroponic herb garden. It always looked like some sort of bizarre garage sale in there. Monty, the gaunt one-eared tortoiseshell cat, was on the piano bench with his paws tucked under him and his tail wrapped around himself. He greeted me with a slow blink of his eyes, and I blinked back.

"We're meeting upstairs in room six," Alvin said, without addressing my comment. "Are you all right on the stairs?"

"I lived in room six when I was here," I said.

Alvin gave a tight little nod that suggested he would rather not discuss my short tenure here and the chaos I'd been involved in (but to be fair, mostly not caused). He politely slowed his pace to match mine as I ascended the broad hardwood staircase, my right leg doing the work and my left leg trailing behind. I ignored the twinge in my lower back; my body was basically held together with duct tape and paper clips, and hardly a day went by when something didn't hurt.

I deliberately kept my head turned to the right as I reached the top of the stairs, but I could still *feel* Teo's room at the other end of the hall, could almost smell the funk of new-adult angst, dirty laundry, hair product, and a whisper of stale cigarette smoke. If I'd expected to run into his ghost anywhere, it would have been here.

My old door lay at the hall's dead end; someone had fixed the brass six so it no longer looked like a nine, and for some reason I took it as a personal affront. They'd been in the process of changing it into an office before I'd even finished wrapping up the Vivian situation, and now it looked as though it had never been anything else.

Caryl was seated at a long table in the center of the octagonal room; the Roman shades were pulled up to let sunlight stream in through the five huge windows. Sitting across from Caryl was a business-casual black woman with a dour expression. Caryl feigned a polite smile of greeting—she clearly had Elliott out—but her companion didn't bother.

"Millie," said Alvin, "this is Tamika Durand, one of the senior agents at the New Orleans office."

"Good to meet you," I said. Tamika just made a little *hm* sound that dripped disapproval. This was off to a fantastic start.

"And this," said Alvin, gesturing toward a laptop at the head of the table, "is Dame Belinda Barker, head of the Arcadia Project, who has been so good as to join us remotely from London despite the late hour."

"How do you do?" said the woman on the laptop screen. I couldn't see her because of the glare, but her voice was clipped and clear as ice; apparently the only thing about this house that functioned properly was the Wi-Fi.

"What an honor," I said, a heavy feeling settling into the pit of my stomach as I took a seat next to Caryl. Serious business indeed.

5

"Have you all been waiting long?" I said as I sat down at the long table. "I was told the meeting was at three."

"That's right," said Alvin. He had a light, chipper sort of voice, but it sounded more like habit than genuine good cheer. "The three of us have been discussing other issues. You're right on time."

I knew scanning Caryl's face to read her mood would be useless, so I cleared my throat and looked at Alvin and Tamika, who had positioned themselves opposite her at the table as though it were an interrogation.

"I assume you want to hear about what happened on stage 13 yesterday?" I said.

"Your version," said Tamika, her tone lending weight to the words.

"All right." I shifted in my chair. "Caryl came to the studio yesterday. I let her into the soundstage, and we went to go look down the well, or what used to be the well. As we were looking, I got kind of a strange feeling on the back of my neck and—"

"What kind of feeling?" Tamika asked. "And where on your neck exactly?"

"Uh—it wasn't that specific. Just that sort of crawly feeling you get when you think you're being watched. I turned around and saw Teo. Thought I saw him, at any rate."

"Mateo Salazar," Tamika clarified in the laptop's direction. I glanced at Alvin. For the Boss of the Entire Nation, he sure seemed fine with Tamika doing all the talking.

"Yes," I said. "I was partnered with him during the time I—"

"We know," said Tamika in a tone that suggested she had been *thoroughly* briefed on the many disastrous breaches of protocol I'd racked up during those few days. "Continue."

"I pointed him out to Caryl, and she said he wasn't really there, that it was a spell. She could see it in my eyes."

Tamika made her little *hm* noise again.

"I sort of freaked out, so Caryl—comforted me as best she could, and after I'd calmed down a little, Teo—the spell—just suddenly went away."

"Caryl 'comforted' you?" said Tamika.

I found myself unnerved by this line of questioning. "She took off one of her gloves and put a hand on my face to sort of steady me." I felt my cheeks warming.

Alvin spoke quietly to Tamika. "Skin-to-skin contact has been shown to ameliorate the effects of psychic spellwork or Gate shock."

Tamika was still looking at me, holding me with her keen dark eyes. "You were comfortable with this?" she asked me. Somehow I *knew* she was implying that Caryl and I were lovers. My face burned even hotter, but this time not from embarrassment.

"Caryl has never been anything but consummately professional, even when under extreme emotional duress." The fact that

I suddenly seemed to have borrowed her vocabulary probably wasn't helping my case.

"Millie," said Caryl.

"No, you heard her," I protested. "Was I comfortable with you touching me? As though you molested me or something. I had just seen a *ghost* for fuck's sake."

"*Millie,*" she said again, sternly, with just a flicker of her eyes toward the laptop.

From my angle the head of the Arcadia Project was little more than an outline and was sitting so still I couldn't tell if her connection was still functional.

"Sorry." I slumped back in my chair.

"Continue," said Tamika.

"That's basically it," I said. "I saw a ghost; Caryl said it was a spell; she touched me; I felt better; it stopped."

Alvin leaned forward onto his elbows; his curiosity seemed to overcome whatever policy or personality trait had kept him silent. "You're sure there was no one else hiding in the soundstage anywhere?"

"Unless they were in the well," I said. "All the clutter had been cleared out; it was just a huge, floodlit, empty room."

"You didn't search the well?" Tamika said.

A sound of disbelief escaped me. "Me personally?"

"Either of you."

"It's a *hole*. A straight vertical shaft that killed the last person who tried to go down it, and that was when it had a platform you could lower, which it doesn't anymore. So yeah, we thought it might be a good idea to call in some backup before spelunking into an interdimensional abyss."

Tamika frowned at me. She had a dire-looking frown, but I

refused to be intimidated. I was right and she was wrong, and it's not often that I'm sure of that in a stressful situation.

"Is there anything else you can remember that might be at all helpful?" she asked, her tone implying that I'd thus far been anything but.

I racked my brain. After a moment I felt a little spark of eagerness as I realized that I did remember something that might be relevant.

"Let me in," I said. "The ghost, or whatever it was, said 'let me in.' I remember it because up until that point I'd been so convinced it was actually Teo, but Teo would never have said something cheesy like that. Am I right, Caryl?"

Caryl nodded blandly but didn't comment. I wished I could see Elliott; he was probably a wreck right now.

Alvin's gentle voice broke the silence. "Caryl, it was an Unseelie spell I'm assuming?"

"Yes," she said. "Unmistakably. A psychic enchantment, cast upon Millie and then dispelled once its purpose apparently failed. Only there was no spell caster present."

Alvin stroked his goatee with the air of someone who really doesn't want to be the guy to say the obvious thing. He was saved the task by the telepresent British woman, whose voice made itself heard, calm and deliberate, from the laptop speakers.

"There was one spell caster present," said Dame Belinda.

Alvin looked at the ceiling. Tamika looked directly at Caryl.

"I did not cast the spell," Caryl said to the laptop.

Tamika looked at Alvin, then back at Caryl, her frown deepening. "Do we have any evidence that you didn't?" Tamika asked.

"Aside from the fact that I was there, and know that I did not, and just told you that?"

"Aside from that."

"I'm afraid not."

Alvin leaned forward on this elbows again, looking at Caryl with an apologetic expression. "We're trying not to talk about your history right now, but we can't overlook the obvious just because it's upsetting. It would make logical sense for your control to start slipping after what happened in June."

"It would make sense," agreed Caryl, "but that does not make it true, and you cannot expect me to idly accept such an accusation. I have no evidence to exonerate me, nor do you have any to convict me."

"I hate to interrupt," I said, which wasn't true at all, "but what reason could Caryl possibly have for tormenting me?"

Alvin gave a slow sigh. "There are elements to the situation, Millie, that you may not be fully aware of. It's not my place—"

"She knows," said Caryl. "Most of it, anyhow. And you're free to tell her anything else you like."

Alvin looked at Caryl incredulously. "Are you sure?"

"Yes," she said. "The cat is largely out of the bag anyhow, and the more she knows, the more helpful she will be."

"All right then." Alvin leaned back in his chair and addressed me. "We normally only discuss Arcadia with people who are under contract with us, but I guess you're—something of a special case."

"So I keep hearing."

Everyone else in the room looked downright funereal, but Alvin actually half smiled at that. "What exactly did Caryl tell you?"

"She said the Unseelie Court kidnapped her when she was a baby, and she didn't come back here until she was, I don't know, eight or nine?"

"Seven," Caryl corrected.

"Right, and then I think she was at the Leishman Center for a couple of years until Martin taught her how to make Elliott. Then she came to the Project and sort of apprenticed under him."

"Except he was a wizard," Tamika said. "She's a warlock. Do you understand the difference?"

"Seelie and Unseelie, basically."

"But it's more than that," Tamika said direly.

"No, no," Alvin corrected her gently. "That is actually the difference, if succinctly."

"But that's not what it *means*." Tamika was adamant. "An Unseelie *fey* crosses a line, and we can rein them in with iron."

My memory vomited forth relevant information for the second time that day. "But Caryl's magic isn't susceptible to iron," I said. "Because she's human and iron is natural to her, or something."

"More or less," said Tamika. "So we have nothing to counter wizards and warlocks. Which is fine for wizards, since they patch up broken bones and make things pretty. But warlocks can do the same kinds of things Vivian Chandler could do, and there's nothing in either world that can stop them."

"Except conscience," I said pointedly.

"You've known Caryl how long?" Tamika said.

Alvin touched Tamika's forearm briefly, and she sat back in her chair, folding her arms. When Alvin spoke, I was struck again by the marked difference in their tones. Clearly they had some practice at this good-cop-bad-cop thing.

"Caryl was put in charge of this office at the age of fifteen," Alvin said softly. "Her whole history has been one exception to the rules after another. We try not to even allow the existence of warlocks, but her years in Arcadia changed her just as surely as if she'd been born half-fey. She can't be changed back."

"I thought even full-blooded fey turned human if they stayed here long enough," I said.

"Adult fey and humans change, one to the other, if they get stranded in the wrong world. But baby changelings have some biological way of buffering iron and norium from each other. We're not sure why or how it happens, but if it didn't, there would be no mixed-blood children at all; the foreign element would be rejected immediately by the mother's womb."

"Are you saying Caryl's half-fey?"

"She isn't, but she was so young when she was taken to Arcadia that her body made the adaptation anyway. Past the age of about two or three, it doesn't seem to happen. The norium in Arcadia would slowly replace any iron in her blood, and vice versa for the fey. That's why we limit visits to a couple of weeks except in rare cases."

"Are changelings common?"

Alvin made a sort of uncomfortable scrunch-face. "There aren't many ethical ways to create one," he said. "But Seelie changelings, wizards, are quite useful, so we haven't outlawed Seelie, uh, liaisons. Just the Unseelie kind. On the rare occasions Unseelie changelings are created, policy is to execute any consenting parents and foster the children in Arcadia where that sort of magic isn't quite so catastrophic."

"But you made an exception for Caryl?"

"Not me personally," said Alvin. "For that you can thank Dame Belinda herself."

I looked at the laptop, making out only a vague grandmotherly frame of silver hair beneath the glare of the poorly angled screen.

"It was not a matter of benevolence," said Dame Belinda, "but of necessity. She was an American-born citizen and a minor who had been abducted. Once she was found, the only lawful course was to return her to her parents."

"Who were more than happy," Caryl noted, "to give me into Martin's care once they saw what I'd become."

"Martin's plan," said Alvin, "was to keep her here and get her whatever kind of care and training she needed until she reached majority, then install her as a liaison at the Unseelie Court."

"But then Martin died," I said.

"There were no wizards available to replace him," said Alvin, "and regional managers have always been spell casters. By then Caryl had proven herself an incredibly capable second-in-command, so despite her age we put her in charge. For four years it worked out just fine."

"And you don't think it's working now?"

Alvin gave a lopsided smile and a shrug: *You tell me.*

Tamika looked at him to see if he was finished speaking, then turned to Caryl. "We've been monitoring the situation here since Vivian's death. Not only has there been very little progress in the follow-up investigation, but there has been turmoil on the Arcadian side; let's not go into the details in present company. Let's just say Duke Skyhollow doesn't feel safe, and I've convinced Alvin that it may be time to consider a change in leadership here in L.A. While I'm no spell caster, my knowledge and my track record with the Project make me a solid candidate."

"Are you here to relieve me of my position?" said Caryl evenly.

Alvin winced. "Let's not go that far yet," he said. "We still have some investigating to do. But there is some evidence suggesting that your powers may not be fully under your control, and now that you've reached the age of majority, I think you should prepare yourself for the possibility that you may be relocated to Arcadia."

I felt a tingling shock in the center of my chest. Elliott, I was pretty sure, had just slammed into me headfirst.

6

Shortly after dropping the bomb that they might be booting Caryl off-world, Alvin and Tamika asked to have the room to confer with Dame Belinda. They wanted me to stay close in case they had further questions, though. Caryl beckoned me with a curt gesture to follow her; I noted the uncharacteristically soft drape of her skirt as she led me down the stairs and into an empty bedroom on the ground floor. The room was on the back side of the house, off a hallway behind the dining room that I'd never explored during my brief residency.

The room must have been Gloria's, since there had been no empty ground-floor bedrooms when I'd been invited to stay. Now there was no sign that anyone had ever lived there; it contained only a twin bed with an olive bedspread. A single window looked out onto a narrow, weed-infested backyard fringed by a row of trees that screened the house behind us from view. Caryl seated herself on the edge of the bed and fixed me with a steady look.

"I am extremely upset," she said.

"Do you want to get rid of Elliott, talk about it?"

"I don't think that's a good idea," she said, examining the palm of her glove.

"I'm not going to let them fire you," I said. "If you were ever going to go crazy and kill someone, it would've been me, crazy as I drove you when we were looking for Rivenholt."

"I handled your hiring badly. I've been handling everything badly for months now."

I moved to lean against the wall by the window, looking at her sidelong. "You're nineteen years old, Caryl. They put too much on you, and nothing that's happened to you has been your fault."

"It's Vivian's fault," she said. "All of it."

"Is she the one who abducted you? I thought she was exiled from Arcadia, like, a hundred years ago."

"Two hundred. But her hand is in what happened to me, though we have no hard evidence. My father was working in research and development at Vivian's company, Cera Pest Control. When I was almost a year old, a former lover of Vivian's happened to visit Los Angeles. The day he returned to Arcadia, my parents' child went missing."

I brushed aside the psychologically fascinating reference to herself as *my parents' child* and moved on. "How the hell did Vivian's ex smuggle you out?"

"We have no idea. Many fey have unique talents; whatever spell he used to hide or disguise me, it must have been very powerful. He took that secret to his grave."

"What was the point of it? Just more of Vivian's random cruelty?"

Caryl hesitated. "I believe it was for the sake of their daughter Slakeshadow."

"Vivian has a *daughter*?"

"Had. When my abduction came to light, Slakeshadow was

executed along with her father. Violations of the Second Accord are punishable by death."

"How was abducting you supposed to help Slakeshadow?"

Caryl smoothed her skirt over her knees, her eyes on her hands. When she spoke again, her voice had an even more detached quality than usual, as though she were reciting something memorized long ago in school.

"Vivian's crimes in Arcadia did not merit execution," she said, "but she was exiled. Her mate and child were stripped of their titles and sent to live in something roughly analogous to poverty. My abduction was part of their plan to win favor with the Unseelie King Winterglass and regain their nobility."

"Wait, what would the Unseelie King want with a human baby? This just got very *Labyrinth* all of a sudden."

"The king was not even aware of the abduction. Slakeshadow used my blood in a potion and supplied it to him regularly without telling him how it worked."

"*What?*"

"In the same way that ingestion of fey blood can inspire a human, human blood can ground a fey, anchor his thoughts. The king's Echo had been dead for more than a century, and while the Echo effect lasts longer for fey than it does for us, Winterglass had begun to lose his memories and his reason. Unseelie are particularly volatile. He had no heir, and chaos was breaking out as his potential successors schemed against one another. Then Slakeshadow came along with a potion that solved all of his problems. Not only did he restore her nobility; he made her his princess-consort and got her with child. Only to execute her six years later."

"Guess her plan didn't work out like she'd hoped."

"Eventually the king discovered me. Heard my screams and followed them." Her gaze drifted toward the window. "I was kept in a wooden crate. One day it opened and—there he stood. As hard as I try, I cannot erase that image from my memory."

"He didn't look like David Bowie, I'm assuming."

"I remember skeletal wings, an owl's skull crowned with antlers. His eyes burned with livid fire."

"Jesus. What did he do?"

"He lifted me out of the crate. Since I could not walk on my own, he carried me to the nearest Gate. The Gate in Saint Petersburg had been destroyed long ago, and so he had to travel to Helsinki; the agents there helped find where I belonged."

"He carried you himself? I didn't think fey monarchs were that . . . hands-on."

"They have not been, before or since. It was a terrible risk; he left the scepter in the hands of his son. For more than a week, the Unseelie Court was ruled by a five-year-old."

"I doubt that," I said. "There must have been someone else calling the shots."

"Not at all. The scepter I mentioned is not symbolic. It is a powerful artifact that grants near-absolute command over all Unseelie fey."

"And the king just . . . gave it to his kid to hang on to while he was gone."

Caryl nodded gravely. "As nearly as I can guess, King Winterglass must have been half-mad with guilt. In a letter once, he wrote me that the moment he caught my scent he knew what he'd been drinking."

"My God." I laced my hands awkwardly in front of me. "Have you seen him since then?"

"Only in nightmares."

"If they send you back to Arcadia, would you be welcome at his Court?"

"Likely," she said. "The king offered to adopt me at the time, but my parents would not allow it. He used to send me the love-liest letters, until I grew old enough to write back and ask him politely to stop."

"Yeah, I'm not sure I'd enjoy being pen pals with a flaming-eyed skeleton either. Do you think the rejection offended him?"

"If I'd seriously offended the king of the Unseelie, I would never have heard the last of it from my superiors. The Unseelie Court and the Arcadia Project are bound only by the delicate thread of the king's word; our power to regulate or even moni-tor the Unseelie is a shadow of what it was in the early nine-teenth century. The loyalty of King Winterglass to the Arcadia Project is all that holds those monsters at bay."

"If you knew that, why'd you tell him to shove off?"

"As grateful as I was to him, I did not want reminders of my trauma. I still do not. If they decide to send me back," she said matter-of-factly, "I shall take my own life."

My breath faltered. "What?" I said. "No, no no no. You do not want to do that."

"While I respect your expertise on suicide," said Caryl dryly, "you have never visited the Unseelie High Court, and therefore cannot fully evaluate my options."

My chest felt tight; my eyes stung. "How can you even say that? How can you tell *me* that and expect me to—" I raked a hand back through my hair, taking short breaths and looking out the window at the weeds. Dr. Davis's voice reminded me to notice the shallowness in my chest, to focus on relaxing my muscles, slowing and lengthening my breathing.

"For the last twelve years," said Caryl, "I have tried to forget what I experienced during my imprisonment in Arcadia. The extent to which I have held tenuously to my sanity is the extent to which I have succeeded."

"So tell that to Dame Whatsit! They can't do this to you!"

Caryl stretched her arms behind her on the bed, then leaned back on the heels of her hands. "Yes, I'll just tell them that they should keep the dangerously unstable warlock on this side of the border because, if not, she may kill herself. I'm sure that will set their minds at ease."

"There has to be something we can do." My palms were getting damp; I wiped them on my work trousers.

"You've already helped as much as anyone could. I think they expected that you would have resentments about the way you were treated, and would be willing to confirm their poor opinion of me. Your loyalty is a powerful statement to my effectiveness as a leader."

"God, I hope so, Caryl. I know I have a lousy way of showing it, but you have to know that I care about you."

Caryl's gaze drifted off in a way that made me sure she was watching Elliott. I wished I could see him too.

"I care very much about you as well," she said.

"I feel like I should give you a hug or something."

"I know." She rose from the bed, placing her back toward me. "But enough of that. There is someone waiting to see you."

For a moment I was confused. Then a little shiver of excitement passed through me. "Claybriar?"

Caryl nodded. "He would have arrived at three, around the time you came into the meeting. I'll tell Phil to let him down out of the tower. Wait in the living room, won't you?"

Monty the cat was still on the piano bench; I gave him a thorough petting to let all the pent-up affection out of my system before starting yet another conversation with someone I couldn't touch.

The last time I'd seen Claybriar, he'd been drained completely of his essence, leaving him no way of maintaining the complicated spellwork that gave him a human facade. His horns and goat legs had freaked me out a little, to be perfectly honest, and if I were to so much as shake his hand, my iron-studded body would disrupt his facade and I'd see it all over again.

The man walking down the stairs now, though, looked perfectly, painfully, messily human. Brian Clay, the fake cop I'd flirted with at a coffee shop. Untidy hair, goatee, soulful dark eyes. At the sight of him, my skin flushed all over with joy.

"Millie," he said when he saw me, and grinned, taking the rest of the stairs two at a time. I realized with a shock that I had never seen him smile before, not really. He stopped a few feet in front of me, hands clasped behind his back, mischief in his eyes.

"Clay," I said, glancing up at him. "You look—exactly the same."

"But this time I came prepared." He held up his hands and flexed them; only then did I notice he was wearing latex surgical gloves.

I laughed in surprise as he held out his hand. I gave it a tentative shake, and when I saw that his facade was still in place, I held on for a long moment. A large hand, made for yard work or carpentry. God, he was so *tall*.

"How have you been?" I said. I gestured to the nearest couch and then sat with him, leaving space.

"I wish I could say great," he said with a wry smile. "But honestly I'm glad as hell to be here right now, and not just because of you."

"What's the matter?" I reached for his hand again, gave it a little squeeze, just because I was so thrilled that I could. He looked at our hands with a sort of pleased awkwardness until I let go.

"I'm practically nobility now," he said then. "I've been the queen's servant for decades, but after the whole mess with Vivian she made me her champion."

"What does that entail?"

"Well, I'm a knight, I guess."

"Nifty! Should I call you Sir Claybriar?"

"If that works for you. But more to the point, being a knight in Arcadia isn't an honorary title. I have to actually go out and slay things."

"*Slay* things? Like monsters? Oh my God. That doesn't sound safe."

"Not even a little. For example: she knows I want to hang around Skyhollow because of you—"

"Skyhollow?"

"The Arcadian side of L.A.; they just call it after the duke. So since I'm interested in the area, she's sent me after this damn manticore, thousands of years old, that's gotten it into his head lately to harass the duke and all his toadies."

"That must be the 'unrest' people were talking about. So it's up to you to kill some legendary beast because, what, you're in the neighborhood?"

"More or less."

"How's that been working out?"

"Well, half of Arcadia is already singing ballads about me. I've slain quite a few fearsome beasties. But this manticore? I've had two actual encounters with the thing so far, and they both ended with me turning tail and scampering."

"Literally turning tail. Because—tail."

"Yes, I have a tail." He gave me a Look. "Though not at the moment."

"Gosh, you're chatty. Almost perky. I hardly recognize you."

He shrugged. "Last time we met, you jolted my brain into gear. I could ride that for years if I had to. But like I said, I'm really glad to be somewhere I'm not expected to kill anything five times my size."

"I wish you could stay forever. I was so lucky to find you, and now you've got me worried you're going to get eaten as soon as you go back."

A shadow crossed his face, and he slowly shifted his hand so that his latex-gloved fingers interlaced with mine, surprising me with a sharp stab of desire. As if things weren't complicated enough.

"I know the feeling," he said. "I worry about you all the time."

"How long do you get to stay?"

"The standard two weeks."

"Not long enough."

"You know how this Echo gig works, Millie. If I stay too long, I lose my mojo. You may as well get used to the idea that we're going to spend more time apart than together."

"This whole soul mate thing is hugely overrated."

"It'll be all right. We'll make the most of the time we have. And I'm still working on finding a way around this iron problem so I can return the inspiration. You could make movies again."

"You're sweet."

"Heh. Further proof we don't know each other well." He gave me another of those impossible grins, then stood, pulling me up with him. "Come on," he said. "I'm starving. I don't suppose you have any peaches?"

"I have no idea. Let's find out!"

In retrospect, that was a terrible plan. I'd been pretty damn close to fine, and then there I went blundering right into the kitchen. Apparently PTSD and grief flunked out of the same charm school; neither of them seems to know when it's cool to drop by.

I saw the Spanish tile and the deserted bar stools, the island stacked with unopened mail, the fine layer of dust on the stove, and something in me collapsed like a dying star.

Teo. Suspicious eyes half hidden by a fringe of black hair, gnocchi sizzling on the stove. The tired old house filled with the smell of garlic and the sound of his manic chatter. He'd been so unfinished, a hanging question, a joyously unstable arc of raw potential. His absence was suffocating, impossible. Residence Four was like a zombie, staggering on empty without its heart.

With no warning at all, I dissolved into ugly sobs.

7

"Millie," said Claybriar behind me, soft and panicked. "What is it?"

"I think I'm going to throw up," I said.

"Oh," said Claybriar. "Uh—trash can? Sink? I don't know; I've only seen this on TV."

I started laughing, then lurched toward the sink. Claybriar rubbed my back awkwardly with one latex hand while my stomach turned briefly inside out; afterward I ripped off a paper towel to wipe my mouth and hunted through cabinets for a water glass.

"Sorry," I said. "That was weird."

"Kind of horrible, actually."

"Sorry."

"But—you're okay now? You're not dying or anything?"

"Just a stress thing," I said, finally locating a glass that wasn't too spotty. "I've never had it happen quite like that before, but then I've never—" My eyes filled up again.

"Maybe you should stay near the sink," Claybriar said gently, making me laugh again.

"Oh my God, you're adorable."

"Thank you?"

"It's Teo," I explained, turning the white-crusted tap in the sink and filling my glass about a third of the way. "You probably don't remember him. The kid who tried to cut off his own hand on the soundstage."

"I do remember that. He died. Were you close?"

"I only knew him for a week, but we were partners. We—" I flicked a glance toward Claybriar's solemn eyes, guilty. "He kissed me once. After I—" My face heated. "I found your drawing of me; we both saw it and—"

"Ah. Arcane friendly fire. I'm sorry."

I took a long drink of water, then dumped the rest out in the sink, leaving the glass there as well. "Aside from that," I said, "we were—sort of becoming friends? But then we had a huge fight. I said some awful stuff. He was pretty much set on never forgiving me, and then—then he died."

"Oh, Millie."

I gestured to the stove. "This was— He was an aspiring chef. Amazingly talented; he fed the whole house. Sunday mornings he did an omelet bar. Every day he was in here, slicing something up, poking around the fridge, complaining about missing ingredients."

I lost it again—just my composure, not my lunch this time. Put my hands over my face and cried, like I hadn't let myself cry in four months. Claybriar was here, and somehow that made it safe.

Apparently he hadn't gotten that memo; he was looking at me as though I might explode into a fine, bloody mist.

"Is there something I can do?" he said.

"I guess a hug's not exactly on the menu."

"It would only hurt me a little," he said. "Not much more than just standing here watching, to be honest."

He came closer, and I closed my eyes so I wouldn't have to see. He folded his arms around me, fierce, and shuddered. I felt no burst of inspiration, but I did calm at the sound of his heartbeat against my ear. Fey had hearts too?

His clothes were part of his facade, so now there was bare skin against my cheek. The hair on his chest was softer than a person's and smelled strange: like bitter tree bark and animal musk. One of his palms rested against the back of my hair; the way my skull fit into the hollow of his hand was almost hypnotizing.

I pulled away as soon as I felt able, because I knew I was hurting him.

"What does that feel like?" I said, looking up at him now that his human illusion had sprung back into place. "Not the inspiration bit, but the iron?"

"Cold," he said. "Sort of numbing, like a buzzing deep into my skin. Toward the end there, I thought I might pass out."

"I'm so sorry."

"Don't be. You feel better, right? And it's gone the minute you let go. Well, I guess I do feel a little sleepy now."

"I seem to have that effect on men." Oh right. Zach. I was definitely not going to bring Zach up right now. "Peaches!" I exclaimed when I saw Claybriar puzzling over my expression. "You wanted peaches."

I opened the custard-colored fridge; the contents were sparse and tragic.

"No peaches," I said a little hoarsely. "I do see one apple, though, with minimal brown spots. You can probably just slice them right off."

"Would you mind doing that?" He gestured to the knife block, and I saw what he must have noticed instantly: the stainless steel stripe going all the way around the length of each handle.

"Oh, damn," I said. "Sure, I can do it. You've touched enough iron for one day. How do fey get by in the modern world, seriously?"

"Rubber-soled shoes protect us from metal staircases and such. We carry packages or walk just behind people so they'll tend to open doors for us. There's a whole handbook for getting by here; we have to pass a test before the Project lets us come."

"I had no idea," I said, slicing two round sections off either end of the apple. "I can't even imagine how someone like Vivian got by for years."

"I guess if she slipped up she just murdered the witness," he said. "Good guys always have it harder."

"Is it really that simple? Good guys and bad guys?"

Claybriar didn't answer, and I looked at him to see if I'd offended him. But he was standing staring fixedly into space as though he hadn't heard me at all. I looked where he was looking, but there was nothing there.

"Clay?"

It took him a moment to drag his gaze back to me, and when he did, he looked pained. "Damn it," he said.

"What's wrong?"

"The queen just summoned me."

"She what?" I forgot the apple on the counter. "How? *Why?* You've been here, like, five minutes!"

"She isn't great at remembering my schedule." He looked sheepish. "I'm so sorry. I'll stay as long as I can, but . . ." He trailed off with a shrug.

"Screw her. She can wait a couple of weeks."

"I'm sure she can," he said, "but I can't. She spoke my name in the Seelie tongue; that's an arcane summons. I'm stubborn enough to put it off awhile, but it's going to needle me worse and worse until I'm standing in front of her."

"Wow," I said bitterly. "It's good to be the queen."

"Anyone who knows my true name could do it," he said. "Luckily, the English translation doesn't have that power, or I'd be crippled, the way you people throw names around."

His choice of the word "crippled" rubbed me the wrong way, but I let it slide. "Who else knows your true name?" I asked.

"Just the queen and my mom, really. And even my mom has probably forgotten it."

"Are you going to tell it to me?"

"I know better than to give you that kind of control." His smile was lopsided.

"But Queen Fairypants gets to know?"

"That's part of the whole champion gig, unfortunately. She can't give me orders unless I'm in earshot, so she has to have a way to order me into earshot."

"What bullshit! You said you were going to stay two *weeks*! Are they at least going to let you come ba—"

I broke off, because apparently our bickering had attracted an audience.

A tall black man was standing in the kitchen doorway, one hand braced on either side of the frame as though it were all that held him up.

"Tjuan," I exhaled in shock. I almost hadn't recognized him. He looked horrible: unshaven, ashy skin, unkempt hair. Because he tended to dress casually, I'd never realized how immaculately put together he'd been last summer until I saw the absence of it.

"You," he said to me by way of greeting.

"Millie. And this is Claybriar, remember him? The fake cop?"

"Hey," said Claybriar sheepishly. Belatedly I handed him the apple, and he looked at it almost reverently before taking a bite.

"Why are you here?" said Tjuan.

There was something disturbing about his manner. He'd always been laconic, but this time it was more than that. His eyes were intent, his head tipped to one side as though he were straining to hear me in a crowded bar.

"I'm meeting with some people from National about a— There's a situation at Valiant Studios. They needed my report."

"So you're not working here." I couldn't tell if he was relieved, disappointed, or confused.

"No, luckily for all of us," I said. "How—how have you been?" His stare got about fifteen degrees colder, but I pressed on. "Caryl says you've been ill?"

He had that look again, as though someone were talking over me, drowning me out. It occurred to me with a chill that maybe somebody was. I'd seen that kind of thing at the Leishman Center when I did my time there after my suicide attempt.

"Hearing voices?" I said sympathetically.

He looked startled. "You hear it too?" The hope in his eyes was so desperate that a lump formed in my throat.

"No," I said. "I'm sorry."

It was as though he saw the sympathy and realized how much he'd given away. I watched him retreat into himself, working the strings of his face until they all went slack again. Then after a moment, he looked directly into my eyes and smiled with one corner of his mouth.

"It gets tedious," he said. "Why can't the voice ever say, *You're all right, Tjuan,* or *Beautiful day,* or *Let's go volunteer at the soup kitchen?* You know, just for a change."

His attempt at humor, of all things, made the tears rush to my eyes. He looked away as though I'd had a sudden nosebleed.

"Tjuan," I said, "if you ever want to talk to anybody, somebody you don't work with—"

By way of answer, he turned around and left. I looked at Claybriar, and his face looked the way mine must have.

"Poor bastard," I said.

"I'll admit I'm not always the best at reading humans," said Claybriar with a mouthful of apple, "but he really does not look well."

"I've got to find Caryl," I said.

Claybriar looked at his apple with a conflicted expression.

"You can bring the apple," I said.

Caryl was seated on the larger couch in the living room, going through some papers in a manila folder. Monty the cat had vanished; most likely she'd shooed him away. He'd belonged to her mentor, Martin, and even after four years, her unmanaged grief made it difficult for her to be around the poor animal. I was starting to understand how she felt.

She looked up when Claybriar and I entered, and a little smile curved the corners of her mouth. She hadn't quite figured out how to make a smile look genuine, but it was new that she was even trying.

"I just ran into Tjuan," I said.

Her smile vanished. "Ah," she said.

"What the hell is the matter with him?"

Caryl hesitated. There were all kinds of Project rules about confidentiality and personal questions, but so long as Caryl was still in charge in Los Angeles, she got to make the call about volunteering someone else's information. After a moment, she seemed to decide I had the right.

"It's some variety of schizophrenia, as far as we can tell, but it doesn't respond to medication. He's been in a kind of remission for years, which appeared to be triggered by electroconvulsive therapy. Unfortunately, his symptoms returned after the trauma on stage 13."

"Could it be a curse?"

She shook her head. "If it were, I would see the spellwork, as I did with you. I think the experience simply—broke him."

I thought of his face when Vivian severed the rope and Gloria plummeted screaming down the well.

"I had no idea he was schizophrenic. He was doing so well when I met him."

"Even now, he's doing his best to hide his symptoms, but I am worried about him."

"Shouldn't he be taking something? I know Project employees aren't supposed to be on meds, but—"

"It's not that simple. Those on active duty have to keep their blood free of controlled substances for arcane reasons, but if I thought medication would help him, I would be the first to make certain he had it, even if it meant he needed to take an indefinite break from active duty. But part of what made his illness so dire when we found him was that he didn't respond to medications. He suffered the worst of their side effects with no abatement of symptoms. It would be cruel to put him through that again, so we shall simply care for him as best we can."

"What if he can never go back to active duty?"

"Part of our mission statement is that so long as you honor

our contract, you are as good as family. We take care of our own."

"Unless 'our own' happens to be a warlock I guess."

Caryl spread her hands in a graceful shrug. "Perhaps. But for the others, the security of knowing they will always be cared for is nothing short of miraculous. Fortunately, we have the gratitude of hundreds of incredibly wealthy people, which means that paying for medical care is rarely a concern."

"You can't tell how well-funded the Project is by looking at the state of this house."

"I think you've just seen why we don't waste our money on wallpaper, Millie."

I hadn't known Tjuan as well as I'd known Teo. But the thought of him as an invalid under the protection of the Arcadia Project made me profoundly sad. He'd been a screenwriter, according to conversations I'd overheard between him and Phil. That was probably shot now too.

"I feel like I should try harder to talk to him," I said.

Caryl stared at me. "And just what do you think that might accomplish?"

A relevant question, actually. One of the things I was working on in DBT was having goals for personal interactions. Borderlines aren't great at healthy interpersonal stuff, and having a set of checklists based on goals is useful to keep us from veering off society's rails. This particular interaction would fall under the heading Relationship Building, though it was odd to think of it that way.

"I was there that night too," I said. "And I'm not his boss. I also lost my partner, and I know it's not the same, but—I don't know. I never made things right with Teo. If I walk away from Tjuan now, leave stuff unsaid . . ."

Caryl studied me for a moment, then said, "Be my guest, I suppose. He is in room two, next to the room where you and I spoke privately before. But don't be disappointed if he isn't inclined to confide in you."

Whatever I was going to say in response was cut off. Somewhere at the back of the house, a woman let out a shrill, harrowing scream.

8

The scream was like something from a horror movie, long and full throated. We all leaped to our feet a quarter second into it: Caryl and Claybriar running toward the sound, me away. No thought; pure adrenaline. No sooner had the scream ended than it was followed by another, just as long, more ragged. I stopped short of actually fleeing the house, but I cowered, forehead against the front door, the heels of my hands pressed into my ears and my eyes squeezed shut. My body responded to echoes of echoes of echoes.

Gloria's scream when Vivian severed the rope.

Gloria shrieking at Phil: *Say it to my face!*

My father shouting into the phone: a deal gone wrong, his voice twisted with hate. The suffocating quiet of the house as he searched for me afterward. *What are you doing under there? I wasn't yelling at you. Get up; you're too big to act this way.*

Eventually I felt Claybriar's hands prying mine away from my ears. His fingers were warm, even through the latex.

I looked up, waiting for a rebuke. Instead he touched my face, the side of his thumb tracing a gentle crescent at my cheekbone.

"A woman has died," he said. "Tamika. Do you know her?"

"She's from—*died*?" I started shivering. "Died how?"

"A spell," he said. "Someone cast a horrible spell."

"What exactly—?"

He shook his head. "You don't want to know."

"Tell me anyway."

"She's—her body has—dissolved."

"*What?*"

"Decayed," said Caryl's husky voice, its emotionless affect particularly unsettling in context as she entered the living room. "A Seelie wouldn't recognize decay, I suppose."

"Are you sure it's her?" I asked.

"Yes," said Caryl. "Same clothes and shoes, same hair. Lying in the room we gave her. The rest of her is nearly unrecognizable."

"Was that—" I felt light-headed. "Was that her, screaming?"

"No. That was Stevie. She found the body."

As if on cue, the distant sound of vomiting came from one of the downstairs bathrooms. This was really turning out to be a vomiting kind of day.

"Where's Alvin?" I asked.

"In there with her."

"With Stevie?"

"With Tamika. It would seem his attachment to her overrides his horror at the state of her body."

But now he was coming into the living room, and he was no longer the soft-spoken "good cop." His eyes were savage, and he raised a finger to point directly at Caryl.

"Lock her in the fucking basement."

"Who?" said Claybriar at the same moment I said, "Basement?"

Caryl lifted her hands in surrender. "I don't need an escort," she said. "I will go willingly until we find out what has happened."

"Until we—" Alvin's fists clenched. "How many Unseelie spell casters are there in the house right now? How many?"

"Caryl was sitting right here when she died!" I protested.

"No," Caryl corrected me, like an idiot. "I was sitting here when Stevie *found* Tamika. I can't say for certain where I was when Tamika died, because there is no way to ascertain time of death."

"You just shut the fuck up *right* now," said Alvin, visibly shaking with rage.

"Right," said Caryl in a clipped voice. "Basement. The lock combination is three seven zero one. You'll want to retrieve me when the time comes to see to her remains."

"*Go,*" barked Alvin; I flinched as though an arrow had thwacked into the wall by my head. "Go, before I tear you apart."

Caryl went. When I spoke, my voice came out a sort of choked whisper. "What are we supposed to tell the poor woman's family?"

"We're her family," said Alvin. And as soon as he'd said it, all his anger drained away and left his eyes hollow. I half expected him to implode, so sudden was the absolute vacuum I saw through those windows.

"There has to be some other explanation for this," I said. "Caryl is not a murderer."

Alvin's eyes sent up another weak flare of anger, but then he just turned and followed Caryl's path to the back of the house, presumably toward the basement prison I'd had no idea existed.

I started to follow him, but Claybriar's latex-gloved hand closed around my forearm, pulling me back gently. Not against him, but almost.

"I wouldn't," he said. "That man's a gun looking for a place to go off."

I met his gaze, having to tilt my head back to do so. "Looks like you picked the worst possible day to show up. I'm so sorry."

"I'm glad you're not alone right now."

Much to my irritation, my left eye chose that moment to release a single tear, making Claybriar's face go all soft and puppy-dog. I wasn't crying, really; that eye's corner was pulled out of shape a little by scar tissue, so it did that sometimes when my head was tipped back.

"Seriously?" I said. "It's me you're worried about?"

"Forgive me for trying to be nice, Roper," said Claybriar, catching the tear deftly on the side of a gloved finger, then flicking it away. "But you're kind of a mess."

"I'm pretty low on the list of who needs pity at the moment."

"Let's go outside for a second," said Claybriar. "Get some air. There's nothing we can do until that man calms down a little."

"Right," I said, moving to the front door and opening it for him. "Fresh air and small talk, I guess. How's your sister?"

"She's fine," he said stiffly, seating himself on the filthy love seat on the front porch. I stayed standing, closed the door behind us. "She's gone back to the Grove," he went on.

I frowned, his words taking a moment to penetrate my fog of anxiety. "I assume you're not talking about the shopping center."

"It's an enclave of my people, near where you grew up I think."

"North of Atlanta?"

"I don't know your cities very well." His tone was distracted, irritable. "East of here a long ways. I was sort of called there when you were born, I guess. My sister came along."

"Called from where?"

"Like I say, I've been serving the Seelie Queen a long time.

We were near the Seelie High Court before that. Daystrike Forest, on the flip side of London."

"Clay?"

"Yeah."

"You were working as the queen's investigator when Rivenholt went missing, right?"

"Yeah. Kind of my specialty."

"Do you think you could investigate now? Help find out what's going on here?"

He blew out a frustrated sigh. "I wish. But even right this second, with my Echo standing five feet away from me and a corpse in a back room, it's taking most of my concentration to do anything other than get up and go home."

"That damned summons."

"Yeah. I'm sorry. I'll stay as long as I can, but my powers of deduction are hobbled to say the least."

I paced back toward the house. "I should see if Alvin's left Caryl alone yet," I said.

"Three seven zero one!" he blurted, like an eight-year-old too excited about knowing the answer to raise his hand.

I stopped. "Beg your pardon?"

"I can remember it," he said. "The code to unlock the basement."

"Nice."

"I've always had a good memory," he said. "But for a faun, that just meant remembering the names of people I didn't live with, or having a vague sense of time passing. Since I met you, information just—collects, like rainwater. How do you people cope with it all?"

I managed a smile. "Your memory's probably better than mine at this point," I said. "In fact—you'd better come with me."

We went back inside, and I poked around the back hallway until I found a likely-looking door with a combination lock
hanging from it. I had Claybriar repeat the combination.

I rotated the numbers until they lined up, squeezed the
lock, pulled it apart. The door opened with a creak, and I held
it for Claybriar. Despite everything, my eyes wandered down
the back of his gray T-shirt and over his jeans as he passed by.
Whoever had designed that ass clearly had it in for me.

The basement was decently lit, as basements go, and tidy
except for some stacked boxes and rolled rugs along one wall.
There was a toilet and an austere utility sink in one corner,
exposed to the rest of the room. The lightbulbs were bare, and
a strong smell of mildew and the appearance of spiderwebs
made the air seem unclean. There was no furniture; Caryl sat
cross-legged on the floor. When we entered, she didn't get up.

"You probably should not be down here," she said. "Alvin
could return at any moment, and I don't want you in the path
of his anger."

"What's he like?" I said, moving to stand in front of her.
"How worried should I be?" Claybriar sat on the floor nearby,
but since I had no idea how long the conversation was going
to last, there was no way I was going to go to the trouble of
getting down and back up again.

"I have never seen him upset before this," said Caryl, looking
up at me with tranquil eyes. "So I cannot predict his behavior.
In the past, I always felt he was trying to give me the benefit of
the doubt. But now? The evidence against me is overwhelming."

"You're innocent, though," I said. "Right?"

She took a deep breath, then exhaled slowly, too deliberate to
be called a sigh. "I cannot imagine how or why I would do this.

Tamika was planning to replace me, which looks like motive, but I've had Elliott this entire time. When I am in this state, rash action, even in self-defense, is impossible. I might stand and watch a train come at me, if I didn't logically know I ought to get out of the way."

"That's a little horrifying."

"My point is, I fail to see how I could commit an ill-considered crime of passion when my passion is not currently accessible."

"Earlier you said Elliott was malfunctioning."

Caryl's gaze drifted over to a cardboard box where Elliott must have been perched. "He's behaving normally at the moment," she said. "Which is to say, he's curled into a ball weeping."

"Dragons can cry?"

"He isn't a dragon. He's—"

"A construct, I know."

"He's what I thought a cuddly pet would look like when I was seven years old."

"Caryl, could you try to go five minutes without breaking my heart?" I messed up my hair with the palm of my hand. "All right, we need to think. What else could possibly have happened?"

"I cannot begin to imagine. To tell the truth, the evidence against me is so strong that even I feel flickers of doubt. So there is no chance that anyone at National or World Headquarters is going to take my side. The man most generally forgiving of me, the man in complete command of every agent in this country, is now doing his best not to kill me with his bare hands. We are past exile; this will lead to my execution."

"What? They can't just kill you. That can't be legal."

"The Arcadia Project is a law unto itself, even more than the military. Our man Adam at the Department of Homeland

Security would ensure that my execution could be carried out without incident even if a mundane law enforcement agency were to somehow become entangled."

I turned away for a moment, rubbing my arms as I suddenly felt the chill in the air. "Unless we prove you innocent," I said, turning back. "How do we do that?"

"For now, the best we can do is delay the proceedings until we can figure out how to assemble a defense. How, I am not certain."

Claybriar cleared his throat. He'd been so still and quiet, I'd almost forgotten he was there.

"Something you want to say?" I asked him.

"I don't really want to say it," he said, shifting his weight onto the heel of one hand. "But there aren't many options."

"What is it?"

"You want to throw a wrench into things, I know a good wrench."

"You want to involve the queen?"

"If she raised a fuss," he said, "they couldn't carry out the execution without dealing with her, no matter how clear-cut the case was."

"Pardon my disrespect," said Caryl dryly, "but Queen Dawnrowan is unlikely to pry her spectacular bottom off of her throne for an Unseelie changeling."

Claybriar tilted his head with a *good point* sort of frown.

"What if . . . ," I started. But then thought better of it.

Caryl tilted her head slightly. "What is it?"

"A terrible idea."

"A terrible idea is better than none," she persisted.

"I just thought . . . Would King Winterglass be upset if he knew they were going to execute you? Would he make scary noises at people? But then I remembered you told him to fuck off years ago, so . . ."

Caryl tapped at her lower lip with a gloved forefinger. "You're right," she said. "It is a terrible idea. But it's a rope, and I am drowning, and so I don't see that we have much choice but to grab for it."

"How would we even get in touch with him?" I said.

Caryl frowned slightly. "That is the difficulty. Even if sending a message to the Unseelie Court were as simple as it is with the Seelie, Alvin would likely guess what we were planning and block the usual channels. To complicate matters, there is no Gate where King Winterglass lives, not so much as a lone Project agent in the whole of Russia, not since the time of the tsars. We'd have to find someone in Helsinki to cooperate, then they'd have to travel the remaining distance overland in Arcadia—"

"Not true," blurted Claybriar.

We both looked at him.

"There's a portal," he said. "In Her Majesty's private quarters. Leads directly to the king's palace. I'm pretty sure it's still functional."

"I did not know that," said Caryl slowly.

"It's ancient, and fallen into disuse," he said. "I'm probably not supposed to be telling you about it, but I've never been specifically forbidden, so—" He shrugged. "There's also a much better-known portal between Duke Skyhollow's estate and the White Rose. The home of the Seelie High Court," he elaborated for my benefit. "So assuming I get permission once I answer Her Majesty's summons, I could get a message to the king in a day or two."

"Can you get permission?" Caryl asked.

"I believe I can."

I turned to Caryl and beamed. "Do I have the most amazing Echo, or what?"

"This is a sound plan," said Caryl. "If a fey witness testifies to the king's displeasure, that should be enough to put fear into Dame Belinda's heart and slow things down. Better yet would be if you could get the king to write a letter of rebuke in his own hand. His letters are so very stirring."

"I'll do my best," said Claybriar.

"Meanwhile, I need some time to myself," said Caryl. "If I do not dispel Elliott soon, he will rupture, and then there will be no getting him back."

"I can stay with you," I said. "If you want."

"I truly do not."

My hands curled into fists, but I nodded. "All right then. Come on, Clay."

I preceded him up the stairs and opened the door for him, then took the time to replace the padlock so that Alvin didn't think I was trying to facilitate an escape attempt.

As I rotated the combination back into disarray, from behind the door I heard the muffled, hoarse sound of Caryl crying.

9

When Claybriar reached for my hand, I moved away. In one of the random mood shifts so common to people with my disorder, I suddenly found Claybriar's presence virtually unbearable. Caryl was crying alone in a basement, and I could do nothing for her; meanwhile some guy I barely knew was hanging around wanting to comfort *me*?

I knew he didn't deserve the sudden intense desire I had to shove him away. One of the first things you learn as a Borderline is that the only way to keep any friends is to act as though you're not feeling what you're feeling at least 30 percent of the time.

I took a deep breath and moved to a window at the front of the house, looking out across the street at the nicer homes, lovingly-cared-for dollhouses with fish-scale shingles and oriel windows. I tried to practice mindfulness, to sink my consciousness into their lovely pastel colors, to the bright blue of the October day above them.

Once I'd tricked my mind out of the death spiral it was trying to dive into, I had at least a vague idea of what I wanted to do.

"Can you wait here?" I said to Claybriar. "I want to talk to Alvin."

"Sure," he said. "Go ahead; I'm good."

Grateful for small blessings, I climbed the stairs in my painstaking half-speed fashion. I could hear Alvin talking on the phone up there, though I couldn't make out the words. As I got closer to room 6, where he was pacing, I heard him imploringly address Belinda, "Dame" and all. I glanced at my phone—Good God, by my math it was nearly one in the morning in London. Someone was not going to be happy. Also, I had two hours to get to my Thursday group therapy. It was too late to cancel without getting charged two hundred bucks for nothing, but how was I supposed to spend an hour with a couple of concerned mental health workers and not mention that I just witnessed a murder? Or that the prime suspect was one of my individual therapist's other patients?

"I'm not saying Gav isn't qualified," Alvin was saying in a placating, sycophantic tone. "He'll do fine until I get back. But this is a demotion, and I'm just wondering if I've done something to— I know, I know. Just, if it isn't too much trouble, could you continue to look for other options? I'll pay someone's moving expenses out of my own pocket if it comes to it. I— Yes, Dame Belinda. Of course."

I lurked in the hallway waiting for him to finish, looking over the balustrade onto the first floor. There was the sound of a key in the front door, and after a moment the Residence manager Song entered, phone pressed to one ear, black-haired baby secured against the opposite hip with a fabric wrap. I instinctively stepped back toward the wall.

"I'm here now," Song said into her phone, then ended the call and jammed it into her pocket, freeing her half-fey offspring from the wrap and setting him down on the floor.

What was his awful name again? I couldn't remember.

I was somewhat surprised to see that he could stand, not only because of what that told me about the passage of time, but because his little jellied legs looked as though they didn't have any bones in them. Looking at his drooping cloth diaper and its bleach-faded greenish stains, I felt a sudden surge of relief that I'd be going home to Manhattan Beach later.

As soon as I heard Alvin sign off with London, I approached the half-open door and rapped on it lightly.

"Yes?" said Alvin. He'd calmed down and now just looked weary; his eyes dull. Their color—a warm, toasty hazel—was part of what had made them seem friendly at first, but now they reminded me of the dead leaves that choked the roof of the house.

"Do you have a minute?" I asked.

"If it's crucial." His jaw worked a little; he was not in a good frame of mind, but it wasn't as though I had the luxury of cornering him sometime when his coworker wasn't dead.

"It is," I said. "I want to help out with what's going on, try to get to the bottom of it."

He turned away from me, walking farther into the room. "Aren't you working full-time at Valiant Studios?"

He hadn't explicitly invited me to follow, but I did anyway. "Yes, but if I tell Inaya what's going on, I know she'll give me the time to look into this."

"I appreciate the offer, but I think that would add to our problems."

"How so?"

Alvin put the conference table between us and gave me a steely look I felt in my solar plexus despite his being about an inch shorter than I was. "It's obvious you're not unbiased in this situation."

"And you are?" I said.

His eyes' hardness went from steel to diamond.

"I'm just saying, it's not possible to be calm about any of this, so let's not pretend anyone is. Even before—before this happened, you came here prejudiced against Caryl, and I'm going to hazard a guess that I've spent more time observing her directly than you have. If we have different opinions of her competence, what makes you so sure yours is correct? You and I are informed in different ways; we could help each other."

"How exactly do you think you could be of help?"

"I can cancel magic by touching it. You know that, right?"

"Yes, that's one of the things Caryl did bother to include in her reports—when they finally came in."

"There's nothing I can do for Tamika, of course—"

"She's long gone." His words were as flat as Caryl's, he'd apparently found some nonmagical place to store his emotions for the time being.

I tried to read him before continuing. Numb and tired was about as close to "fine" as he was likely going to get in this situation, so I ventured onward.

"On top of my potentially useful hardware, I also have personal experience working with Caryl, and she cares for me. If she needs to be talked into something, I'm your woman."

"Can I ask you about that? When you say she cares for you . . ."

"We're not—involved. She has a crush on me, but it's the sort of crush a child would have."

"It still makes me uneasy."

"Please tell me you're not one of those people who classifies same-sex attraction as a weakness of character."

Alvin gave me a long look, his jaw working as he weighed his response. "You don't know me," he said finally, "so I'll just let that one slide."

"You're right; I don't know you. For all I know, you could be a raging homophobe."

"Not that I'm obligated to defend myself, but among the many hats I wear on a daily basis, I'm on the Outreach Committee for the LGBT Community Center of New Orleans."

I felt suddenly shy, my face flushing. "Oh. You're gay?"

"I'm trans."

"Trans?" I blinked, looking him up and down. My face went from warm to hot. "You—used to be a woman?"

"That's debatable. But I do have a sash full of Girl Scout badges."

"I—wow, I—"

"My point is, Caryl's sexuality, or yours, doesn't enter into this. It's your working relationship and her PTSD that concern me."

"Okay, but—" I'd had another point, but it was gone now. I didn't know how I was supposed to react to the information Alvin had just given me. I suspected that I wasn't supposed to react at all, but I was failing at that and was preoccupied with that failure. My brain was a snake eating its own tail.

Alvin smoothed a hand back over his silver hair, looking twice as tired as he'd looked at the beginning of the conversation. "Okay but what?"

"I don't remember. I'm sorry. I've got brain damage, so if we switch topics . . ."

There was a barely perceptible softening around his eyes.

"All right," he said. "It's okay. We were talking about why you thought you could help. You mentioned that you can cancel spells and that you have influence over Caryl."

"Right!" I must have smiled pretty huge with relief, because he smiled back a little, as though involuntary. "Whatever's happening right now?" I said. "Dollars to donuts this has something to do with the shit that went down on stage 13 in June. Everything has been screwed up around here since then, and I don't think it's coincidence. Tjuan's had a relapse, the soundstage seems to be haunted, a manticore's trying to eat the duke, Caryl's familiar is on the fritz—"

"On the fritz how?"

Shit. I hadn't meant to rat her out. "I don't know exactly," I said. "It might not be broken at all; she may just be feeling some very strange emotions that are manifesting visually, the way the spell is designed to do."

"What exactly did she tell you?"

I considered my options. I hated to betray Caryl, but Alvin's objections seemed to revolve around the idea that I was on Caryl's side and not Dame Belinda's. If I was going to help Caryl, I needed the Project's goodwill. As much of an asshole as I was for thinking it, I knew I could get Caryl's forgiveness a lot easier than I could get Alvin's permission.

"She said Elliott was frightened around Tjuan or something. And sometimes becoming aggressive toward Caryl herself."

Alvin stroked his goatee. It was closer trimmed than Claybriar's, more distinguished than hipster—wait, he had a *goatee*. Now my brain was considering hormone treatments and hair plugs and wandering way, way off into the weeds while Alvin was continuing to talk to me.

"It's ambiguous," he said thoughtfully as I struggled to focus. "It could be a manifestation of Caryl's discomfort about Tjuan's condition, and the aggression could be from some form of externalized self-recrimination."

He was starting to sound like Caryl, but I wasn't about to tell him that. "Could well be," I said instead. "But I haven't even finished getting to my third point, which may be the most important. If all this links back to what happened with Vivian, I'm the only person left you can work with who was actually there."

Alvin lowered his hand from his chin and gave me a long, steady look. "We've been following up on Vivian at the international level," he finally admitted. "Looking for conspirators at Cera. Do you know of Cera?"

"I feel like I've heard the name, but it's slippery."

"Exterminators," he said. "An international company, but Vivian held a controlling interest. We assumed Cera's COO, Garcia, might be carrying on with the plot you uncovered, but all our investigations made him look completely ignorant of whatever she was scheming. And yet there's still odd activity among the lower-level employees that we can't understand and can't dismiss."

"Like what?"

He opened his mouth to answer, but then a wary expression crossed his face. "I think I've told you enough, unless you want to sign a contract with us."

"That would require me to live in a Project Residence, and there aren't any near where I work. Among other problems."

"Then you'll have to make do with what I've told you, most of which I shouldn't have. I have to draw a line somewhere. If you prove yourself helpful, maybe I'll tell you more."

"All right," I said. "For now then I guess I just, what, go home and wait?"

"Home," said Alvin. The weight of it all seemed to crash back down on him in that single syllable. "I'm not making it back in time for my anniversary, am I."

"You're married?"

"Not yet," he said. "Been with my girlfriend a year next week." He rubbed at his forehead as though trying to erase the lines on it. "I fucking jinxed it by making reservations."

For some reason I'd assumed he'd been involved with Tamika; I guess I didn't have a lot of experience with close bonds that didn't involve sex. I tried to think of something comforting to say, but I got the strong vibe from Alvin that he was tired of talking to me, so I mumbled "sorry" and went back downstairs.

Claybriar wasn't in the living room where I'd left him; he was sitting at the dining room table drawing. All of my irritation vanished as a warm blanket of awe and lust settled over me. I had never actually seen him at work before, only the finished products.

A few strands of hair had fallen over his eyes, but I could still see his intent, transported expression as the tip of his pen flicked across the paper with effortless precision. The undone top buttons of his shirt revealed a tempting wedge of skin, but honestly, his complete inattention to my existence was the most erotic thing about the whole scene.

I edged closer, trying to muffle the sound of my shoes against the floor, a harder task than it would have been in the days when my body was a single coordinated machine. I didn't want to disturb Claybriar, but I was desperate to see what he was drawing.

It turned out to be a tall, skeletal figure clothed in shreds of black, great antlers curving from its hook-beaked skull. Malevolence burned in its eyes, and power—power beyond anything I'd experienced.

No doubt about it; this was Winterglass, king of the Unseelie Court.

And I had just asked my Echo to deliver that guy some really bad news.

10

I wanted to say something to Claybriar, but I wasn't sure it was safe. He was casting an actual spell as I stood there; Teo had explained to me how empathy charms worked. Claybriar was binding his emotions into the drawing even as he was making it. From the expression on his face, I believed it; his look of concentration went beyond what you might expect even from an artist. There was something almost prayerful in it.

I watched him as he filled in the last shadows under the king's feet: jagged, slanting shapes that made it look as though the light source were low on the horizon behind him. There is something humbling about the presence of genius; I felt vulnerable and a little sick at myself for the way I'd dismissed him mere minutes before.

At last he finished the drawing, shuddered, and pushed it away like a plate he'd cleaned too fast.

"You okay?" I asked him softly.

He lifted his eyes to look at me, his expression unfocused. It reminded me disturbingly of the way Tjuan had looked at me when he was hearing voices.

"Yeah," he said roughly. "Just not used to— I've never used Unseelie magic before."

"Wait, *what*?" I went to the table and sat with him. "You can do that?"

"Yeah. I'm not great with the Unseelie tongue, but I guess I managed." He surveyed the drawing and shuddered again.

"Where did you learn to speak Unseelie?"

"It's not like human languages. It just sort of comes to you, if you're attuned."

"But you're Seelie."

"Seelie and Unseelie aren't nationalities; they're different kinds of magic. Most types of fey have potential to do one or the other. But if you use too much Unseelie magic it twists you, turns you ugly, so different species tend to have different preferences. It gets political, though, because of the king and queen. They serve as . . . the embodiment of each power, I guess you'd say, and you can't serve both. You have to choose."

I looked at the drawing again. He'd written REIGN OF SHARDS beneath it. The paper seemed almost saturated with fear and hatred.

"Why did you draw him?" I asked him.

"It's for the queen," he said. "When I ask to go and see Her Majesty's rival, she'll fear betrayal. I'm bound to her by choice. If I swear loyalty to him instead, she'll lose her power to command me."

"Do you even speak enough Unseelie to swear loyalty?"

"Wouldn't have to. All I have to do is prostrate myself before the king in a certain ritualistic way and boom, I'm Unseelie. They made it easy, so whole armies can do it at once."

"I can see why she'd be worried."

He looked down at his work, traced the edge of the paper with a fingertip. "That's why I need her to know how I feel about him."

"Just tell her. Fey can't lie, right?"

"Fey language isn't for—conversation," he said haltingly. "Our language shapes reality. Look what saying my name can do. We have other ways of communicating besides speech. The ones you call the *sidhe*, our rulers? They can get right into your head, share thoughts directly. I have my drawings, and I can also make other objects communicate in different ways. Nothing too powerful."

"That's *very* powerful," I said, gesturing to the drawing. "Remember, your drawings are what brought me to you."

He gave an awkward shrug. "The fact that they last awhile is useful. Her Majesty can hold on to it while I'm gone. Her memory isn't great, which is part of the reason she needs me." I thought I saw something like tenderness in his expression, which made me unaccountably jealous, but before I could have another mood swing he picked up the paper and folded it, putting it into his pocket.

I stared at it. "Uh, what did you just put that drawing into if your pants aren't real?"

He burst into laughter. I loved his laugh; it always sounded like some caged thing breaking out.

"My clothes are real enough," he said. "I bought them at Old Navy. I mean, the body under them's pretty real too. It does— most of the body stuff."

"If that's a real body, where does it go when I touch you?"

"It goes wherever my real one is right now. I mean, I guess it does? I just wear the stuff."

"You're honestly not even curious?"

"Yeah, but it's over my head. All I know is that they adapted the spell from creatures that naturally shape-shift. So now

I've got more than one body, and they just rotate into place as directed by the spell. Except one of my bodies isn't natural to me since I wasn't born a shifter, so the spell's required to make me change to it."

"But where did the body *come* from?"

"There's specialists at the Courts who make 'em."

"People who create *entire functioning humans*?"

"The bodies at least, if they have the right blueprint. But they can't *animate* them. Even the *sidhe* can't manufacture sentience. So you don't need to worry about some soulless army of artificial humans marching against you."

"I—really wasn't until right this second."

"I guess my work here is done."

I sighed. "Your work here probably *is* just about done, right? Thanks to Her Majesty's short leash. And I've got to get to therapy or I've flushed two hundred bucks."

"I'll see if I can convince Duke Skyhollow to let me come back once I've reported to Her Majesty and delivered your message to the Unseelie High Court."

"But I want you *now*."

I'd chosen my words poorly; his eyes flared with a sudden naked lust that made me all too aware of what he really was.

"It would be worth it," he said quietly.

I looked away. "Pfft. I'd kill you or something."

"Nah," he said. "It'd just hurt me like hell. And I might be human by the time we were done. And probably in a coma. I'd be stuck in Arcadia for, I don't know, decades, recovering."

"So, not worth it."

"Not for you, since you've only got eighty years to live." His grin this time was decidedly feral.

I fanned myself dramatically, trying to cover my discomfort. If he could have held his current form, I'd have been all over it. But the thought of—no, just no. I was not touching the goat half of him, not like that, not ever. The realization was pretty depressing.

"Walk me back up to the Gate?" he said.

His surgical gloves were lying crumpled on the table; he started to put them back on. I liked his hands—long fingers, strong knuckles. Ideas started to come to me and sent the blood rushing to my cheeks. But no. I couldn't very well ask him to do things for me that I wasn't willing to do for him. Even though I knew he *would*. Especially because I knew he would.

"Come on." He held out his hand and I took it, lacing my fingers between his.

He was patient with me on the stairs, letting me lean on our joined hands a bit.

"I don't actually know how to get into the tower," I said. "The door is warded so I can't see it."

"I can," he said. "Just have to shift my focus a little. Hold on."

He stood for a moment in the second-floor hallway and stared at the wall as though it were a stereogram.

"Aha," he said. He stopped right before room 6 and opened a door that absolutely wasn't there, a door behind which was a spiral staircase. I let out a little grunt of astonishment; I'd walked by it dozens of times and never had the faintest clue.

More stairs, more leaning. He smelled so good I got a little light-headed.

The floor of the tower room was actually the ceiling of room 6. Unlike room 6, this room had windows on all eight walls and was empty except for the Gate in the center and a single tiny desk at one side. At that desk sat Phil, who had apparently been having a nap; he furtively wiped drool from his salt-and-pepper beard as he sat up.

I'd seen a Gate once before at Residence One in Santa Monica, and this one was enough like it that I couldn't identify differences from memory. It was semicircular, with a large enough radius that Claybriar would be able to pass under it without ducking. On the outside, it was made of a staggering number of small, precisely shaped blocks of graphite covered—via some magic or other—in an unbroken veneer of diamond. The interior of the Gate was what you didn't want to look at; it was a pulsing, roiling, impossible worldless nothingness that would make your brains leak out your eye sockets if you looked too long.

"Is there a problem?" said Phil, narrowing his eyes at Claybriar. "You're here for another two weeks, right?"

"Summons from the queen," Claybriar said. "I don't have much choice."

Phil cocked a bushy brow. "La dee dah," he said. "I guess there's no rules about going back early, but you do understand that once you're gone you're gone. You can't just pop back over here. The grand dame's watching this area pretty sharp; you gotta get a new exit permit, gotta fill out a new I-LA4—"

"I understand. Uh—could you give Millie and me a minute? To say good-bye?"

Phil looked between us, and his air of irritation hardened into something downright resentful. For a moment I thought he was going to object, but instead he just gave a stiff shrug.

"Fine," he said. "Just don't tell Caryl I left the Gate unattended."

Did he still think Caryl was in charge? Did he not know his partner had found a dead body? How long had he been up here? I sure as hell wasn't going to be the one to break the news. "Thanks" was all I said.

"After the fey goes through," said Phil, "write it down in the log here. Should be self-explanatory. I'm gonna see if I can slip past Caryl for some coffee." With that he trudged out, closing the door behind him.

"He's about to be in for a shock," said Claybriar ruefully.

"He's had worse," I said. "He was Gloria's boyfriend."

"Oh."

I looked down at my hands. I was suddenly aware that it was just the two of us in the room and felt the weight of expectation.

Claybriar took a half step closer to me. I inhaled tensely, then felt his gloved fingertips slide into my hair. He stroked them over my scalp; I exhaled and my eyes closed. This wasn't the hircine lust I'd seen in him downstairs, but something tender and human that took me completely apart.

"Is this all right?" he asked.

"It's fine," I said weakly, my eyes still closed. "It's just—normally—" I felt groggy; I couldn't find the words.

"Normally what?"

"This seems like a kissing moment. But—"

He leaned in, brushed my lips with his. His exhale of surprised pain was tinged sweetly with apples.

"How about that?" he whispered, his breath warm against my mouth. "Was that all right?"

"Yeah," I whispered back. "But I don't want to hurt you—"

He answered by wrapping his other hand around my arm

and pressing his lips to mine again. And again. Then just the faintest teasing flick of the tip of his tongue; if I'd had toes, they'd have curled. I opened my mouth, inviting him, but he drew back—likely pausing for relief, but gorgeously tantalizing all the same. He steadied himself for a moment before coming in again.

"God," I whispered the next time he drew that half inch back. I had quite literally never felt anything like this in my life. He put both hands under my arms, because I was starting to list to one side. Finally he drew back all the way and looked down at me, smiling a little.

"You okay?"

"Today is—not quite what I was expecting," I said. "On a number of levels."

"Was that too far? I've been wanting to do that since—well, I guess since I saw you in that resort in Santa Barbara."

"It's fine," I said. "It's good. It's great. Just—well, fuck." I let out a shaky laugh. "Bye, I guess."

His smile took on a tinge of sadness. "Take care of yourself, okay? I promise I'll be back."

I was still too high to be sad about how long it might be. Borderlines live in the moment, and in that moment all was right with the world. In truth I'd lived long enough to know that soon the high would wear off and I'd crash hard, but it was easy not to care about that.

"Watch out for that minotaur or whatever," I said with a faint, tipsy smile.

"Manticore," he said, and made a face. "Thanks for reminding me. Would have been really awkward to go through the Gate with a massive hard-on."

"Oh God!" I said, pulling away from him. "Get the hell out of here."

So he did.

After fibbing my way through group therapy and tossing and turning my way through nightmares of rotting corpses, work on Friday was even more excruciating than usual. On top of the standard stress and nuisances, I had the constant awareness in the back of my mind that Caryl was locked in a basement and there was jack-all I could do about it.

Things at Valiant weren't exactly lining up to make me feel competent either. Since stage 13 was no closer to ready for Naderi, I managed to arrange an afternoon meeting with some guys from Wendigo Digital about doing green-screen work. Inaya even made a point of showing up personally. But instead of recognizing this as a gesture of respect, Naderi treated it like we'd sprung an intervention.

It didn't help that Rahul, the guy doing most of the talking for Wendigo, was the single most arrogant prick I had ever had the privilege of dealing with in years of working in entertainment. He kept staring at Naderi's cleavage and spoke about television as though it were some poisonous ghetto where Wendigo's reputation was in danger of being drive-by shot. If Naderi hadn't made such a name for herself in film, I probably wouldn't have even gotten Rahul to take the meeting, and as it was, I'm pretty sure he was high as a kite.

Keeping the peace was like trying to juggle a razor, a bowling ball, and a vibrating dildo, and just as things were teetering on the edge of getting ugly, my phone buzzed against my thigh. I ignored Rahul's frown and eased the phone just far enough out of my pocket to look at it. I didn't recognize the number, so I declined the call and pushed the phone back into my pocket.

"Look, sweetheart," Rahul said to Inaya while I was too distracted to stop him from addressing her directly.

"I'm sorry," Inaya interrupted. "Did you just call me 'sweetheart'? Are we courting?"

Rahul laughed. Inaya didn't.

"You seem to forget," Naderi said, "that you're here to sell *me* on this half measure, this *expensive* half measure, when all I really want is space to build actual fucking sets."

"And you seem to forget," he countered, his friendliness evaporating instantly, "that my company doesn't need a glorified soap opera to make its reputation. I'm here out of respect for your track record, and out of respect for the numbers that your show is pulling in, and because it's Friday afternoon and the man I wanted to be meeting with decided he'd take off early for his brother's gay wedding in San Francisco."

Before Naderi could respond, I cleared my throat to pull her attention. "I know this is not what you wanted," I said to her. "That's on me. And I get that no one here is going to be best friends. But we still have no ETA on getting stage 13 up to code, and this would at least allow you to keep shooting. Wendigo does top-tier work, and consider for a second how improbable it is that we even got a meeting with them today. I think someone up there is trying to tell you something."

Playing on Naderi's religious convictions and Rahul's vanity in one stroke seemed to ease the tension in the room a notch. I was just starting to consider myself not entirely incompetent when my phone buzzed its quiet little song again.

"So sorry," I said, and disabled the ringer entirely. Whoever it was could wait.

Apparently the caller didn't agree, because when Rahul and Naderi finally agreed to meet again next week to talk numbers, I returned to my desk and saw that I had seventeen more missed calls from the same person.

I called back, half angry and half panicked. I didn't recognize the voice of the guy who picked up.

"Who is this?" I asked irritably. "And what's the big goddamned emergency?"

"Assuming this is Millie," said the mystery caller, "I would be the person you tried to talk into working with you less than twenty-four hours ago."

Oops. Alvin.

"I'm so sorry," I said. "I was in a meeting at Valiant, and I don't have you programmed into my—"

He brushed right past my apology. "You need to come to Residence Four right away," he said. "There's someone here to see you. And *only* you, apparently."

"Claybriar?" My heart kicked against my chest.

"I wish. No, Millie, you have the indescribable and non-negotiable honor of explaining yourself in person to King Winterglass of the Unseelie Court."

11

The cab driver managed to get me to Residence Four just before five p.m., but already the October sky was looking wan and sunsettish. As I got out of the cab, a great flock of rasping crows wheeled across a patch of leaden cloud, as though I weren't quite creeped out enough. The looming Victorian residence had never looked more haunted; it seemed to grow taller as I approached. The leaves in the yard were piled high enough in some places to tickle the remaining nerve endings just below my right knee as I trudged through in my work slacks.

I knocked on the front door, half expecting the porter from *Macbeth*, but Alvin answered, of course. He looked grim.

"Come in," he said. There was something subdued in his manner, almost as though he were slightly afraid of *me*. He stepped back to let me in, and as he did so, he gestured to the couch that faced the door.

I didn't have to ask if I was looking at a king. I was so struck by the man on the sofa that it took me a moment to even process that Claybriar was in the room as well, leaning against a far wall.

The king's facade was that of an Asian man around my age, certainly not past thirty. The top section of his hair was pulled back from a pale, sorrowful face and held with a wooden clasp. The rest of his hair fell over his shoulders like satin. He wore a long black jacket over a poet's shirt and slim charcoal-colored trousers; his hand rested lightly on a walking stick with a translucent blue sphere at the top.

"King W— Your Majesty?" I had no idea how to address him, and Claybriar looked faintly disgusted by my choice.

Winterglass took a long moment to study me. When he spoke, his voice was as cold and soft as fresh snow.

"You are no subject of mine," he said. His accent was hard to place; he sounded like a foreigner making an almost-flawless attempt at British Received Pronunciation.

"What do I call you?"

"For this time and place I have been given the unlikely name of Feng Morozov," he said. "I suppose Mr. Morozov will do."

"Pleased to meet you, Mr. Morozov," I said. "You can call me Millie."

"You are a friend of Caryl Vallo," he said. "I would give you my hand in greeting, but the iron in you sings like a struck bell."

"Touching me would be unpleasant for both of us," I agreed, remembering Claybriar's drawing of the king's true form.

The artist in question was leaning on the wall, looking resentfully at his subject; when he caught my eye, I smiled uncertainly. "I'm glad you came back," I said.

Claybriar grunted, softening a little. "I've been given leave by Her Majesty to help your investigation until I've healed well enough to hunt again."

"Healed? You're hurt?" I went to him instinctively, as though there were anything I could do.

"That manticore waylaid us on the way to the Gate," he said. "I managed to heal the worst of it with magic, but my back's still clawed up pretty good. Was mostly occupied with keeping my organs inside me, so I saved the back for last, and then it was too late."

"But it was your fey body that was injured, right? This one's okay?"

"They're linked. What happens to one happens to both."

"Oh no! Did you kill the manticore, at least?"

"Nah. I dazzled it with a flash of light so I'd have the advantage, but the damn thing just bolted away, blind. I couldn't have kept up even if I hadn't been bleeding everywhere."

"He saved my life," said Winterglass, his eyes distant.

"Not on purpose," said Clay. "His life just happened to be near mine at the time."

The king gave a single sharp laugh, like ice cracking in a thaw.

"Mr. . . . Morozov," I said. "I'm sorry for keeping you waiting. I wasn't expecting you to show up here. To be honest, I'm not sure of the protocol." I looked back at Alvin, but he gave me a *you made your bed, you lie in it* kind of look.

"Some matters cannot be left to lesser hands," said Winterglass. "My purpose here is to help Miss Vallo and ensure that the true"—he hesitated for a moment, shrewd black eyes searching mine as though they were a database—"perpetrator of these crimes is found."

This marked the second time this man—or whatever you'd call him—had spontaneously abandoned his kingdom for Caryl's sake. Worth noting.

"You don't think your absence will cause problems?"

"I dare not linger indefinitely," he conceded, "but as I have brought my scepter with me in the form of this staff, I at least cannot be usurped in my absence. Any matters of state will have to be postponed until my return."

"So the staff will work the same way here that it does in Arcadia? Make people obey you?"

"Only Unseelie fey, but it also prevents Unseelie fey from commanding me or causing me harm."

"It was a good idea to bring it with you," I said. "Caryl mentioned before that you'd left it with . . . your son? Seems like a lot of trust to put in a child."

Winterglass looked slightly disconcerted and took a moment to frame his reply. "That was a mistake," he said, "but not because he is unworthy of trust. It would be my honor to put my realm in the hands of Prince Fettershock again, but he is . . . traveling." The king gazed for a moment at his own hand where it rested atop the milky-blue orb. "Caryl has told you of her abduction?"

"A little," I said. "Have you spoken with her yet?"

His eyes sharpened, held mine. "Where is she?"

I looked to Alvin. "You didn't tell him?"

"I didn't even know he was here to see her," said Alvin. "He wouldn't say a word to me other than to keep demanding that I produce you. Thanks a heap for that, by the way. You'd better have a plan."

I smiled slyly and hoped he'd infer that I did, because I hadn't the faintest idea what to do next, other than the obvious.

"If you'll follow me, Mr. Morozov," I said, "I can take you to see Caryl."

"Three seven zero one," said Claybriar helpfully.

I smiled at him. "Are you good to stay for a while?" I asked.

"Yeah. Once I reported to the queen, the summons was dispelled."

"Then you come too. And Alvin? I'm going to need a pair of fey glasses."

Caryl sat on the basement floor with her arms wrapped around her knees and her forehead resting on them. She didn't look up as I came down the stairs with fey glasses clutched in one hand; I half wondered if she was asleep.

Winterglass breathed a single word in the viscous Unseelie tongue, and Caryl sat bolt upright as though she'd been jabbed in the back. She scrambled backward until the wall stopped her, and then she cowered there, looking up at him.

"Caryl!" I said. "It's okay—I'm so sorry; he decided to come here himself."

"It's fine," she rasped, tears overflowing and streaming down her face. She began to shake convulsively. "It's only that I don't have Ell—" And then she fainted, hard and fast enough that I couldn't stop her before her head hit the basement floor with an audible thump.

Winterglass swept across the room and knelt beside her, sliding his arms beneath her and cradling her against him. He laid a palm against the side of her head where it had struck the floor. It looked as though it might bruise but wasn't bleeding.

"Caryl," said Winterglass, followed by a stream of murmured words in what sounded like Russian. Then he seemed to remember himself and switched back to English. "Caryl, you are safe. Call your familiar."

Her eyes fluttered but didn't quite open. She groaned, then murmured dark words under her breath. Slipping on the Project-issue mirror shades Alvin had let me borrow, I saw Elliott appear. I'd kind of missed the little guy. He gave a stretch of his batlike wings and fluttered to my shoulder, unsurprised to see me, since he was just a facet of Caryl's mind.

Caryl sat up and pulled away from Winterglass, who stared at her with a desolate expression. Both, through the fey lenses, were veiled in the green-purple haze of Unseelie magic.

"I apologize," said Caryl. "Thank you for sending the message, Millie, and thank you, Your Majesty, for coming."

Winterglass didn't correct her form of address; perhaps because she used Unseelie magic, he considered her his rightful subject.

"You're a grown woman now," said the king. "All this time in my mind, you remained the same."

"The cliché of the estranged parent," said Caryl dryly. "But let us not dwell on it; you would not be here if there were not urgent matters on the table."

"You have only to tell me what you need," he said, "and it is yours."

She looked at him for a moment while Elliott, still perched on my shoulder, blinked a few times in bashful surprise.

"I need you to stall the wheels that are grinding toward my execution," Caryl said. "I stand accused of killing a human agent of the Arcadia Project, and believe myself to be innocent of this crime."

"Why do they believe you responsible?"

"She was killed by Unseelie spellwork, and I was the only practitioner of Unseelie magic in the area."

"Well," I interrupted, "Claybriar can cast Unseelie spells, but he never left my side between the time he arrived and the time her body was found."

"What sort of spell killed the woman?" asked Winterglass.

"A somatic enchantment," said Caryl. "A lethal one that instantly decayed the flesh."

I interrupted. "Somatic means what exactly?"

"A spell cast on the body," Caryl explained, "as opposed to a psychic spell. I should mention that I was also the only spell caster present in an abandoned building the day before, when Millie fell under a psychic enchantment."

"A dangerous one?"

"If it was meant to be, it failed. She saw a vision of a man she knew who had died there."

Winterglass made a low, thoughtful sound. "A haunting, then."

"Haunting?" echoed Caryl. "The Arcadia Project has never found any evidence of the existence of ghosts. The human soul isn't even—"

Winterglass made a dismissive gesture. "Hauntings are not caused by human souls but by wisps, charges of arcane energy that have been drawn to your world from ours by miraculous or catastrophic events. The energy becomes"—he paused for a moment, searching Caryl's eyes just as he'd searched mine earlier, as though finding the word there—"imprinted by the event that drew it. This wisp of energy echoes the event again and again to any mind that carries the appropriate emotion."

"So it really wasn't Teo I saw. Just . . . escaped energy?" I glanced at Claybriar, but he was busy glaring at Winterglass as though taking notes for an even less flattering drawing.

"Escaped but temporarily bound," the king said. "Just as light is only seen when reflected, magic cannot be sensed until it is bound in a spell. Oddly enough, a caster is not always required to bind it. As water flows downhill and ah"—he paused again, rubbing his fingers together as though trying to find the metaphor physically in the air—"lightning will leap from earth to sky, arcane energy seeks emotion. You were . . . sad, or fearful perhaps, and so you drew the energy into yourself. Once it was in your mind, it flowed into the structure it found there, forming a spell."

"So I cast a spell on *myself*?"

Winterglass drew back as though affronted. "If you wish to simplify it to the point of absurdity."

"Either way, it lets Caryl off the hook."

Winterglass shook his head. "I am still troubled by the death here. Flesh does not have its own awareness, and so a somatic spell would require craft. Someone killed your agent with purpose."

"But not Caryl," I said.

"Not Caryl," Winterglass agreed.

"What do we do?" I asked him. "How do we find out who killed Tamika? The two things have to be related. Could we have let the energy out of there somehow when we opened the door, turned it loose, given it different powers?"

"No," said Winterglass firmly. "It was not the door that trapped it. Think of emotion as water. In Arcadia, emotion flows in streams through the very air; living things can be buffeted by fear or joy with no cause, as by a wind."

"I can relate."

"Yes, it feels like madness to your kind. But wisps of arcane energy use these streams to travel anywhere, fast as thought. Your world, on the other hand, is a dry wasteland. A wisp in your world is as a fish who has been drawn from its stream and deposited onto a beach. Its fins are useless."

"So if the metaphorical fish couldn't pursue me, it must still be flopping around in there."

"Yes."

"Shouldn't we go toss it back into the Arcadian water?"

Winterglass rose to his feet and paced thoughtfully toward the wall Caryl had been leaning against, lacing his uncallused fingers behind his back. "Because wisps lost to your world are an ongoing occurrence, the Seelie Court regularly performs a ritual to call them back. This is done twice a year, just after the spring and autumn convergence."

"You mean the equinoxes?"

Again Winterglass gave me that odd searching look, as though his answer could be found in my thoughts somewhere. Given his inexplicable fluency in English and the tidbit I'd learned from Claybriar about *sidhe* getting inside people's minds, it occurred to me that he might be using me as a sort of translating device.

"No," he said. "Each year, sometime between your equinox and ours, the two worlds draw close enough that tremendous amounts of energy slip over, even without traumatic events. As part of the Second Accord between our worlds, the Seelie Court routinely does a drawing ritual to 'tidy up' after each of these convergences. The next ritual should rid your world of any stray arcane energy, including the wisp that haunted this building of yours."

"When is that?"

"I do not know. Fey do not keep calendars; the ritual is a purely reactive event. We sense the convergence, and the Seelie respond. But it cannot be long. It is 'autumn' here, yes?"

"But if it wasn't an energy wisp that killed Tamika, the

ritual won't help us. You're sure it wasn't a wisp? Something invisible that you only see once it casts a spell? It makes sense in both cases."

"Again," said Winterglass, his tone taking on a hint of condescension, "a mind is required to craft a spell. Your emotion drew the nearby energy, and your mind shaped it. But flesh cannot shape a spell; it has no will, and the energy itself has no will or desire, any more than light does."

"I need some air," said Claybriar, heading toward the door, which had been left slightly ajar. He'd gone so quiet I'd almost forgotten he was there.

Winterglass drew himself up to his full height, clearly taken aback by Claybriar's rudeness. "Did I offend you, faun, by debunking your quaint superstitions?"

"We forest types get claustrophobic in basements," Claybriar said without looking at him. But the way he kicked the door closed behind him suggested he was editing the truth: the fey version of a lie.

"What faun superstitions were you talking about?" I asked.

Caryl cut in, her voice sharp and her eyes on Winterglass. "His Majesty was simply reminding the queen's champion that he comes from common stock, despite the fact that he has proven himself as rational and intelligent as any human or *sidhe*."

Winterglass waved it away. "His origins are a matter of fact and not opinion, but if you desire, Caryl, I will refrain from mentioning them in future. Anyhow, I am certain that no wisp caused the somatic spell you describe. If you require an elegant answer to both mysteries, I suppose any number of sentient beings might have enchanted you on the soundstage."

"There was no one there besides Caryl and me," I protested.

"I can attest to this," said Caryl.

Winterglass spread his hands. "Then what you are describing is impossible."

"If you do not believe me," said Caryl, "feel free to search the area yourself. I, on the other hand, must stay here so long as I am under suspicion of murder."

"I understand," said Winterglass. "Perhaps I shall investigate, provided the humans can offer safe transport."

"I'm in," I said. "We can go anytime tomorrow; I don't work Saturdays. But I want to bring Claybriar, too, if you two think you can manage not to get into a slap fight. As for logistics, let's hope Alvin's not too mad at me to help with that."

As if talking Alvin into letting the Unseelie King loose in Manhattan Beach wasn't hard enough, His Majesty took exception to the entire concept of a scrunchie.

Caryl had been able to give me the number of a place that was willing to lend us a couple of navy blue fire inspector uniforms, and Winterglass put on the shirt and trousers without complaint. But for some reason, the moment I started to explain to His Majesty what he needed to do with his conspicuously dramatic raven locks, he dug in his heels like a toddler.

"This cannot possibly be necessary," he said acidly as Residence Manager Song hovered around him making uniform adjustments. "This is an arbitrary humiliation."

Song awkwardly ran a lint roller over the back of His Majesty's Dickies, and I would have exchanged a sympathetic look with her if she'd been willing to make eye contact.

"You two are supposed to be city fire inspectors," I explained, "because that's what a certain nosy disaster of a showrunner is expecting to see. And city fire inspectors don't generally walk around looking like they just stepped off the set of a *wuxia* movie."

"I understand almost nothing in that sentence."

"Look, no city employee would have hair this long at all, but I've been led to understand that your facade's hair doesn't actually *grow*, so we're not going to cut it all off for the sake of one ruse. And we can't use hairpins; they'd hurt you. Just let me show you how to twist it up so it'll stay under your hat and not be *flowing* everywhere. All right?"

Perhaps because I'd invoked the horrifying specter of hairpins, King Winterglass deigned to let Song use the scrunchie to twist up his silken locks under an LAFD cap. He refused to leave his walking stick behind, since it had been fashioned from his all-important royal scepter, but he was able to put a charm on it that diverted eyes away.

Claybriar looked way more at home in his uniform despite the goatee; he had an honest working-man's vibe. Sadly, we didn't have an appropriate vehicle. Since none of us could drive, I had to call a cab.

Valiant was by no means deserted on a Saturday, even though I was personally off the hook; Inaya made do with just Araceli on weekends. Inaya was clued in to our little ruse, so she'd given security the names Clay and Morozov and their fake reason for being on the premises. Just to be safe, I waited for a moment when no one was watching the soundstage entrance to unlock it and usher the boys inside.

Because I was terrified of receiving another visit from "Teo," I'd come armed with every tool Dr. Davis had given me for controlling my emotions—distress tolerance techniques, she called them. Even so, as I smelled the dust of the place and switched on the quavering floodlights, every muscle of my body tensed from trying so hard not to fear the thing that fear would make me see.

I led the two fey toward the center of the cavernous space. "We were standing by the well when I first saw the—whatever it was. You all right, Clay?" My voice sounded small in the emptiness.

"I'm fine," he said, but didn't look it. I could have kicked myself for not at least walking him through distress tolerance in the cab. He'd been beaten half-dead and imprisoned in the well with his sister; my PTSD was probably nothing compared to his.

"I promise no one will push you down the hole this time," I said weakly. "Morozov, do you see any arcane energy floating around?"

"That is the difficulty, is it not?" said Winterglass, his eyes roaming the farthest shadowed corners of the stage. His cheekbones were breathtaking in the dim light. "Energy cannot be seen with the naked eye," he said. "Unless it is moved to action, we have no way of knowing it is here."

"Moved to action?" I stared at his delicate profile as Claybriar wandered away toward the hole in the floor. "Are you suggesting that I should deliberately freak myself out so that I can suck that creepy stuff back into my brain?"

"I have only the dimmest notion what you have just said, but if I understand you correctly, then yes."

"Not a chance," I said. "I'm supposed to be *tolerating* distress, not swimming in it. You want someone to have a horrible vision, do it yourself."

"I am not afraid," he said. "I have no weakness that the creature can exploit."

"Oh, I'm weak now?"

Winterglass gave an eloquent shrug.

"Millie!" Claybriar's panic sliced through the silence like a hot knife. He was kneeling by the edge of the well.

"Never mind," I said to Winterglass, moving toward my Echo. "Looks like we have a volunteer."

12

Claybriar knelt, calling hoarsely down the well in the Seelie tongue, then looked up over his shoulder at me as I approached.

"We need rope," he said.

"Your sister?" I guessed.

"Yes. Find some rope!"

"It's the haunting," I said. "It's in your head now."

He shook his head irritably. "No, she's down there in the well. She must have fallen in from the Arcadian side. Listen!"

I listened; Winterglass approached to stand just behind me and listen too. The only sound was Claybriar's rapid breathing.

"Aren't you going to do something?" Clay swiveled on his knees to face us; he was clearly starting to panic.

"We can't hear it. Only you're hearing it. Cover your ears."

Claybriar put his hands over his ears—futilely, I watched him realize, just as I'd realized when I'd closed my eyes to block out Teo's apparition. Claybriar's whole body contracted with dismay. Meanwhile Winterglass got that strange unfocused look that Clay had worn when looking for the tower door in the Residence Four hallway.

"The faun is enchanted," the king said. "I see the spellwork."

"Make it stop!" Claybriar cried, hands clutching his ears, head bent almost to his knees.

I started to reach down and touch his hair, but at the last minute pulled my hand back and turned to Winterglass. "What do we do?"

"Something is very wrong." The king's tone was flat, cold. "What I am seeing makes no sense. This spell has been *crafted*. By an Unseelie fey."

"How do you know?" I turned a full, slow circle, my eyes scanning the soundstage, looking for somewhere, anywhere that a person could hide.

"It is a sort of 'handwriting,' simply put. A spell caster leaves traces of his essence in his work."

"Signed in blood?" I said with a shiver. I'd heard Arcadia Project members use the word "essence" to describe what ran through fey veins.

"That's not entirely inaccurate," the king conceded.

"Is it anyone you know?"

"No."

I turned my back to the well. "Is someone here?" I called out. Silence.

Winterglass lifted the scepter that I'd forgotten he carried. I was as susceptible to the charm he'd placed on it as anyone else.

"Author of this spellwork," he called out in a ringing voice, "by your essence I know and command you. Reveal yourself, and kneel before your king!"

Nothing happened except that Claybriar gave a terrible, convulsive shudder and looked up at us. A strange, cold hunger twisted his face, made it *wrong*. When I met his eyes, there was no hint of recognition in them.

"Morozov . . . ," I said, backing slowly away from Claybriar. "What the hell is *happening* right now?"

"I—do not know," said Winterglass.

"Really not what I want to hear."

"I no longer see any sign of spellwork upon him."

"Well clearly *something's* wrong!" I studied Claybriar from a safe distance; he had gone still, his eyes fixed on Winterglass. "And the mystery spell caster doesn't seem in the mood to obey you."

Winterglass shook his head with a touch of contempt. "So long as the scepter is mine, my command over Unseelie fey is absolute. Unless—no."

"What?"

"Nothing relevant in this case," he insisted with the air of a man who had no intention of elaborating.

"Are you sure? Because something is clearly up. Maybe your scepter doesn't work on Earth? Maybe the caster isn't Unseelie?"

"Or," said Winterglass thoughtfully, "perhaps he is already kneeling." With a dramatic sweep of his arm, he indicated Claybriar.

"What?" I blurted. "He's not Unseelie! He's the queen's champion for fuck's sake. Unless—he's on his knees; does that count as prostrating himself to you? Did he just switch teams?"

Winterglass looked at me in alarm. "You know far more about fey rituals than any outsider has a right. But no. The gesture you describe is quite specific, kneeling directly to a sovereign with forehead to the ground. Your faun has not pledged himself to my Court. But is that your faun? Are you certain?" We both turned to look at the man kneeling by the well.

"It—yes," I said. "Claybriar, it's you, right?"

Claybriar's eyes were still on Winterglass. "I am and I'm not," he rasped. "Is coffee a cup? Is light a lamp?"

"What the hell are you even—"

A savage smile split his face. "Ah, it feels so good to talk to someone. Too quiet for too long. Go on, ask me something else! If you're good, maybe I'll even give him back to you."

Goose bumps rose on my arms. "Oh my God. Someone's using him as a puppet."

"Someone is speaking *through* him? How?"

"I don't know! You're the expert."

"There is no *expertise* in this situation, Lady Roper. I have never seen its like. Even I cannot command speech."

"Who are you?" I asked Claybriar, or whatever was looking out of his eyes. "Puppet-master-person. Where is your body?"

"Which one? I've used a few." Claybriar smiled. Or his face did, anyway.

"*Your* body," I insisted. "The one you don't have to steal. Where is it?"

"I borrow bodies when I need them. I don't have one of my own."

Winterglass took a half step back, and his expression, for lack of a better word, was *lost*. If the king of the Unseelie Court was lost, I was decidedly fucked.

"Clay, are you still in there?" I asked. "Can you hear me?"

"He can hear you," Claybriar's mouth said, "but I'm not letting him talk."

"Rise," said Winterglass, and Claybriar did. "Miss Roper, tell it to kneel."

"Kneel," I said. Claybriar ignored me.

"Kneel," said Winterglass, and Claybriar did.

The king began to pace. "The creature we are addressing," he said, "is an Unseelie fey bound to the Accord. Otherwise it would not respond to my commands. A consciousness with no physical form? A 'spirit'? That is the stuff of myth."

"And yet we're interviewing one."

The king stopped his pacing to glare at me.

"Think about it!" I said. "Three people died on this soundstage in horrible ways, and now some . . . incorporeal *thing* has possessed my Echo. Classic ghost story. Not to parrot my shrink, but would it be too much to ask for you to practice some radical acceptance, dump the denial, and start looking for solutions?"

Winterglass turned to Claybriar. "What manner of creature are you, when you are not possessing someone else's body?" he demanded.

"I never had a word for it." The creature used something very like Claybriar's casual cadence, as though it were filtering its thoughts through his brain. "But she called me a wraith."

"Who called you a wraith?"

"The exiled countess."

"Vivian Chandler?" I blurted.

"That's the name you gave her, yes."

My fists clenched. "You were working with Vivian."

"Yes."

"And now that she's dead?"

"Now we're working without her."

Every word in that sentence sat poorly with me, "we" making the top of the list. Claybriar gave me another chilling smile.

Meanwhile, Winterglass seemed to regain some of his composure. "How did you get inside the faun?" he asked.

"I opened him."

"How did you 'open' him?"

"I found his deepest sorrow."

"Let me in," I murmured, half to myself. "This fucker was trying to possess *me* before."

Something seemed to shift inside Winterglass; his eyes lit with understanding. "This thing," he said, "this *wraith*, is constructed of arcane energy, just as we are constructed of flesh. It travels on currents of emotion, just as arcane energy does, and is invisible to human and Arcadian eyes, just as arcane energy is. But where did it come from? In all of Arcadian history no one has ever reported an encounter with such a creature."

"I'm less concerned with where it came from and more concerned with how to get it out of Claybriar."

"I have no answer for that, either. I learned of wraiths mere seconds ago; it is too soon for me to have worked out the mechanics of their possession."

I reached out and prodded Claybriar's chest with three fingers. His facade flickered away during the brief moment of contact, then returned, with no change in his expression.

"Pretty sure that didn't work," I said. I shifted my weight onto my AK since my knee was starting to go wobbly. "Which means I may not be safe either. I suppose this is where we panic?"

"No need," said Winterglass with a sly smile. "If this creature is subject to energy's natural laws, then the solution is the same as for a haunting. When the Seelie Court performs the drawing ritual, this creature should be pulled back to our world."

"Even though it's inside a person? How exactly does this drawing ritual work?"

"That information is privileged to the High Courts."

"Privileged my ass. If something's supposed to help Clay, I need the details."

"You are entitled to nothing."

"Didn't you have an Echo once? Surely you can imagine what this feels like for me."

Something flickered over the king's face: not softness exactly, but a kind of sad uncertainty. At last he spoke, with the air of someone who knows he is Breaking the Rules.

"Not in front of this . . . creature," he said. I couldn't be sure if he meant Claybriar or the thing possessing him, but he was already stalking across the soundstage. I glanced worriedly back at Claybriar before following Winterglass at my own slower pace.

Once I'd caught up to the king in what he seemed to consider a distant enough corner of the room, he leaned in and whispered to me, his eyes still on Claybriar. He smelled strange this close, like old stone and peppermint.

"At the Seelie Court," he said, "there exists a relic from the Time of Beasts, from before civilization in Arcadia. Its name translates roughly as the Bone Harp."

"I'm assuming it's not an actual harp."

"But it is. Legend says it belonged to the Beast Queen and was given to the Seelie Court as part of the First Accord, ending the war between the Courts. When played, the harp draws arcane energy to its location—even energy that has escaped to your world, which is why its use after convergences was written into the Second Accord."

"What about energy that's inside people, though?"

"I have never faced that precise phenomenon, but any energy not bound in spellwork is always drawn back to Arcadia by the harp's song."

"Isn't possession a spell?"

"It would seem not. Notice that your touch did not disrupt it. I saw spellwork when the wraith was enchanting the faun to hear a voice from the well, but now there is none. The faun has simply become . . . the wraith's *location*, as the soundstage was before."

"And once the harp stops playing?"

"The energy it drew is freed."

"But it'll be in Arcadia, where the harp is. So it would have no easy way back over here."

"Correct. In time, rare events may once again pull wisps across to your world and strand them here, but since the ritual is performed twice a year by your calendar, the losses are always recouped."

"But you said you don't know when the next ritual is. In the meantime, what the hell are we supposed to do with a possessed faun?"

"The Arcadia Project has a prison, does it not?" said Winterglass with sudden bitterness. "It should confine him as well as it does Miss Vallo."

I gave a little snort of outrage. "I'm not throwing everyone I care about in the same basement. Furthermore, I can't imagine the queen is going to be fine with you locking up her champion. Can't you just order this wraith-thing to leave Claybriar alone?"

The king gave a deliberate, patient sigh that made it strangely easy to picture him raising a kid. "If it leaves," he said slowly, "we can neither see it nor communicate with it. We'll have no way of knowing for certain if it has been drawn back to Arcadia once the ritual is performed."

"So you're completely comfortable using my Echo as a storage device for an evil spirit."

"So it would seem."

I felt fury rising and groped for body awareness, tried to force my muscles to relax. Pissing off the Unseelie King was not going to help anyone. I took a couple of slow, deep breaths and then, once I had enough of my brain back to control my prosthetics, crossed the room to address the wraith again.

"How long have you been here on this soundstage?" I asked.

The wraith had been staring at Winterglass, who followed close behind me; now it shifted its gaze back to mine. "I don't know," it said.

"How did you get here?"

"Wasn't my idea. I was in Arcadia, waiting for orders."

"What kind of a thing are you when you're in Arcadia?" I asked.

"Same as I am here. I was waiting, watching. Then some goddamned human took a knife to himself."

My emotional preparation had been eroded by the most recent series of shocks; I flashed back to Teo staring at his own hand in horror because of Vivian's spell, driving his pocket knife into it as though it were something alien that needed killing.

"His desperation when he died," the wraith went on. "It grabbed me, and suddenly—I was here. But he was dead. I had nowhere to go. Please, I need to *move*. If you want your friend back, help me get out of here."

"You'll leave his body? What exactly are you asking us to do in exchange?"

"No," said Winterglass. He held up a hand toward the wraith, palm out, as though telling a dog to stay. "So long as it has a body, it can be questioned, can be studied."

"That 'body' happens to be my Echo!"

"I understand that it is painful to watch him suffer, but

sometimes we all must endure pain for the greater good. The wraith's control of the faun's body is all that allows us to hold this conversation, and so long as I can converse with the creature I can give it orders."

"Please," said the wraith, sounding almost frantic. "I can't stay in this room another minute. If you let me out, I can help you find another one."

"Another room?" I said.

"Another wraith. It was here with me that night, and it got out. I can help you find it, if you'll help me leave."

I turned to look at Winterglass; his eyes were positively *sparkling*. I looked back at the wraith uneasily.

"If you'll give Claybriar back control of his body," I said, "I'll find a way to get you out of here, I promise."

"Nothing you promise matters," said the wraith. "You can lie."

"Then trust the word of your king," said Winterglass carefully. "I promise to help you to leave this room on the condition that you personally accompany us to find the other wraith you mentioned and release the faun from your control once you have found the wraith. I promise nothing beyond that."

"That's enough," said the wraith. "I'll take it. Okay." Carefully it got to its feet, eyeing Winterglass warily as though it expected him to object.

"What can you tell us about this other wraith we're hunting?" I said. Because right now, as far as I was concerned, that thing was Suspect #1 in Tamika's death.

"When Vivian died," the wraith said, "it found itself inside a *chapel*."

"Holy ground," I said, remembering. "That hurts Unseelie fey."

"Hurts Unseelie *bodies*," said the wraith. "Bodies resist. A wraith has no resistance, it's just—repelled. It shot out of the doorway and into the man standing outside, where it became . . . very disoriented."

I drew in a sharp breath. "Tjuan. He's not relapsing; he's possessed. The wraith is *still in him*."

"And may have cast the spell that killed that woman," said Winterglass.

"We've got to tell Alvin right away," I said. "We need him to let Caryl out of the basement if she's going to help us figure out how to stop these things."

"Stop them from doing what, exactly?"

"They're still carrying out Vivian's plans, or trying. And as of last June, Vivian was planning to destroy every noble estate in Arcadia."

From the king's expression, this was the first he'd heard of it. "Impossible," he scoffed. "The protective wards on noble estates are tied to the fey who own them; it is impossible to unravel them while their owners are inside."

"She wasn't going to undo any spellwork. She was collecting fey blood, lots of it. You know what happens when fey blood is spilled on the ground here, right? All she'd need to do would be to find the right spots on Earth and boom, mass destruction in Arcadia."

"Also unlikely," said Winterglass. "Without a pair of Gate builders it is nearly impossible to map an Arcadian location to its precise counterpart on Earth."

"Well, Vivian knew at least one pair of Gate builders; that's how this well got here. The fey half of that pair was executed for breaking the Accord, so they won't be any further help. But they must have some other way of moving the plan forward, because you *just heard this one say that they're carrying on without her.*" I turned to the wraith. "What's the plan?" I demanded. "How are you going to destroy the estates?"

"I only agreed to lead you to the other wraith," it said. "I never agreed to betray the countess."

"Morozov, make him talk."

Winterglass slowly shook his head. "I cannot command speech."

"I thought Unseelie had to obey the guy with the scepter."

"There are limits to its power. My subject must be able to hear me, for instance. And I am forbidden to command speech—which in Arcadia is synonymous with spell casting. If I could command speech, I would have the power to cast any sort of spell known by any of the near-infinite variety of Unseelie fey. The architects of the Second Accord were not willing to grant that much power to any one fey, even a king."

"Ugh." I clawed my hair back from my face. "I'm beginning to see why Caryl got so annoyed that I killed Vivian before the Project could question her."

Before Winterglass could so much as draw breath to respond, Claybriar lunged at me, knocking me to the floor.

13

As my bolted-together skeleton made impact with the wooden floor, the full-body pain was so intense that at first I didn't notice Claybriar's hands around my throat.

"YOU killed the countess!" the thing possessing my Echo growled.

Weakly I tried to pry loose his fingers, but I was already starting to lose my vision at the edges.

"Release the human!" Winterglass cried out sharply, several seconds too late by my count.

The wraith did as the king commanded, and I gulped a desperate breath. My windpipe felt like it was full of wet sand. I curled onto my side, gagging, trying to get air to flow again. Every cough felt like it was severing my spine.

"Do not move *a single limb* until I tell you that you may." The king's voice was so icy that I froze for a full second before realizing that he was talking to the wraith.

My legs still seemed to be nestled firmly in their prosthetic sockets, which seemed like good news until I tried to sit up and found out why. I'd landed almost entirely on my back and thrown out something badly in the process. Any attempt to get myself off the floor was like a lightning bolt to my entire nervous system, so I lay faceup on the floor, moaning and watching Winterglass pace back and forth like a panther in a cage.

Clearing my throat also hurt. My voice came out rough.

"Surprise surprise," I said. "Maybe the queen's hard-bodied champion isn't the best wraith container."

"Do you propose a better one?" said Winterglass.

"I propose we kick it out of him and just leave it here. I don't much care what that thing wants anymore."

"I am bound to my promise that I would help it leave this soundstage, and to do that it needs a body."

"*Not* Clay's."

"Do you volunteer, then?"

"No!"

"You must admit, that would limit its power, particularly if we were to remove your artificial limbs."

"I—" My heart sank. It was a horrible thing for him to say. It was also sickeningly *true*. "I just—God, I'm already so messed up in the head . . ."

"It seems it must be you or the faun," said the king with a cold smile. "Just how devoted are you to your Echo?"

I realized with a sick wave of self-loathing that I was not devoted enough. Maybe if I'd had access to the magical part of our bond I'd have been less selfish, but the thought of taking off my legs and letting that thing— No, I couldn't. I lay there burning with shame; I couldn't admit my weakness to King Winterglass, but he was smiling as though he already knew. I had the sudden uncontrollable urge to find his own weak spots, to *hurt* him.

"Maybe you should bring Caryl here," I said, "and give it *her* body. It wouldn't be the worst thing you've ever done to her."

I wasn't actually expecting the barb to hit home, but it did. He took a step back as though struck in the chest. Remorse choked me instantly.

He murmured something in Russian I couldn't understand, but it conveyed so much pain that my eyes stung with tears. As hard as it was for me to apologize, I was working myself up to it when the king gave a weird shudder. At the exact same time, Claybriar went as limp as though someone had cut his strings.

"Clay!" I called out from the floor. My throat still hurt a little from where his hands had been wrapped around it. He lay senseless, but I could see him breathing steadily. I tried to move, but pain jolted through my spine again, and I could do nothing but lie on my back, eyes filled with tears.

Then I heard King Winterglass begin to laugh. The sound made my blood run cold.

"Oh shit," I said. "*You're* possessed now."

"Oh, it tried," said Winterglass in a strange, brittle voice. "That's what's so . . . delightful." He smiled, gazing into the middle distance. "Oh yes, I feel you struggling, little one. Stay there inside me until further notice." With that alarming command, he swept across the floor to kneel next to Claybriar, turning his limp body over. "Don't worry about your faun; I think he is merely stunned."

"Explain what just happened," I said between clenched teeth.

"The wraith rode the current of sorrow you so helpfully provided," he said. "I can feel it in me now, fighting the inevitable, but it is trapped. You see, my little subject can neither command me nor cause me harm. I am in full control."

"How do I know you're not the wraith cleverly pretending to be you?"

"Because I just told you that I was not, and neither I nor the wraith can lie."

"Oh, right."

Winterglass continued to examine Claybriar, listening to his breathing, gently lifting one wrist and then the other.

"What's the matter with him?" I said.

"He seems unharmed; he should come round any moment."

"And you? You seem strangely okay with being possessed."

"It has not 'possessed' me. It would be more accurate to say that I possess *it* for the time being. I could not have been certain of this beforehand, but I can feel now, as clearly as I can feel my own breath, that because of the scepter it cannot control any part of me. Not for want of trying."

"And yet you can still carry it out of here, fulfilling your promise."

"Then decide at my leisure how to dispose of it."

"Well. You're welcome, I guess."

King Winterglass looked up from his examination of Claybriar to fix me with a chilly look. I averted my eyes.

"Let's make sure Clay's okay," I said, "and then get the hell back to Residence Four so you can order the other one out of Tjuan and 'dispose of' them both."

"Agreed." With that, Winterglass gave Claybriar a smart slap on the cheek. Claybriar groaned and levered himself to a sitting position, looking bewildered.

"Thank God you're all right," I said.

"What happened?" said Claybriar, cradling his head in his hands as though it hurt.

"Weren't you *aware* that whole time?" I asked. Hadn't the wraith said as much?

"What whole time?"

He'd clearly missed at least the last bit, given that he wasn't immediately falling all over himself to apologize. "What's the last thing you remember?" I asked.

"The well," he said vaguely. Then his gaze sharpened. "My sister!"

I shook my head. "It wasn't your sister. It was a spell, like the one that made me see Teo."

"What happened to you? Why are you on the ground?"

I touched my fingertips to my throat and exchanged a glance with Winterglass. The king spread his hands in a graceful shrug.

"Let's—let's talk about that a little later," I said. "We need to get back to the Residence as soon as possible."

"But you're hurt."

"Just a little. Mostly my back. I fell."

"Let me try and fix it."

"Fix it?"

He shrugged. "Seelie thing. If I catch an injury before the mind gets used to it, I can convince the body it never happened. I'm not *great* at it, but—"

"I don't think any kind of body magic works on me. What did Caryl call it? Somatic spellwork?"

"Let me at least try."

He came and knelt beside me; his face took on the same distant, reaching expression I'd seen when he was drawing. After a moment, he shook his head.

"You're right," he said. "I can't get the spellwork to hold. It just sort of melts on contact with you. But there doesn't seem to be any serious damage. Bump on the back of the head, bruising around your throat but no real damage to the windpipe. Your back is what's going to give you trouble, but even that will be fine in a few days."

"In the meantime," I said, "I'm going to be even slower than usual. Let's call a cab and get back to the Residence." I hesitated, then looked between the two of them. "I hate to do this to you boys, what with my iron and all, but . . . I'm going to need someone to help me up."

By the time we got back to Residence Four, my back hurt so badly that getting out of the cab took three tries and brought tears to my eyes. It was bearable if I sat down and rested against something upright, so I made a beeline for the couch as soon as we were inside.

I'd already texted Alvin, who was busy doing Caryl's managerial maintenance stuff at Residence One. He'd promised to be there by a quarter to two, which meant I had at most fifteen minutes to pull myself together. Winterglass went down to the basement to speak with Caryl while I sat on the sofa and tried to breathe. Monty the cat decided this would be a great time to jump onto my lap; I grudgingly stroked my fingertips down his bony spine as Claybriar settled onto the other end of the couch.

"Well," I said. "Turns out King Winterglass is a pretty useful guy to have around. Thanks for fetching him."

"Fetching?" His gaze was a little sullen. "I'm your dog now?"

"For a guy who speaks English as a second language, you're annoyingly alert to nuance."

That got a smile. "Sorry. I'm cranky. *Sidhe* make me uncomfortable, and Unseelie make me *really* uncomfortable, and Winterglass is the ultimate example of both."

"Explain again how some kind of Irish fairy ended up in Russia?"

"What?" Claybriar looked baffled.

"*Sidhe*," I said. "That's an Irish word, right? But isn't his palace in the equivalent of Russia somewhere?"

"Well, *sidhe* isn't *our* word," said Claybriar. "When stuff got named by the Arcadia Project, it got named whatever the people in London thought it should be named."

"So what are the *sidhe* exactly?"

"I dunno. Just a kind of fey. The assholes who rule everything."

"But they didn't always? Winterglass said something about the Time of Beasts, and a Beast Queen."

"Yes, yes, I know how the *sidhe* see the world. I've worked for them all my life."

"Is there some other version of the story?"

"Can we not talk about this?"

I stared at him. "I said something wrong, didn't I?"

"It's fine. You didn't mean any harm. This is just me being dumb. I was raised—I was raised a certain way, and sometimes it's hard to shake off."

"What do you mean?"

"I don't want to talk trash about my own people," he said. "But the *sidhe* aren't all wrong when they think of us as animals. We're not as much like humans as the *sidhe* are. Not sure if that's because we hardly ever interact with humans, or if our idiocy is the reason we don't interact. Either way, most fauns have awful memories and no ability to reason. Can't learn about arcana or science or how things work. So we just—make up our own stories based on how things *feel*."

"And part of you still believes these stories?"

"No," he said emphatically. "No, now that I can think clearly, I understand the logic of it all. But I remember how the old beliefs *felt*, and—I don't know—sometimes I miss it. Is it weird to miss ignorance?"

"Not at all," I said gently, starting to reach out before I remembered he didn't have his gloves on. I returned my hand to the half drowsing cat in my lap. "I understand wanting to unlearn something. Like . . . Professor Scott."

He turned his eyes to me, something like anger still faintly simmering in them. "The guy you jumped off a building over."

"It's complicated. I didn't jump because of him, but because of the—brutality of that paradigm shift. I had this idea of who he was: a tortured angel, keeping his heart locked away to protect himself. Turned out he was more like—an abandoned house where nothing worked anymore except the security system."

"Ouch."

"What destroyed me more than losing him was having to go back and rewrite everything that had ever happened between us, everything I'd thought was romantic and magical. To see it from his perspective and realize how hollow and sleazy it all was. It broke me."

"Ah, Millie."

"It's all right. A bunch of people worked pretty hard to put me back together. I'm not the same person, but maybe I'm better. My point is, I know what it is to just think, *Please, let me go back to believing the lie.*"

To my surprise, Claybriar's eyes filled with tears.

"Oh no," I said. I shifted awkwardly, not sure what to do, and I was rewarded with another twinge of agony from my back.

"I'm fine," he said. "Just don't say anything to Winterglass about my weird fits of nostalgia. He already thinks I'm an ignorant savage."

I was about to tell him exactly how little I cared about Mr. Morozov's opinion, but then I heard a key in the front door. After a few failures, it finally unlocked and opened to admit Alvin Lamb.

"So," he said, shoving what I recognized as Caryl's key ring back into his pocket. "I really hope the 'smoking gun' you referred to in your text message was metaphorical."

"Mostly."

"This had better be good," said Alvin. "Belinda's called a summit in London, and I need to have something to tell her."

"King Winterglass is in the basement with your prisoner," I said. "I suggest you bring them both up here for this."

"If you don't mind," said Alvin while his eyes said *even if you do*, "I'd rather leave Caryl in the basement until *after* I've seen this smoking gun of yours. I hope you'll forgive my skepticism."

Not only did I forgive it, I was fully prepared to give it last rites. I rested my back until Alvin and Winterglass returned, and then recounted the day's events to Alvin, only skipping the part where Claybriar had assaulted me. I also glossed over how we'd arrived at the decision to trap the wraith inside King Winterglass, since I didn't think His Majesty would appreciate my explaining that I'd managed to hurt his feelings. When I was finished, Alvin stared at me for a long moment.

"*If* this is true," said Alvin, "then it sheds doubt on Caryl's guilt. But you have to understand that from my point of view this sounds like the most utter, irredeemable bullshit."

"Confirm with His Majesty, if you like," I said, trying not to sound smug.

Everyone turned to look at Winterglass.

The king's eyes widened. "This puts me in an awkward posi-tion," he said.

"What's so awkward about it?" I asked.

"Perhaps more than anyone here, I wish to see Caryl's release. But as much as I might desire it, I cannot confirm your story, as I lack the ability to lie."

My gut dropped to my knees. Apparently the ace I'd thought I had up my sleeve was actually a poisonous snake.

14

"What are you doing?" I snapped at Winterglass. "Just tell Alvin what happened. You were the one who figured half of it out."

Winterglass gave me an incredulous look. "What madness is this? You know I am a poor accomplice in fiction."

My heart started to hammer in my chest. "What the fuck is going on? Claybriar, what is he doing?"

"Millie," said Claybriar gently, "you know I'd help if I could, but I was out like a light for most of it."

"But *you* were wide awake!" I said to Winterglass, hearing my voice start to rise in both pitch and volume. "You were *right there*! Just tell him!"

"Please do," said Alvin. "I would like to hear your version of events."

"We entered the soundstage," said Winterglass. "There was, in fact, a haunting; I witnessed its effect on Claybriar. He thought he heard his sister in the well. Millie attempted to pull him away, and he attacked her, pushing her down onto the floor."

"I did *what*?" Claybriar protested, rising to his feet.

"You were *possessed*!" I said. "The wraith did it! And before it attacked me it gave that whole damned *speech* through you, about Vivian, about Tjuan being possessed, a speech that Winterglass is *really fucking inconveniently* leaving out!"

"There was no speech," said Winterglass. "And this 'wraith' idea is absurd."

Had the wraith somehow taken control of Winterglass? No, that didn't make sense; it couldn't lie any more than he could.

"The events happened exactly as I relate them," the king went on. "When Claybriar assaulted Millie, I believe it somehow broke the spell the haunting had placed upon him. After that, Mr. Lamb, Millie asked to return here to speak to you, and we complied."

I felt a twinge of horror at the expression on Alvin's face, because a significant slice of it was *pity*.

"I can understand," he said to me, "why you might enhance the story a little, since the actual events don't clear Caryl's name. I could forgive it as an act of desperation—*if* you hadn't just shoved Tjuan under a bus. Because that's what you're trying to imply, isn't it? You're taking advantage of the fact that he's ill to shift the blame onto him. I'm going to have to ask you not to interfere further in this investigation."

"I'm not making this up!" I said. "I swear to God, Alvin!"

Unexpectedly, Winterglass stepped in. "She's confused," he said. "Panicked. Her emotions suggest this was not a calculated act of deception."

Alvin studied me, seemingly unwilling to argue with Winterglass on any point.

"You do seem sincere," he said at last, in a careful tone I'd heard a lot when I was ranting at the Leishman Center. "Maybe when your Echo attacked, it was traumatic enough that your mind created an alternate narrative that excused his actions."

"You think I'm crazy," I said, hearing my voice quaver with the threat of tears. Damn it.

"If this is honestly how you remember it," he said, "then you're not to blame."

"I didn't *hallucinate* this! I'm Borderline, not—whatever it is you're telling me I am!"

"Millie," said Alvin, "listen to me for a moment. This isn't an attack; this is a discussion."

I bit down on my lip to keep from talking, nodded stiffly, let him continue.

"I don't talk about this very much, but I went through a rough time before my transition. I attempted suicide twice; it was my second attempt that brought me to the Project's attention, when I was nineteen. My family had disowned me, so I had nowhere to go."

I wavered between pity and a profound unease. *No family, nowhere to go* seemed to be a distressingly common thread among Arcadia Project employees.

"Between the stress of that," he said, "and of having to face all this new information about magic and parallel worlds—there was a period of time when my perceptions and my memories got . . . weird. I started thinking I'd woken up and started my day when I was still dreaming, or worrying that I was dreaming when I was awake. It passed after a few months, but I still remember how terrifying it was. I—I shouldn't judge you."

Tears slipped down my cheeks; I was a hot mess of gratitude and fury and humiliation. Alvin was being incredibly nice *for all the wrong fucking reasons.*

Or were the reasons wrong after all?

No, Millie. Stop it. Remember what Dr. Davis says. Others can't change the truth just by denying it. Your thoughts and feelings are valid.

Except when they weren't.

I tried to stay calm. "I—can see why this looks bad," I said. "But what I've told you, it explains everything."

"It explains what you desperately want explained, at the expense of everything we know. Sentient creatures without bodies? King Winterglass, is that even possible?"

"It's folk tale nonsense in either world," said Winterglass. "Everything attributed to 'ghosts' and 'spirits' has consistently been proven to have more rational causes."

But you fucking spoke to one, I didn't say. Because that would make Winterglass a liar, something else that was supposedly impossible by all the laws we knew.

Unless.

If this is honestly how you remember it, Alvin had said, *then you're not to blame.*

Either I or Winterglass clearly had a fucked-up memory of what had happened—and only one of us had a wraith hitching a ride in our head. Unseelie magic could mess with memories; I'd heard people talking about Vivian using this power. And Claybriar had supposedly been aware while the wraith was talking through him, but remembered nothing of it later. While my own memory was a little patchy at times, I had no precedent for *inventing* memory whole cloth. It made much more sense for a wily wraith to snip and edit things to protect itself. It wasn't a command, or technically even harm, so the scepter could conceivably have allowed it.

But it was my word against a king's. Alvin didn't trust me and was heavily invested in good relations with Winterglass.

Caryl would believe me, but her hands were tied. I was going to have to find some way out of this other than continuing to argue for what sounded like delusion.

"I'm sorry," I said at last. "What you're saying makes sense, and I'm not trying to cause trouble. Just—I got hurt pretty badly trying to help. Don't make it worse by booting me off the case. Give me one more chance."

"If you didn't lie on purpose . . ."

"I didn't. I think you can see now that I honestly remember it that way. But if Winterglass remembers it differently, we need to go with his story."

Alvin let out a long exhale; I hadn't realized until that moment how upsetting this whole confrontation had been for him. "Thank you," he said. "I know how hard it must be not to defend yourself, and that makes me want to give you another shot. I won't mention this at the London summit, but please, *please* be more careful."

"What we *do* know," I said, "is that there is some misplaced arcane energy causing trouble, and that Queen Dawnrowan can do a ritual that will pull it back to Arcadia where it belongs. I don't think we should wait; I think we should send word to the Seelie Court to do it as soon as possible."

That would likely fix Tjuan and stage 13. Caryl, however, was still up a creek, and I had no idea how to help her.

After our meeting, Alvin declared his intention to take the two fey to Residence One to fill out some paperwork and then drop them off at their hotel. So much for a private attempt to straighten things out with Winterglass.

It became obvious the minute I tried to stand up from the

couch that I was going to need some heavy-duty pain medication, but I was pretty sure those sorts of substances weren't allowed in an Arcadia Project Residence, so I asked Alvin about it on his way out.

"The Residence manager should have some locked away," he said as he held the front door open for Winterglass and Claybriar. "Unless Caryl's been slacking on that, too."

Residence manager meant Song. She was a gentle creature, seemingly incapable of anger, and I had a feeling she'd lived through far worse abuse than I'd dished out back in June. But the guilt and self-loathing I felt in her presence were suffocating, and it ironically made me even more prone to treating her callously.

At the moment my back pain trumped my guilt, and so I went to knock on her door on the east side of the lower floor. Softly, in case her baby was asleep.

As it turned out, he was. The two of them apparently shared a double bed, because he was still sacked out on it, and Song looked as though she'd just peeled herself away. She had a freckled, pixie-ish nose and narrow, dark eyes; her pillow-mussed hair was not quite black. She'd thrown on a T-shirt, but quickly and half asleep, to judge by the tag sticking out at the front of the collar.

"Have they hired you back?" she murmured to the floor.

"No," I said, and her shoulders lowered a half inch. "Just helping with the Caryl situation. I'm sorry to wake you, but I need some pain medication. I've hurt my back pretty badly."

Finally she dragged her eyes up to mine; hers were full of suspicion. "There's Aleve in the kitchen cabinet."

"I think this is beyond that," I said. "I fell down on a

hardwood floor, flat onto my back. Was pushed, actually."

I saw a shock of sympathy in her face; the thorough swiftness of it confirmed some of my suspicions about her background. "Who pushed you?" she said, taking a half step closer.

"Someone under an Unseelie spell," I said. "He feels awful about it now."

Without another word, Song went to the back of the room and opened the closet; the safe was in there. She rooted through it and came back with a couple of little white pills. "These should be good for about six hours," she said. "I'll come find you before they wear off."

"I'm . . . actually not staying here."

"You should until your back is better," she said. "I can take care of you. I'll put the air mattress in the living room; it'll be quiet there at night."

"Thank you," I said, warmed and a little shaken by the way she had instantly dilated her protective instincts to include me.

I went to the kitchen for some water, took my pills, and rested on the couch until they kicked in. As soon as I was able to stand up without wishing for a swift death, I made my way toward the back of the house.

Even though I was slightly afraid of Tjuan now that I knew what was inside him, and even though I didn't expect him to believe me, I needed to tell him that he was going to be all right. I had no idea how long it would take to arrange the drawing ritual, but it didn't seem right for him to have to live in despair in the meantime if he could have the slightest bit of hope.

His door was closed, which didn't surprise me in the slightest. I knocked, and after a moment I heard a creak of bedsprings, followed by shuffling footsteps. Tjuan opened the door a couple of inches and stared at me through it. The skin under his eyes looked bruised.

"Hey," I said.

"What?" he replied.

"Can we talk? I know we're not exactly best friends, but I'm worried about you."

"Get in line," he said. "I'm at the front."

"Can I come in?"

Instead of answering, he squeezed through the door and shut it behind him as though to keep a tiger in the room. With a quick beckoning jerk of his head, he shuffled to the kitchen, looking exhausted. He placed the island between us, slumping and leaning his elbows on it.

"I'm sorry you're having such a hard time," I said. "I wanted to tell you, I think we might be able to help you. Maybe."

"Electroshock?" he said.

I winced. "That's what they did to you before." I'd spent some time in a loony bin myself, but I hadn't so much as heard about anyone using ECT; the images that came to mind were all from melodramatic movies.

Hostility sparked through his eyes for a moment, then died, leaving him with a thousand-yard stare.

"I'm sorry," I said. "We won't talk about that." I looked at him and tried to figure out how to even raise the subject of possession. I found myself at a loss. "I never thanked you for your help with Vivian," I said. "The world's better off without that monster."

"We're all of us monsters of some kind," he said.

I was feeling less and less competent to converse with him at every moment. Not that I'd ever been great at it.

"I guess that's true," I said. "I try not to even think about some of the stuff I've done."

"Ever killed anyone besides her?" he said to the countertop.

Once again I found myself blindsided. "Myself, I guess, or at least tried pretty hard."

His eyes wandered down the length of me, a disinterested cataloging of the damage. "I didn't know that," he said.

"I told you about my fall, but you probably—"

"You said 'fell,' not jumped."

My surprise tempted me to find out what else he remembered, but I recognized it as Borderline emptiness, the craving to be filled with someone else's picture of me. I pushed past it.

"Besides that, no, I've never tried to kill anyone. You?"

"No."

"Why do you ask, then?"

He lost focus, and I realized that he was probably, as we spoke, trying to keep the thing inside him from taking the wheel. How was he even succeeding at that?

"Tjuan," I said. "I know why you're hearing voices and how to make it stop. You're not crazy."

"Explain."

"There were . . . some kind of arcane-energy creatures on the soundstage in June. Two of them. The Unseelie King got one of them to talk this morning; it called itself a wraith. It said one of its little friends hitched a ride out of the soundstage in your brain."

Tjuan exhaled like I'd punched him in the stomach. "Oh my God."

"Alvin doesn't believe me," I said, "and I think the one in the king's head messed with him so he can't back me up."

Tjuan drew in a shaky breath, then let it out. "First thing that's fucking made sense in four months. So what do we do?"

"Winterglass talked about a 'drawing ritual' he has to get the Seelie Court to do. It should pull any arcane energy back to Arcadia, including these guys. I don't know how long it will take, though; I'm sorry."

"I've held out this long," said Tjuan.

I stood for a moment a little awkwardly. "You're a hell of a guy, Tjuan," I said.

"Don't think you know me enough to say."

"I know you helped me bring down Vivian, and that you've been fighting a wraith for four months now after I saw one take over the Seelie Queen's champion in seconds. How are you doing that, anyway?"

"Practice?" he said wanly. "It's not that different from the shit I dealt with in the hospital."

"Well, as far as I'm concerned, you're a goddamned superhero."

"Think whatever you want," he said, and with that, shuffled wearily back toward his room.

15

Caryl sat reading an L. M. Montgomery novel by the light of the bare basement bulb, dressed in comfortable-looking gray sweatpants and a T-shirt. There was even an empty teacup resting on a crate in one corner; Song must have been bringing her things. Caryl lowered the book as she heard my careful steps on the stairs; I was trying not to reawaken the pain in my back. I could tell at a glance that Elliott wasn't out; Caryl's face lit up when she saw me.

"I didn't mean to disturb you," I said. "Uh, I think you're going to want Elliott. I've got heavy-duty news."

Caryl exhaled a little petulantly, then murmured the words of the spell. I didn't have fey glasses on, but the way the light drained out of her eyes told me that she'd transferred all her most inconvenient mental processes into the construct.

I kept my summary of the situation as brief and nontraumatic as I could, but there was one aspect I couldn't leave out, and it made my stomach congeal into a cold lump just thinking about it.

"The worst thing," I said, "is that even if they manage to get these wraiths back to Arcadia, you're still on the hook for

Tamika." Realizing this would likely not be a quick meeting, I carefully lowered myself to a sitting position on the chilly basement floor so I could be at Caryl's eye level.

"If you think *that* is the worst thing," said Caryl, "your priorities are severely misaligned. What concerns me is that allegedly Vivian's plan is still underway. You do remember what her plan was, don't you?"

"Large-scale property damage." I shrugged. "So warn the nobles, and they can evacuate before their fancy houses blow up."

"The estates are not simply houses, and they would not 'blow up.' That interdimensional void you see—or rather don't see—inside a Gate? Arcadia would be riddled with vast tracts of it. Permanently."

I took a moment to let the image sink in. "Okay. I'll admit that sounds a little worse than an explosion, but it's still kind of an 'over there' problem. I'm pretty good at not caring about 'over there' problems."

"It becomes an 'over here' problem very quickly. Without the protection of their estates, the *sidhe* would be defenseless."

"Against what?"

"In Arcadia, what we diplomatically refer to as 'commoners' are a huge and widely varied population that includes manticores, sea serpents, gorgons, any creature that has ever haunted a human nightmare. Even the less monstrous commoners resent the *sidhe*'s power and knowledge to varying degrees, and far outnumber them. Without their estates to protect them, the primary species we interact with would become extinct, leaving thousands of brilliant human minds severed from their Echoes. Human progress as we know it would grind to a halt."

"Okay, that's definitely an 'over here' problem. But if it's the wraiths carrying out the plan, this ritual with the harp should solve it."

Caryl paused for a moment, her eyes unfocused in thought. "I was about to argue that the wraiths cannot be her only conspirators, but in truth, the baffling results of our ongoing investigation suddenly make sense if they are."

"What's so baffling?"

"We quickly put together that if Vivian intended to commit terrorist acts on a global scale without leaving the Southern California perimeter, she would need to mobilize her only international network: the employees of Cera Pest Control. But Vivian seemed withdrawn from the company in recent years, giving orders largely through her chief operating officer. We assumed he had to be in on her plan, passing along instructions to the various branches, but I rifled his mind a bit, and he proved shockingly and disappointingly ignorant of the entire affair. There were no signs of alterations to his memory."

I leaned away from Caryl pointedly. "Rifled his *mind*?"

Caryl ignored me. "Vivian wouldn't need to directly order employees if she could send wraiths to possess whomever she needed, but I'm still unclear on the mechanics. It seems from your story that wraiths cannot move about on their own on Earth unless they take over a human body."

"Right. They're stranded flopping fish, like the king said, and I guess people are fishbowls on legs."

"But possession can apparently take place only under very specific circumstances."

I leaned back in toward Caryl, tense. "How long has Vivian been working on this? And how long has she owned that company?"

Caryl was silent for a long moment, and she must have been thinking what I was thinking, only without the inconvenience of horror. The idea that Vivian might have been methodically planning this for decades, and that we only stumbled onto it at the eleventh hour because she took the wrong person's sister prisoner . . . If she'd messed with anyone but Claybriar, no one would have investigated. The first we'd have heard of her plan would have been when estates started dropping off the map— *with their owners inside them.*

"I don't like this," I said. "If she managed to slip that much by us for that long, how much are we still missing? I thought I was holding a rope, and now it looks like a tiger's tail."

"We cannot let our dismay get in the way of—"

"Wait." I stopped her with a hand. "Let's get back to your reading the COO's mind for a second."

"You oversimplify. In rare cases, a combination of suggestion and—"

"Not looking for a tutorial here. I'm asking, is he local?"

"Ah. Yes, Cera's international headquarters are in Santa Monica, since Vivian has never been permitted to leave the Southern California perimeter. A few months ago I cloaked myself and entered the building in an attempt to investigate, but sadly I could not break into any locked doors without destroying them in a way that would have revealed our interference. I was reduced to weeks' worth of unimaginably dull eavesdropping before deciding that Cera was a false lead after all."

"But Cera has to be the key," I said. "If we can find some hard evidence there of what Vivian's minions are up to, it might prove I'm telling the truth and shed enough doubt on your guilt that we could get you out of here."

Caryl steepled her gloved fingers and stared at them vacantly. "If only I had found a way into Vivian's files while I was there."

"I'd try and get in there for you, but I'm sure someone else has moved into her office by now."

"Possibly not. She still has not officially been declared dead."

"Seriously? You guys did fine coming up with fake stories about Teo and Gloria."

"We had their bodies. Not only are piles of dust difficult to interrogate, but they make accident-staging problematic."

I blew hair out of my eyes. "How many times do I have to apologize for that?"

"But in Vivian's office, there *must* still be correspondence and records in hard copy. Vivian was less technophobic than most fey, but I can virtually guarantee that since she died unexpectedly there will be an interesting paper trail. Unfortunately, I have no access."

"I'll find a way," I said. "I've always had a gift for getting in where I don't belong."

Since Winterglass had arrived through Gate LA4, Arcadia Project protocol dictated that he had to depart through the same Gate. This meant that I was in the perfect place to intercept him on his way out on Sunday morning. Alvin dropped Winterglass and Claybriar off for their departure but didn't stay himself; he was off to the summit in London, along with every other national head in the Arcadia Project, apparently.

Winterglass was not pleased about being detained by the likes of me; I could see the contempt in every line of his beautiful face as he loomed over me in the living room. Claybriar wasn't around to defend me; he was busy in the kitchen hunting apples.

"Just hear me out," I said to Winterglass. "If your memory's being tampered with, you'd want to know, wouldn't you?"

"Of course."

"You remember Claybriar pushing me. But you don't remember what we were talking about before that?"

"Do you?"

"Not photographically, but I know we were trying to get the wraith to tell us Vivian's plan, and it wouldn't. You said you couldn't force it to speak. Remember that?"

"You may be recalling a conversation you had with someone else," he said. I thought I detected the faintest uncertainty in his tone.

"The Bone Harp," I said. "That's the relic they use in the drawing ritual."

This time he looked decidedly disconcerted. "Where did you hear this?"

"You *told* me. My Echo was possessed and I was freaking out and you told me so I'd understand that he would be fine."

"I have no memory of that," he said. He stood still for a moment, his expression blank, as though he were searching inward. Then his eyes widened. "I *felt* something. Faintly, for a moment. Something in my mind . . . resisted me."

"That's your wraith."

"Why would I *do* that? Why would I allow a hostile presence inside my mind?"

"It . . . was kind of an accident at first." I didn't elaborate. "You let it stay because it's one of your subjects. It can't command you or cause you harm. Unfortunately, now it's loopholing its way through your memories."

Winterglass began to look genuinely alarmed, his eyes still

unfocused, attention turned inward. "*Sidhe* must use spellwork to affect memory. I see none here. But if this 'wraith' is, as you told Alvin, a form of energy in itself, and if it has assimilated itself into my thoughts . . ." He clenched his hands into fists. "I must find a way to perceive its presence more securely."

"It knows you need to do that, so it won't let you. There's another wraith here in the house that hasn't seen your facade yet, might not recognize you as king. If I could trick it into showing itself in front of you, would that let you command it?"

"If it commits any action, I should be able to address the actor."

"Then follow me. I have the beginnings of an idea."

Tjuan was in the kitchen with Claybriar. They weren't talking; Tjuan was leaning his elbows on the kitchen island and staring at half a piece of toast, and Claybriar was munching an apple as though any minute someone might take it away.

"Mr. Morozov, this is Tjuan," I said. "He's the one with the unwanted passenger."

"And," said Tjuan, "it's trying to talk me into some horrible shit right now. The sooner we can end this, the better."

"It wants to kill me, right?" I said, backing up a step. "Because it was *there* when I killed Vivian. It watched her die, heard her screaming."

"You're making it worse," said Tjuan irritably. "Settle down; it can't make me do anything. Got plenty of practice ignoring voices."

One of the king's brows shot toward his hairline. "You have been possessed before?"

"No," said Tjuan. "Or—" A strange look came over his face. "Actually, I don't know."

"Whatever was wrong with Tjuan," I said, "he recovered. Electroconvulsive therapy. Would that get rid of a wraith?"

Winterglass looked at the same time intrigued and troubled. "In theory. Arcane energy is Arcadia's analog to your electromagnetic spectrum. The two are incompatible in a similar way to iron and norium."

Tjuan frowned. "If you're suggesting that I stick my finger in a light socket I'm just going to go ahead and walk out of here."

"No, no," I said. "I— Tjuan, I need you to trust me for a minute."

He looked at me flatly.

"I know. I know trust isn't really your thing. But I'm the one who found out what's wrong with you, right? Now I need you to . . . relax your control. Let the wraith take over. I need to talk to it directly."

Tjuan looked wild-eyed for a moment, backing toward the sink. The counter's edge stopped him; he flexed his hands, then curled them into fists.

"Did I not just say it wants to kill you? It does *not* want to talk."

"I'll be fine," I said. "I'm immune to somatic spells."

"Yeah, that's why it wants *me* to kill you."

"I won't force you to do this, Tjuan," I said. "But I need you to trust me when I say I'll be fine. Think back. How many times have I steered us wrong?"

Tjuan considered this for a moment, scratching anxiously at one hand with the other. He glanced at Claybriar, who had begun to edge closer to me, protectively.

"Are the three of you prepared to take me down?" Tjuan said, his voice tight. "I am stronger than I look."

"So am I," I said. "I promise, that thing can't take me. I killed

Vivian, remember? What's a wraith, to me? I need you to trust me, Tjuan. Just let go. Let me talk to it."

"If you're sure," said Tjuan. "Just don't—hmm." He stopped, clearing his throat, looking up at the ceiling. His face went through a few contortions; then he said quietly, "Whatever it says, just know it's not me. It is *not* me."

"Of course it isn't, Tjuan." I tried not to show my sudden surge of sympathy, because I knew he'd take it for pity. "You're an asshole, but you're no murderer."

He did not seem to appreciate my humor. "This is my worst nightmare," he said.

"At least you've got your clothes on, and all your teeth." This time he smiled faintly, but I could tell it was an act of charity rather than amusement.

"You keep saying it'll be all right," he said. "When it comes down to it, somehow I believe you. So . . . all right." No sooner had he spoken than he slumped so dramatically that I thought he was going to collapse to the Spanish-tiled floor.

Just as Claybriar moved to help, Tjuan straightened, eyes hungry. He *smiled* in a way that looked wrong on him, and, with astonishing quickness, he vaulted straight over the kitchen island toward me.

16

I let out a squeak and stumbled backward even as Claybriar and Winterglass moved with unexpected synchronicity to seize Tjuan. Their combined strength was barely enough to keep him from struggling free.

"Be still, wraith!" Winterglass barked at Tjuan, and, like magic (because it was), Tjuan stopped struggling. "Cast no spells, alter no memories, nor move that body's limbs until I give you leave to do so."

"Just get it out of him!" I snapped. Winterglass turned to fix me with a glare that could have sent a tank full of fish belly up.

Claybriar cleared his throat. "Much as I hate to take Mr. Morozov's side," he said, "you might want to go easy on the whole ordering-kings-around thing."

"If he can give that invisible son of a bitch orders," I said, "why is he still leaving it inside him?"

"I have questions," said Winterglass.

"Because that went so well last time? Oh, right, you don't remember."

"You," said Winterglass to Tjuan. "Wraith-creature who

possesses this body. Did you cause the death of a human woman in this house?"

"That would make things nice and tidy, wouldn't it?" That smile again, so wrong on Tjuan's face. The smile—and the evasion—reminded me of someone.

"Vivian?" I half whispered. "Is that you, somehow?"

"No." Its smile widened. "But I've been inside her."

"Gross!"

"And enlightening," said Winterglass coolly. "This supports the part of your story regarding their collaboration."

"Of course it does," I said irritably. "I didn't make any of that up." I turned back to Tjuan, trying to keep my temper. "Look, ghostie. If you ever want to see Arcadia again, start talking. Did you kill—"

I paused, remembering how important wording was when asking questions of the fey. Vivian had promised not to hurt anyone, but it had been the bottom of the well that *hurt* Gloria. Vivian had only severed the rope.

"Did you cast a spell that caused harm to Tamika Durand?"

"Nope." Big smile.

I stood there for a moment, wondering what I'd said wrong, how the thing was tricking me. "Did you do *anything* that may have contributed to Tamika's death?"

"Why, yes I did."

I ground my teeth. "*What* did you do that may have contributed to Tamika's death?"

"My friend advises me not to tell you."

"What, you've lawyered up now? Who's your 'friend'? Tjuan?"

"No, the one you brought with you."

"The one— You mean the wraith? The one in Winterglass? You can *talk to each other*?"

"Of course."

Well, shit. It hadn't occurred to me that I'd be enabling the two to *cooperate*. I was even less enthusiastic about this interrogation now that I knew I could only hear half the conversation.

"I need to know exactly what happened to Tamika," I said. "Will you tell us the details if one of these fey promises to return you to Arcadia afterward?"

"Nope." Biggest smile yet.

I had the sudden, counterproductive urge to punch Tjuan in the gut. I took a deep breath, picturing the snowy little cabin in the woods that Dr. Davis and I had been mentally decorating just for these occasions.

"Okay then," I said. "I guess we'll just row you out to the middle of the ocean somewhere, and His Majesty will order you to vacate that body you've borrowed. Do wraiths float or sink?"

The wraith's horror showed on Tjuan's face, but only for a moment.

I had a sudden razor-sharp memory of Teo saying, *I would have said there was no one in the world who would be worse at Good Cop than me.*

"No," the wraith said once it had found its calm. It was hard to tell if it was bluffing; it had hijacked someone with a spectacular poker face. "You can't get me to turn. Torture me however you like; you've only got so long to do it, and who am I to shrink from that when Vivian was willing to lay down her life for the cause?"

"I wouldn't say she was *willing*," I muttered, making Tjuan's face contort with the wraith's frustrated urge to throttle me. "Why would we only have 'so long' to torture you?"

It closed Tjuan's mouth firmly and pointedly.

"The drawing ritual," said Winterglass. "I believe it has just confirmed that the wraiths will be recalled at the autumn ritual."

"How many of you are there?" I asked the wraith.

"I'm sure you'd love to know."

"Not that I really need your help," I said, taking care to sound as smug as possible, "because I can figure it out on my own. Three people died that night, but your friend only mentioned two wraiths. One got pulled over when Teo died, and one when Vivian died. That means there's one more somewhere."

"Wrong," said the wraith acidly.

"Make as many vague denials as you want," I said. "I know how you bastards' half-truths operate, and I know I'm right, and the king here is going to give you a hell of a dunking in the Pacific until you tell us where that third one is."

The wraith hesitated for a moment. I suspected it was conferring with its friend. "I'll tell you where your logic breaks down," it finally said, "if you promise both of us that you won't strand us here. That you'll either give us bodies or take us back to Arcadia right away."

I sighed and turned to Winterglass. "Is it worth making a deal with this asshole?"

"Any information is better than none," he said, "and returning these creatures to Arcadia ahead of schedule is far from the worst outcome. Wraith, here is the agreement I propose: explain this human's mistake to her satisfaction, and I will ensure you return to Arcadia within the week."

Tjuan grimaced. "A week?"

"At the latest. As soon as it would not disrupt my own mission," said Winterglass. "That is the best I can offer. Accept or refuse."

"I accept," growled the wraith, then heaved a huge sigh. "The woman who fell down the well? Her death was fast. She didn't suffer enough to bring a wraith across, even though a whole crowd of them were just on the other side waiting for Vivian's orders. My friend and I"—here it gestured to Winterglass—"are the only two wraiths who got stranded in your world by the deaths that night."

Winterglass frowned. "Your specificity implies that you are leaving out important information."

"I've answered the question I said I would answer. Now you must honor your promise."

"Forget it, Jake," I said to Winterglass. "It's wraith-town. I wasn't expecting it would give us anything too useful. But now you have proof that these things exist and that they had something to do with Tamika. *Before we do anything else,* would you mind telling any and all wraiths in this room not to fuck with anyone's memory again?"

"I have already asked this of Tjuan's passenger, but I still have no grasp on the one inside me. I fully believe that it is here, but cannot sense its presence in any way that allows me to address it."

I sighed. "Then let's just use your body as jail for both of them and get them out of here."

"We can't share a body," Tjuan's wraith interrupted.

"You mean we have to find *another* mule? Why? What would happen if you shared?"

"The new one forces the old one out."

"The way you ricocheted out of the chapel because of the holy-ground thing? And you ended up—" A bolt hit me from the blue. "Claybriar, go stand next to Winterglass."

I wasn't sure whether it spoke well of me or ill of him that he did it without question.

"Now, Mr. Morozov," I said, careful not to order him, "would you please tell Tjuan's wraith to enter your body?"

Claybriar made a sound of dismay. "But then won't the—"

"Do you trust me?" I interrupted before he could reveal my line of thinking to the wraiths. I moved to stand near the refrigerator, putting some space between myself and the fey.

Claybriar looked grim. "Of course."

I was half expecting to get into another debate with the king, but before I could even confirm Claybriar's consent, Winterglass murmured something in the Unseelie tongue. Tjuan's knees went out from under him, and he sank to the kitchen floor. At almost the same moment, Claybriar snarled and lunged toward me. I opened the refrigerator door, ducking behind it as I pushed it into Claybriar, sending him staggering back. It wasn't much of a defense, but it was enough of a delay for Winterglass to realize what had happened.

"Stop, wraith!" he cried at Claybriar. The wraith we'd brought from the soundstage, seizing the chance to attack me when it found itself inside a free body, now had no choice but to obey its king.

"Dumbass," I said to it, trying to hide how badly my hands were shaking as I closed the refrigerator.

The wraith snarled at me. "Better to get trapped than waste a chance to end you. You don't even know what you've done, by killing the countess. You—"

"Silence," said Winterglass.

"Well there you have it," I said to him with fake nonchalance. "Both wraiths identified. Take out their claws however most pleases you, Your Majesty."

As Winterglass processed what I'd done he looked poleaxed,

maybe even impressed. Reluctant to look at Claybriar, I moved toward Tjuan, who sat on the floor with his head tucked between his knees. When I tried to bend down, a cruel twinge in my spine made me suck air between my teeth. I straightened up again quickly.

Winterglass began to murmur something to Claybriar—or to the wraith inhabiting him—in the Unseelie tongue.

"You okay?" I asked Tjuan.

"Head hurts like *fuck*," he groaned. I opened the cabinet where harmless quantities of over-the-counter pills were kept and got a couple of Excedrin, then filled a water glass. Tjuan watched me through pain-squinted eyes without getting up, then took what I offered. As he quickly downed the pills, I turned back to look at the two fey.

"It is done," said Winterglass. "I have specifically forbidden either wraith to cast spells, alter memories, take control of their host bodies, or even to communicate with other wraiths until released in Arcadia."

"Why free them, then? Once they're free, what do you suppose they're going to do?"

"I have no idea, but commands must have limitations included, and that seemed a reasonable one. I have no thoughts on how to control them aside from imprisoning them in a body—which has drawbacks—or stranding them in an abandoned building such as your soundstage, which I have already promised not to do to these. The best I can do is take Claybriar back to Arcadia with me and release the both of them there. I do not suggest that this is a solution to our problem; it is simply my only reasonable option."

"How soon can Claybriar come back? I need him for something

tomorrow. Actually, you would be useful too, but I understand if you need to get back to ruling the world or whatever."

"There are travel formalities to which rank-and-file fey are bound, in these matters. Monarchs are free to come and go as they like, in theory, though I am the only one who has ever done so. If Claybriar leaves, he would not be able to return by tomorrow."

"I'll need him for this. Can you both stay another day?"

Claybriar winced. "I don't want to get in trouble."

"With whom? Caryl's been relieved of command by Alvin, who just flew off to London. Who does that leave in charge?"

"Phil," said Tjuan from the floor.

"You and Phil are pals, right?"

"We get along."

"So tell Phil how we cured you, then talk him into sending these two back tomorrow night instead of this morning. Morozov, are you and Claybriar safe with the wraiths in you until then?"

"Until they reach Arcadia, they can take no action at all," said Winterglass. "They will, however, be able to see and hear whatever we do and say. I've no idea how to blind or deafen something that has no eyes or ears."

"You're saying you *could* blind them if they had eyes? Remind me not to get on your bad side."

"He can't do anything to you, Ironbones," said Claybriar with a wry smile. "So what's this plan you're plotting?"

"Do you still have the fake LAPD badge you used on me last summer?"

In answer, he whipped it out of seemingly nowhere, holding it up about two feet from my face.

"Whaaat?" I said. "You just carry that thing around with you?"

"What thing?" I was now staring at his empty hand.

"Wait, that was an illusion? That time on the street, too?"

"One of the easiest spells there is. I don't even have to detail it; your mind does that."

"You are dangerous," I said. "Tjuan, you feeling up to working with us on this?"

He hesitated, elbows resting on his knees. "What do you need me for, besides handling Phil?"

"Handling doorknobs, cars, that sort of thing. And me if necessary."

Tjuan gave me a long, wary look, but after a moment's hesitation began pushing himself to his feet. "If it'll help stop these things," he said, "I'm on board. But let me get cleaned up first. I smell like Satan's gym bag."

"I wasn't going to say."

"Good call."

"You talk to Phil; I've got to call Inaya and find out when would be the best time to duck out of work and do a little snooping."

The international headquarters of Cera Pest Control was located in a business park in Santa Monica, its looming corporate evil just a stone's throw from a 24 Hour Fitness and an El Torito Grill. Of the four of us, Tjuan not only had seniority with the Arcadia Project but was also the only one with a car, so he ended up in charge by default even though the plan was mine.

The building was shaped like a Tetris S-piece, four stories high. I hadn't expected it to be quite so large, but given that it was the center of administration and R&D for a couple dozen different countries around the world, it shouldn't have surprised me.

Until I'd done some research, I'd had no idea how huge Cera's reach was, because in Los Angeles it wasn't the first or even the third name that came to mind when people found swarms of ants in their kitchens. But while most chain pest control companies were owned by larger corporations that handled other types of business, Cera was unique in that it specialized in wholesale critter slaughter and had a presence in more countries than any other exterminator in the world.

Its founder? A woman. Pretty outrageous in 1970. Edna Cera

had started the company out of her home with the help of her common-law husband as front man. He'd died once the company had gained a solid footing, and in 1998 the increasingly reclusive Edna had passed control of the company to a newcomer, Vivian Chandler.

Of course, both Edna Cera and Vivian Chandler were just two in a long line of facades for Countess Feverwax, exile of the Unseelie Court. There was only so long a woman could live among humans without aging before people would begin to notice—even in Beverly Hills.

Now the L.A. headquarters was a hive of international activity; much of its workforce was involved in navigating legal and cultural landmines, as well as undertaking groundbreaking research and development. As the four of us walked blithely through the front doors of the building on Monday morning— appearing to be two of us, thanks to some don't-look-at-me magic Winterglass had cast on Tjuan and himself—I felt my nerves fail me and my hands get cold and sweaty.

Master magician Winterglass had fine-tuned the invisibility spell so that our own team wasn't fully affected but instead saw the enchanted ones in a hazy, grayed-out fashion that let us know the spell was still working. The original idea had been that Claybriar and the newly groomed Tjuan would be visible and pose as cops, since L.A. was full of white guys with goatees and clean-shaven black guys. Neither of them would call that much attention. But the snag was that the king couldn't cast a don't-look spell on me, which meant I had to pose as a cop instead of Tjuan. Even with trousers concealing my prosthetic legs, I was going to be memorable thanks to the scars on the left side of my face.

At the last moment Claybriar had come up with a genius idea. I'd borrowed a really nice ginger-colored wig from Valiant, and Claybriar had cast one of his charms on it. Anyone who noticed me would now be so mesmerized by my beautiful hair that it would be all they remembered. All the same I'd put on about six tons of stage makeup, and I tried to keep the right side of my face toward the security guard as Claybriar flashed his "badge" and asked how to get to the office of Adal Garcia.

"I don't like this," said Tjuan in the elevator. "Not even a little bit." He was starting to look wild-eyed, which was vastly preferable to the dead, distracted look he'd had while possessed. All the same, it was probably just as well I had to play cop instead of him. Tjuan's new close haircut looked sharp, but he was at least a month away from healthy. Even back in the summer, the man's cheekbones could have cut glass; now they looked downright ghoulish.

Meanwhile the fey were instinctively crowded together at the center of the elevator; their distaste for metal had the two foes all but cuddling.

"We'll be fine," I said. "Anything bad happens, Morozov can make it disappear. Right?"

"Do not spend my talents recklessly," said Winterglass in a resonant murmur that made gooseflesh rise on my arms. "Unseelie energy is a poison to this world."

"It is?" I said in alarm. I'd stood right next to Caryl casting spells back in June. "How, exactly?"

"Shh," said the king as the elevator doors opened onto a gray hallway.

Vivian must have thrived off the existential despair of her employees, because there was no art hanging on the walls, not even the most perfunctory attempt at warming the space. Just a long, ash-colored corridor with charcoal-colored doors set into it at regular intervals.

"There aren't even names on the doors," I said as I emerged. "No wonder Caryl had so much trouble."

"Vivian must have been worried about corporate espionage," said Tjuan. "Cera has some proprietary stuff that's been giving them an edge in the last few years."

I raised a brow at him. "You know about Cera?"

"You can't work for the Los Angeles Arcadia Project and not know *all* about Cera."

"What kind of stuff are they protecting? Maybe it ties in."

"Whole different approach to pest control. Plague, not poison. Contagious diseases that are harmless to humans but wipe out colonies of ants, termites, whatever."

"That's so Vivian."

"Environmental disaster if you ask me, but customers love it because after one visit you won't see an ant for years. But then of course some ants survive, and evolve, and they have to come up with new plagues—so their R and D is pretty intense. They—"

Tjuan's mouth clamped shut as a door opened down the hall. A tired-looking bald man began to head toward us with the expression of someone lost in his own thoughts. I tried to figure out how to look more like a plainclothes cop, but then the guy turned at the T-intersection and I let my breath out.

"Let's get this over with," I said.

When we got to Garcia's suite, I turned the metal door handle, since the only other human was functionally invisible. The three men went in ahead of me, Winterglass and Tjuan trying to position themselves out of the way as Claybriar and I approached the desk in the cramped, drab reception area. It didn't look as though they expected to entertain many visitors.

The young Indian woman in the burnt-orange jacket at the reception desk took one look at Claybriar and turned up her smile about eight hundred watts. I glanced at him to remind myself of what she was seeing for the first time. His facade wasn't L.A. gorgeous, but it was nice enough if you liked blue-collar boys.

"Hi," she said. A handmade placard at her desk, a stubborn flag of individuality planted on a barren landscape, told me her name was Pooja. "What can I do for you?" she said to Claybriar.

He held up his "badge"; I couldn't see it since he wasn't casting the spell on me, but I saw Pooja's face change as she "recognized" it.

"I'd like to speak with Mr. Garcia as soon as he's available," Claybriar said. Then he smiled, and Pooja's expression shifted yet again.

"Is everything okay?" she asked, unconsciously winding a strand of hair around her finger.

"He's not in any trouble. We're just looking into what happened with Vivian Chandler."

"Oh, isn't it horrible?" said Pooja. "I've been carrying pepper spray. I really hope you can find out who's behind all this."

"All this?" I said.

She turned to look at me, and her gaze went straight to my wig.

"Yes," she said to my bangs. "The abductions or whatever they are. Do you know they're happening in other countries too?"

"Our main focus is on Vivian Chandler," I said, "but anything you've heard might help."

"Well it's not just women disappearing," she said. "A guy in New Delhi was missing for three days and then came back to work, with no idea what had happened to him. Didn't even realize he'd missed three days. They've put him on medical leave or something, tried to hush it up, but a friend of my family works with him and says that he had weird cuts and bruises. He couldn't explain those, either, said he just woke up with them."

"And you think it's related?" Even though she was still staring at my hair, I did my best to keep my scars angled away. That meant looking at her in a sidelong fashion that gave me a permanent look of skepticism.

"If it were just the one thing," she said, "I'd write it off. But I've heard of three different employees in different cities disappearing temporarily, and at least five—not counting the New Delhi guy—having weird injuries they didn't remember getting. And well, of course, the owner of the whole company disappearing *permanently* as far as anyone can tell. Those are just the ones they didn't hush up, and all this in less than a year? I've been sending out my resume, and I'm not the only one. Honestly, it's weird you guys don't know about it all."

"Officer Clay is better informed than I am," I said. "I'm just the rookie tagging along."

"Don't worry," said Claybriar, leaning slightly on Pooja's desk in an obvious gambit to get her attention off me and my wig. "I'm aware of the man in New Delhi, and the other disappearances; and I'm investigating how they might be connected. Chances are we're not going to be able to solve this without some international cooperation, but for now we're gathering all the information we can about the local missing person."

"Well, I wish you all the luck, seriously," Pooja said, picking up a phone at her desk and pressing a button. "Mr. Garcia, the LAPD is here about Vivian again."

Again. Of course the cops had been here before. Oh God, there were so many ways we could screw this up.

After a few moments of small talk with Pooja, we were greeted by Adal Garcia. A stout man with tired eyes and a neatly-groomed iron-gray moustache, he shook both of our hands briskly and then invited us back to his office.

It must have been the most comforting, homey place in the entire building; it felt like an anti-Vivian zone. Potted plants adorned every surface, and the walls were littered with pictures of what were presumably a wife and three children. From his choice of decor, he didn't seem like the sort of man who would devote his life to wholesale extermination.

"I figured the FBI would have taken this over by now," he said. "Or Interpol."

"We have no concrete proof yet that the crimes are linked," Claybriar surprised me by saying. I found myself wondering just how many cop shows he'd binge-watched during his long visits here searching for me. "Ms. Chandler's disappearance, especially, doesn't match the details of the other crimes, and it's still under the LAPD's jurisdiction."

"Do you have new information?" Garcia asked.

"I can't go into the details," Claybriar said, and I tried not to frown as I remembered him using that line on me in June. "But we do need to take a look at Ms. Chandler's files. We have reason to believe that she may have been complicit in some illegal activities."

Garcia looked uncomfortable. "You have a warrant, I presume?"

Claybriar held out a handful of nothing toward Garcia, who actually took hold of the near "end" of it as he leaned forward to examine it. After he had finished skimming the illusory paper's imaginary contents, he "took it" from Claybriar and set it on his desk.

"Right this way," said Garcia. His manner was decidedly less cooperative now.

I squinted at him. "Is there some reason you don't want Ms. Chandler's files searched?"

"Naturally I'm protective of our company's interests," he said as he withdrew his keys from his desk. He had yet to even look directly at me, so in his case I didn't have to endure a weird obsession with my wig. "It's taken thirty hard years—most of which I was here for—to fight our way to the number three spot, and we owe that to Vivian as much as to Edna."

Six of one . . .

"Vivian worked here part-time at best," he went on, "because of her other job, but it's her innovations that got us to where we are. I'm pretty sure she was killed for them, and that our employees are being targeted by some kind of environmentalist wackos for them, so you'll excuse me if I'm not thrilled at the idea of the people rifling through everything in her office."

"We're not here for your research," I said. "All we care about is finding evidence of any crimes that have been committed. If you're right about what's happening, we won't find anything. If Vivian has stepped outside the law, then your cooperation with us might be all that keeps your company together."

"You're right," said Garcia. "I'm sorry." He led us out of his office and to another door in the same suite. "Please understand, this is not how I wanted to take over the company. I've been keeping her things locked up, haven't stepped into her role in four months, thinking she'd turn back up eventually, like the others."

Good luck with that.

"I don't know what we're going to do without her," he said as he unlocked the door. "Go ahead; I can open up her desk for you; the keys to the rest of it should be in there."

"Also," I said, "if you could get an IT guy to log us into her computer, that would be helpful too."

"One of them's on this floor right now, actually," he said. "She's on the stubborn side, but I'll see if someone can track her down."

There were no photos in Vivian's office, no greenery. It had the look of a place where she did not expect to spend much time. It was, however, jammed *full* of filing cabinets. This was going to be a long, boring errand.

As we worked, I spent a lot of time musing about what would happen if Garcia found out we weren't with the LAPD before we finished.

"Morozov," I said, breaking a long silence as my painfully dry fingertips sorted through an incomprehensible stack of papers. "When we're done, can you make Garcia forget we were here?"

"I dislike doing that," he said. There was a tension in his voice; I got the feeling I'd brushed against an iceberg under the water. "It is not 'erasing' a memory, it is planting something in the mind, a barricade of sorts. If not placed to absolute perfection, it can have disastrous results."

"Since when do Unseelie care about that? You're not exactly known for your warm fuzzies."

"Not all Unseelie are like Vivian. While we embrace fear and sorrow and other energies that your kind consider 'negative,' not all of us force them upon those who fail to appreciate them."

"Appreciate them?" I said, hearing a snappish edge to my voice. "I used to 'appreciate' negative emotions. I used to chase them down with hounds. All it got me was a seven-story trip to the pavement."

"This is what I alluded to in the elevator," said Winterglass. "Human physiology is not built to sustain the sorts of energies that I work with." As he had on the soundstage, he suddenly looked so deeply, powerfully sad that I felt a pulse of concern for him. Before I could ask him what was on his mind, Tjuan made an odd sound across the room.

"Oh, this is something," he said in an ominous tone, staring at a little spiral-bound notebook he'd pulled out of Vivian's desk drawer. "This is definitely something."

18

As I approached Tjuan, he turned the notebook so that I could see. It appeared to be a handwritten list of locations, taking up many pages. Some were street addresses; some looked like geographic coordinates. Some of them had people's names written beside or underneath them, along with contact information.

"What do you think that's about?" I asked.

"Look where some of these are," he said, flipping through the pages to point out the relevant ones. "Los Angeles. New York. New Orleans. London. Nairobi. Singapore. Hong Kong. Helsinki. Lagos. A lot of these locations seem to be clustered around Gate cities. Just the way noble estates tend to be."

"Can I see that?" Tjuan handed it to me, and I looked through it. "Some of these are residential addresses, some commercial. This set of coordinates here with all the question marks says it's a lake. What's with the random?"

Tjuan shrugged. "The worlds aren't a perfect parallel," he said. "The Seelie and Unseelie royal palaces are in the same spots as palaces here, but it doesn't always work like that."

"So these are Vivian's targets. Where she was planning to drop the fey blood."

Winterglass looked up from the pile of paper he was sift-ing through, his expression profoundly skeptical. "One of her wraiths could easily find a noble estate—arcane energy can travel Arcadia at the speed of thought. But given the difficulty in arranging an event that could draw energy across, it would likely have to wait for a convergence in order to slip across the barrier. And once it arrived, it would be a stranded fish, yes? And wraiths cannot seem to communicate with any greater range than any of us. So how would they reach Vivian to tell her of their findings?"

"Remember the one in the soun— No, of course you don't. Anyway, I think it said it was in Arcadia waiting for orders from Vivian. That a bunch of them were crowded on the other side of the Earth/Arcadia border from where she was. That suggests that they were somehow able to communicate with her across the border, but they had to be close. So picture this: they find a good bombing spot during the convergence, and then once they're back in Arcadia they just swim to Vivian's location and report from across the border."

Winterglass seemed to find this idea profoundly unsettling.

Tjuan made a thoughtful sound. "If she can get reports from anywhere in Arcadia anytime," he said, "it might even explain how she could match up Echoes so easily for her clients. We were never sure how she was doing that."

I held up the notebook. "If this is her to-do list, you should check this against a list of known noble holdings and see if you can figure out which—"

I cut myself off as the office door handle gave a loud thunk, and the door opened to admit a stocky middle-aged woman with a paisley button-down shirt and streaks of teal green in her salt-and-pepper hair. Tjuan and Winterglass immediately flat-tened themselves against the nearest walls to assist in their invisibility.

"I'm Chin Ju," the woman said, arms folded across her chest. "IT girl. Garcia said you needed my help with something; can we make this quick?"

"I'm Officer Clay." Claybriar put out his hand, and she unfolded her arms to give it the briefest possible shake before closing herself off again.

"Officer Mills," I improvised.

She asked to see both our badges, which made me sweat bullets, especially when she narrowed her eyes in scrutiny of my empty hand. I knew Claybriar was doing the magic on her brain and not on me, but I was still half-afraid my iron would mess it up somehow. Finally, Chin Ju let out a pacified grunt and settled herself at Vivian's workstation.

Still clutching the notebook, I came around the desk to observe her at work. As my eyes fell on the keyboard, I noticed faint but unmistakable impressions there, little scars where Vivian's nails had eroded the plastic.

Those perfect, tapered, burgundy nails. Memories stabbed me like shards of crystal. Vivian sipping champagne in a hotel room or relishing a slice of chocolate cake at Gotham Hall. Hints of raspberry red in her dark hair, black stockings with a seam up the back. That light, lilting voice.

Darling, I'm the hero of this story. I know I don't look the part.

Her perfect nails had clawed at the floor of the chapel as I crawled toward her and—

"Millie?"

Claybriar's voice. I looked at him and saw the concern in

his eyes. Of course he was watching me like a hawk; of course he could tell that my throat had closed up, that my heart was hammering.

How could I explain? Four months' dust had settled into the impressions she had left. She hadn't been a monster to the people here; they were still half hoping she'd turn up with bruises and a wild story.

But she wouldn't. Because I'd crushed her throat, watched her turn into a bat-winged mantis-creature and then crumble into grit and ash. In one moment of wrath, three centuries of life had disintegrated like a kicked sand castle.

"What is it exactly I'm looking for?" said Chin Ju. She hadn't so much as glanced at me.

I did a frantic mental inventory of my DBT skills, but all I could find was a phrase that was useless out of context: *Be effective. Be effective. Be effective.*

What did that even mean?

It meant: Do what you're supposed to do, regardless of what you're feeling. Regardless of whether it feels right or wrong in the moment. Ignore your thoughts. Just Do the Thing.

"Scheduling," I said. "I need to check for appointments at specific locations."

"During what time frame?"

"Future appointments," I said, "or things still in progress."

"What could future appointments possibly have to do with her disappearance?" Chin Ju asked.

I wrestled my brain into the present; I could hardly remember our cover story. "We're checking up on the possibility of sabotage," I said. "A competitor might have sneaked some dangerous substances into your warehouses with plans to see them used."

"Why is the LAPD investigating international crime anyway?" asked Chin Ju.

Ugh, smart people. I didn't have the time or mental focus to deal with this.

"We work the case until we're told otherwise," I said, trying to sound impatient and on the verge of arresting someone.

Chin Ju did not seem particularly intimidated. She was looking at me now; not at my wig. At me.

"Can you please help me check the appointments?" I prompted.

"Sure," said Chin Ju. But I didn't like the slight hesitation before she turned back to her work.

She was suspicious, and her job was about sniffing out inconsistencies, solving problems, identifying threats. Right now I felt like a bug she was minutes from squashing.

"Give me a location," she said.

"Uh, Singapore," I said. I paged through the notebook, found an address there, read it off to her.

She opened an application, tapped some keys, sifted through what looked like a color-coded database. But then something in her posture changed subtly. If I hadn't been scrutinizing her, I'd have missed it.

"Find something?" I asked her.

She turned slowly to look over her shoulder at me. Her expression suggested she'd just received a shock that had taken her higher thought processes momentarily offline. "Can I talk to you for a second alone?" she murmured, glancing behind me at Claybriar.

"He's safe," I assured her. "You can trust him."

She shook her head firmly. "I can't. I can't talk about this with him here. Just us girls, for a second?"

I looked at Clay, and he shrugged. Since he couldn't touch the door handle without going faun-tastic, I moved to it and held it open for him.

"Just for a minute," I murmured to him. "Just wait there in the hall, and I'll let you back in once she's ready."

"Please don't be too long."

I nodded, closed the door behind him. Chin Ju beckoned me back over to the desk. She'd risen from her chair, looking tense, and she pointed to the screen. I came around the desk to look; the font on the spreadsheet was so tiny I had to lean in close to look, putting Chin Ju behind me.

Which was dumb, of course.

My cheekbone slammed into the wood of the desk hard enough to make me see stars. The burning in my scalp suggested that Chin Ju had used my wig as a handle to put me there, and the pins had ripped at my hair. My back surged with a fresh crescendo of pain from Saturday's injury.

"What has that fey done to it?" her voice hissed close to my ear. "Why won't it answer me?"

I didn't even have time to figure out what the hell she was talking about before the two people she'd had no idea were still in the room pounced on her and dragged her off me. Her blind punch caught Tjuan right in the mouth, but to my surprise His Majesty avenged Tjuan with a vicious uppercut that left Chin Ju reeling.

I heard Claybriar pounding on the door outside. Rubbing the bruised side of my face—ugh, she'd ruined my good side—and futilely trying to straighten my wig, I made my way unsteadily to open the door while Tjuan and Winterglass secured Chin Ju against the far wall.

In her struggles the front of her button-down gaped open,

and I saw a mess of crisscrossing superficial scars. Self-harm? Or torture?

"She's possessed," I said.

"Obey me, Unseelie creature," Winterglass said to her, shedding his invisibility spell with a graceful shrug as though throwing off a cloak. "Cast no spell until I give you leave to do so, and neither cause harm to nor alter the memory of anyone in this room without my permission."

Chin Ju stilled, but the look she turned on Winterglass was twisted with hate. "Enjoy your power while you can, *Your Majesty*," she said. "Your time is ending."

"Your leader is dead," said Winterglass. "Every power in two worlds is aligned against you. But if you provide the Arcadia Project with information, they will be merciful."

Chin Ju just snarled.

"What are we supposed to do with another wraith?" I said. "We've got nobody left to transport this one back to Arcadia. Unless—" I glanced at Tjuan.

"No," he said.

"Yeah, I didn't think so."

"I don't just mean 'hell no,' which by the way, *hell* no, but also they took my visa away when I started hearing voices. The only guy who could give it back is across the pond by now, so I won't be going to Arcadia any time soon."

"So leave the wraith here," said Claybriar to Winterglass. "You haven't made it any promises. Kick it out of this woman, disable it, lock it in the office."

"No!" blurted the wraith. Its rebellious snarl turned to a look of abject terror so swiftly it was almost comical. "Don't leave me here. Please."

"They'll be doing a drawing ritual in a couple of weeks," I said. "You'll get to go home, not that you deserve it. Why so panicked?"

The wraith didn't answer.

"The one on the soundstage was like this about being locked in there, too," I informed Winterglass, since he'd been divested of that memory.

He looked thoughtful. "It must be a kind of torment," he mused. "A creature without form or boundary, accustomed to riding the endless currents of emotion in Arcadia, now stranded, paralyzed and suffocating in the emptiness."

"My heart's breaking," I said, rubbing at the bruise on my cheek.

"Tell us how to stop the destruction of the *sidhe* estates," said Winterglass, "and I will allow you to stay passively inside this woman's body until you are called home."

"Are you serious?" I said. "You're going to willingly let an innocent woman walk around with a wraith inside her?"

"First," said Winterglass, "the wraith will not harm her if I so command it. Second, what it gives us in return for this small favor would save the Arcadia Project and both of our races. Third, you seem to forget that you have no authority to command me. You may waste your breath debating with me if you choose, but it will avail you nothing."

"It doesn't matter," said the wraith. "Nothing you could offer will make me betray the cause."

"What cause? Watching the world burn? Because I'm not understanding how random destruction is a 'cause.'"

Apparently, launching a glob of spit toward my feet didn't count as causing me harm. Great.

"There is no point in trying to make the likes of *you* understand," the wraith snarled.

"Then you have made your choice," said Winterglass. "Leave this woman's body. Do not possess, enchant, nor cause harm to anyone who is now in this room, nor to anyone who should later enter it." He said it again in Unseelie for good measure, or at least I assumed that's what he was saying. I wasn't ready to discount that he could have been betraying me somehow.

Even as he finished his last sentence, Chin Ju shuddered and staggered backward. She looked at Winterglass, then at myself and Claybriar, her eyes full of confusion and her jaw swelling up from the blow Winterglass had dealt her.

"You . . . hit me," she said to Winterglass with a kind of astonishment that was rapidly building to outrage. Oh right. Winterglass had ordered it not to alter her memory. She looked at Claybriar, at me. Tjuan was still invisible. "You *let* him."

I moved to Winterglass, leaning as close as I could without touching him. "I know you're not keen on the idea," I whispered, "but maybe you should—"

Chin Ju bolted. None of us had time to consider how and whether to stop her; we just stood there with dumb looks on our faces as she disappeared out the door.

"She's probably headed straight to Garcia," I said, starting in the direction she'd gone. "We need to catch her, wipe her memory. Do the same to Garcia if she gets there first."

"No," said Winterglass. "They are blameless."

"You were willing to leave her possessed, but you won't spare her a horrible memory?"

"Argue when we are safe," Winterglass said between clenched teeth. "We need to flee this building before we are cornered."

"But we're not done here," I said. "We've barely—"

"Bridge burned," said Tjuan. "Let's move."

Tjuan was in charge, and he was also my ride, so I did as he said, even though everything in me was screaming to catch her, fix this. She had to know I was wearing a wig now. Had she noticed my scars? She'd seen Winterglass, too; surely someone here would be making a call to the LAPD with all of our descriptions.

Winterglass drew another don't-look spell over everyone but me; I felt insanely conspicuous as I made my way as swiftly as possible to the elevators and jammed my finger repeatedly on the button with the down arrow. It felt like three days before one of the sets of doors finally opened and we were able to slip inside.

The fey hogging the center of the cramped space meant I was forced to stand almost between the elevator doors. To my horror, from my vantage point I saw Chin Ju and Garcia appear around the corner of the hallway. I ducked around and squished myself against the wall of buttons with a muttered, incoherent prayer, frantically stabbing the door close button. When the last sliver of hallway disappeared and the floor began to sink, I shuddered with relief. But the elevator was so slow Tjuan had time to straighten my wig; it seemed likely they'd beat us by taking the stairs.

Good news: they didn't. Bad news: apparently, they alerted the guy at the security desk in the lobby, because as I got off the elevator, there he was, standing in my path.

"Ma'am, can I see your identification please?" said the security guard in a brisk but friendly tone.

"Sure," I said. I could have flashed my empty hand, had Claybriar do his trick. But I knew damn well this guy wouldn't just nod and let me by. We'd assaulted an employee; even if he believed I was a real cop, he'd want to talk to supervisors and things I didn't have.

So instead I reached behind me and grabbed Winterglass by the wrist. The king's don't-look spell dropped, along with his facade. Almost immediately Winterglass wrenched his arm from my grasp, but it was too late.

The security guard staggered backward until he slammed up against the desk he usually sat behind, preventing him from fleeing farther. His mouth opened, but nothing emerged except for a high-pitched whine, and then his legs gave out completely, forcing him to sit down hard on the floor. I guess it was a pretty rough way to force a paradigm shift. The man didn't raise an objection as I walked briskly out into the parking lot with the boys close behind.

"To the car," said Tjuan. "Fast as you can go."

19

I took a moment to adjust the valve on my prosthetic knee, then broke into a respectable jog under the fading late-afternoon sky. My heart was hammering from more than exertion as Tjuan and I opened the back doors of his gray Camry for the fey, then let ourselves in the front.

"Morozov," Tjuan said sharply, starting the car and peering out the window toward the Cera building. "Can you hide the license plate until we've cleared the parking lot?"

"I cannot cast spells upon steel," said Winterglass.

"Caryl could have done it," I said sullenly.

Something about my comment seemed to light a fire under Winterglass; he murmured a few words in the Unseelie tongue. I shivered as the stretch of sunbaked asphalt between us and the building was suddenly wreathed in a toxic-looking smog.

"Not exactly subtle," said Tjuan, "but it beats getting tracked to the Residence." And then he peeled the hell out of there.

As much as I was tempted to pop some pain meds that night, I'd been too long away from home and a decent shower, so once

Tjuan was sure we weren't being followed, I asked him to take me back to my apartment in Manhattan Beach.

On the way I saw a whole new side of Tjuan; our little adventure had left him almost giddy. As he bounced theories off us, one hand occasionally leaving the steering wheel to gesture emphatically, I suddenly had less trouble picturing him as a writer. I was so exhausted and so fascinated by the excited-geek vibe he was putting off that I had some trouble following what he and Claybriar were heatedly debating.

"It doesn't matter," Tjuan said. "They wouldn't need appointments. They've got uniforms, trucks, and equipment with a recognizable brand name; if they just show up when no one's home and start spraying the yard, who in the neighborhood's going to call the cops?"

"So why haven't they?" said Claybriar. "She's had all those locations for at least four months. They've obviously infiltrated the hell out of Cera. If it's not a scheduling issue, what are they waiting for?"

"Damned if I know," said Tjuan.

It was full dark by the time we got to my place, and Claybriar asked if he could walk me to my door. I suppose I didn't think it through too well; fatigue left me feeling more brain-damaged than usual. As we climbed the exterior stairs and passed into the radius of Zach's porch light, I saw his curtain flicker aside for a moment, then fall back. A twinge of guilt left me feeling a little queasy.

"What's the matter?" said Claybriar as I started to unlock my door. His constant scrutiny of me was both flattering and inconvenient.

"I can't talk out here," I whispered. "Step inside a minute."

He did, and I closed the door behind us. Somehow the simple act of putting that slab of wood between us and the others shifted the mood to something dangerously intimate. He felt it too, and stepped closer, so that he was a couple of inches from pinning me back against the door.

"I—I should tell you," I said hurriedly, "I've been—my neighbor and I are . . ."

"Fucking?"

I stubbornly lifted my chin as though my face hadn't just gone tomato red. "It's just a—you know, it was a convenience arrangement. I should have told you right away. I just—"

"I'm going to stop you right there," Claybriar said, stepping back a little, palms out. "You do *whatever* you want. Seriously. Whatever and whoever."

My queasy feeling intensified. I tried to read his face, but he seemed relaxed, even amused. "You don't care?"

"Don't make it sound—I just mean, you and I obviously can't—and it's not as if I . . ." He didn't seem to know how to finish.

"It's not as if you what?"

He shrugged and addressed his next words to my shoes. "Well, I'm a faun. Right? I—frolic. That's pretty much how fauns kill time."

"Oh." I let out a short, awkward laugh. "So you—get around."

"Does that bother you?"

"No, no, I mean, who among us hasn't had an orgy in a magical forest, right? Good on you." I ransacked my brain for signs of jealousy and surprised myself by finding none. Did I expect a damned *goat-man* to become celibate the minute he met me? Of course not. I hadn't changed my ways; why should he? I turned it over and over, looking for hallmarks of denial, but it felt pretty solid. Whatever he was giving all those Arcadian nymphs, I didn't want. And if I needed my bell rung, I knew where Zach lived. So that was that. Right?

"You should get back," I said. "You and Winterglass need to get back to Arcadia and dump those wraiths, get the Seelie Court to do the ritual."

Claybriar groaned and rested his eyes in the palm of one hand.

"What? You can come back, right?"

"Probably. It's just—that means we've got to get past the damn manticore again."

"Can't Winterglass call it off?"

"No, that's the weird thing. It ignored his commands."

"Wait. How? It's not an Unseelie fey?"

"It sure as hell *spoke* Unseelie."

"The thing *talks*? What was it saying?"

"Winterglass didn't translate."

"Did he say why he couldn't command it?"

"That seemed to surprise him as much as it did me. He panicked and yelled something about beasts, but I didn't really catch it; I was kinda busy fighting and casting spells and whatnot."

"Damn it! Am I sending the two of you back to get eaten?"

"It'll be fine, Millie. The only reason that was such a close call is that Mr. Arrogant had figured he could just order it away. He and I know what to expect this time; I'm better prepared, and I suspect he is too."

"Just be careful," I said. "And see if you can find out what the manticore's deal is and why it won't obey. Ask Winterglass to translate. That thing starts going crazy right after Vivian dies? It could be involved in this mess somehow."

"Winterglass didn't seem to think so when it was yelling at us before. But I'll see what I can find out."

"Please do—so long as it doesn't get you killed."

He stepped closer, his eyes soft and his voice low. "You are not going to lose me," said Claybriar. "I don't want to put you through that."

"Is that a promise?" I said, and then immediately realized what I'd asked. I held my hand up in front of his mouth even as he drew breath to answer. "No," I said. "Don't bind yourself. Just do your best to stay alive; that's enough for me."

It was a little dizzying to realize that he'd been willing to promise me that he'd never leave me, and that unlike the others in my past he'd be bound to that promise. It was tempting, in a dark sort of way. But I wouldn't let him do it any more than I'd let him chain himself in the hold of a sinking ship.

Once we handed the list over to the Arcadia Project, for a couple days, everyone there seemed to forget I existed. The fey got busy back in Arcadia, and the humans got busy studying the list Tjuan had found. I had almost started to settle back into a relatively stable rhythm at Valiant by Thursday, around the time Parisa Naderi decided that breaking and entering was the answer to her problems. Just before lunch I got a call from Sam the security guard alerting me to the fact that Naderi—who we'd all thought was safely tucked away in her office writing—was apparently trying to find a way to pick the lock on the side door of stage 13. Where there was still a treacherous pit leading to another dimension.

"Jesus Christ on a moped," I said. Inaya wasn't there to take offense at my blasphemy; she'd been called away an hour ago to an emergency meeting at the Arcadia Project's Residence One in Santa Monica, of all places.

"Don't shoot the messenger," said Sam on the phone. I loved Sam; there was literally no one high enough on the totem pole that he wouldn't spy or tattle on for me, and I had no idea why. I think he just enjoyed getting important people in trouble.

"I'm more likely to slip you a big fat wad of cash," I said. "You've saved me some huge drama if I can get there in time."

I hopped into the less sluggish of the two golf carts parked outside the building and floored it, but even so, by the time I got to the soundstage, Naderi was nowhere to be found. I prayed that meant she'd given up, but a quick check of the side door found it unlocked. God damn it.

"What the hell is all this?" Naderi greeted me as I stepped inside. She'd turned on the floodlights and was staring not at the hole in the floor but at the mural David had painted on every square inch of wall.

"Ask David Berenbaum, if you can find him," I said. "If you want evidence that he was starting to lose his marbles when he left, you're looking right at it."

"David painted that?" She looked like she couldn't decide whether to be angry, bewildered, or impressed. "In a soundstage? Why?"

"Again, you're barking up the wrong tree."

"This isn't so bad, though," said Naderi. "We can work around this. All of this," she added, gesturing to the center of the room. So she'd seen the hole, too. Hard to miss, I suppose.

"No, we can't work around that hole in the floor," I said

through gritted teeth. "Not if it goes against city ordinances, which it does. Please, you can't keep taking things into your own hands like this."

"Who else am I supposed to trust?" she said.

"Try trusting the woman who got you a meeting with Wendigo, the woman who is busting her ass to keep your show on the air while interest is still hot. That would be me, if you're not keeping track."

I had never spoken to her quite like this, but it was doing what I wanted it to do, i.e., making her mad enough to quit staring at the soundstage and focus on me.

"Rahul is an asshole," she said. "I'd rather take the show off the air than work with him."

"Look. I'm in full agreement with you that this never should have happened to you. This soundstage should have been yours from day one. But—have you ever heard the term 'radical acceptance'? I heard this from someone with a PhD in psych. Psychology is useful to writers, right?"

"I'm not sure I like where you're going with this," she said.

"Hear me out. The idea of 'radical acceptance' is that sometimes in order to reduce suffering, you have to stop fighting the situation and do the counterintuitive thing. Wholeheartedly embrace reality, spiky bits and all."

As I talked, I eased my way back over to the soundstage door and held it open for her. Distracted by my words, she unconsciously took my body language cue and walked through it as I continued.

"There are similar ideas in scripture," she said.

"Exactly," I said warmly as I led her down the steps. "Will-of-God type stuff, right? When you stop saying, *I shouldn't be in this mess!* and start saying, *I am in this mess; what next?* supposedly it sets you free, makes things much less painful, and your eyes are clear to see solutions."

"Solutions like that jackass Rahul?" she said warily.

"I could be wrong here, but I think half of what's making this so stressful for you is that you can't give up on the idea that you can have it the way it *should* be. We all know how it should be. But it isn't that way, and you're tearing yourself apart with the idea that you can force it into being. You're a hell of a woman, Naderi, but you're not God." I sat in the driver's seat of the golf cart, swiveling toward the passenger's seat as though she were already sitting in it. Distractedly she slid in beside me, and I started the motor.

Naderi looked a little depressed, but that was good. It meant she finally understood that she wasn't in control.

"It's going to be all right," I said to her as I drove back toward her bungalow. "Maybe this first season you have to do green screens. Maybe things don't look exactly how they should. But first seasons are always awkward, and anyway let's not kid ourselves that people are tuning in for the visuals. You've got them hooked on the *drama.* And you need to keep them hooked a little longer. You know how viewer attention spans can be, and how many options they have nowadays."

"I know," she said. Huge exhale. "I know."

"We reel in the fish this season, end on a cliffhanger, and in season two we can wow them with production values. And you get to tell this whole sad story in the DVD commentary so there will be no question about whose fault it was that season one wasn't up to Parisa Naderi's standards. The fans will eat it up."

I could have been wrong, but I swore I saw a hint of a smile at one corner of her mouth. I was *nailing* this, and I couldn't even brag to Inaya, because that would involve telling her that Naderi had broken into the soundstage in the first place. If I wanted to be a good assistant, I'd have to make it seem like I wasn't doing anything at all.

I barely got back to my desk in time to give Araceli the nut-shell version and then make myself look busy before Inaya burst back onto the scene, her arm wrapped firmly around a gorgeous strawberry blonde. I raised an eyebrow for half a second before I registered two important details: first, that the woman had scratches across one side of her face and was leaning on Inaya heavily, and second, that I recognized her, or her facade anyway.

Baroness Foxfeather. Inaya's Echo.

20

"What fresh hell is this?" I greeted them, rising from my chair.

"In my office," said Inaya with a jerk of her head.

Araceli gave me a wide-eyed look I couldn't quite read as I followed the two of them. Inaya must have caught it, because she said, "Honey, could you run down to the Jamba Juice and get my friend here a smoothie? That orange-blueberry one." Araceli hopped to it, seeming to sense the pained urgency in Inaya's tone.

"What's going on?" I said as soon as Inaya's office door was safely between us and the rest of the world. Foxfeather sank into the plush upholstered chair in the corner with a little whimper, then abruptly pitched forward, face in her hands, and began to sob. Inaya stroked Foxfeather's reddish hair in a way that made a throb of jealousy rise up through my confusion.

"Poor Vicki is a refugee," said Inaya, referring to Foxfeather by her alias, which was too much like Vivian's for my liking.

"Refugee from what?"

"There's some kind of monster loose in fairyland," said Inaya. "Something I'm led to understand *your* Echo was supposed to be taking care of."

"The manticore?" I said in shock. I moved to Foxfeather, trying to adopt a comforting posture without touching her. "Did it hurt you?"

"My estate," she said, looking up at me with streaming eyes. "It's *gone*."

My hands went cold. "Gone? As in . . . big interdimensional void?"

"No, just . . . a rotting wreck . . . uninhabitable! The manticore destroyed it!"

"Destroyed your *house*?"

Foxfeather just buried her face in her hands again.

"It wasn't exactly a house," Inaya said tentatively. "Or so says Luis at Residence One. It was some sort of oasis: trees and vines and a magical spring, all protected with spells. It's where Vicki and her family and her—what did you call them?"

Foxfeather looked up again. "Vassals."

"Her vassals lived. A dozen people. All refugees now."

"All except the two the manticore *ate*," sobbed Foxfeather. "My bard and my aunt!"

"Oh my God," I said. "I thought *sidhe* estates were impregnable or something!"

"Only if I'm inside it!" she sobbed. "But I thought it was safe to leave! The manticore had always been *nice* to me."

"Wait, what?"

Foxfeather nodded solemnly. "It's been wandering Skyhollow for years. It was always ugly, and smelly, and ate some of us— but some of us got along with it just fine! It let me ride on its back once!"

"What the fuck?" I said. "And now it suddenly turned on you? Where was Claybriar during all this?"

"At the High Court," sobbed Foxfeather. "If he'd been there, he could have slain it! But it ate through my wards, rotted all the trees, poisoned the water. We had to run, all in different directions. Dreamapple and Bellgreen didn't make it. I saw it swallow Bellgreen whole!"

"Did it hurt you, too?" I said, pointing to the ugly scratches on her cheek.

She touched her own wounds, looking shocked. "No, no, Ironbones. If the manticore had clawed me, I would have no *face*. A nasty little common Seelie creature did that to me on my way to the Gate."

"A Seelie fey? Why?"

"Because it could! The commoners will get you if you don't keep to the roads. But if I'd kept to the road, the manticore would have spotted me."

I peered more closely at her wounds. They looked painful, even had the faint smell of dried blood. "It's like Claybriar said," I observed. "Your facade mirrors your injuries. That's so weird."

"No it's not," she said, looking at me as though I were criminally stupid. "If they didn't design them that way, everyone who gets a facade would be immortal!"

I hadn't even thought of that, when I'd killed Vivian. So, somewhere in the weird pocket-dimension where the facade got stashed, I had created a second pile of human dust?

"I can't take her to a hospital," said Inaya, possibly misreading my expression. "Luis at Residence One said it's not allowed, because the second any part of her is removed from her facade—including a blood sample—it turns fey again. But Luis is blind; he couldn't look at her injuries, and the other lady there is just—crazy. Scary crazy. I didn't know who else to go to; you know more about fey than I do. Is she going to be okay?"

"Are you hurt anywhere else?" I asked Foxfeather.

The fey took a slow inventory, running her hands over herself in a way that was a little bit distracting. "Just my ankle, where I turned it," she said at last.

"She'll be fine," I said.

"When is Claybriar returning to Skyhollow?" Foxfeather asked fretfully. "The commoners are so much calmer when he's there."

"I—I don't know," I said. "He's got some business with the queen, and also here."

"I don't know what's going to happen to those other people," said Inaya. "Nine of them; some of them didn't even have facades. They're all in this little three-bedroom house in Santa Monica with a Gate right there in the living room like some kind of—" She shuddered.

"Can't they take shelter in someone else's estate in Arcadia?"

"Apparently it's not that simple to change estates; there's rituals or something? Luis said he'd contact Residence Five, see if they can send a messenger to Duke Skyhollow, convince him to give Foxfeather's people asylum. But I wasn't just going to leave her there in that house."

"Take her to your place," I said. "I'll cover for you while you're gone."

"God bless you," she said. "I'll be back just as soon as I can."

The rest of the workday seemed dull by comparison, but I was surprised by a text from Tjuan around three. We'd exchanged numbers the night before so he could contact me when he had word from Claybriar. He was the only agent in L.A. who knew the entirety of what was happening right now, so between that and the manticore disaster, when I heard the unique chime I'd set up for Tjuan's number, I almost sprained my wrist in my hurry to get my phone out of my pocket.

do you like chinese, the message said.

After allowing my adrenaline to dissipate, I took the plunge and assumed this was not a race-related question.

sometimes why

He didn't answer. I kept checking my screen periodically for a few minutes, then figured I wasn't going to hear back. An hour later my phone chimed again, kicking my heart back into high gear.

nm, it said. Never mind.

Staring at the screen, I was reminded that I didn't understand Tjuan, not even a little. Even when he wasn't possessed.

tjuan what's up, did you hear about foxfeather

This time it only took him eleven minutes to answer.

burbank is handling it. phil's getting chinese later tonight do you want some or not

yes ffs

Over the course of another half hour, I managed to wrangle the name of the restaurant out of him and put in an order. It wasn't exactly the warmest dinner invitation, but given my previous interactions with Tjuan I felt like he'd just given me a big mushy hug. A thank-you for de-possessing him, perhaps?

Too late, I remembered I had group therapy after work. I didn't want to rack up an absence over something trivial; enough of those could get me kicked out of the program without a refund, and I had a feeling that things were only going to get uglier as the wraith situation progressed. I did, however, adjust my ETA for Tjuan and then duck out of the session early by saying that I had a rare opportunity to mend a relationship with a former coworker. The session leader allowed me to leave, but only if I'd share the results with the group next week. That was problematic on several levels, but I'd cross that bridge if it ever came.

When I finally arrived at Residence Four a little after eight o'clock, Phil, Tjuan, and Stevie were already gathered around the table. Phil was the only one who greeted me, and it was more of a grunt than a greeting. I sat down and commenced to eat the most awkward dinner of my life.

Phil, apparently having spent his limited goodwill toward me on his hello grunt, spoke only to Tjuan for the rest of the night. Stevie, a tiny brunette who appeared to be pretty deeply placed along the autism spectrum, didn't speak to anyone, just stared at me unnervingly. Tjuan only addressed me a couple of times, mostly to have me pass him something or ask if I was going to eat that. He ate as though he'd only just remembered he had a digestive system; it was grimly fascinating.

The worst thing though was the way Teo's memory hung over the table. Dinners at Residence Four had once been so spectacular that Caryl would leave her luxury apartment and drive an hour in peak traffic just to sit at the table. Only twenty-two, and he'd been the best chef I'd ever met. Now Caryl was in the basement while I ate gelatinous Chinese takeout and tried not to think about how dead Teo was, how all his fire and snark and culinary snobbery had been reduced to bones in a box.

I didn't eat much. More broccoli beef for Tjuan.

I waited for everyone else to leave the table before I gave up. I took my plate to the trash can by the kitchen sink and scraped it; Tjuan came in and leaned on the kitchen island.

"Morozov's back," he said.

"What? They came back already?"

"Just Morozov. Clay's going through entry and exit procedures like a good boy, but His Majesty bounced back like a bad check as soon as he dumped his wraith. I had to drop him off at the Omni so he'd quit hovering over Caryl."

I sighed and continued scraping my plate. There was a moment's silence, but Tjuan just kept leaning on the island like he was working his way up to something.

"You know T. J. Miller?" he finally said.

I set my plate down in the sink, turned to look at him. The name nagged at me, but so vaguely I couldn't even come up with a decent bluff. "Not intimately," I said.

He snorted. "You're not wrong. I meant, you know the name?"

"Yes," I said as my brain frantically sorted it from other similar names, rejecting mismatches, frantically scrabbling for the correct data folder. "Yes, I do."

"Not many people could tell you who wrote a screenplay," he said, "but I figured you being a film student, you might pay more attention."

Screenwriter! It snapped into place. "*That's* who you are," I said, pleasantly shocked. "I read a couple of your screenplays when I was binging on action scripts for a class project. And you've been on staff on a couple TV shows, right?"

"You do pay attention."

"Writing was never my strength, so I used to kid myself I should learn all the writers' names, since I might be working with one someday."

"Well now you are," he said.

"Not exactly what I had in mind. But I'm guessing it wasn't your Plan A either."

"My last staff writer job, I got . . . sick in the middle of the season. So now I work under the radar. Uncredited rewrites."

I stared at him, inferring the tale of abject humiliation that lurked between those sparse words. I felt a sudden urge to bridge the distance, give him a pat on the arm, something. But I didn't think that would go over well.

"I see," I said instead. "I guess you know my story already."

"Yeah."

"Nice to get a little quid pro quo."

"Yeah, well, if they hire you back, we'll probably be partners, so I thought I ought to—"

"Oh, no, no, I've got another job now. Full time. Sorry if that wasn't clear."

His expression went strange. Very strange. Abruptly he turned away, bracing both hands on the counter.

"Tjuan? I hope—I didn't mean that personally. I mean I'm sure you'd be a great— Tjuan?"

This wasn't disappointment I was seeing; in fact I was pretty sure he was no longer hearing me at all. He shuddered and sagged against the counter, then turned back toward me, looking through me as though I weren't there. The expression in his eyes was familiar, but it wasn't what it looked like. It couldn't be.

"Tjuan. What is it?"

He forced his eyes to focus on me, and his mouth worked a few times before he could get the words out.

"It's back," he said.

21

"There's a wraith in your head again?" I said, backing away a little. This time Winterglass wasn't nearby to keep the thing off me.

"Same one," he said, forcing the words out as though they hurt.

"Are you sure? Because Clay took it back to—"

"I'm sure," he snapped.

"But no one's been tortured, or—"

"It just called me its Gate."

"What? Why? Because it's been in you before? That makes you a pathway?"

"That's what it says."

"So as soon as Claybriar let go of it, it could just fucking transcend dimensions and hop right back into you? That means that every single person at Cera who—"

"Stop. Talking. To. Me." Tjuan put his hands on his head as though to keep it from shattering into pieces.

"I'm sorry," I said. "God, Tjuan, I'm so sorry." And then, not knowing what else to do, I backed out of the kitchen.

The Seelie Court's ritual was useless, then. How many hosts were out there, and where?

I made a beeline for the basement, too panicked to feel guilty that Caryl had been dozing on her cot before my heavy tread on the stairs woke her. She rubbed her eyes and muttered Elliott's summoning spell without my even having to ask. When she'd finished, she stifled a yawn with the back of her hand.

"We're screwed," I said.

"How this time in particular?"

"Tjuan's possessed again."

"What?" Now she was awake. "How is that possible?"

"I have no idea. I'm panicking."

"Panic will not help us." Caryl's expression showed only puzzlement. "Tjuan was perfectly lucid when he briefed me about Vivian's list of addresses, not more than two or three hours ago. Then he asked Stevie to match the addresses up with nobles' estates. I'm assuming this possession is very recent?"

"It just happened. Where are we with Alvin? Does he even believe in wraiths yet?"

"When last I spoke to Tjuan, he had not yet succeeded in reaching Mr. Lamb."

"And now we've lost Tjuan. We need to go get Winterglass, see if he can help."

"You're missing the more urgent problem."

"What's more urgent than what's happening to Tjuan right now?"

"Tjuan existed in that state for four months without harming himself or others. Meanwhile you've just told me that the drawing ritual cannot keep the wraiths from carrying out their plan, a plan which may take place at any moment."

"Right." My gut still insisted that Tjuan's suffering was the higher priority, but that's the trouble with guts sometimes.

"Then we need to find out *immediately* what's been holding the wraiths off," I said, "and make sure it keeps holding until we can figure out a way to stop them."

"They may be waiting to complete the list," said Caryl. "They would need to strike every location within a day or two of one another, since the moment the collapses begin in Arcadia their secret would be out."

"But their secret's already out," I said. "And they know it. They've got nothing to lose by proceeding. So what are they waiting for?"

"I see your implication."

"You do? Let's pretend I don't, for a second."

"Their delay suggests they await a signal or call to action. Which suggests that someone has taken Vivian's place."

"You think so? Who?"

"Now that you have burned our bridges at Cera—yes, Tjuan briefed me on that as well—I have no idea how to proceed in identifying conspirators."

I let the rusty gears in my brain turn for a few. "What about the manticore?"

Caryl lifted a brow at me. "I was not aware that the thing had leadership qualities."

"I don't mean that it's the leader. Though I suppose it could be. I just mean, maybe it knows something. Don't you think it's suspicious, the timing of its attacks? How long has this thing been alive?"

"At least a millennium, as I understand it."

"But it chooses *now* to start raising hell? Foxfeather said it's been chilling in Los Angeles awhile."

"Skyhollow, you mean. Manticores aren't native to the area;

this one's very arrival decades ago could be interpreted as an aggressive act."

"But suddenly it's escalated things. Maybe we should find out why it's mad, what it wants."

"Wants? Millie, we're talking about a creature the size of an elephant with three rows of serrated teeth. It wants to eat. Without chewing."

"But it *spoke*, Claybriar said. That implies higher thought. Winterglass didn't translate, so we have no idea what it was trying to say. It spoke first, got ignored, and *then* attacked them."

"Where is His Majesty, by the way?"

"Tjuan dropped him off at the Omni, he said."

"You will need to find someone to drive you there, and you will need to figure out how to get the king to cooperate."

"Caryl, *you* speak Unseelie, and you're already on board. Is there any way you could protect yourself if the manticore tried to attack you?"

"Yes. But King Winterglass could simply command the creature's obedience."

"Actually he can't. Claybriar said the manticore just ignored his orders."

Caryl sat up straighter, her eyes sharpening with what must have been, given Elliott's presence, sheer intellectual curiosity. "That's not possible," she said. "Unless . . ." She traced her lower lip with a fingertip, her gaze losing focus.

"You have a theory?"

"It must have to do with the creature's age," she said. "The current power structure in Arcadia dates back to sometime in Earth's first millennium A.D. But if the manticore was already alive before the scepters were even made, and if it did not explicitly agree to accept that shift in Arcadia's reality . . ."

". . . then it's a *perfect* candidate to inherit leadership of Vivian's rebellion."

"There is a certain logic to that."

"Imagine if you were the one to find this out, to prove it. It could only help you."

"Not if I flout authority to do so. I am not permitted to leave this room."

"Alvin doesn't even have to know. We get Phil to sneak you across, find out what we need to know, and then once you know what we're dealing with, we figure out some legal way to get the same information to Alvin."

"Arcadia Project rules are not arbitrary. Breaking them would set a dangerous precedent; I cannot agree to this."

"Caryl, we can't *stop* the wraiths unless we cut this thing off at the head. And we have no idea how much time is left. If we wait to debate this up the chain of command, it might be too late."

"You could have King Winterglass here within two hours."

"The guy who provoked it to attack before? And who doesn't have the queen's champion to save his ass this time?"

Caryl was silent for a long moment. The advantage of Elliott was that it kept her from panic, which kept her from denial, which sped things along.

"I will go," she said, "but on the condition that you come with me. The steel hardware in your body will make the creature think twice about eating you. And if the manticore can speak, it can cast spells. If it enchants me, I could use your help disrupting the spellwork."

"You want me to go— to Arcadia? How is that even possible if I explode magic?"

"To be more precise, you disrupt *spellwork*. Every square inch of Arcadia is not covered in spellwork any more than every square inch of Earth is covered in power lines. It will be awkward, but not impossible. The most difficult part, I suspect, will be convincing Phil to let us through."

Caryl had predicted correctly. In the tower, he stood quite literally between us and the Gate, scowling behind his unruly dark beard. Outside the windows the night was pitch black, reminding me how very late it was and that I still had work in the morning.

It was possible that Tjuan might have been able to soften up his friend a little, as he had when we'd delayed Winterglass and Claybriar's exit, but under the current circumstances Tjuan wasn't likely to even leave his room, and Phil wasn't bending an inch for either of us.

"Do you really want to piss Caryl off?" I said to him. "She was your boss up until last Thursday, and there's a good chance she will be again."

"Not likely," said Phil. "Alvin's next in line, from what I understand, and Alvin was *really, really* specific about Caryl. If she doesn't get back in the basement I'm going to have to call London and report the both of you. Do you have any idea what time it is in London right now?"

"Arcadia is in serious danger," said Caryl. "There is no telling how much time we have left to avert it. We need to speak to the manticore that has been harassing Skyhollow, because we believe it may have information that can help us."

"If your business is legitimate," said Phil, "then call Alvin and get clearance."

I snarled in frustration. "Even if he was answering his phone, you know he'd never let Caryl out of there! He thinks she killed Tamika!"

Phil gave a little shrug.

I narrowed my eyes at him. "Do *you* think Caryl killed Tamika?"

"I just work here. I'm doing what I was told, because if I fuck up, I don't have much hope of another job. If you want to cause trouble, do it on your own time and don't involve me." His tone was unambiguously final.

I turned to Caryl. She seemed remarkably calm.

"I understand the position you are in," she said calmly. "I will do you a favor by taking the decision out of your hands."

Phil had just enough time to realize how ominous that sentence was before Caryl muttered a few Unseelie words and sent him collapsing to the floor.

"Oh my God!" I said. "Caryl, what did you do?"

"A sort of spinal anesthesia," she said. "He'll be fine until we return, but he won't be able to make it down the spiral staircase."

"Caryl, what the *fuck*! What if the manticore eats you while we're over there?"

"Then I'll be dead, and my enchantment will be broken."

Phil swore and tried to use his elbows to drag himself across the room toward the desk, which only drew our attention to the phone sitting on it. On the edge of hysteria, I nabbed it and stuffed it into the pocket that didn't already have my phone in it.

"We'll be back soon," said Caryl. "Try to relax."

Then she stepped through the Gate, and the void swallowed her.

"Oh boy," I said, hugging myself and twisting back and forth in the way I'd started to do when freaking out, now that pacing required way too much front-of-brain thought.

"She's crazy," whimpered Phil. "Alvin was right. She's going to kill us all."

"She's not going to kill anyone!" I said. "Relax, I can fix you I think." I moved to him and bent, slowly and painfully, to touch him on the shoulder. "Better?"

"No!" he grunted.

"Oh shit, right, because—changeling. Iron immunity. Shit. Look, I'll go get her back, right now. I'll bring her back and she'll undo this."

I stepped toward the Gate. And stopped.

I couldn't even look into it. It was like going blind, like falling, like being punched repeatedly in the brain. I was supposed to *walk into that*?

No. There was no way.

But there was no choice, either.

"Here I go," I said. Maybe to Phil, maybe to me. But I still didn't go.

It was like standing on the highest high dive of all time, with a line of people waiting behind you, and suddenly realizing you had no idea how to swim. I let out a high, keening sound of terror. Someone was going to have to push me, but the only other guy in the room couldn't even sit up. So I let Dr. Davis push me. *Be effective.*

The sensation could best be described as a painless explosion that vaporized my entire being, then said "just kidding" and casually put me back together in the same arrangement I started with. I imagine dying must feel similar.

My first impression of Arcadia was that it was impossibly *bright*. Not painful like sunlight on sidewalks, though. The radiance had a hyper-real, blooming quality that reminded me of my most vivid dreams.

The sky there was the shade of a ripe peach. The Gate was the only thing that looked the same; I stood next to it on a great craggy golden promontory in the middle of a desert. Nothing about the landscape was bleak or barren, though; the shimmering golden sands were littered with rock formations and alive with palms, succulents, and cacti whose huge bright blooms swarmed with butterflies.

Wait, not butterflies. One fluttered by my head; its diaphanous wings were attached to a tiny childlike body, moving too fast for me to catch any details.

"Holy shit," I said.

"I wasn't certain you were coming," said Caryl's voice.

She was standing on the rock some distance off to my left. Even she looked different, like an oil painting of herself. She pointed behind me, and I turned and looked down at the landscape to see a shimmering river of distorted light, moving like water over the sand.

"That is the path to Skyhollow Estate," Caryl said. "But you cannot take it without destroying it, and we are not looking for civilization just now at any rate."

"Right," I said. I took a deep breath and immediately regretted it; the air hit me like laughing gas.

Caryl stepped to the very edge of the high rock, turning slowly around to survey the area. "We should stay near the Gate in case we need to escape."

"What's to stop the thing from just leaping through the Gate after us?"

"There is a powerful ward drawn about this rock; only humans and those with facade enchantments may pass through it."

Caryl led me carefully down a steep path to the sand below. I'd had a little practice using my prosthetics on sand, but this felt all wrong; the ground was strangely spongy under my feet.

"Ugh, this place." Carefully correcting my balance, I turned around to look at the promontory behind us, but it was gone. I cringed back from what looked like a hundred foot sheer drop to an emerald sea.

"Uh, Caryl? Where did the rock go?"

"It is still there. The illusion keeps most fey from wandering too near the ward and becoming curious about it."

"So . . . to get back home, I have to convince myself to jump off a cliff?" I laughed out loud. And then I kept laughing and couldn't stop. My lack of control over it scared me more than the cliff did.

Unfazed by my hysterical mirth, Caryl turned to look out over the desert, and I followed her gaze. On the far distant horizon, in the direction that the mirage-road seemed to travel, I thought I could make out walls and towers, but they were cloaked in a scintillating apricot haze. The warm, dry wind brought a strange smell, somewhere between smoke and cinnamon.

"How large is this territory?" I asked Caryl when I had calmed my giggle fit enough that I could speak. "How are we supposed to find the manticore?"

"I shall lure him to us," said Caryl.

22

I looked over at Caryl. Somehow in the blushing golden glare she had gone from nondescript to heartbreakingly beautiful.

"You're sure you want to bring it this close to the Gate?" I said.

"Yes," she said, and then began a droning incantation in the Unseelie tongue, gazing at the upturned palm of her hand.

"Is it safe to cast Unseelie spells around me? King Winterglass told me they're poisonous or something."

She halted her incantation. "My spells are not as strong as his," she assured me, "but even so I take care not to cast too often in one spot. It can create a sort of . . . psychic aura around a place that depresses and demoralizes those nearby."

"Lovely."

She restarted her incantation. When she was finished, she said, "I doubt you recognize the words, but this is the same construct I used to find Vivian at Regazo de Lujo."

Without fey glasses, I couldn't see anything, since a construct was pure spellwork bound only to itself. "And you're going to follow it?"

Caryl shook her head. "We will wait here. The construct is

a sort of calling card. When it arrives at its destination it will allow the recipient to retrace its path and find us. That was the danger I spoke of when I sent it after Vivian."

"Did you dissolve Elliott to make it this time?" I said, studying her face for signs of distress.

She shook her head, then gave her hand a graceful upward motion as though releasing a bird. "When I summoned it at the resort, my reserves had run out after hiding the car. I had to reappropriate Elliott's energy in order to cast."

I watched Caryl turn sharply to the left as though watching the thing speed away. "And you're . . . fully charged now?"

"'Charge' doesn't even matter here," she said. "I can draw arcane energy from the very air. Every spell I cast here is more potent, more precise, and costs me nothing."

"So you could cast a thousand of those."

"I cannot cast duplicates of a spell. The first word of each spell is unique, and if I speak it again it simply starts the spell over. I could, however, cast one copy of each spell in my repertoire. I do not hold enough arcane energy within me to do that at home."

"It must be almost disappointing to go back."

Caryl turned and gave me a slow appraisal that carried a tinge of disapproval despite her expressionless face. "Perhaps it would be," she said, "if power were something that concerned me. But I am no tyrant. And whatever I am, I was born human. I need a world where things are what they seem, where no amount of wishing can make them anything other."

"Wishes come true here?"

"In a manner of speaking," said Caryl. "You could not wish for a rain of gold and have it suddenly appear. But Arcadia reflects the aggregate of its citizens' desires and expectations. Reality here exists largely by consensus."

"So . . . basically Arcadia is what my college friends thought the world was like when they'd smoked enough weed."

"If you say so."

Caryl gazed out across the rippling sand, and I watched her profile. I realized that part of what made her so difficult to describe was that her every facial feature was the definition of "average." Her mixed ancestry made her a blend of India and Africa and eastern Europe, a visual mean of humanity. She was indistinct, forgettable, and yet somehow in this light, perfect. I couldn't stop staring at her.

"Caryl," I said. "About what you said, at the soundstage."

She held up a silk-gloved hand to forestall me, not having to ask what I meant. "I consider the matter concluded," she said. "You were correct, and if I'd had Elliott I'd have understood that immediately."

Something in me twisted a little. "You're saying I was right about not being relationship material."

"That's a harsh way of putting it," said Caryl. "But you and I are both very ill in different ways, and my prefrontal cortex is underdeveloped even for a nineteen-year-old."

"But you can *be* grown-up temporarily. For long stretches of time."

She shook her head. "Absence of emotion is not maturity," she said, "though it's easy to mistake. Part of maturity is learning to deprioritize emotion, prevent it from taking the reins. But a large part is perspective, long-term decision making. While my duties over the last four years have helped develop my decision-making faculties, there are no shortcuts to perspective. Even without my emotions, I often make poor decisions, simply because I lack the life experience to inform them, and because I am more intelligent than most people I stubbornly resist outside advice."

I only partially heard what she was saying, because the entire time, I was staring at her profile and teetering on the precipice of touching her, turning her toward me, shutting her up with a kiss. There was no thought behind the impulse, no decision; it was driven by that sense of reckless impunity you feel in a dream.

I might have done it, if not for the noise.

We both heard it at once, coming from the direction where Caryl's construct had disappeared. It was somewhere between the deep, coughing roar of a lion and the blast of a brass band. If sudden panic had a sound, that would be it.

The hairs stood up on the back of my neck. I crowded close to Caryl. "Was that . . . ?"

"I believe so."

And then we saw the thing loping across the sand. My Wikipedia research had in no way prepared me.

It moved like a lion, muscles shifting under its bloodred hide, but its approach was faster than physics could account for. Its batlike wings were half unfolded, and its tail bristled with glasslike quills (venomous, and launchable, if the legends had it right). Its face was the worst part: big as a café table and human enough to plunge deeply into the uncanny valley, with a mouth that stretched from ear to ear. Its mane was matted and wild, the color of a dried wound.

"I think I might be sick," I said.

"This is a predator," said Caryl. "Show no weakness."

"Maybe I should wait on the other side of the Gate," I squeaked.

"You can report back." Even if the cliff behind me had been real, I would have seriously considered jumping off it to get away from that thing.

"I need you here if it tries to enchant me," said Caryl.

I crossed my arms over my chest. "Right," I said. I started shivering convulsively. "I want to say for the record that I don't think a thing should be allowed to have venomous tail spines *and* magic."

Caryl hadn't taken her eyes off the beast. When it drew close enough, Caryl called out to it in the Unseelie tongue. It halted its approach and began to pace back and forth at shouting distance, its baleful crimson eyes fixed on us.

"I told it we've come to submit to its demands," Caryl said quietly. "Though that's only a rough translation; fey languages do not work the way that human languages do. A conversation is rather like grappling; each utterance is an attempt to secure a position."

I was still crowding her, but she hadn't drawn away. She probably had worse emotions for Elliott to carry just now than claustrophobia.

The breeze carried a rank, leonine scent as the creature slowly began stalking toward us. Its paws were velvety red, each the size of a tea tray, with claws like meat hooks. The sheer weight of the creature turned my joints to jelly; I could feel the impact of each foot vibrating through the ground.

It stopped about fifteen feet away, braced its feet against the sand, and let out the same horrific roar, this time at close enough range that it rattled my rib cage.

When the air calmed, Caryl released a few more sibilant, bone-chilling syllables in the Unseelie tongue. For a moment the manticore stood very still, only its tail lashing back and forth. The whiplike motion was so sharp that I expected quills to fly off in every direction. Then the manticore spoke to us in a deep, brassy voice.

"Talk," it said. "I'm listening."

Caryl and I both stood there in absolute silence for a full seven seconds, then turned to stare at each other. The manticore was surprisingly patient during this little display of idiocy, which is to say it didn't eat either of us.

"Greetings," Caryl said, always first to find her composure. "I—did not expect that a manticore would speak English."

"I'd say I didn't expect a human to be ignorant," said the manticore, "but I don't have your gift for lies."

Spells, venomous spines, *and* sarcasm. Great.

"I shall not tax you for an explanation," said Caryl. "I came here as a translator, but I see my services are not required. Allow me to introduce Baroness Millicent Roper."

"Save it," said the manticore. "The only reason I haven't already eaten you both is the stench of iron. I don't answer to the ones who play at king and queen, so why would I give a damn who calls herself a baroness?"

"Just as we thought," Caryl murmured to me. "It does not recognize the king's authority."

"I'm not an 'it,'" the manticore snapped, and then reared up briefly on his hind legs to show us.

I made an exaggerated display of being cowed by the magnificence of the monster's genitals, and then he did the last thing I could possibly have expected. He laughed, a great rumbling sound that sent me into a fit of nervous giggles. Slowly he lowered himself back to all fours.

"I like your pet," he said to Caryl.

"I'm Millie," I said. "What should we call you?"

"I haven't been named by your little 'Project,' if that's what you mean."

"But you must have a name. How do fey address you?"

Without warning, I found myself plunged into a waking nightmare.

Red-hot cords wrapped around me; my entire body spasmed in agony, leaving twisting burn marks where the cords inched over my thrashing limbs. No sooner had a scream ripped out of me than the image was gone. Breathless and filmed with cold sweat, I looked down at my arms and found them unmarked.

Caryl looked vaguely disoriented, which suggested that she had been subjected to the image as well.

"I should have warned you not to ask that," she said. "This is how fey are named here. A fey mother adds a word to the language to describe something for which there was formerly no word. Others are allowed to know the definition, but not the word itself."

"Because the word would give them power over the person."

"Yes. And so the Project approximates an English translation. Rivenholt, for example—a small, close-growing group of trees bisected by a seismic fissure in the earth. Without such a word, we can only address fey as the fey do, via the image or experience the word denotes. That can be . . . impractical."

I rubbed at my arms. "You are the Grand Duchess of Understatement."

"It isn't often that I find myself in the position to name a fey," Caryl said to the manticore, "but may we call you Throebrand?"

"I couldn't care less."

"You must consent, or the name will not function as truth."

The manticore rolled his great red eyes heavenward, then exhaled a weary-sounding stream of Unseelie words. The neglected-refrigerator smell of dark magic wafted through the air.

"The naming ceremony is usually more formal," said Caryl, "but that will suffice."

The manticore's tail curled up and over his back in a way that was equal parts curious cat and angry scorpion. "What are you after?" he asked us. "You don't expect me to believe you're really here to help me."

"We didn't even know you needed help," I said. "But we do know you're angry enough to destroy people's homes and eat them alive, and you have been ever since V—uh, since the death of the exiled Countess Feverwax."

"*Vivian*," said the manticore as though he were spitting out gristle.

"So you're acquainted."

"I served that woman and her pathetic revolution for half a human's lifetime."

I felt an almost tangible click as things fell into place. "That explains a lot," I said, "including your Valley accent."

"When I got tired of her delusions," said Throebrand, ignoring my smart-ass remark, "she made me a promise that tempted me to carry her little revolt through to the end. But then she died. Even I can't call in a debt from the dead."

"What did she promise?" I said. "If we can help you, maybe you'd consider helping us in return?"

Throebrand made a percussive choking sound; I backed up a step, expecting the world's largest fur ball.

"You?" he roared. "Vivian was *sidhe* garbage, but at least she was bound by a promise. Nothing can bind an iron-monkey."

"What's the harm in telling us what she promised?" I said. "Worst case, we can't help you either, and you're no worse off."

"Except that your little *Project* now knows what I want and can use it to manipulate me. In other words, that thing you're trying to do right now."

"All I want is to stop the carnage you've been causing, and the even worse destruction that's going to happen thanks to Vivian's plan. A plan you're up to your ass in, apparently."

Slowly Throebrand's mouth stretched into an ear-to-ear grin, exposing his yellow bear-trap teeth.

"So you know what's coming," he said. "And you also know that there's exactly *squat* you can do about it."

"Is there any point in even trying to explain to an Unseelie fey why it's *wrong* to hurt innocent people?"

"Nope," he said, then made another scoffing hair-ball sound in Caryl's direction. "You thought your pet monster would intimidate me, changeling?"

"Wait, *I'm* the monster? Says the guy with shark teeth?"

"You're in Arcadia, Ironbones," said Throebrand. "I *belong* here."

"Not in Skyhollow you don't," I said. "I may be an ignorant human, but I've picked up on that much. And if you won't run after a carrot, that just leaves us the stick. I'm going to do everything I can to help Claybriar make an end of you."

The manticore's horrible red eyes narrowed. "You know the queen's so-called champion?"

"You could say that. He's my Echo."

Throebrand's face went perfectly blank and his body still; even his tail stopped twitching. As shocked as we'd been when he first spoke English, it seemed I'd managed to turn it around on him. A series of expressions fought each other for control of his face, and finally he spoke in a careful, even growl.

"What is it you want from me exactly?" he said.

"Information. Also to stop attacking people."

"Define 'people.' I do have to eat."

"Uh . . . anything sentient?"

"What qualifies?"

"Just—don't attack anything that could sit down with me for a game of cards, okay?"

"You've just described every source of meat in Arcadia."

"Oh." I scratched at my hair. "Uh, any chance of you going vegetarian?"

"Nope."

I looked at Caryl. "This isn't going well."

"When you say *people*," Throebrand interrupted, "what you really mean are the damn *sidhe*. I might agree to leave them alone, for now, under certain conditions."

"And fauns," I said. "I'm pretty sure I don't want you eating fauns either."

"Fine. But I'd need something in exchange."

"Why do I have the feeling I'm not going to like this?"

"I want to visit your world."

"Buh," I said. "Uhhhh."

"That is impractical, to say the least," Caryl filled in for me.

"Those are my terms," said the manticore. "Take them or leave them."

"That would be our cue to leave," I said. "Nice talking to you, Smiley."

"Wait," he said. "You said you need information. I have it."

"Information you had no interest in giving us until you found out Claybriar was my Echo. Why does that make a difference?"

"Gee," said Throebrand. "That sounds like information. And I'm pretty sure you're not interested in dealing with me."

"Not interested enough to set an elephant-size predator loose on the streets of Los Angeles. Nothing you could possibly have to offer could be worth making a deal like that."

"You think that," he said, grinning ear to ear again, "because you don't know what I know, and how little time you have to figure it out."

"You know when they're going to bomb the estates."

"Among many other, much more useful things."

I hesitated. "If you tell us when the bombings are planned, I will *reconsider* making a deal with you. Otherwise I'm walking right now, and we're done."

"Halloween," he said.

"What the *fuck*?"

"Yeah, I thought you'd like that."

"That's—what, a little over a week, now? Jesus Christ!"

Throebrand gave a massive leonine stretch, feigning a yawn. What a pain in the ass.

Caryl looked thoughtful. "It makes sense. Without Vivian to give a signal . . . and some of them would not have a way of following a calendar. The convergence at Samhain would be a palpable event to them, a cue they could all act upon no matter where they were, and use to coordinate their strikes."

I considered Throebrand for a moment. "Not that I'm condoning it necessarily, but . . . could we even make a facade for . . . something like that?" I murmured.

"I—am not certain. We couldn't expect it to master bipedal movement in the time allotted." Caryl tilted her head, studying Throebrand dubiously.

"So give me four legs," he suggested cheerily. "What sort of creatures do you have over there?"

"Not very many that could just walk around L.A.," I said. "Maybe a dog? A big-ass dog. Nah, I seriously doubt it."

"I don't see why not." Throebrand lashed his tail. "Pretty please? I promise to be a good doggie." He gave me a horrible open-mouthed grin, showing all three rows of teeth.

"There's not enough *nope* in the world," I said.

"Hold a moment," said Caryl. "This could conceivably work, if we had a promise of proper behavior and a willing facade crafter. Skyhollow's people would of course have nothing to do with him. But perhaps I could persuade King Winterglass to contact the people at his High Court."

Throebrand bristled. "*Sidhe* usurpers," he growled.

"Beggars can't be choosers," I said, trying to hide how unnerved that simple display of aggression made me. "How long would this take, Caryl?"

"I am not certain, as the entire process is known only to Dame Belinda and the High Courts. I do know that a human mind is required to create and hold the image, and the crafter must join with the human's mind and make the image flesh, with constant feedback to shape the creation. Depending on how cooperative the various parties are, it could be anywhere from twenty-four hours to never."

"Worth a try," said Throebrand. "Get me to your world, give me a little tour, and I'll tell you exactly what the wraiths are up to."

"I don't see that we have much choice," I said. "If you promise not to attack any *sidhe*, fauns, or humans between now and Halloween, we'll contact Winterglass and do everything in our power to make this happen."

"Pleasure doing business with you," said Throebrand. He turned and began to stride away, then paused to look over his shoulder. "Just make sure it's a *really* big dog."

23

The moment we got back, Caryl removed her curse on Phil, but either the paralysis had spread to his vocal cords or he'd simply decided never to speak to either of us again.

"We have until Halloween to stop the destruction of Arcadian civilization," Caryl explained to him. "I am sorry for taking drastic measures, but you had no right to prevent the regional manager from accessing the Gate, and I have not yet been officially removed from that position. Until Alvin officially takes over here, we are in a sort of Schrödinger's box that makes it difficult to tell which of us violated the rules."

Phil responded to that by turning his back on us and sitting at his desk as though we weren't even present.

"If you want your phone back," I said, patting my pocket, "you may want to cooperate."

"Keep the phone," said Caryl. "If he reports us, Dame Belinda will further hinder our investigation, and that could cost countless fey lives."

"He can just use another phone."

"He would be in contract violation if he did so. We have already established that he will not risk loss of employment."

"He can get fired for using a different *phone*?"

"Employee privileges and promotions are linked to behavior rather than diagnosis. Phone usage patterns are an important part of our evaluations."

"Just leave me alone," said Phil.

I knew he was going to be trouble, but it was already midnight, and we still needed to talk Winterglass into cooperating and get me home in time to grab a few hours' sleep before work in the morning. So I contented myself with keeping Phil's phone hostage.

Luckily, Alvin had left Caryl's car keys on their usual hook in the kitchen. Her SUV was still parked on the street; it had a ticket on the windshield from street cleaning two days before.

The Omni was about ten minutes from Residence Four, but Caryl's SUV wasn't cleared to park in the hotel's garage, which meant that by the time we even got to the front doors my lower back was a throbbing nightmare from dragging my prosthetic legs over five blocks of sidewalk.

The hotel intimidated me with its grandeur, even (or maybe especially) in the dead of night. Its concave, modern facade was lit by a row of fan-shaped lights atop three-story columns; the lobby's interior was a sprawling golden palace accented by arrangements of enormous red flowers. I felt like a gnat.

Caryl and I didn't speak in the elevator, and we slipped through the impeccable fourth-floor hallway toward the king's room like a pair of thieves. Even if Caryl hadn't known the room number I could have guessed which one was set aside for the Arcadia Project; at the very end of the hall stood a door with an old-fashioned wooden knob. Gently I rapped on the door, hoping it would be enough to wake Winterglass without alerting his neighbors.

The king of the Unseelie came to greet us half-asleep, in what I was beginning to surmise must be the fey's usual private mode of dress. I wish I could say this was the first time I'd been greeted by a stark-naked *sidhe*. I kept my eyes on his face, but that helped less than you'd think. He'd taken the clasp from his hair, and it fell forward to half veil one eye.

"Sorry to wake you," I whispered. "May we come in?" I stood aside so he could see that Caryl was there too. At the sight of her his sleep-dulled eyes brightened, and he moved back to let us pass. The room was softly lit and surprisingly minimal, decorated in shades of beige, gray, and slate blue. It wasn't even a suite, just a king-size bed and the usual assortment of hotel furniture, all made from the finest woods and richest upholstery.

Once he closed the door behind us, I returned to a more conversational volume. "Could you put some clothes on, please, Mr. Morozov?"

Winterglass looked down at himself. "Ah." His tone perfectly blended sympathy with contempt. He nabbed his dark trousers from the back of a chair with a swift motion of one leanly muscled arm. Turning his back to us, he stepped into them, hiking them gracefully up over his perfect ass and buttoning them before turning back around. He didn't bother with a shirt, and I tried not to think too hard about the fact that he was going commando under there.

"We're going to need your help with a couple of things," I said.

"I promise nothing, but I am listening."

"First, Tjuan has been possessed again."

"Are you certain? How?"

"I think it's because you released the wraith in Arcadia. It was able to travel back to Tjuan's corresponding location and essentially use him as a Gate. Because it had been in him before."

"But if they have that ability . . . this means—"

"Yes."

Winterglass lifted his hand to cover his eyes, a picturesque pose of despair. He took a slow breath before lowering it, and when he did, his expression was calm. "I can disable the wraith the next time I visit the Residence. Was there anything else?"

"We'll need your assistance in getting a facade for someone," I said. "A custom facade, in secret, and as quickly as possible."

"Are there not procedures for that sort of thing?" He was ostensibly speaking to me, but his eyes were on Caryl.

"We can't let the Project know," I said. "I'm doing this behind Alvin's back."

Winterglass frowned, lowering himself to perch on the bed. I remained standing, but Caryl seated herself on the edge of the chair his pants had just vacated.

"This bodes ill," the king said. "I am no criminal, to skulk about hiding my plans from my allies. Why the secrecy?"

"To tell Alvin why we need the facade would require telling him that Caryl and I have already violated Project protocols. We had to do it; there wasn't time to wrestle with bureaucracy. We found out we have until Halloween to stop the wraiths from destroying every noble estate in Arcadia."

"Halloween?" said Winterglass blankly.

"The autumn convergence," clarified Caryl.

"Which happens in like a week," I added. "So you see the urgency. What we're asking is unprecedented, and I'd rather get forgiveness once we've saved Arcadia than riddle the place with holes while we're waiting for permission."

After a moment's icy pause, Winterglass exhaled, relenting. "Tell me what you need."

"We need the facade of a large dog. A facade the manticore could use."

Winterglass looked as though I'd slapped him. "Are you mad? You are. You've gone mad."

"No," said Caryl gently. "I wish we had another option, but I was there. I spoke to the beast myself. It may be the best source of help."

"You let it *speak* to you?" His eyes smoldered with the first flames of a towering rage. "That thing is a savage beast mimicking speech to mock its betters. You're *both* mad."

"No, we're not," I said as patiently as I could manage. "The thing—the manticore—Throebrand, *he* speaks perfect English. He's apparently been working with Vivian for decades, and he was every bit as reasonable as any other fey I've talked to, which is to say, not very. But he has agreed to give us information about what Vivian was planning before she died. He knows *everything*, Morozov; he was part of it. But he won't tell us squat unless we bring him here."

Winterglass rose from the bed, more than a hint of anger animating his lanky frame now. "This is idiocy. You play right into that animal's claws."

"I don't have time for your classist bullshit," I said, my own temper fraying around the edges.

I'd pushed it too far. I hardly had time to blink before Winterglass had me pinned against the wall. It probably hurt him more than it hurt me, but it was a little hard to think about that when I was staring into the fiery blue eye sockets of an antlered nightmare creature. I whimpered, and he let go almost immediately, raking one perfect hand through his inky hair.

"That thing will never help you," he said, moving away. "It is distracting you with this—*assignment* so that you look the other way while it plots something foul."

"Distractions?" I said with a nervous laugh. "Plots? According to you, it's just an animal."

"Animals can play tricks," said Winterglass. "Wolves on the hunt work together to trap their prey. Birds lay eggs in other birds' nests. And this beast wants nothing but our destruction."

"It's the best lead we've got, Morozov, and you are the only person who can make this happen for us."

He turned to me, his eyes boring into mine. "I will not do it."

"You'd rather watch all your friends' homes, probably even your own palace, disappear into an interdimensional void? You would rather the nobility of Arcadia be homeless? What do you think the commoners that you've spit on all these years will do to you once there are no walls to protect you?"

"Do you think I am a fool?" he hissed, his entire body trembling with something that was beyond rage, beyond panic. "Do you think *I* do not know what they will do? I, who stood and watched my king bleed in the street like a dog?"

I stood dumbly, not taking my eyes off him. "Caryl," I said, "what is he talking about."

"Tsar Alexander II," she said, her calm seeming out of place.

"Narodnaya Volya," Winterglass said, the Russian words bittersweet like dark chocolate in his mouth. "Rebels, you would call them. I have seen what the 'will of the people' will do. The tsar *freed* the people. The tsar had plans to remake the government to give them voice; he would not listen to me when I told him it was folly."

"You were pals with the tsar of Russia." I suppose it shouldn't have surprised me. "Was he your Echo?"

His eyes suddenly filled with tears. He turned away from me and went to the window, pulling aside the curtain so that he could stand gazing out at the lights of the skyscrapers like some goth-girl's fan art.

"No," he said. "Fedya was my Echo."

"Fedya?"

"Fyodor Dostoyevsky," said Caryl. "The novelist," she clarified, as though I and not she were the one who'd grown up on another world.

"He was already dead when they slew the tsar," Winterglass said in his softest falling-snow voice. "He had been ill, and Narodnaya Volya hunted me to Fedya's doorstep. Or hunted the man I pretended to be. In those days I went by the name of Snezhan Leonidovich Raskolnikov."

"Raskolnikov?" I repeated in a half whisper. "Why does that ring a bell."

"*Crime and Punishment*," Caryl replied softly. "The name evokes shattered glass; Dostoyevsky apparently found it pleasing."

"I stayed in Petersburg," Winterglass went on, lost in his reverie. "Even after Fedya left us, I stayed to protect his king from these animals, because I had promised. I promised! But the *people*"—he all but spat the word—"they were worse than children: children with fire! They threw it at his carriage, at him when he tried to flee. His legs were shattered. So much blood . . ."

Winterglass stared out the window but didn't seem to be seeing the city.

"That's a hell of a memory to carry around," I said as gently as I could into the silence.

"Memory," he said with a bitter laugh, "is the splintered glass that keeps me on the throne."

"I'm—I'm sorry," I said. "I feel for you, I do. But—"

Caryl cut me off with a sharp gesture before I could continue. I turned to her in irritation, but she only shook her head. She rose from her chair and went to his side. To my shock she reached up and began to comb her fingers through his hair. He closed his eyes.

"My poor king," she said in a velvet voice. "No one should have to carry the sorrows, the responsibilities, that sit on your shoulders." She slid her hands beneath his hair to massage the shoulders in question—bare, perfectly sculpted shoulders. This had suddenly gotten very hot, very fast.

"Only an animal avoids responsibility," said Winterglass, but the venom had left his voice.

Caryl slipped her arms around him and leaned her head against his back, cheek resting on his satiny hair. "You know I would not ask this of you if I did not believe it could save you and everything you love."

"Narodnaya Volya thought murdering their king would save them. And look what has become of Russia. Once a center of art and faith—what has come from it since the 'people' had their way?"

I decided that bringing up ballet and space travel and about a thousand Olympic gold medals was probably ill-advised. And I did see his larger point.

"I am not asking you to trust the *people*, Your Majesty," said Caryl. "I am asking you to trust *me*."

Winterglass pulled free of her arms and turned to face her, slipping a hand beneath her jaw to tilt up her gaze. I had a sudden erotic terror that he was going to French-kiss her right there in front of me, but instead he touched his lips to her forehead, fatherly, and then gazed intently into her eyes.

"You know I would do anything you ask," he said sadly. "Please do not ask this of me."

"I have no choice," Caryl said. "But I promise, I will ask nothing more of you. If you can see to it that a facade is made for Throebrand in time, then I will consider you free of your debt to me."

His eyes filled with tears again. "What if I do not wish to be free of it?" he said.

"You cannot punish yourself forever," said Caryl. "Not for Fedya, not for the tsar, and not for me. Let me settle this debt for you, lighten your burden at least a little."

He seemed to consider it for a long moment, stroking Caryl's cheek with infinite tenderness as he did so. At last he nodded.

"I trust your promise," he said. "You are, I think sometimes, more fey than human."

"I'm sure he means that as a compliment," I said, reminding them pointedly that I was there. "How fast can you have this thing made?"

He turned back to the window. "Give me two days," he said. "I will return to Arcadia first thing in the morning, and disable your friend's wraith on my way out."

24

On Friday I could barely keep my eyes open. So of course, as luck would have it, I got called into Inaya's office just before lunch and informed that the entire staff of Wendigo had been subjected to drug tests as part of the big buyout, and everyone who had failed had been let go. Including Rahul. So we'd made a deal with a ghost, and guess whose job it was to deliver the news to Naderi in person.

Somehow her numb, quiet resignation was worse than the anger I'd expected.

"That's it, then," she said, settling into a cushy chair in her office while I remained awkwardly standing. "Nothing left to do but go on hiatus until we have enough in the can to keep going."

"I'm still working on stage 13," I said. "I'm not going to give up on this."

"Radical acceptance," Naderi said bitterly to a painting of an antelope getting its jugular ripped out. "This is the reality. We yank the show off the air before the cliffhanger I'd planned, and hope the fickle fans are still around when we get back."

Somehow, when it came down to it, it was me who was having trouble accepting the finality of the defeat.

"They will be," I said, unaccountably morose. "It won't be a long hiatus, and it's a hell of a show."

Naderi stared at the doomed antelope for a moment longer. "This is one of those days," she said, "when anyone else would just break open a bottle of whiskey."

"I don't drink either," I said. "Want to take off early and get totally not-smashed together?"

Naderi gave me a hard sidelong look without even moving her head. "You're trying to make *friends* with me right now?"

"Despite what you think," I said, "we're on the same side. I hate this whole situation."

"*Hole* situation," said Naderi, with a punch-drunk little chuckle. "Because of the soundstage floor. You ever going to explain what happened in there?"

Half of me wished I could and was exhausted enough that I was tempted, but she wouldn't believe me anyway. I shifted my weight awkwardly. "Vivian Chandler was doing something in there before she died. Can't very well ask her what it was all about now, can we."

"I wonder if it was something for me," Naderi mused.

A weird feeling crawled across my skin. My Arcadian-bullshit sense was tingling something awful. "Why would you say that?" I said, my gaze drifting back to the disturbing painting.

"Eh, just thinking out loud. About six months ago, back when we weren't even sure *Maneaters* would get picked up and they were still building Valiant here, Vivian said she had a huge surprise for me once the construction was finished." Naderi glanced at me again, and this time her gaze latched on. "I'm sorry—were you and she close? I didn't mean to—"

"Oh no, we weren't. God no."

"Okay. Because you look like you just sat in a bowl of ice."

"It's—unrelated," I lied. Less smoothly than usual, judging by her steady gaze. "I—remembered a thing I forgot. Kind of a crisis thing actually. I hate to be rude, but—"

"Go then. I'm sick of looking at you."

Of course no one at Residence Four would take my call. Caryl must have locked herself back in the basement like a good little prisoner. I thought about calling Alvin, but even if I succeeded in reaching him, I couldn't figure out a non-incriminating way to lead into the revelation I'd just had. So I had to mentally commando crawl through the rest of that agonizing day as though my brain weren't tumbling in circles. I went back to Wikipedia and every other link I could find, and just as soon as I could leave work I took a cab straight to the Residence.

Of course when I got there, Phil wouldn't let me in. He pulled aside the little curtain on the front door, took one look out onto the porch, and walked away.

"Damn it, Phil!" I yelled, and pounded on the door some more. "Open up! I'll give you back your phone!" Nothing.

So I kept pounding. When one fist got tired, I used the other. When they were both throbbing, I turned around and surveyed the porch for a likely bludgeon. Nothing looked suitable, but I did spot an abandoned teething ring, which made me remember Song's baby, which made me remember the sliding glass door at the east side of the house not far from Song's room. I circled around the wraparound porch, found the side door, and pounded on the glass.

Eventually a bewildered and slightly miffed Song appeared, baby on her hip, to open it and find out what the hell I wanted. She stood so as to block my entrance.

"Sorry to bother you," I said. "I've got to talk to Caryl, and Phil's being an asshole and won't let me in."

"Boo," said the baby, tugging his mother's hair.

"I'm not supposed to let you onto the property," Song said with her usual lowered eyes and apologetic tone. "I got a call from Alvin; he's on his way back from—"

"I don't have time for this," I said, taking care to keep my voice calm. "A bunch of invisible terrorists are going to blow up Arcadia in a little over a week. The manticore knows stuff, and I know how to get it out of him, but Alvin won't listen to a damn thing Caryl or I say, so we're on our own. Please, Song. Remember what happened when they told you to fire me last summer? I saved the day anyway. Don't be the bureaucrat this time; that's not you. Don't make saving the world harder than it has to be."

Song teared up. "I'm sorry," she said, cradling her son close. "I need this job. I can't let you in."

"Song—"

"But!" she blurted desperately. Then she lowered her voice until it was barely audible. "Sometimes Stevie uses this door and forgets to lock it behind her. If you were to come and find the door unlocked, and sneak past me when I was busy with the baby, that wouldn't really be my fault."

"Are you saying what I think you're saying?" I said.

"I'm not saying anything," she said. "I'm going to my room to try to get Sterling to nap." *Sterling*. That was his name. Poor kid.

Song closed the door in my face, but by an astounding coincidence, she left it unlocked.

Out of consideration for her sense of propriety, I waited for her to disappear into her room before quietly sliding the door back open, letting myself inside, and locking it behind me. I kept a sharp eye out for Phil as I headed for the basement, but he must have gone upstairs.

The basement seemed especially dank and musty today, or maybe it was just my mood. Caryl summoned Elliott at the sight of me, then sat cross-legged on her sleeping cot, spine straight and expression attentive. "Do you know Alvin is returning?" she said.

"Someone might have mentioned it."

"How did you get in?"

"The side door was unlocked for some reason." Might as well get used to the half-truth while it wasn't crucial. "Caryl, I think I know what Vivian promised to Throebrand. I think she was going to introduce him to his Echo."

"His Echo?"

"Don't laugh," I said, as though she were in any danger of doing that. "That's what Vivian did, right? Echo matchmaking? And manticores are creatures from ancient Persian legend, which suggests that they're common in that part of the world, or what's parallel to that part of the world. Right?"

"Yes."

"This particular manticore came from his homeland 'half a human's lifetime' ago? Around the same time Parisa Naderi and her family oh-so-coincidentally moved from Iran to Los Angeles."

Caryl's gaze took on a sharp, fixed quality that could almost be mistaken for excitement. "This would explain why Throebrand suddenly became eager to work with us when he found out that Claybriar was your Echo."

That one threw me a little. "It would?"

"This world often parallels Arcadia, you see, at least roughly, in events and relationships. Claybriar is Throebrand's current nemesis, and so Throebrand would have reason to believe that you might have a similar relationship with *his* Echo."

"So he wants me to give the tour because he thinks I'll lead him straight to her without even knowing."

"And you could. Purposefully, now."

"Should I?"

Caryl considered. "This is powerful. We can use this as leverage. If he knows we can deliver what Vivian promised, then there is likely little he would not do to see it happen."

"I know this is a weird thing for me to balk at, given my history, but—I don't want to promise this unless I can deliver. My pride smarts at all that crap he said about humans being liars. Can we actually introduce them? It'll be good for them both, won't it?"

"I—honestly cannot say," said Caryl. "Those with Unseelie Echoes tend to lead miserable, chaotic lives. Dostoyevsky is one of the few who died by something other than his own hand, and that, I think, only because his Echo is—well, you have seen his peculiar sensitivity."

I wrapped my arms around myself uneasily, then shook my head. "Naderi is strong. She's managed to keep some kind of moral center despite years in the entertainment industry, and she has nerves of steel. She's gotten this far in life without an Echo or really much support from anyone; I think having access to a powerful partner could only make her stronger."

"To say nothing of the fact that it would end the problems that Throebrand has been causing in Skyhollow."

"Claybriar wouldn't have to kill him anymore?" I said. "Then there's no debate. Let's do this."

"The first step of the plan is already underway," said Caryl.

"In the meantime, we still have another problem to address."

"Alvin?"

"Alvin. He is returning from London this evening, and I understand that he will be bringing Dame Belinda with him."

My jaw went slack. "Whaaaat?"

"Phil did not say why, exactly. I think the only reason he even informed me of that much was in hopes of frightening me."

"Did it work?"

"Quite effectively. Dame Belinda is intimidating enough on a laptop screen; I am not looking forward to meeting with her in person."

"Maybe she'll be shorter than you and smell like prunes."

"I fail to see how that will matter, as she has the power to order my execution."

I inhaled sharply, then slowly exhaled, relaxing hands that were trying to curl into fists. "I'm not letting that happen, Caryl."

"It's touching that you would say that, but I hope you realize you have absolutely no power to prevent it."

"People are always telling me what I can't do, and it hasn't done much to stop me."

"Yes, well, as commendable as your confidence may be, let us not forget that it comes with occasional collateral damage."

For a moment I couldn't catch my breath. That was the problem with logical-Caryl; when she was disconnected from her emotions, she disconnected from everyone else's as well, couldn't see the way her words might ricochet into ugly places. I knew she hadn't explicitly meant to blame me for Gloria's and Teo's deaths, but if she'd had her heart in its proper place she'd have known better than to say something that would catapult me directly to that conclusion.

When I finally got air into my lungs, my eyes flooded, and Caryl studied me, one brow lifting about a quarter of an inch.

"I've hurt you," she said. "I apologize."

"For someone who claims to love me," I said, "you sure don't mince words."

"How many times must I apologize?"

"For what? Loving me? Saying so? Or reminding me of shit I'm already sick with guilt about?"

"I do not wish to have this conversation."

"If we were in a relationship, it would be your responsibility to have this conversation. So keep that in mind next time you want to get all starry-eyed at me."

"I dismissed Elliott at the soundstage because it was the only way to *help* you," she said. "The repercussions were not entirely under my—"

"You said you didn't want to talk about it, so let's not talk about it," I said, well aware that I was being an asshole as I flounced out of the basement. Sometimes you have to assist people a little bit in the process of getting over you.

I did stick around the Residence for a while, though. Neither Song nor Caryl had said exactly when Alvin was going to arrive, but I had a feeling he'd be stopping by as soon as he could, due to the irregularities that had been going on with this particular Gate.

I was a little relieved, to be honest, when he came through the front door alone, just before nine p.m. I'd spent the intervening time chewing my nails to the quick at the prospect of meeting the Grand High Pooh-Bah of the entire Arcadia Project; now I just had to cope with Alvin's look of mingled shock and outrage when he saw me relaxing on the larger of the living room sofas.

"How did you get in?" he asked.

"The side door was unlocked for some reason." Practice had helped; it was butter smooth.

"Well, this saves me the trouble of calling you," he said. "You and I need to have a conversation."

"Is this a conversation about trespassing that's going to end with me in jail?"

"I don't think I could make a trespassing charge stick," said Alvin, sitting on the other couch opposite me, "given that your pal Caryl's name has been on the house deed since shortly after her eighteenth birthday."

"Well, there we go. So assuming Phil tattled somehow, that only leaves you yelling at me about unauthorized use of the Gate, but that's debatable too. The only reason Caryl isn't in charge right now is a false accusation that we're in the process of disproving. She had every right to schedule an emergency trip."

"But not to bring an uninitiated human to Arcadia. That's a serious infraction no matter how you try to spin it, Roper." His words were grave, but there was something in his eyes that put me at ease, maybe the cinnamon-toast color, or maybe a little spark of amusement lurking in their depths. I had the sudden certainty that everyone in the New Orleans office adored him. I always seemed to find myself facing down people who had way more friends than I did.

"What exactly are you going to do? You don't have any authority over me."

"Not technically," he said. "But technicality doesn't matter. Your actions have narrowed your options down to two, and you aren't going to like either very much. Either way, you're done at Valiant."

"I beg your pardon?"

"You've seen Arcadia. The rules are clear on this; uninitiated visitors are not allowed. My good friend Adam at the Department of Homeland Security would back me up here, I'm afraid, and the DHS *does* have authority over you."

"Jesus Christ." I sat up straight, arms prickling with goose bumps. "You have my attention. What are the two options?"

"Option one: You sign a contract with the Arcadia Project. The contract is for life, and among its provisions is that you consent to be tracked by the Project if you leave the perimeter, in the same way that fey are. It also states that you will remain bound by the rules and regulations of the Arcadia Project and the Accord, even if you should later leave our direct employ."

"A lifelong contract? Is that even legal?"

"It doesn't matter. It's arcanely binding whether it's legal or not. Once you sign, you are committed to everything in its text, so I suggest you read it thoroughly."

"Is there wiggle room in any of the—"

"No."

"Okay then. What's my second option?"

"Unfortunately, due to the way the Accord is structured, if you insist upon remaining free of the Project's oversight, we will have to secure all of your proprietary knowledge."

"Secure my . . . knowledge. Wipe my memory."

Alvin wrinkled his nose briefly. "There's no *wiping* involved. We have someone lock down the mental pathways leading to those memories. It would be complicated, and there's a definite risk that it would increase your mental instability. You would also be useless to Inaya West, and therefore you'd lose your job either way."

"And my apartment. At least the first option leaves me a job, and housing. I don't see how I really have two options at all."

"You *can* choose to forget about us and walk away," said Alvin, something sad touching his face for a moment. "People have. And I can understand why, even though it leaves you very alone in the world. For some people, freedom is more important than security."

"People who have no idea what a real lack of security feels like," I said bitterly.

"That's my take on it," he said. "It's not very American of me, but I'd rather live under a thousand stupid rules and know I'm safe than be 'free' to blunder into an oncoming train."

"I'm not sure which is worse," I said. "But in this case, I don't get to be free either way. Living with six months of my life missing isn't exactly freedom."

"I wish I could give you more choices than that," said Alvin. "I also wish you hadn't painted yourself into this corner. Caryl should have known better. You don't know the Accord, but she does. She knew what she was doing, taking you there."

I looked down at my hands. "She knew what I'd choose. She wanted me back."

Alvin was silent for long enough that I eventually looked up at him.

"Do you see why I was concerned," he said, "when you told me she had a 'crush' on you? She's a teenager, Millie, a wickedly smart one who's used to wielding life-and-death power. She's manipulative, and calculating—"

"And she's my friend," I said. "I'll yell at her about it later, but right now my priority is getting her off death row, and dealing with what I found when I was in Arcadia."

"Which is?"

I stared him down, clamping my lips shut.

"Fine," he said. "Once you sign the contract, you'll have to tell me anyway. I'll go prepare it. You're not squeamish about needles, are you?"

"Not really," I said. "Uh, why?"

"Because this," he said, "is not the sort of contract you sign with a ballpoint pen."

25

I was up until two a.m. just reading the damned contract; it was forty-six pages long and written in near-microscopic type, in language that made standard legalese read like a comic book. All the convoluted, dry verbiage in the world couldn't disguise what I was actually doing, though, which was signing my life away.

Let's be real about it, though; I'd done that back in June, the minute I'd agreed to meet some weird stranger named Caryl Vallo in a park in Santa Monica. But this was the first time I'd fully faced that realization, seen in literal black and white.

There was one ray of hope, a distant one. Apparently, if I earned my way to senior agent status and then found a full-time job outside the Project where I could be useful—like Spielberg, or this Adam guy at the DHS—I'd no longer have to serve as an agent. They'd still track me and I'd still be bound to secrecy on pain of brain-wiping and all that, but I'd no longer have to live in a Residence or deal with arcane craziness on a day-to-day basis; I could live a basically normal life unless the Project needed a favor. But it would have to be a much more influential job than I had any prayer of getting. And so long as I was still an agent, any outside employment had to be short-term or part-time. Sorry, Inaya.

When I was finished reading, I went to the dining room as instructed, with the papers in hand. Stevie was waiting there, sullen and silent as usual; everyone else had gone to bed, I guess. She presented me with an ostentatious quill pen. The pen appeared to be filled with the blood Alvin had extracted from me when I started reading, hours earlier. I thought about asking what he'd done with the rest of the blood, but even if Stevie had answered me, something told me I wouldn't have wanted to know.

I signed my name, disturbed by the way the "ink" sat wetly on the page, refusing to sink into the fibers. I left the paper at the table to dry and made my way to room 6, my old room at the base of the tower. My one non-negotiable request had been that they put my air mattress in there and not ask me to sleep in Teo's or Gloria's old room.

Alvin had enough heart to grant me that request, but he did not have enough heart to let me sleep past eight a.m. the next morning. My phone rang at about three minutes to, and I was so groggy it took me a few minutes to understand what he was asking and that by "peninsula" he meant the hotel, with a capital P.

"Today?" I said stupidly. "High tea in Beverly Hills *today*? My clothes are all in Manhattan Beach, and I'm not sure I even have anything there that doesn't have holes or coffee stains."

"I've given you as much warning as I could," said Alvin. "I didn't think you'd want me waking you any earlier."

"You guessed correctly," I grunted. "Unfortunately the only person who can drive me anywhere is possessed. Do I need to explain that?"

"The king briefed me."

"But he hasn't come to help Tjuan yet."

"He will. I'm assigning Tjuan as your partner."

"He said you might. But he's not taking me anywhere this morning, I don't think. Is Caryl allowed out of the basement, or do I have to call a cab?"

"Cab," said Alvin. "Caryl is still our only murder suspect."

"Guilty until proven innocent?"

"It's not as though Tamika was stabbed," said Alvin. "And yes, there was a wraith there, but we already know it didn't kill her."

"We can argue about this later," I said. "I've got to find clothes."

"First," said Alvin, "now that you've signed the contract, it's time for us to discuss what you learned while you were in Arcadia."

"Will you even believe me? You don't have a great history when it comes to that."

"Do me a favor and drop the attitude. I'm either your boss, or your boss's boss, depending on how events fall out. And the sooner you get used to taking orders without making personal drama out of it, the easier your life is going to be."

"Is it too late to put that signature back in my veins?"

"I know you think I'm the bad guy," said Alvin, reminding me unpleasantly of Vivian, "but I'm just trying to prepare you. If you think I'm a hard-ass, I'm not sure you're going to survive ten minutes with Belinda. She wasn't knighted during World War Two for patching up soldiers, you know. She was a god-damned sniper."

"Fine, boss. No need to get so dire about it. What do you want to know?"

"Everything. But do me a favor and let me decide what parts of your story to tell Belinda. I don't want you in her sights unless it's absolutely necessary."

Dame Belinda Barker was not shorter than Caryl, as it turned out, nor did she smell like prunes. Her white hair was flawlessly curled; her dress was impeccably tailored and a vaguely military shade of blue.

"There you are," she said as Alvin and I approached across the Peninsula's Living Room; my boots were indecently loud on the oak parquet.

Belinda's age was not evident in any hand tremors or grandmotherly absentmindedness that might have stirred my sympathy, but in the almost alarming transparency of her skin, which held on to her bones for dear life. Half-hidden by tired, pinkish folds were two of the sharpest, most relentless gray eyes I'd had the misfortune of meeting. According to Alvin's heads-up in the rental car, she was all but blind on the left side, but I couldn't have guessed it by the way she held my gaze.

At Alvin's gesture, I seated myself on the honey-colored sofa across from her and arranged my skirt awkwardly as Alvin took a seat next to me. I'd managed to find a flowered dress from my UCLA days when I'd been twenty pounds heavier, and I'd stuffed my prosthetic feet into a pair of brown leather boots. Combined with the now greenish bruise on my cheekbone from Monday's encounter with the possessed IT lady, the effect was as gruesome as one might imagine.

Next to us was a cream-colored marble fireplace; on the mantel a white orchid gazed demurely at its own reflection. On the low table between us was spread the glory of the Living

Room's traditional high tea. But it was Saturday, not Sunday, and no one else was gathered nearby enjoying the same. I had the distinct impression that Belinda had simply stared down the hotel staff until they'd brought her scones and clotted cream with due ceremony.

"Millicent Roper," she said. She did not offer me her hand, as hers were occupied with cup and saucer. "I am pleased to hear from Alvin that you chose to come work for us."

I wanted to say something steely like *It wasn't as though I had a choice,* but instead I said, "You are?"

"Of course," she said. Her accent wouldn't have been out of place at Buckingham Palace. "It's rare to find someone who possesses both useful talents and the proper circumstances to make an appropriate employee of the Project."

Again, something stopped me from making a bitter commentary about "proper circumstances."

This kind of instant deference to a fellow human being wasn't like me. But here was a woman who had lived through bombings, been *knighted by King George*, for God's sake. She was the closest thing my species had to what the manticore was in Arcadia—a relic of another era.

"Given our time frame," Dame Belinda said once I'd politely refused a cucumber sandwich and stumbled my way through pleasantries, "we are left with very few options, and only one that has any hope of saving the Arcadia Project."

I sat up straighter, then glanced around the room again. We were the only three in the entire lounge, and I began to suspect that this, too, was a situation that Dame Belinda had stared someone into submission to arrange.

I'd expected to have to explain *my* plan; it had never occurred to me that while I was trespassing in Arcadia and making deals with demons, the bureaucracy might *also* be doing something. I didn't have much hope that their plan would address the scope of the problem, but I was willing to grasp at any possibility that meant I didn't have to offer up my alternative.

I hadn't told Alvin about my plan to bring the manticore through the Gate. It was a lie of omission, but one I thought necessary given his emphatic disapproval when I'd confessed to interviewing the thing. So all I'd told him, aside from the all-important time frame, was that Vivian had made the manticore a mysterious promise, and that Throebrand was deeply pissed off that she couldn't deliver.

"I am led to understand," said Dame Belinda, "that these . . . *wraiths* King Winterglass discovered have the ability to possess sentient beings, and to repossess their hosts on Earth if set free in Arcadia."

"Unfortunately yes," I said. "It happened to Tjuan."

"But the wraiths are helpless on this side. Stranded, unable to move or possess anyone beyond a certain range."

"Yes, when they've possessed someone, they've always been sort of . . . adjacent. At least in my experience, and I've been present at more possessions than anyone else in the Project."

"That does allow us one course of action that could be implemented within the week, but it is a less than satisfactory one."

"Which is?"

"To bring the Bone Harp to the soundstage at Valiant Studios, and have the Seelie Queen's harpist play it there."

"I—what?" I'd been expecting some kind of myopic garbage: an elderly reactionary's denial of the situation's urgency. This was—not that.

"Was I unclear?"

I looked at Alvin; he just gave me a barely perceptible shrug. I looked back at Belinda. She cranked one white brow upward in a way that impelled me to speak.

"I understand what you said, but—maybe I'm not clear on what the harp does. I thought it drew *all* arcane energy to its location."

"That is correct."

"I also understood that arcane energy on this side gets trapped where it came through."

"Yes."

"So—if the harp is over *here* . . ." I looked at her, waiting for her to explain where my logic had gone wrong.

She just stared me down with her pale, sharp eyes.

"You'll be taking *all* of Arcadia's magic," I finished. "And storing it on a soundstage in Manhattan Beach."

"I did say it was a less than satisfactory solution."

"I—can't really disagree. This is—kind of the nuclear option, isn't it?"

"If you have other ideas, now would be the time to mention them."

I drew in a long breath, considering whether or not to speak. Dame Belinda waited patiently, but in the end I couldn't do it. There was no way I could make my idea sound palatable, and if she flatly forbade it, that would take it off the table.

"Your idea would stop the attacks," I ceded, "but then what? What happens in Arcadia if there's no arcane energy?"

"Existing spells would be unaffected, as only energy unbound by spellwork can respond to the song. But no further spells could be cast until the energy is released. In an emergency case, a less important spell could be unraveled and its energy repurposed, but all working of spells would have to be carefully rationed and controlled."

"I have a hard time imagining Arcadia agreeing to this idea."

"Arcadia already has," said Dame Belinda. "Both the king and queen have given their approval to the measure, with the understanding that the Arcadia Project's top priority thereafter will be finding a way to separate these 'wraiths' and safely contain them, so that the harp may be returned and used as before."

"How long do you suppose that'll take? Keeping people out of stage 13 has already been a challenge for Inaya, and she loses my help on Monday. Are we talking days here? Months?"

"I cannot begin to imagine," Belinda said. "Until two days ago I did not know there was such a thing as a wraith. We are at a new frontier. If the circumstances were not so appalling, it would be exciting." She could not possibly have sounded less excited.

"What do you need me to do?" I said. "I assume there's a reason it's me at this meeting and not Phil or someone."

"You are here because I wished to hear your opinion."

"My—opinion?" She was speaking English words, but I couldn't process their meaning.

"Of everyone in the Arcadia Project, you have the broadest experience with the current problem. You were the last to see Vivian Chandler alive. You were the first to see a wraith, and as you just stated, you have witnessed more possessions than any other individual. You may be our newest employee, but I would have to be blind in both eyes not to see your value."

Of all the people to give me validation out of left field— Dame Belinda Barker, head of the Arcadia Project? Yet another crucial thing I wouldn't get to bring up in therapy Tuesday night. Dr. Davis thought the Arcadia Project was some sort of cult that had brainwashed Caryl; she'd been thrilled when I'd left them back in June.

I looked at Alvin; there was something a little strange in his smile.

"I appreciate the vote of confidence," I said. "But as far as what I have to say, it's nothing you don't already know. This is an awful idea, and would be catastrophic to Arcadia, at least temporarily. But I have nothing better to offer, and it's reversible if we come up with something better, right? Just a matter of taking the harp back to Arcadia."

"In theory," said Belinda. "In truth, the transport of the harp disturbs Arcadia's leadership more than the temporary rationing of magic."

"Why? Is it that fragile?"

"No more so than any other ancient relic, but imagine if the Mona Lisa or the Rosetta Stone were being shipped temporarily to a war-torn third-world nation, and you'll have an inkling of their concern."

"So this thing matters that much to them?"

"Yes. It belonged to the last Unseelie Queen."

I let that sink in for a moment. "Why *aren't* there Unseelie Queens? Or Seelie Kings, for that matter?"

"It's rather a complicated story."

"I have time," I said, hoping I had the patience to match.

Dame Belinda set down her empty cup and folded her hands in her lap, looking thoughtful. "The Unseelie we deal with today are . . . troublesome, but they were once truly evil, ruled by monsters. In those days the *sidhe* were one of many races, Seelie aligned, and relatively weak. The fey call this the Time of Beasts. In that time, the law of succession was based solely upon each monarch's ability to murder his or her predecessor."

"Charming."

"Quite."

There was an unused cup and a half-full teapot, so I poured myself some tea, though I wasn't a fan of the stuff. I was feeling a strong need for caffeine.

"The last Unseelie Queen, creator of the Bone Harp, was a monster of legend," Dame Belinda said. "Her name is lost to memory, as is the power she used to create the harp. All that is spoken of her today is that she had an insatiable appetite for war and the ability to silence all other spell casters."

"By playing the harp." The tea was still scalding hot and smelled surprisingly good.

"Its empirically demonstrable power does help to corroborate the myth," she agreed. "According to the legend, she could stop even the Unseelie King from casting spells, though he was otherwise immune to his queen's powers of command. Monarchs cannot command one another, you see."

"But the harp would target arcane energy itself, not the king. He couldn't cast anything because there'd be no free energy to use."

"Precisely. With this power in play by the Unseelie, the Seelie were spectacularly losing the war between the Courts, and since the Unseelie King himself was concerned about the lack of checks on his mate's power, he struck a deal with the enemy to stop her."

I took a careful sip, steam warming my face. It wasn't coffee, but it was the best damned tea I'd ever tasted. "How did the Seelie stop her, if she could silence them?"

"The details of their plan are lost, because they were doomed to failure. The Seelie King betrayed both sides by informing the Beast Queen of the plot against her."

"Wait, the *Seelie* King? Why would he do that, if his own people were losing the war?"

"No one knows for certain. There are too many variations at this point in the story for a logical mind to trust any of them. The version I've heard most often suggests that the Seelie King was a monster himself, more kin to the Beast Queen than to his own mate, who was *sidhe* in every version of the story. At any rate, the Beast Queen escaped the trap by taking her own life. In some versions a Seelie noble tried to seize the harp and use it in revenge against the Unseelie, but the Unseelie Queen must have foreseen this possibility. She appears to have cursed the harp so that *sidhe* cannot touch it."

"What happens if they try?"

"Instant death. Or on rare occasions a dangerous, terrifying madness, as in the case of Countess Feverwax."

I set my cup down so fast a bit of tea sloshed over the rim. "*Vivian* touched the harp?"

"Two centuries ago," said Dame Belinda, looking at the spilled tea with profound disapproval. "She subsequently destroyed her own estate, unleashing a lethal plague that killed her vassals to the last man."

I sat back, seeking the support of the cushion behind me. "That's what got her exiled," I said. "This harp—it started *everything*."

26

"Yes," said Dame Belinda. "The moment Countess Feverwax touched that harp, she became completely unhinged from law and reason. Due to the nature of her powers there were terrible repercussions in *both* worlds. This provoked a unanimous amendment to the Accord—Unseelie fey are no longer allowed to touch the harp at all. Its power, combined with their abilities, is catastrophic."

"What happens if an Unseelie touches it now?"

"They simply cannot; they are repelled. This is why the Seelie Queen employs a harpist who is loyal to her Court, but not one of the *sidhe*. The queen herself, being *sidhe*, cannot touch it."

I considered all of this, leaning forward to retrieve my teacup and take another sip. I was starting to notice subtleties in the flavor; was it possible I only *thought* I disliked tea because most American tea was crap?

"Did the harp drive the Beast Queen mad too?" I asked. "I mean, suicide seems like a weird reaction to being told people are trying to kill you."

"Her suicide was motivated by purest spite. You see, since succession passed in those days to whoever killed the queen, no new queen could be crowned after her. The entire order had to be rebuilt."

"No more Seelie Kings either?"

"Both from a sense of balance and to punish the betrayer, there was a unanimous decision among the Seelie to depose and then execute their king. It sounds brutal, but it was the end of the great ongoing war, and the beginning of peace. The First Accord was struck between the two Courts. It held that only *sidhe* would be permitted to rule in the future, in large part to keep the harp out of the hands of monarchs. Another provision of the Accord was that the harp would reside at the Seelie Court."

"Because Unseelie can't touch it?"

"That came later; this was more . . . reparations of a sort."

I was curious what the tea might taste like with a lump of sugar in it, but when I reached toward the bowl Belinda frowned subtly. I took this as a hint and pretended I'd just been trying to adjust the bowl to a more advantageous position on the tray.

"In this same spirit of peace," Belinda said, "royal succession would now take place on both sides via the transferal of a charmed object, a scepter. Of course, succession by murder was not unheard of thereafter—for example, an assassin from one Court might dispose of the monarch of another—but nor was it strictly necessary. It opened the fey to more civilized possibilities, and for the most part succession is now hereditary or by consensus. When the Arcadia Project was organized along its current lines during the Renaissance, the Accord was expanded to establish peace between both Courts and our world—we call this the Second Accord—but it is essentially the same ancient document."

"So the harp was an instrument of war that eventually became a symbol of peace."

Dame Belinda nodded solemnly. "And even if it were not, it would still be priceless simply by virtue of its age. For fey, artifacts from other ages are keys to memories otherwise lost. Even the few fey who were alive before the Accord have no memory of those times."

"That's a shame," I said.

"Perhaps. Perhaps not. The older I become with my mind stubbornly intact, the more certain I become that the fey's amnesia is all that permits them to live so long."

"Well," I said, setting down my cup and sitting back again. "I guess it goes without saying that I should stay twenty feet away from the harp at all times."

I could tell from the way Dame Belinda's face twitched that this was a disaster she had not even contemplated.

"Yes," she said after a moment. "We shall not involve you in anything to do with its transport or use."

"Fine by me," I said. "In the meantime I'll work on trying to come up with better ideas. I'm . . . sorry about breaking the rules earlier, by the way."

"Before, you were not bound to the rules," said Dame Belinda. "Now you are. And you understand that if you are to be removed from the Project for any reason, we will be forced to block access to related memories. This is not something we care to do, or to do often. The more memories we tamper with, the greater the chance of serious side effects such as epilepsy or dementia."

"Forgive me for asking, but why would you do that to me, if you know it's a risk?"

"You know where the bodies are buried, both literally and

metaphorically, and you have a history of impulsive, vengeful acts. So long as we employ you and keep you secure, our security is your self-interest. If we are forced to release you, you would have nothing further to lose by exposing us."

So much for warm fuzzies.

"Understood," I said stiffly. "You'll have no trouble from me."

"Now," said Belinda. "You have already met the king of the Unseelie Court and the head of the Arcadia Project; are you ready to meet the Seelie Queen?"

Apparently, for the time being, Arcadia was leaderless. For even one monarch to leave Arcadia was virtually unprecedented; now Los Angeles was hosting them both at once. Part of me was shaken by the realization that I was living through Historic Times, but most of me was selfishly focused on my upcoming visit with Queen Dawnrowan.

I insisted on bringing Claybriar back through LA4 to smooth the introduction and potentially act as translator, but if I'd thought his presence would put me at ease, I was sorely mistaken. He and I sat in the back of Alvin's rental car on the way to the Hollywood Hills, and the entire ride consisted of Claybriar rattling off incomprehensible rules of fey etiquette that I should not violate under any circumstances. But he said them in no particular order and so rapidly that there was no way my slippery brain was going to hold on to any of it.

"Settle down," I said. "Why are *you* so nervous about this, anyway?"

"Imagine I was your boyfriend," said Claybriar. "And you were about to meet my mother."

"Ah, I see."

"Not yet, you don't. Now imagine that your boyfriend's mother ruled the entire world, and was crazy as a bag of cats, and could compel your boyfriend, if the whim struck her, never to talk to you again."

"Oh," I said. "Maybe I just—shouldn't say anything while we're here."

"That would offend her worst of all."

"Fuck," I said. "Can you boil it down to one simple rule? Or . . . three rules? I can probably remember three rules."

"Okay," said Claybriar. He raked a hand back through his hair. "Simplify? I can do that. Rule one: act like she's the pinnacle of all creation and worship her with every nuance of your being."

"Uh . . . okay, gotcha."

"Rule two: don't show the slightest hint of unhappiness, stress, or impatience—act like we're all going to live forever and everything is peachy, and we're all just here to have a good time."

"Ho boy."

"Rule three—probably the most important: do *not* be boring."

"I . . . really don't want to do this."

"You just broke all three rules in one sentence."

I considered hitting him, but then got distracted as I looked out the window at the rose-painted late-afternoon clouds and felt a sense of déjà vu about the winding street we were ascending. "Why does this look familiar?" I said uneasily.

Alvin glanced over his shoulder at me from the driver's seat. "Did you ever go to David Berenbaum's house, when he lived here?"

"Uh."

"Ohhhh," said Alvin. "Right. You—smashed up his car or something."

"That's what got me fired in June, yes."

"Well, if it makes you feel any better, the car went with him to the emu ranch. And once you step inside the house, you won't recognize it. Her Majesty has been here less than a day and she's already . . . redecorated."

"I can only imagine."

"No, no, you really can't."

The house's exterior was familiar enough to send a twist of anxiety through my gut: peach stucco and a carefully land-scaped yard full of succulents and native ground-cover plants. But when Alvin found the key and opened the door, there was none of Linda Berenbaum's country-chic decor behind it. In fact there was no house at all.

Well, of course there was a house. There had to be. But what-ever Queen Dawnrowan had done to it had me thoroughly con-vinced that I'd stepped into a sun-dappled forest. Near enough to scent the air, a rainbow-misted waterfall splashed invitingly into a crystalline pool.

As Alvin ushered us in and eased the front door shut behind us, I watched a towering oak swallow up a rectangular slab of fading Los Angeles sunlight. For the convenience of visitors, the doorknob remained visible as a bark-covered protrusion, marking the illusion's exit point. I clasped my hands behind my back and kept them there, trying not to touch any walls; in my experience that's where the fey anchored these sorts of spells.

"I really hate when they do this," Alvin said, his hand linger-ing on the doorknob. His voice carried as though disappear-ing into the forest that appeared to surround us, not bouncing back from the walls I knew were there.

"There was a room like this upstairs when I was here before," I said. "Viscount Rivenholt's doing. Linda had me break the enchantment."

"Ward," corrected Alvin. "If the spellwork's anchored on a place rather than a person, it's called a ward."

"I imagine the queen will be upstairs," said Dame Belinda, seeming not at all fazed by the pair of blue butterflies doing a mating dance around her head. She gestured toward a rocky, tree-covered slope to the right of the waterfall that I could only assume was actually the staircase.

"I'm bad enough at steps when I can actually see where I'm going," I said uneasily.

"Attitude," said Claybriar softly in a warning tone. "Now might be a good time to adjust it."

"Now would also be a really bad time for me to fall flat on my face."

"I'm not kidding, Millie," said Claybriar, looking almost panicky. "Don't even think stuff like that. Happy thoughts only."

"What, is she going to read my— Oh right. She can."

"She won't go into your head without permission," said Claybriar. "Which is why we need a translator; she can't just go rifling through your head for words the way Winterglass does."

"I *knew* he was doing that!"

"But she's also not stupid, and she can read your mood the same way a human would. So seriously, cheer up."

"Be happy or else?"

"Pretty much."

I was on the verge of declaring this impossible until Dr. Davis's voice gently reminded me that I was the boss of my brain. I relaxed my shoulders, took a deep breath, plastered a huge, ear-to-ear smile on my face, and waited for my mood to catch up. Once I got closer to the slope, I could see where the steps were; a serpentine path had very carefully been designed to look like randomly placed rocks and tree roots and somehow preserve the exact shape and distance between stair treads. So long as I followed the eccentric zigzag of the path, I could see exactly where I needed to step. The surfaces only looked wet; they weren't actually slippery. All the same, I'd have killed to know where the handrails were.

The upper floor appeared choked with dense growth; the occasional gaps in the brush must have been doorways. Dame Belinda seemed to know her way around pretty well for a half-blind old woman.

"How can you tell where you're going?" I asked her.

"I supervised the spell casting," she said. "It is forbidden even for a monarch to cast a ward on this world without the supervision of a high-ranking member of the Arcadia Project."

In one spot, two enormous trees had leaned together, growing into one twisted trunk about seven feet from the ground. Dame Belinda led us through the gap between the two and into what was clearly the master bedroom, because Queen Dawnrowan hadn't concealed the bed. It was strewn with rose petals, and its posts were wound about with flowering vines, but it was most definitely a California king with a hand-sewn quilt. Her Majesty lounged there propped on one elbow while a child around three years old ran the wrong side of a brush carefully over her sovereign's hair.

The queen's facade was Paltrow blond, lithe and languid with heavy-lidded eyes. My first impulse, shockingly visceral, was to crawl into bed with her. But no sooner had the feeling washed over me than it was chilled by a deep sense of how utterly out of my league she was.

"I'll be communicating your words to her nonverbally," Claybriar said to me. "Just say what you want to say directly to her, and I'll tell you her replies."

I fought the feeling of awkwardness that threatened to overwhelm me, focusing on the soothing sound of running water and wind through leaves. "I'm so honored to meet you, Queen Dawnrowan," I said. "I'm Millicent Roper, Claybriar's Echo."

"The woman with iron in her bones," said Claybriar after a slight pause. Speaking for Dawnrowan, I could only assume. His flat tone seemed to convey a slight distaste which also may have been hers, given the way she was looking down the dainty bridge of her nose at me.

"That's right," I said as cheerfully as possible.

The little girl shrank behind the queen for a moment, looking shy. She had cherub cheeks, devil eyebrows, and tiny pigtails the color of root beer.

"What an adorable little girl," I said, since most normal people found children adorable. "What's her name?"

"Uh . . . that's hard to translate," said Claybriar. "She said, sort of—Blesskin, I guess?"

"I love her pigtails," I said to the queen. "Is she yours?"

"Yes," said Claybriar. Then he quickly added, "She means it's her servant, not her daughter. Blesskin is the harpist."

I turned to him in astonishment. "A *child*?"

"No. I'll explain later," he said between gritted teeth. "Attention on the queen, please."

Right. I turned back to her, though my main impulse was to get out of the room as soon as possible. "I love what you've done to the house," I said brightly. "You've really improved it."

The queen's gaze wandered. "Yes," said Claybriar, followed by, "She's getting bored."

"What should I talk about?" I whispered.

"I don't know!" he whispered back. "If I could predict her, my job would be a thousand times easier."

"I saved Claybriar!" I blurted. "Do you remember when you sent him to find his sister and the other missing commoners? A very generous thing to do, by the way. I'm the one who rescued him from the well. He was very brave about the whole thing."

Queen Dawnrowan turned her eyes back to me, studying me. "He travels this world easily," Claybriar said for her. "He knows its secrets, speaks its language— Uh, okay, her tone here is really boastful, but I don't feel comfortable trying to reproduce it."

I laughed a little, despite myself, and although the queen had no way of knowing what had amused me, her face brightened with what appeared to be a genuine smile.

"You're proud of him," I said to her. "You should be. He had me fooled into thinking he was a real human! An officer of the law, in fact. It was brilliant. Your smile is devastatingly beautiful, by the way, and Claybriar, please don't translate that if it's rude."

The queen burst into a peal of delighted laughter, and behind her, Blesskin burst into the kind of uncultivated baby giggles that are irresistibly, empirically cute.

"You totally translated all of that, didn't you," I accused Claybriar. "Including the part about me asking you not to translate."

Claybriar gave me an innocent look and a shrug; between his expression and the giggling three-year-old, I smiled a little myself. It seemed like the right sort of mood; the queen's eyes had lighted on me with obvious interest.

But then I relaxed a little too much and thoughtlessly touched a tree to steady myself. A tree which of course was actually the bedroom wall.

The queen's carefully crafted illusion melted like a torched cobweb, and suddenly we were standing in the Berenbaums' master bedroom, minus the Berenbaums and most of their stuff. Just the essential furniture remained, including the bed, which was now noticeably absent of rose petals and climbing vines. Compared to the masterpiece that Dawnrowan had made of the place, it suddenly looked like a prison. The expression on the queen's face made me feel a bit like Alice in the courtroom in Wonderland.

"Oh, *shit*," said Claybriar, and I was pretty sure he wasn't translating.

27

Claybriar began to pace, addressing me in a panicked tone. "Why did you do that, she's demanding to know. What have you done, you've ruined everything, she spent all night on it, et cetera."

"I'm so sorry!" I said. "I didn't mean to! It's the iron . . . and I forgot that this all wasn't real. . . ."

Claybriar suddenly fell to his knees, pressing his palms and his forehead to the floor.

"What are you doing?" I asked him, baffled.

"Trying to distract her by reaffirming my oath of loyalty," he said. "But it doesn't seem to be working. It's not me she's worried about."

"I've screwed us, haven't I."

"I translated your apology, but she doesn't trust humans because of the whole lying thing. She thinks you did it on purpose."

I felt as though a hand were squeezing my chest. The queen was going to tell Claybriar never to talk to me again. I looked behind me to Alvin and Belinda for guidance and wished I hadn't. Belinda looked like an ice sculpture, and Alvin had dropped his face into his hand in despair.

"If she doesn't trust me not to lie, then how am I supposed

to—" On an impulse, I painfully lowered myself to the floor, arranged my prosthetics into a kneeling pose, and pressed my brow to the smooth-finished hardwood, mimicking Claybriar's pose. "Your Majesty," I said, "I am your loyal servant."

I closed my eyes, breathing deeply and feeling the wood against my forehead, the twinges of protest in all my joints. There was a long silence, and then Claybriar's voice, warm with relief.

"She's delighted," he said. "This is the first time a human has ever sworn fealty to her. This is in no way arcanely binding, Millie, but you know she's going to take you up on it, right?"

"I'll play along," I said, a little shaky with relief. "I'll do whatever makes her happy. Unless what makes her happy is for me to ever get up off this floor again, because I'm pretty sure we're going to need a crane."

Since only the one room was ruined, we moved downstairs for dinner, which consisted of berries and spoonfuls of honey; then we all parted ways amicably for the night. I managed to get away with no more arduous duties for my new pretend sovereign than a promise to return sometime and babysit Blesskin.

Claybriar explained that Blesskin was actually a full-grown fey of some native Skyhollow variety whose temperament, intelligence level, and natural size were best represented by the facade of a human preschooler. And like many preschoolers, Blesskin was cramping her caretaker's style and limiting her opportunities for tourism. I promised I would come back sometime and watch the runt for a little while, give Dawnrowan a chance to at least wander the neighborhood and gawk at its spectacular view of the city.

• • •

What was left of the weekend revolved largely around getting me moved out of my Manhattan Beach apartment. Zach was a big help getting the boxes into Tjuan's car, but he seemed strangely depressed about the whole thing.

"You're not getting attached, are you?" I teased him when we were upstairs out of Tjuan's earshot. "Should we swap numbers or something?"

"I . . . wouldn't mind that, actually," he said, not meeting my eyes. Even as I gamely added him to my contacts, I found myself disconcerted by the idea. If I actually made arrangements to see him on purpose, wouldn't that mean we were sort of *dating*? I wasn't sure how I felt about that, and it set off a whole cascade of other worries.

As much as working at Valiant had frazzled my nerves, it was slowly beginning to dawn on me that quitting was going to be even worse. I was losing my personal space, my comfortable income, and my veneer of normality. Fear began to gnaw at me to the point that I felt it physically; my hands were clumsy and sluggish, my gait lopsided. And no one I cared enough about to go to for comfort could even touch me.

All I could do was try to force my mind into other channels. There was certainly a lot to do; they were going to put me back in room 6, which meant not only moving in furniture for me, but moving office furniture out. I was going to have to put a real bed in there, not just an air mattress. Because this time I was staying.

Though I'd sooner have stuck a fork in my eye, I owed Inaya the courtesy of quitting my job in person on Monday morning, and so I forced myself to get dressed, comb my hair, put on makeup, and call a cab. I hadn't calculated properly for rush-hour traffic from North University Park to Manhattan Beach and ended up walking into the office twenty minutes late. Araceli was already on a call, but the chilly look in her eyes spoke volumes. I walked right past her and through Inaya's open door.

"Oh thank God," she said when she saw me. "I thought something had happened to you."

"Traffic," I said vaguely.

"I just talked to Naderi. How the hell does she know about the hole in soundstage 13? Never mind that, we've got to talk about next week, and I'm already running late for my ITV meeting."

"Yeah, about next week . . ."

"Araceli's going to be sitting in on a whole series of late-afternoon meetings dealing with international sales, and so I'm going to need you to cover the phones."

"Oh boy," I exhaled, looking at the floor. "Here's the thing." I shifted my weight onto my AK. "You and I both know I'm not very good at this job, right?"

"You mean the phones? You seem to do all right. What's the matter?"

"I don't just mean the phones. I mean—all of it."

"Honey, that's not true. I know you've got some handicaps, but you've done a really good—" She stopped then, eyes narrowing. "Wait," she said. "Oh no you don't. I know what this is."

"I had to sign a contract with the Arcadia Project," I said. "I broke some rules, and—I saw too much, I guess—so they gave me the option of working for them or having my brain wiped. Either way, I'm not going to be any use to you."

"Uh-uh," she said, pulling herself up to her full height. Even without the aid of magic, my boss was a stunning creature of legend when angry. I half expected an icy wind to come howling through the office to stir the twists of her hair. "No, *ma'am*."

"I don't quit—I'm fired?" I said, almost hopefully.

"No. Not a chance. I don't want to hear this Arcadia Project bullshit right now."

"It's true. I wish it weren't true, believe me. I'm sorry."

"Don't give me sorry. Don't you dare. I picked you up out of the gutter. I mean for fuck's sake *literally picked you up out of an alley with piss all over you* and gave you a job you are seriously underqualified for—"

Now she admitted it? I felt like she'd yanked the floor out from under me. I'd come here out of respect for what I thought was our relationship and ended up trapping myself in a devastating psychological corner.

"—and you tell me you're leaving and that you're *sorry*? Don't give me sorry, give me two weeks' fucking notice and a proper replacement."

"How am I supposed to—"

"*Figure. It. Out.*" She turned away, took two deep breaths. Then she turned back to me, her voice suddenly smooth as silk. "I understand things are falling apart over there. A woman's been killed, my Echo's homeless, and there's ghosts or something. I'll give you as much leeway as I can to help Arcadia out. But you will be here when I ask you to be here, and you will not leave this lot until I clear you to go, until you have someone *trained* to replace you, because I do not have time for this shit right now."

I could almost physically feel a wall against my back; my eyes filled with tears of panic.

"I got by—oh honey, don't! Don't you do that. This is on you—I got by without an Echo for thirty-seven years, and I will *salt and burn* the Arcadia Project if they fuck with Valiant, do you understand me?"

"Loud and clear," I said, digging my nails into my palms.

Inaya gave me a long, hard look. "Good," she said. "Now sit the fuck down at your desk and do your job."

I did. I did my job. I went into the ladies' room first, though, and pounded my fists against my skull until the pain made me stop needing to scream and break everything in the building. It bordered on self-harm, and I knew Dr. Davis wouldn't approve, but I didn't have a convenient sink to fill with ice water and plunge my head into, and I was really not in the best state of mind to go down the whole list of other distress tolerance skills. So I punched myself in the head a few times, told myself I deserved every bit of this, cried violently for twenty seconds, and then went back to my desk. All things considered, my performance that day could have been much worse.

I didn't return to Residence Four until around a quarter to eight, and when I got there, Claybriar and King Winterglass were sitting in the living room listening to Phil play the piano. The first *Goldberg Variation*, precise and sprightly. As much as I hated for Phil to be a source of distress tolerance, his nuanced playing did a lot to loosen the knots the day had put in me. My father had only played piano when he was happy, and so my visceral reaction to the sound was a rush of relief: no one was angry; everything was going to be all right.

Claybriar smiled when he saw me but didn't get up. Winterglass looked transfixed, as though Phil were working an enchantment. The king didn't seem to notice my entrance, even when I lowered myself onto the couch between him and Claybriar. Claybriar instinctively scooted farther away, but at the same time he reached into his pocket to put on his surgical gloves. The gesture made me a little bashful; I turned to look at Winterglass.

"Don't you boys have music where you come from?" I asked.

Winterglass raised his hand sharply. I shut up.

Phil's eyes were closed, his head bobbing as he played, like a small hairy craft on a rough sea. He was almost smiling. I'd never noticed how elegant his hands were; it had never occurred to me to wonder what Gloria had seen in him. I glanced from his hands back to his face and realized that he'd lost some weight since summer. Quite a bit, actually, although the beard did a lot to disguise the sharper contours of his cheeks and jaw.

When Phil had finished playing, Winterglass turned to face me in the ensuing silence.

"We do have music in Arcadia," His Majesty said haughtily, as though I had just spoken. "But what I just heard was not music; it was *engineering*." I couldn't tell if his tone indicated awe, contempt, or some mixture of the two.

"Caryl likes Bach," I said.

Phil scowled. There, now I recognized him.

"You should probably avoid playing Baroque music," I said to Phil. "She might hear it down in the basement and have a moment's enjoyment."

Phil swiveled fully around on the piano bench. "She fucking *paralyzed* me," he said.

All the anxiety his music had relieved came back with a jolt. "You're fine," I said. "She wouldn't have done it if it would really damage you."

"*Now* I'm all right," he said. "But she had no fucking right to do that to my body. So let's not act like I'm holding a grudge for no fucking reason." As he walked away, he added, "Bitch."

"Wow," I said, staring after him with my heart racing. "I'm so glad I live here now."

I glanced at Claybriar, and sort of wished I hadn't; the cold rage in his eyes as he watched Phil leave was decidedly Unseelie.

"It's all right, Clay," I said quietly. "I heard worse every day at Valiant."

He reached out to touch my arm and said nothing.

I turned to King Winterglass and tried to focus on taking slow, deep breaths. "Are you back from Arcadia already? Or have you not left yet?" I seriously hoped it was the former; our time frame was pretty tight.

"I have been and returned."

"And you fixed Tjuan, I take it?" I asked him.

"I banished the wraith to a locked storage closet and have specifically forbidden it to repossess him, or to possess any other human being so long as I reign."

"Is Tjuan okay? Where is he?"

"He is resting now. But I also have news." Winterglass rose from the couch and slipped his hands deep into the pockets of his long swishy jacket, which he'd apparently been wearing indoors for who knows how many hours.

"Is it about the—" I hesitated, then lowered my voice. "Let's go down into the basement."

The king nodded and turned briskly on his heel. Following us, Claybriar murmured the combination under his breath.

Winterglass walked ahead of us down the stairs, and Caryl rose to her feet when she saw him. She looked equally prepared to kiss his hand or cower under his wrath; obviously she didn't have Elliott out. This made me wary; I stood half behind Claybriar as though shielding myself.

"The manticore's facade is ready," Winterglass said. "I worked with a human agent from Helsinki on this; she has sworn not to share the information with anyone else in her office. I have done my best not to alert your queen to our activities, but if—"

"Wait, *my* queen?" I said. "You know that whole fealty thing is all just in Dawnrowan's head, right? It's not binding."

"He means Dame Belinda," said Caryl. "We indicate the Project's hierarchy to the fey by giving employees titles parallel to their own; it helps them understand who outranks whom and the deference due."

"I bet Belinda loves that."

"Can we keep to the topic at hand?" said Caryl irritably. It made me wonder how often Elliott masked her irritation with me. I probably didn't want to know.

"Sorry," I said. "So the facade's ready. How do we get it connected to Throebrand?"

"I took the crafter through the portals to Duke Skyhollow's estate," said Winterglass, "explaining to the duke that we were conducting an investigation in his lands in an attempt to solve the manticore problem. I did not expand upon this. They had no authority to detain me, but it is safe to say their curiosity is aroused. The crafter is prepared to meet you in a protected wilderness shelter and cast the enchantment. The manticore cannot enter until you dispel the wards I cast."

"Tell me about this crafter. Does he or she speak English?"

"Yes." Winterglass hesitated, then answered quietly, "The crafter is my son."

28

"Prince Fettershock is young," said the king, "but very skilled, and he speaks your language well. There was no one else I could trust with a matter at this level of delicacy."

"How old is, uh, Fettershock exactly?"

"Seventeen."

"What? What is that in fey years, like, three?"

"I do not understand the question," said Winterglass.

"You guys live forever—I assume you grow up more slowly than we do."

"A fey matures as rapidly as his experience permits. My son has been given a great deal of responsibility to groom him for his future role, and he has been in regular contact with his Echo since he was four years old. He is sufficient to this task."

"So what's next?"

"I will enable Claybriar to locate the wards I set around the cave, and once you find them you will disable them. I shall leave it to you to summon the manticore. If my son is so much as bruised, I shall withdraw my support for this venture and report your actions to your queen. I shall also demand that everyone involved be executed."

"Wow. Nice working with you."

"You doubt that you can control the creature?" Winterglass said with a raised brow. "If I am so blindly elitist, and your manticore is such a reasonable sentient creature, you should have no fear of this meeting."

"You're using your own son as a *bluff*?"

"It is no bluff, if you are competent and trustworthy."

"Don't worry your pretty head over it, Mr. Morozov," I said with a tight smile. "The manticore and I are best buddies. His name is Throebrand, by the way."

"I could not possibly care less what it calls itself. Put the monster in contact with my son, and my son will bind it to its facade. After that, his role in this farce is finished, and so is mine."

"Are you returning to Arcadia, then?" asked Caryl with big soft eyes. Wait, wasn't she turning those same eyes on *me* just last week?

"Not yet," he said. "I shall be supervising the transport and care of the Bone Harp. But make no mistake—you and I are no longer allies." At this, he turned a dry-ice look on Caryl. She utterly *wilted*.

"That—seems harsh," I said, concerned about the expression on her face.

"I will always rue what Slakeshadow did in my name to that innocent child. But Miss Vallo is a child no longer, and it took me only a few hours to realize that I had been manipulated. I must seem quite the fool to you."

"Your Majesty, I never—" she began, her eyes filling with tears.

"Silence," he said. "My divided nature was my undoing. I failed to remind myself that love is as much poison to my kind as fear is to yours. You would think, after everything I suffered with Fedya, I would remember."

"I can see that you're hurt," I said, since Caryl seemed incapable of reply. "I'm genuinely sorry if we salted old wounds. But we're still on the same side here, aren't we? My priority is to prevent a crisis in Arcadia, and preferably without devastating it by sealing all its magic away."

The king was still looking at Caryl. The softness that usually blunted his edges when he looked at her was gone. She saw the change too, and she looked pale to the point of fainting.

"Please forgive me, Your Majesty," she said.

"Of course I forgive you," he said, colder than ever. "You are what Slakeshadow made you. But there are only so many times that a reasonable man can make the same mistake. Farewell."

I stared after him as he ascended the stairs.

"Drama king," said Claybriar scornfully. "What did all that even mean?"

"I'm not entirely sure," I said. "You okay, Caryl?" Since she didn't have Elliott out, I risked a gentle pat on the shoulder. She drew away from me subtly, but noticeably enough that I pulled my hand back.

"I'm fine," she said, wiping at her eyes. "It's my fault. I have neglected and manipulated him by turns—I suppose even an immortal has limited patience."

"I'm sorry," I said quietly. "I've been where you are right now. More times than I can count." Claybriar was watching me like a hawk, so I turned back to him. "Are you going to be safe at this meeting with your nemesis?" I asked him. "I know I at least won't get eaten, but I worry about bringing you into range of those teeth."

Claybriar tipped his head. "Huh. You're right; he *can't* eat you."

"I'm honestly more worried I'll stumble into important spells somewhere along the way and screw them up."

"I can help," said Claybriar. "There's some really nice areas, pure wilderness, untouched by spellwork. Give me some time to work out a route and I'll get us there safely."

"Is this a date? If so it's an incredibly crappy one."

"I don't know; a scenic suicide mission sounds pretty romantic to me."

"I'm not going to let anything happen to you, Clay. If Throebrand so much as licks his lips in your direction he's going to be choking on iron."

"I love you," said Claybriar.

He just . . . said it. He made it sound so natural, so free of angst. As though it were nothing to be ashamed of, nothing with repercussions, nothing I was even supposed to answer. He just felt it, and said it, and he was already walking up the stairs.

I looked at Caryl. Her eyes were wide.

"Well," she said quietly, maybe bitterly. "You're a very lucky woman."

I don't know what made me do what I did next. Damned Borderline impulses, they're like grenades whose pins fall out at random and you have to decide on the spot whether to blow yourself up or someone else. In this case I lobbed the thing at both of us by moving in to kiss her.

I stopped just in time, but she kept standing there, looking at me. Very still, her wide gray-hazel eyes just a hand's span from mine.

"I dare you," she said in a strange tone.

So I kissed her. Quickly, almost vindictively, fingertips resting for just a moment at the back of her neck. And then I turned and hobbled up the stairs, not looking back at her, already hating myself. I barely made it to the couch before everything buckled.

Claybriar sat next to me. "You okay?"

"Not really."

"What's the matter?"

I already knew I wasn't going to tell him.

"Just—Inaya won't let me quit," I babbled. "It was rough today. I'm still shaky. What Dr. Davis would call 'emotionally vulnerable.'"

"Do you need anything?"

"I need to figure out how to plan this meeting with Prince Fettershock around work and therapy. Ugh. This isn't going to be good, Clay. I don't have time to fall apart right now. The things I do when I get like this—"

"Like jump off buildings?"

"No. No, never again. But I have other ways of destroying myself. Don't let me, okay? Keep an eye on me. Lash me to the mast."

His gloved hand found just the right spot between my shoulder blades, moved gently back and forth. "I'm here," he said. "I'll hold you together better than all the steel screws in the universe. But if you're not up for this meeting with the man-eating monster, I'd understand. Maybe I can take care of it on my own."

"You think I want to miss a chance to face down a giant monster that's afraid to eat me? Not a chance. In fact, I think that's *exactly* what I need right now. I'll make it work tomorrow. Somehow."

. . .

I'd run through several scenarios of what the Unseelie King's seventeen-year-old son might look like, but none of them remotely resembled the person who waited for us the next afternoon in a dry, pleasant little cave an hour's walk from the Arcadia side of the Gate. The young prince could just as easily have been an Asian-American kid plucked straight off the streets of L.A.

His sneakers were red and orange; his asymmetrical bangs were dyed navy blue at the fringes. Everything else he wore was black. He was crouched on a red-gold rock at around my eye level, illuminated by a natural skylight in the cavern, with a huge burlap sack lying on the ground underneath him. When we entered, he began to speak in what I eventually recognized as fast, accented English. Not British; Chinese, maybe?

It was a struggle just to be mentally present, much less adapt to his speech patterns. Negotiating with Inaya to leave work early had been ugly, and unless everything here went like clockwork I still wasn't sure that I'd make it back to the real world in time to see Dr. Davis.

"You're the queen's champion," Prince Fettershock was saying to Claybriar when my brain finally caught up.

"That's right," Claybriar said.

The prince stabbed a finger at me. He had the same slender, beautiful hands as his father, which, after a moment, I realized was exceedingly weird.

"And you're Ironbones. Cool. I hardly ever see other Echoes together. My Echo is in graduate school for architecture. You've not heard of him yet, but you will. I'm Shock, or that's what I go by in Hong Kong. Good to meet you."

"Are you—human?" I said, baffled.

"Not yet," he said. "This is my facade. Do you like it? I made it myself; it's one of my talents. I made one for my father as well."

"That explains a lot."

"Well he can't visit Los Angeles looking like some nineteenth-century Russian."

"What do you mean you're not human *yet*?"

"I'm stuck at Court for another year; the *sidhe* have borrowed this 'age of majority' nonsense from humans, and so I don't get to decide anything about my own life even though I have more brains than most of these politicians put together. Where is the monster?"

"Throebrand?" I said. "I don't know. Stuck in traffic?"

"My father would not understand that joke."

"Your father doesn't understand a lot of things."

"True. Would you like to see the dog?"

"Uh—okay."

Shock hopped down off his perch and opened the bag, hauling out what looked for all the world like a massive, recently-dead Irish setter.

"I love big dogs," he said, giving the huge limp body a hug, then giving its fur sweeping strokes of his graceful hand. "I can't have one in my Earth apartment, unfortunately. This was so much fun to work on. Setters are not normally over thirty kil—uh, seventy pounds or so. This one is around, mmm, ninety? I don't think I could get away with a bigger one, and I'm not skilled with wolfhounds. Also I thought he would like the fur. He is red, correct? The manticore?"

"Very," I said. I was fighting a sudden sadness; the chatty kid reminded me way too much of Teo.

"So once he shows up I will cast a spell to link this body to his soul—we are assuming he has one, right?—and when I do that the dog will disappear. Or at least it will look like that; it will really be hidden somewhere else on the v-axis. It will switch with the manticore body automatically when he goes through the Gate."

"Why is your facade still active?" I said. "You're in Arcadia. Shouldn't you be reverting to your fey form?"

"I spend far too much time in your world," he said. "I've managed to attend the Hong Kong International School for two years now, using only seasonal breaks to return to Arcadia. The Project shouldn't let me, but it's like they're afraid of making me angry. So I have a weak link to my fey body; sometimes it takes days for me to change back. You should be happy I haven't; the real me is hideous."

"What an awful thing to say about yourself."

"Thank you, Mother," he said. "Just kidding; my mother would never have said things like that. She was too busy cutting up babies. Good riddance to all this, honestly. I wish my eighteenth birthday would come faster."

"If you're leaving when you reach majority," I said, "who's going to be king after your father?"

"I don't know," he said. "Father can have another child, or hog the throne forever. Not my problem."

"You are not at all what I expected. Your father described you—a little differently."

"I guess fey are allowed to lie, as long as it's to themselves." He stopped, and for a moment I saw a hint of the maturity his father had mentioned, a brief calm in his eyes. "I guess you must think Father is a bad person," he said. "Humans think that about all Unseelie. But honestly he's just broken; he's seen too much, and there's too much pressure on him. I look at him and I—I don't want to end up like that."

"Can't say I blame you," I said.

"You know," Shock said, "you're not so bad."

"You were expecting something different?"

"Maybe," he said. "Father made it sound like—"

I never got to find out what Winterglass made me sound like, because the air suddenly vibrated with a familiar coughing, brassy roar.

"Here comes our monster," said Shock. Then he yelled something in the Unseelie tongue, heading for the mouth of the cave.

"Throebrand speaks English, you know."

Shock stopped in his tracks, then swiveled on his sneakers to face me again. "Are you kidding?"

"Your dad didn't tell you?"

"Not even a hint."

"Why am I not surprised." I sighed deeply.

Throebrand approached the mouth of the cave and loomed just outside it. It wasn't a huge opening, and with him standing in front of it, he entirely blocked our view of the desert outside.

"You don't actually want me to go in there, do you?" the manticore rumbled, tail lashing back and forth.

"Don't like confined spaces?" I said, willing my body not to panic at the sight of the massive predator.

"I was thinking of you," he said. "If I step in there, I'll be the cork in a bottle."

"Wow, it *does* speak English," breathed Shock. "Like, TV English."

"I'm fine with you staying outside," I said. "Throebrand, this is Prince—uh, this is Shock. That dead dog on the ground over there is apparently your shiny new Los Angeles body."

"Kind of small, isn't it?"

"I'm afraid they don't make dogs your size," I said. "Not outside of hell, anyway."

"Fine, fine," said the manticore in his distant-thunder voice. "Going to be weird looking up at you people though."

Shock rubbed his hands together, all business, and launched into a rapid-fire orientation speech.

"Okay, now, you were supposed to undergo some training. But we don't have time to go through all of it. Given the body, I suggest a leash. Leather only. Avoid contact with car exteriors, tools, anything with iron or steel. Aluminum's okay but you can't always tell what's what by looking. So if it's metal, avoid it. Don't take him on an escalator or allow him to walk over a grating; we can't put him in rubber soled shoes. If you forget for a second it's no matter; just move away from whatever metal you touched. Humans will forget what they saw all on their own, if it's quick enough."

"Why are you addressing this whole speech to *her*?" growled Throebrand. "I'm not an actual dog."

Shock turned to Throebrand, not missing a beat. "Give yourself twelve to twenty-four hours to get used to operating this body. Maybe more, since it's so different from yours."

"And so much smaller. I want to emphasize smaller."

Shock cracked his knuckles. "Are you ready?"

"Ready as I'll ever be," said Throebrand. "Dog me."

29

When we returned through the Gate with a staggering, panicked, drunk-looking Irish setter, Phil pointedly ignored us. He just sat there at his desk in the tower room, filling out paperwork.

"You're going to tattle on us, aren't you," I said.

"Right," Phil said bitterly. "So you can tell Caryl I was the leak, and she can give me spleen cancer. I'm staying the fuck out of this. Not even looking."

I turned back to Claybriar. "I'm not going to be much help with the—dog," I said, "since I can't touch him, and I can understand why it's awkward to put him in your care. Maybe we should take him to Tjuan?"

"Sure," Claybriar said. "But I'd like to keep an eye on him too, since it's my job to keep people safe from him. I'll stay in one of the empty rooms here till this is sorted out."

Throebrand slipped, hitting his chin on the floor. "Fuck," he said.

"Gah!" I took a step back. "Oh my God, you can still talk? *Don't do that.*"

Throebrand grunted, and tried to get up, but his paws slipped out from under him again on the polished hardwood floor. Splat.

"You might have to carry him," I said to Claybriar, and winced at the look he gave me.

The queen's champion reluctantly heaved his nemesis off the floor and headed for the stairs. I lingered for a moment, watching Phil's back and trying to figure out some way of getting through to him, but finally decided that it was pointless.

I also realized that the real reason for my hesitation was that I didn't want to go where logic told me I needed to go next. Unfortunately, I didn't have a lot of choice in the matter.

Caryl's nose was buried in a copy of *Rainbow Valley* when I arrived. For a moment I thought that she, like Phil, was simply going to pretend I wasn't there. On the off chance that she was absorbed in her reading, I stood politely and waited for her to notice me. Eventually, she closed the book and looked up at me but didn't stand. She also didn't summon Elliott.

"Hello," she said cautiously, her posture tense with expectation. "Do you have news, or—?"

"News," I said. Her posture loosened a little; did I detect a hint of disappointment?

"Go on then," she said, and wrapped her arms around herself. Her teeth chattered slightly.

"Are you cold?"

"No."

"Caryl—I'm sorry. About—"

"It's all right. I'm the one who should apologize."

"What?"

"I goaded you," she said. "I know you think of me as a victim, but you forget that I am extremely intelligent, and that I have been studying you since before I hired you. I impulsively attempted to—provoke a response, and it worked."

Of all the conversations we could be having about this, this was not the one I'd been expecting.

"So," I said with a trace of irritation. "You think this is a sitcom, where people kiss and then just kind of say 'oops' and move on? As far as I'm concerned, you're my goddamned *boss*. Everything we're doing here is about trying to reinstate you. And you're telling me right now that you intentionally sexually harassed me?"

She looked suddenly fretful, and I regretted my harshness. I wanted to ask her to summon Elliott, but I realized that I was starting to use the familiar as a crutch even more than she was. They were her feelings; she should be the one to choose whether or not to feel them.

"I didn't think it through," she said. "I'm still trying to learn how to function without Elliott."

"I wasn't exactly blameless here either," I said. "No one twisted my arm. But we have got to figure out a way to work together without this being a source of—whatever." I gestured vaguely.

"What exactly would you like to do about it?"

I looked at her, at the exposed edge of her collarbone, at the soft round edge of a breast under her gray sweater. I let her see me look. She started shivering again.

"I'm trying to get out of the habit of doing what I'd *like* to do," I said.

"It seems to me that the healthiest thing would be for us to attempt an actual relationship," she said. "There is nothing in the Project's contract to forbid it. And so long as we manufacture obstacles for ourselves, the temptation will only be stronger."

"And then what happens when the relationship implodes? I don't have a convenient place to stash the pain while I continue trying to work with you."

"It has already imploded," said Caryl, so calm she almost sounded like her adult self. "We cannot un-ring a bell."

"There's also this whole thing where I kind of have a boyfriend now."

Caryl's eyebrows shot toward the ceiling.

"Well, a guy I've been sleeping with for a few months, anyway. We just exchanged contact info, so now it feels like I'd have to officially dump him to get involved with someone else. And then there's Claybriar."

"You and Claybriar cannot consummate a physical relationship," she said. "And you will remain devoted to each other regardless. There is nothing you and I could do that would change Claybriar's status. He will always be your Echo."

I shook my head, frustrated. "When it comes down to it, Caryl, it isn't about anyone else, or even about you being my boss. Or about you being nineteen. Seven years is a big age gap but it's not—I mean, you're legal, and—that's not it."

"Then what is it?"

"It's the fact that I *know* myself. And don't give me that starry-eyed look of denial, because I mean it. You know what borderline personality disorder is. I punish myself by destroying anything good in my life. The closer you are to me the worse your life is going to get. Zach isn't close enough to me to get hurt, and Claybriar can take it. You I'd rip to shreds, and if I cared about you even a tiny bit less, I'd be fine with that. But we've been through too much for me to treat you the way I do everyone else."

Caryl's eyes welled up. Damn it. I waited for her to object, but she didn't, just looked up at me, tears slipping free down her cheeks.

"I can't force you to give up on me," I said. "I've been where you are, so I know better. I can only tell you that eventually you'll get over it. You'll probably go through a phase where I completely disgust you, and then hopefully you'll come out the other side and we'll be friends. But don't make me tell you no again. I can't guarantee I'll never slip, especially if you *deliberately* mess with me. It still wouldn't change anything. We're not going to be together, Caryl. Not now, not ever."

Watching her face was like watching her fingers slip from the edge of a cliff. Quickly, hoarsely, she muttered the words of Elliott's spell, the ripcord to her parachute. And then she was as calm as the Dead Sea.

"Tell me your news."

It was for the best, really. I'm not sure how a heartbroken Caryl would have reacted to the whole drunk, man-eating Irish-setter thing, but I'm guessing it wouldn't have fallen under the heading of Professional, and I had to wrap this up in time for therapy. Under the circumstances, Caryl agreed that our next step was definitely to bring Throebrand into Naderi's proximity and see if the sight of her rang any bells. But Inaya and Foxfeather's accidental introduction last summer notwithstanding, this was usually something that was supposed to be supervised closely by high-ranking Arcadia Project officials, and there was no way in hell Alvin was going to be on board with this.

So now, on top of the egregious breach of protocol we'd probably committed by bringing a manticore over here in the first place, we were going to have to let the jailbird drive.

· · ·

"I would like to file an official complaint about the role I've been assigned," said Tjuan, sitting in the backseat of Caryl's SUV with the dog on Wednesday afternoon.

"Noted," said Caryl. "If I am ever officially in charge of the Los Angeles Arcadia Project again, I shall make certain to put it in your file."

This was as close as the two of them came to banter, and it made me feel, irrationally, that everything was going to be all right.

"It's the smell, isn't it?" said the dog, whom we'd decided to call Brand for short. "I've stopped noticing it, but when Shock first put me in this body I almost threw up."

"As dogs go," I said, "you smell pretty nice."

"It's the *talking*," said Tjuan. "That is just not right."

"Eh, what's the point of going to all this trouble to get information if he's mute?" I said. "I'm going to side with Shock on this one. So long as Brand's just here in the car with us he can talk all he likes. Once he gets out, though, he has to play the part, or he gets shipped right back home."

"Fine," said the dog.

When we drove through security, I leaned over so the gal in the booth could see me. I looked oh so sharp; I was even wearing a skirt.

"They're friends of Inaya's," I said, and she waved me through. Inaya had made it pretty clear to everyone on the lot that I was Not To Be Questioned About Anything, Ever, and it was one of the few things I was really going to miss about the job if she ever let me leave it.

I started to direct Caryl toward Naderi's bungalow, but as we turned the corner of soundstage 6, I spotted the showrunner herself.

"Stop!" I cried, and Caryl did, on a dime. If not for Tjuan's intervention, Brand would have abruptly joined us in the front seat. "There she is," I said. "This is perfect. We don't even have to get out."

"Where?" said Brand excitedly.

Naderi was standing on the sidewalk by soundstage 8, in animated conversation with someone who looked awfully like the guy who'd played Dwight on *The Office*, though it was hard to tell as he mostly had his back to us. Naderi had on a light leather jacket with a bloodred shirt underneath it; her face was lit with excitement and framed by wild corkscrews of escaped hair. I couldn't really blame Brand if he found her beautiful.

She was best seen out of the driver's-side windows, and Brand was on the passenger's side, so he had to clamber into Tjuan's lap.

"Great," said Tjuan, lifting his hands as though the animal's glossy, perfect coat were covered in mud.

Brand made a smeary nose print on the window. "It's her, isn't it! It's her! In the red shirt! She's even wearing my color!"

"She does wear a lot of red," I mused. "And her office is full of lions. Hey, Caryl, maybe open the window before Brand wears a hole in it with his snout?"

"Only if Brand promises not to leap out the window the moment I get it down."

"I promise not to jump out the window," said Brand.

"This would be a good time to practice wagging your tail," I said to him as Caryl pressed a button and the window began its long descent with a *zzzzzzzzhhhh*. "That's what dogs do when they're happy, and people are going to expect it of you when you're happy in public."

"*Wag* my tail?" said Brand, looking over his shoulder at me where I sat riding shotgun. "Like this?" He gave his long, beautifully-fringed tail a slow wave back and forth, like a cat. It was surreal as hell.

"Faster, like this." I demonstrated by flapping my hand.

Brand tried it out. "Oh, interesting. I don't think I could do that with my real tail. How's that?"

"You got it."

He turned back to look out the window, keeping his tail going. "Wow," he said. The window was all the way down, and he stuck his head out. After a moment he drew back inside the car and turned to me again. "You know her? You can introduce us?"

"I'm welcome in her office basically any time, as long as I have good news. If not, she'll throw things at me until I leave."

"She's here," Brand said, his voice soft. "I didn't believe you. Vivian told me that humans lie all the time. But you didn't. It's her; I can *feel* it. I don't believe it." He turned back to the window and gazed at her with *actual* puppy-dog eyes. "What's her name?"

"Parisa Naderi," I said. "You'd call her Parisa, I guess. I call her Naderi because I'm kind of afraid of what she'd do to me if I dared to be on a first-name basis."

"Parisa," said Brand softly.

At just that moment, Naderi finished up her conversation with the guy she was talking to and gestured toward stage 8. The two of them turned and began to head toward it.

"No!" said Brand. "She's leaving!"

"It's okay," I said. "Once you've told us what we need to know, I'll introduce the two of you. I gave you my word, and I intend to keep it."

"No!" said Brand, barely listening. He shifted back and forth in a sort of panic, his paws digging into Tjuan's thighs.

"Settle down, you," said Tjuan. "Caryl, you'd better put the window back up."

At that, Brand shoved his head all the way out. "PARISA!" he yelled.

Tjuan had tackled the dog almost before he got to the third syllable. He wrestled all ninety pounds of him into submission on the passenger's side of the car while Caryl rolled up the window.

Naderi had heard the voice, though, and turned.

"Noooo!" howled Brand in the backseat, as though Tjuan were drawing and quartering him. The sound was half-human, half-canine.

Naderi had no way of recognizing the SUV, but she still kept staring right at us. She said something to possibly-Dwight, putting a hand on his shoulder, and started to walk toward us. There was something intent in her expression, as though she knew who had been calling her.

"Oh no," I said. "Don't let her see us right now, not like this, not with the dog. Drive, Caryl. Drive!"

Caryl stepped on the gas and got us out of there, with Brand sobbing and howling in the backseat all the way.

30

It was starting to get dark, cloudy too. I had Caryl drive us through Wendy's, and we even got a burger for the dog. He ate it bag and all, much to Tjuan's very vocal horror, but it seemed to make him feel better. When we pulled into the driveway of Residence Four, I noticed Alvin's rental car.

"Shit," I said, and looked at Caryl.

As if the clouds agreed with us, it started to rain. Real rain, not a halfhearted Los Angeles spritzing. It pattered on the roof of the SUV.

"I'll cast a spell to make myself unseen," said Caryl.

"Can you hide the dog, too?"

"I would not care to risk the divided focus. The dog can be explained so long as it does not *speak*; my escape cannot. If we run into Alvin, distract him while I return to the basement. If he has already checked and found me absent, I'll claim that I used spellwork to hide."

Not only was Alvin right there in the living room when I came in and shook raindrops out of my hair, but Dame Belinda was sitting next to him. Despite the teacup in Belinda's gnarled hand, it didn't look as though they'd been having a casual chat.

"Sorry about the dog!" I said brightly, as Tjuan tightened his fingers on Brand's collar. "Friend of Tjuan's roped him into watching this guy for a few days."

Neither Alvin or Belinda knew Tjuan well enough to know that he didn't have much in the way of friends, but they still looked a little too suspicious.

"Have you seen Caryl?" said Alvin.

I paused in what I hoped looked like confusion. "No," I said, finally letting the tension show on my face. "Are you saying she's not in the basement?"

"She appears to have escaped," said Belinda, "and there are only so many people who know the combination to the lock."

Without further ado I made a beeline for the basement, hoping I looked panicked enough. I unlocked it and opened the door, and I can only assume Caryl walked in ahead of me, because she suddenly appeared at the bottom of the stairs. I mimed sleeping and pointed to her cot, then left and locked up behind me.

"Uh, Alvin?" I said. "She's down there. I think she's asleep."

"What?" said Alvin, rising from the couch. "Not possible. I've been down there three times in the last hour."

"I don't know what to tell you," I said. "Anyway, Tjuan and I are going to strategize upstairs for a bit about how to replace me at Valiant, feel free to join us if you want."

As I headed for the stairs, I really hoped Alvin wouldn't call my bluff. Tjuan held Brand firmly by the collar, nearly choking the poor animal. Brand moved with all the grace of the recently anesthetized, and to make matters worse, he started to grumble an objection. Tjuan swiftly closed a hand around his muzzle, then scooped the dog up into his arms. I looked back at Alvin and Belinda; they were staring at us as though we'd brought in a live nuke.

"It'll be fine!" I called over my shoulder. "It's just for a few days, and he's housebroken and everything."

Alvin and Belinda just stared at me for a moment longer. Then Alvin moved toward the basement—thank God—and Belinda followed him.

In the upstairs hallway we ran into Claybriar, who'd heard voices and come out of Teo's old room, and also poor Monty, who hissed and puffed up like he'd jammed his paw into a light socket.

"Aw, what a cute little guy," said Brand.

"Brand, you have *got* to shut up!" I whispered. "Seriously, do not talk unless we give you direct permission, or so help me we will toss you right back through that Gate."

"Don't test her," said Claybriar, following us. "Or me, for that matter."

Brand let out a menacing growl, though a pretty weak one if measured on the manticore scale. After that he did us all the favor of keeping his trap shut until we got inside my room and closed the door.

Glancing at a south-facing window, I spotted my ghostly reflection. I moved toward one of the bamboo shades and pulled it down over the rain-spattered glass. If it was dark enough for me to see myself in the window, that meant anyone across the street could conceivably peek over and watch our little meeting.

"All right," I said, moving to do the same to the other south-facing window. "Brand, tell us everything you know about Vivian's plan. For starters, who is in charge now?"

"Nobody," said Brand. "It was always just Vivian and the—what did she call them?"

"Wraiths." I turned back to the others; Tjuan had let go of Brand's collar, and they both stood there looking at me while Claybriar paced near the north-facing windows.

"Wraiths, then," said Brand. "Used to be, Vivian would direct them. Tell them where to go and so on. First scouting. Then they looked for people vulnerable to possession, anywhere, anyone. Then they'd take over those bodies and use them to find Cera employees. Abduct them, torture them until they broke enough to get possessed. Then she'd send them back to work, so she had easy access to them at any time. Took years, but she got wraiths in just about every office of Cera."

"God," I said. "How many?"

"I don't know. Hundreds."

"We already have a way to stop them," I said, "but kind of a horrible way. Do you know about the Bone Harp?"

"The what?"

"I figured you'd know more about it than I did, since you're so old. It's a relic of sorts, dates back to when the Accord was made."

"I've got a pretty good memory," said Brand, "but it doesn't go *that* far back. Maybe if you introduced me to Parisa . . ."

"Are you fucking with me?" I said. "If you remember something important, you'd better tell us now and not dangle it."

Brand let out a little doggy snort. "I honestly don't remember. Could I lie? Believe me, I wish I knew all about the Accord. I wish I knew how to undo it and everything it stands for. That's why I joined Vivian in the first place. She said she was going to tear it all down, bring down the *sidhe*."

"If that's your goal," I said uneasily, "we have a problem. The *sidhe* pretty much *are* the Arcadia Project."

"Look," Brand said, "I've got no love for the nobles, but I'm not that passionate about ousting them either. They can't control me, because I didn't buy into their Accord, so they're more of an annoyance than a threat. I'd have gotten bored with Vivian's crusade years ago if she hadn't told me she knew my Echo."

"What was your part in this exactly? What did you do for her?"

"Well, sometimes wraiths would get stuck Earthside, right? My job was to call them back to Arcadia."

"How?"

"Vivian would send a wraith to tell me the name of whoever was stuck, and I'd say the name out loud, which would pull it right to me. Then I'd let it go free about its business."

"Wait, when you say she told you their *names* . . ."

"It's like when the queen summoned me," said Claybriar. "Vivian must have known the true Unseelie name of every wraith she was working with. It would give her absolute control over them."

"But the one thing she couldn't do," Tjuan piped up, "is get them back to Arcadia, because she was stuck on our side."

"You said she sent a wraith to tell you the name," I said.

"That's right."

"If the wraith knew the name, why couldn't it do the summoning?"

"Summon it to where? A summons has to come from a location. In Arcadia, a wraith doesn't really have a *where* the way it does here. It's like asking where the air is in a room. That's why she needed a physical person on the Arcadia side to help her."

"It could have been anyone, then?"

"I was local, I wasn't bound to the king and queen, and she knew my Echo, so I was kind of the obvious choice."

"You must know pretty much all the wraiths' names by now!"

"Well, no," said Brand. "I'm a fey, remember? Crap like that tends to float right out of my head. It was a lot of names."

"But once we introduce you to Parisa—"

"From what Vivian said, yeah, it's pretty likely I'll remember their names. Remember every damn moment of my life, in fact."

"It gets weird," Claybriar said, sounding almost sympathetic. "Fair warning."

"This is perfect!" I said, feeling vindicated in all my rule breaking. "You could isolate the guilty wraiths by name, trap them here. We wouldn't have to use the harp!"

"Explain this harp thing?"

"The Bone Harp. The Seelie Court has had it since the Accord. If you play it, it pulls *all* arcane energy to its location. And they're bringing it *here*."

"What? Why?" Brand looked baffled.

"Because it's the only way they can think of to stop the wraiths," I said. "If they're on this side, they're beached fish. They can't even flop their way to their old hosts to repossess them."

"You're going to trap all the spirits *here*?" Brand's ears and tail drooped; he looked as though someone had just caught him chewing a table leg. Claybriar surprised me by reaching out to stroke the dog's head, fingertips gentle on the slightly pointed peak of its skull. Brand and Claybriar exchanged a brief look, puppy eyes looking into puppy eyes. *Yeah, I know,* Clay's look seemed to say. Something strange and brief and almost *friendly* passed between them, but then Brand's stance shifted.

"Hey, Champion?" he said to Claybriar.

"Yeah?"

"Don't ever fucking *pet* me."

Claybriar took his hand away, but the corner of his mouth turned up in a half smile.

"Stupid Seelie cream puff," said the dog.

"Play nice, boys," I said. "And I agree the harp thing is a pretty fucking dystopian solution. That's why I'm looking for another way. And I think you're that way."

"Yeah," said Brand slowly. "I couldn't give two shits what happens to the *sidhe* or their estates, but absolutely nothing good can come of this plan they've cooked up, so count me in to stop it."

"We're going to need some kind of a promise from you," I said, "given the whole Unseelie-monster thing."

"Fine," he said. "I promise you that I will do everything in my power to stop the wraiths from destroying the *sidhe* strongholds—without using that harp," said Brand. "Beyond that, I think I'm going to reserve judgment about how deeply I want to get involved in this Arcadia Project of yours, at least until I've figured out if there's any way to communicate with my Echo other than using you idiots as go-betweens."

"You know, if you ever turn on us," said Claybriar, "I'll be obligated to hunt you down again."

"Look me in the eye," said Brand, "and tell me how scared I look about that."

"Hey, I might not have succeeded in killing you yet," said Claybriar in a dangerous tone, "but don't be under the impression that you've seen my best effort."

"Pah. You're tied to the Seelie Queen's apron strings, but face it—you're more like me than you are like her, and you know it."

The two stared at each other for a long moment, and then

Claybriar turned away, pacing toward a window. Brand's words seemed to have upset him more than I could account for, but I doubted he'd admit why in front of Brand.

"Tjuan," I said, "can you keep taking care of Brand while he's here? I would, but, you know." I flicked Brand on the ear; for a split second his true form *exploded* into the room, forcing Tjuan to stagger to the side, pushed out of place. Then Brand was a dog again.

"Jesus Christ!" said Tjuan. "I see your point. Maybe don't *demonstrate*."

"Sorry," I said. "Anyway, I feel like I can trust you to be careful with him. And, uh, take him for walks or whatever."

"You owe me *huge* for this," said Tjuan. "Manticore huge."

"Yeah, yeah," I said. With a growl of frustration, Tjuan grabbed Brand's collar and hauled him away.

Claybriar was standing at the window farthest from the door, looking out into the dark. I had never heard this kind of rain on the roof and windows of Residence Four; the water's onslaught pattered and crackled in surround sound on all that glass, invasive and intimate and slightly frightening.

I wanted to go to him, but his expression was so dark it made me hesitant. I waited to see if he'd unburden himself, but he just kept staring out at the gloomy weather.

Not knowing what else to do, I left, brushed my teeth for bed, peed and whatnot, gave him some time. But when I came back he was still standing in the exact same spot, with the exact same expression.

"All right," I said to him, closing the door behind me and leaning on it. "Time to talk to me."

31

"Don't pretend to care," Claybriar said, his face as impenetrable as the view outside the glass. "I know I don't matter to you the way you do to me."

"What the hell? This sudden complete lack of confidence is the opposite of attractive, Sir Claybriar."

He fixed me with a simmering look, not in the least amused. "You think I don't know?" he said. "You told me, the first time I ever touched you. The magic doesn't work both ways. I'm just any other man, to you. Any other fey."

"Clay. *What?* Hold the phone a second." I moved closer to him, reached out instinctively, but kept my hand back at the last minute. "You're not just any other man. Just because I don't get high and go make *Reservoir Dogs* when you shake my hand, that doesn't mean you're *nothing* to me. You're gorgeous and talented and sharp and—deep and passionate and—you kiss like a shot of fucking whiskey. Your magic doesn't work for me, but *you* work for me."

If my words had any effect on him, it wasn't evident. Which annoyed me, because I thought they'd been pretty good words. I wasn't sure I could find better.

I exhaled slowly and moved to the air mattress, lowered myself down onto it. A hard thing to do in a skirt without showing Claybriar my underpants, but I was in this conversation for the long haul, so I might as well get comfortable. Maybe a little *too* comfortable. I didn't quite think about what I was doing until he turned and I saw his face change. I'd already released the suction on my right prosthetic and eased my shin stump out of the socket, as casually as I'd slip off my shoes.

I almost stopped when I realized I had an audience, but something new had streaked across the mix of emotions in his face, and new was good. So I just kept going, massaging the circulation back into the skin and scar tissue that covered the asymmetrically tapered dead end just below my right knee.

"I still believe," Claybriar said into the silence.

"Believe what?" I said, moving to my left leg and pushing the release pin on my AK to lift it off my liner-covered thigh.

"In the spirits," he said. "The fauns' . . . gods, or whatever."

"I didn't know you had gods."

"It's what I was talking about before. The old superstition Winterglass taunted me about. I feel like touching you should have cured me of it, the way it lets me—choose, when I see someone I want to—" He raked a hand through his hair, pacing again.

"Slow down, Claybriar. It's all right. Just talk."

He took a deep breath, stilled. "At home," he said, "when I wanted to fuck, it was just, that was everything. I never forced anyone—the Seelie don't. I don't usually have to. But if I ever wanted someone who didn't want me back, the feeling just completely consumed me until I couldn't see them anymore or smell them. It was misery."

I reached for the little bottle by the mattress, slathered up my skin with goo to help peel the silicone liner off my left thigh. "Believe it or not, I kind of get it."

"Since I found you," he said, "it's different. It's a choice; I can choose what to think about. I'm in command of my own mind; to me that's magic. And I thought everything would be like that, but I can't—with the spirits, what I grew up with, it's gotten into me somewhere so deep I can't tear it out of me."

I looked into his face as I towel-dried and massaged my thigh. I was baffled by his manner; he spoke as though he expected me to spit on him, send him away.

"So you have faith in something most people don't believe in anymore," I said. "So do Naderi and Inaya, and they've done all right. I don't judge them. I'm just . . . one of those people who can't make myself truly *believe* something unless everybody agrees that it's sitting right there."

"That's sensible."

"No, it's *necessary*. Because my brain is so fucked up, I can't afford to argue with other people's perceptions. It's all that's kept me between the lines of normality most of my life."

"I envy that," he said. "I wish someone could make me see the truth, so that I wouldn't keep clinging to this—whatever it is."

"Relax about it, okay?" I said. "It doesn't bug me, so try not to let it bug you."

Lightning flashed, briefly revealing the shuddering shapes of trees, and then a harsh clap of thunder sounded. It was such an impossible and almost supernatural sound in Los Angeles that I really wished I'd could go back and say something amazing right before it.

"I mean," I went on lamely, "you're not entirely wrong. There's the wraiths. We still don't know exactly where they come from, or if there are more things like them. Maybe there are good ones too, who don't go around possessing people."

Claybriar turned away, flinching as though I'd struck him, and it sounded a genuine chord of sorrow in me.

"I think that's what's making it worse," he said. "Dealing with the wraiths; they're like a parody of everything I used to believe in. The spirits I imagined weren't like that; they weren't so calculating. They weren't just—Vivian without a body. They were wild. Innocent. Pure. Drifting through the world waiting for something to entice them. Every time we cast a spell, we thought we were reaching out to them, offering something, and when one 'accepted,' it was such a thrill. Spell casting was—well not to be a horny goat about it, but—"

"Kind of like making love," I finished for him. "No, it's a beautiful thought, and I see no reason why you shouldn't keep thinking of it that way."

"Because it's not true!" he blurted, whirling around and suddenly so angry I shrank back from him, even given the distance between us. I must have looked frightened; I saw the guilt flicker over his face.

"I'm sorry," I said, not sure what I was apologizing for.

"No, no, I—" He let out a stormy puff of breath, scrubbing a hand over his face and then raking it back through his hair. "It's just—lies are such a casual thing for you. To others, to yourself. You can just tell yourself whatever makes you feel best, and I wish I could do that, but I can't."

"That's just the thing," I said. "You're a fey; you can't lie. If you were absolutely a hundred percent sure that spirits like the ones your people believe in don't exist, then you couldn't lie to yourself about it, right?" I wasn't sure that was true—Shock had claimed that the king was lying to himself about various things—but Clay was listening with something like hope in his eyes, so I went with it. "And if it might not be a lie, then you might be right and everyone else, even your fucking perfect queen, might be wrong. And wouldn't that be a kicker."

There was a softness in Claybriar now; I'd worn away the jagged edges of whatever had been lacerating him. But he also looked weak and shaky, as though he'd confessed to a murder. My heart went out to him, and I didn't know how to make him feel better, how to take away his shame.

"Want to see me naked?" I said.

He blinked.

I turned my face away with a little shrug. "I don't show people, usually. Which is to say, not ever. It's always lights-off with Zach. But I can show you, right? It's you. I sort of—I wonder what it would all look like to you."

His eyes on me were steady; a strange calm had settled over him. "I could draw you, and then you'd know."

I laughed, unbuttoning my shirt. "Oh, no. I'd be too worried about the drawing falling into the wrong hands. I'll take your word."

I was careful not to prolong it, not to make it a striptease. I took off my clothes as though I were at the doctor's office, shrugging off the shirt and glancing up at him as I reached back to unhook my bra.

His expression wasn't at all what I expected. He was so still, every muscle slack except the ones required to keep him standing. His eyes weren't hungry at all, but touched with something almost like sadness. Not pity though; that would have buttoned me right back up in a hurry. No, there was a kind of humility in it.

I took off my bra, then leaned back on my elbows and hooked my thumbs into elastic, wriggled out of my skirt and underpants at the same time. I used the remains of my right shin to gently kick the rest of my clothes to one side, and there I was, naked on my air mattress, a crazy quilt of scars with three-quarters of a right leg and a quarter of a left one. Drastic weight loss hadn't been kind to my breasts; they sat a little lower than they ought to for their size, and me not even pushing thirty very hard. Below them, slightly asymmetrical ribs were visible—a good portion of the steel in my body had gone to putting them back together—and the skin of my torso was painted, especially on the left, with pale pink whorls and knots and stripes of scar tissue.

Also, I hadn't shaved in months.

"Ta da," I said weakly.

Claybriar walked toward me as though I were a wild bird who might fly away. I wondered if he was going to touch me, and decided that I was okay with it. I hadn't meant for this to be a sex thing, but I was surprised by my lack of disgust at the idea.

He lowered himself to his knees next to me. His expression reminded me of a consumptive from some nineteenth-century novel: eyes all fire and light, cheeks flushed, but dying inside.

"I'm starting to think this was a bad idea," I said, but it came out husky.

Claybriar made no move to touch me, simply knelt there, letting his eyes move over me as though he were, in fact, planning to draw me. Which he probably was, the sneaky bastard.

"If you tell me I'm beautiful," I said, "I will bona fide slap you."

"If there's a word for what you are," he said, "I don't know it."

"Disaster?"

"That'll do," he said. "Hurricane and aftermath, all at once."

I shivered and felt his stillness pass over me like a cloud; his reverence was infectious. I felt the same cognitive dissonance I had when I'd seen the portrait of me he had dropped at the train station in June: a sudden flood of love and respect for someone who was also, somehow, me.

But there was no magic this time. Just the nearness of an otherwise sane man who was genuinely, thoroughly weak-kneed with adoration. I would have let him have me, horns and all, if he could have.

"I do love you, you know," I said. He closed his eyes.

There was nothing but the sound of rain for a little while. It would have been a good time for a thunderclap, maybe a quiet one rumbling along the horizon, but the weather did not oblige me.

"I want to sleep here," Claybriar said.

"Okay."

"Just right here on the floor, at the foot of your bed."

"Okay, Crazypants," I said more hesitantly.

"I'm a faun," he said. "I'm used to sleeping on the ground."

"But you know, this does kind of hinder my masturbation plans."

Claybriar let out a gunshot laugh. "It—doesn't have to."

"We're not quite there yet, Clay."

"Okay. Gotcha. Well, good night then."

"You don't need to . . . wash your face, brush your teeth?"

"Nope."

"Oookay then. Uh, good night." I found the wadded-up mess of my sheet at the foot of my air mattress, straightened it out a little, and then pulled it over me, curling awkwardly onto my side and listening to the rain.

The weirdo actually fell asleep, almost right away. I could

tell by his breathing, audible but not quite a snore. The last few days had been exhausting for everyone, and our conversation must have untied some knots that had been keeping him from proper rest. I waited a little while, then whispered his name a couple times to make sure he was really out. He just kept right on breathing.

And so, because there was no way I was going to sleep otherwise, I quietly carried on with my evening plans.

32

By the time my alarm went off in the morning, Claybriar had already slipped out. Remembering the previous evening, I felt a queasy, hope-laced embarrassment. I got dressed for work and went downstairs; Claybriar was in the kitchen with Tjuan, who had apparently made him a smoothie.

"What are you up to today?" I said to Tjuan, suddenly too shy to even look at Claybriar.

"Writing," Tjuan said. "Now that I can."

"Where's Brand?"

"Still asleep in my room."

"In the afternoon, do you think you can bring him by the studio?"

"No problem."

I had to practically straddle Claybriar to get to the coffee cups behind him; he didn't move away, leaving me to keep the necessary half inch of air between us.

"Hey, Hurricane," he said quietly. The warm smile he gave me washed all the queasy away. "Am I invited to the big intro?"

"Sure."

I grabbed my usual coffee and banana, and when my cab

showed up I gave Claybriar an air-kiss good-bye, smugly uncaring of Tjuan's thoughts on the gesture. Claybriar seemed so much happier this morning, more serene. It pleased me to believe I was a big part of the reason for it.

At work, too late to matter, I utterly nailed everything Inaya asked of me. It almost made me wonder if I could have stuck it out there for real, but I knew myself better than that. My competence tended to come in irregular streaks.

What pleased Inaya more than anything, though, was when I told her I was about to solve the Naderi problem permanently, and that the two of them were going to be closer friends than ever when I was done. I didn't tell her exactly why and how, though—I had no idea how long it would take Naderi to adjust to the massive paradigm shift she was about to experience.

Getting Naderi to stop writing and come meet me at stage 13 for some Really Important News was about as difficult as getting a teenage boy to stop mowing the lawn and come make out with the prom queen. I'd already let Brand and the boys into the soundstage where they wouldn't call any more attention, so it was simply a matter of waiting for Naderi to show up. I stood outside enjoying the autumn sunlight, watching for her, wanting her to see me before she saw them. She came alone in a golf cart, parked it crookedly, and then vaulted up the steps toward me in a way that made me envious.

"Hello," I said with a dopey grin. "Allow me to introduce you to some people who are going to be very important to you in the near future." I opened the door to the soundstage and let her in.

Once her eyes adjusted to the comparatively dim interior, Naderi stopped in her tracks. "What's with the dog?"

Brand had been instructed, under pain of dismemberment,

not to say a word until we specifically cleared him to do so, but at the sight of Naderi he seemed to lose control of his motor functions. He tried to wag his tail but ended up sort of scooting across the floor like a hydroplaning sedan, and then collapsed onto his side, tongue lolling.

"That's Brand," I said. "He's a very special dog, as you're about to find out. This is Tjuan, and this is Clay."

"Hi," said Claybriar. Tjuan just sized Naderi up suspiciously. Only when I saw him looking at her the way he used to look at me did I realize that we'd sort of become friends, somehow.

"What's so special about the dog?" said Naderi, smiling a little despite herself as Brand rolled over onto his back to show off his magnificent doggy bits. "Besides the fact that he clearly hasn't been neutered yet."

"He's magic!" I said.

"Funny."

"No, seriously. Go pet him."

Naderi gave me some pretty epic side-eye, but with a shrug she moved toward the dog, wary.

"Good boy," she said. "Are you friendly?" With understandable caution, she squatted next to him and lowered a hand to his belly, giving it a little rub. As she made contact, she sucked in her breath.

"Oh my God," she said. She paused, breathless, her eyes misting, and then sat down hard. Brand wriggled his way into her lap, and she threw her arms around him, burying her face into his fur.

"See?" I said to her.

Naderi's whole body was suddenly racked with joyous sobs. "What the hell?" she said, muffled by his luxurious coat. "I don't know what's the matter with me."

"I do," I said. "You're happy." I may have gotten misty too, watching the two of them.

After having a bit of a cry, Naderi pushed the dog back so she could look at him in wonder, caressing his ears. "I love him," she said. "I want to keep him."

"He's all yours," I said.

"Seriously?"

"Well, it's complicated—" I began.

But then the dog blurted, "I'm actually much bigger than this!"

Naderi screamed and leaped to her feet, backing up until she hit a wall.

"Don't be scared!" said Brand, cowering against the floor in a submissive posture and looking up at her. I didn't even bother trying to shut him up; too late now. "I'd never hurt you!" he said. "But if you ever need me to hurt someone *for* you I will. I've got really sharp teeth. I'm not actually a dog at all."

Naderi was crying again, this time not entirely joyfully. "What the *fuck*?" she said. "What is happening right now?"

"I wasn't kidding about the magic," I said. "Sorry. Brand is a sort of—mythical creature. A manticore. The whole dog thing is a disguise. But he does belong to you, in a manner of speaking."

"Oh my God," Naderi said. She slid down the wall until she was sitting again. Brand hovered, concerned, pacing like a lion in a cage.

"There's a whole other world," I said. "The hole in the sound-stage floor leads to it. That's what we've been trying to figure out how to deal with. All kinds of shit is hitting the fan right now. There're these things, these wraiths on the loose, and Brand is here to help us stop them."

I'd thought the scenario couldn't get any weirder, but as usual, I was wrong.

Naderi's face suddenly went slack, unnaturally so. I didn't have quite enough time to process the eerie familiarity of that sudden shift before she *lunged* across the floor at Brand and wrapped her hands around his neck.

"Traitor!" she snarled at him.

Claybriar and Tjuan immediately pounced on her, prying her off the confused and terrified animal. Once they'd separated them, Brand slunk over to a corner, letting out a series of hacking dog coughs and telegraphing the deepest, most wounded betrayal.

Tjuan wrestled with Naderi, pinning her arms. "Is there anyone left in the fucking universe who hasn't been possessed?" he shouted.

I buried my hands in my hair. "And I just told that thing that Brand is working for us now."

Claybriar looked Naderi up and down, strangely calm. "How long have you been in there?" he asked.

"Not long," said the wraith, twisting Naderi's face into a chill smile. "But long enough." It turned and spat in Brand's direction. "Just wait until the others hear. You're dead, monster. One of us will find you. We'll make it *slow*."

Brand bristled and stared Naderi down. "And just how do you expect to get out of this place without me? How do you expect to do *anything* without me? You have no idea how much trouble you're in. That's my Echo you've taken over. And she just gave me my memory. *I know your name*."

A look of slow, creeping horror came over Naderi's face. "I—"

"Talk," said Brand. "Tell us everything you've made Parisa

do. Or I will make you wish you had a body that could die."

"Nothing, I swear!" said the wraith. "I've just been waiting inside her. Listening. Until now."

"How did you even get into her?" I interrupted.

"She came to the soundstage," said the wraith. "Alone, until you arrived. She was so afraid, so hopeless, it was easy. I helped her get just a little more afraid, and then she was mine."

"Wait," I said. "You were here when she broke into the soundstage? That's not possible. Both of the soundstage wraiths were elsewhere by then."

"There were three."

"No!" I said. "The first wraith I talked to here said that only Vivian and Teo's deaths pulled wraiths over."

"Only the boy's, in fact. Two of us were already here."

"We? There were *already* wraiths here that night? Why?"

"Just the two of us. Remember that lovely ward Vivian used to hide the soundstage? And the curse hidden inside it, the one that almost killed your little friend?"

I backed up a step as though punched. "Vivian—she—she bound *living creatures* into her spells?"

Naderi laughed. "Stupid girl," the wraith said. "What do you think spells *are*?"

I turned slowly to look at Claybriar, who'd gone pale. Then I looked at Brand. "What is it talking about?" I said to them. "Spells are not *creatures*."

"They're spirits," said Claybriar dully, standing with his arms slack at his sides.

Brand tipped his head at me. "You didn't know that?" he said. "I always figured you guys knew and just didn't care."

"Arcane energy," said Claybriar. "It's alive. All of it."

"Wait, so—spells are—wraiths?"

Naderi scoffed. "Most are only *spirits*. Wraiths are the ones Vivian drew *inside* her. The ones she woke up."

"Woke up from what exactly?"

Brand growled. "She taught some Unseelie spirits this possession trick," he said. "It's changed them somehow."

"Evolved us," said the wraith. "We can think, now, like Vivian did. We have all your human intelligence, all your memory, but you still can't see us or hurt us. We can go anywhere, do anything. We don't die. We'll never die. There's nothing you can do. We'll outlast you."

"Yeah, you're tough," growled Brand, "till someone binds you in a spell or strands you on the wrong side of the border."

"Always temporary. We can wait."

"I still don't understand," I cut in, noticing the acceleration of my pulse. It was as though my body understood before my brain did. "Every spell—Claybriar's drawings, the ward in the hall at Residence Four—you're saying there's something *alive* inside there?"

"Spirits," Claybriar said again. He looked strangely patient now, and a little dazed.

"But how did they get in there?"

"The *sidhe*." Naderi's eyes burned with the wraith's hatred. "You taught the *sidhe* how to remember. They learned our names, studied them, learned writing to lock them down. And they taught the language to you, your wizards, your warlocks. *Sidhe* and humans command us, and we can do nothing. Generations passed, and even the *sidhe* forgot why their magic is so powerful, so dependable. But it was revealed to Vivian, when she was young. They called her mad, and exiled her. And now she has used *sidhe* spellcraft, the masters' very tools, to help set us free."

I stared at Naderi for a long time.

"Claybriar," I finally said. "I need to get to Caryl. Can you and Tjuan find some way to help Naderi?"

"I can help!" said Brand. "I can bind this wraith; I know its name. I'll get it out of her, turn it into a nice ward or something."

"No!" the wraith cried. "Please, not again."

"Cry me a fucking river," said Brand.

"Wards are against the old beliefs," said Claybriar softly. "Prisons for our gods."

"Oh *now* you're keen on the old beliefs?" said Throebrand. "You're not going to tell me what an ignorant animal I am?"

"Shut up," I said. "Both of you. I have to go to Caryl. I have to tell her that Elliott really is alive."

33

I couldn't very well tell Caryl to summon Elliott before I broke the news. All things considered, she took it surprisingly well.

I leaned against the basement wall watching her pace back and forth, fiddling with the cuff of one of her gloves.

"This—explains many things about the way *sidhe* and human spell casting works."

"Such as?"

"The vocabulary. The first word of an incantation is the most important; the rest can be 'paraphrased,' as it were. And one can't cast two copies of the same spell. They've never explained why, but clearly each incantation begins with the name of an individual spirit. The *sidhe* have—assigned us slaves."

Finally she started to cry. I was almost relieved. I tucked my hands between my ass and the wall to remind me to keep them to myself.

"There's no way you could have known," I told her.

She wiped her eyes, then made a forestalling gesture. "I'm fine."

"It isn't your fault."

"I—I doubt most of the *sidhe* even understand anymore." Even without Elliott, even with tears streaming down her face, Caryl seemed to have an ingrained muscle memory of poise that kept her from collapsing completely. "They turn by rote to an ancient archive, their Words of Power—spirit names!—and don't even remember what they mean anymore. This cannot continue."

"Maybe you can learn to do it the way Claybriar does," I said softly. "I've seen him. He just—asks. Like a prayer. I think they come to him because they want to."

Caryl studied me, her teary eyes thoughtful. "I am going to try something," she said.

She closed her eyes, murmured three syllables in the Unseelie tongue, and then opened them again.

"What was that?"

"The first word of the spell I use to summon Elliott. Presumably his name. If so, I have summoned him but not told him what to do."

"Is he here? Can you tell?"

"No," she said. "If he's not bound into a construct, I cannot see a spirit any more than you or the fey can."

"So what's the point? All you've done is trap him."

"He was already trapped, don't you see?" She began to wring her hands. "When I dismiss him, I have no way of sending him back to Arcadia. He will be trapped wherever I released him. Now I've at least made certain that he is nearby, can hear what we're saying. That he knows I had no intention of—"

She broke off as Elliott suddenly appeared on a nearby crate, rustling his wings and blinking his beady iguana eyes. *Appeared.* I wasn't wearing fey glasses. If I hadn't been leaning on the wall I might have fallen over.

"Hello," said Elliott. *Said Elliott*, in Caryl's voice.

Her own mouth hung agape. Elliott's form seemed to

shimmer in and out of existence as I watched, but from what I could see, he definitely looked the same as the construct had through fey glasses.

"Uh . . . Elliott?" I said. "Why can we see you?"

"You cannot," said Elliott, his voice occasionally glitching even as his image did the same. "I have proj . . . llusion to facilitate communication. Unfortunat . . . quite skilled enough to make it clear . . . people at once."

"Elliott," said Caryl, starting to cry again. "I didn't know."

"Please don't cry," said Elliott back to her in that same familiar throaty rasp. He still couldn't seem to hold his form steady. "Do you tru . . . would suspect malice of you? Who knows you better than I?"

"So help us understand," I said to him. "Every spell we cast has a *person* inside it?"

Elliott scratched his scaly chin with a foreclaw. "While certainly dist . . . viduals capable of feeling and thinking, most spirits are decidedly less 'personlike' than I," he said. "Caryl used me to . . . of her cognitive processes, and so they became a part of me."

I tried to piece together what he was saying. "She sort of . . . imprinted you?" I said. "So now you think like a human?"

"A reverse possession," said Caryl. "Instead of entering a human mind, a human mind entered him."

"It changed me," said Elliott agreeably. "But I have helped Car . . . llingly as I would help myself. The distinction between the two of . . . fact a bit fuzzy, after all these years."

"It shouldn't be," said Caryl. "What I've done to you is wrong."

"It cannot be undone," said Elliott. "Do not waste en . . . regret. Let us deal with the situation at hand."

"Which is?" I said.

"I have been trying to find a . . . municate with Caryl since she returned from soundstage 13." He turned his reptilian head back in her direction, glitched out of sight for a particularly long moment, and then reappeared. "I tried to warn you that Tjuan was pos . . . bindings limited my ability to communicate. You also need to know . . . one possessing Stevie right now."

"Wait, what the *hell*?" I said, levering myself off the wall to approach him, as though it would help me hear his fractured speech. "Did you just say there's a wraith in Stevie?"

"Yes."

"How? When?"

"When she disc . . . ka's body. It is the same wraith . . . side Tamika when she arrived here."

This was like talking to ER staff over the worst phone connection ever. "*Tamika* was possessed?"

"Yes. I overheard snatches of her wraith's—'conversation,' I suppose you . . . with the wraith inside Tjuan, when the two humans were near enough . . . other for their 'passengers' to communicate."

"Tjuan's did that same thing with Claybriar's during an interrogation."

"I was unable to linger and listen, as Caryl . . . way elsewhere, but I heard enough to realize that they were planning . . . gether, and to understand that the wraith had influenced Tamika to accom . . . vin here. It was trying to reach Los Angeles to gath . . . ligence inside your organization."

"And once it got there it—disposed of its host. Jumped into Stevie."

"I am not cert . . . the initial plan," said Elliott, "but I do know that the wraiths framed Caryl delib . . . to get her out of the way."

"Why was Caryl such a danger to them?"

"She wasn't." Elliot blinked out for a full two seconds, then returned. "I was."

"Because you're just like them, but you're on our side. God bless you. Can you testify about this to Dame Belinda and Alvin? Especially the whole part about all arcane energy being *sentient*?"

"That presents difficulty," said Elliott. He was suddenly missing a tail. "I know of no way to prove that I am not . . . struct cast by Caryl herself."

"Ah," I said. "That would be a problem, since they're already blaming everything on her. But we have enough pieces now that even if we can't fit everything together into a perfect whole, it's got to at least create reasonable doubt."

Caryl began to pace again. "Our first priority," she said, "even before we decide the matter of my guilt, is to stop the use of the harp. In light of these revelations, Dame Belinda's planned course of action is utterly unconscionable."

"Right," I said. "We're no longer just talking about bleeding Arcadia dry; we're talking about mass torture."

"It will be worst for the most innocent ones," said Elliott. His head floated bodiless for a moment, like the Cheshire cat. Then he winked out entirely. Eventually just his wings appeared, even as his voice carried on. "Those spir . . . never used possession. They . . . memories, and so after a few . . . torture will be all they know, everything . . . may never recover." I guessed Elliott was distraught, judging by how haywire his spell casting had gone.

"Settle down, Elliott," I said as soothingly as I could. "We can't understand you right now."

"Give me a few . . . compose mys . . ." He flickered out completely. How very Caryl.

Caryl smoothed her hair and took a deep, shuddering breath. "The wraiths will act in two days," she said, "which means the harp will be employed sooner than that."

"If we tell Dame Belinda, do you think she'll call off the ritual? She seemed reasonable enough."

Caryl shook her head slowly. "Reasonable, yes, but calling her 'conservative' is putting it mildly, and she has already been asked to accept the existence of wraiths. A leap I don't think she could have made without Winterglass to confirm it."

"Will he help us?"

Caryl stiffened. "Even if he weren't already furious with us for working with the manticore, think about what we would be asking him to accept. What we are asking them all to accept."

Somehow I'd been so fixated on preventing giant holes in Arcadia that it hadn't occurred to me until just this moment that—*best*-case scenario—the Arcadia Project was going to have to make a decision whether or not to continue participating in the trafficking and enslavement of sentient beings.

"Yeah," I said. "There is no way Dame Belinda is going to take this gracefully."

"Go to Alvin first," said Caryl. "He is still grieving and angry, but reasonable. Tell him whatever you feel will not incur further punitive measures. Test the waters. See if we can get him on our side. If not . . ."

I waited a moment to see what Plan B was. But she couldn't seem to come up with one.

"I'll convince him," I said. "I've been talking a lot of people into a lot of improbable stuff lately. Just leave it to me."

"Go now, if you can," said Caryl. "In the meantime, I shall stay here and wait for Elliott to return. There is a great deal I would still like to know . . . and to apologize for."

I checked in with Tjuan first to find out the situation with Naderi. He'd had Brand turn the wraith into a nice, subtle maybe-you-should-go-somewhere-else ward on the soundstage door, and Naderi was recovering in Inaya's office. Also writing, apparently. Charged up by contact with her Echo, she'd already churned out forty pages of new script on her tablet, much to Tjuan's obvious, visceral envy. That was Naderi for you. No time to bellyache about possession or reality being turned on its ear; she had work to do.

There was no way I could meet with Alvin and still have time to attend group therapy that evening, so I used up my last allowable absence and texted the facilitator to let her know I wouldn't be present. I felt a twinge of anxiety about it, especially since I'd left early the week before, and if you wash out of DBT they don't let you back in. Best not to think about that now.

To my surprise, when I called Alvin, he didn't ask why I wanted to talk to him without his boss present. I felt a twinge of hope that maybe his nose wasn't as firmly wedged in her posterior as it seemed. There were a limited number of places we could speak freely about Arcadia Project matters without worrying about other Project people overhearing us, so we ended up meeting at his room in the Omni while he had room service deliver dinner.

"It's just us," he assured me as I settled into the chair opposite him with a Caesar salad. "Dame Belinda's all wrapped up trying to keep the king and queen from killing each other, or maybe making out. French fry?"

"Thanks." I nabbed one off his plate, buoyed by his friendly manner.

"So what's on your mind that you can't talk to the others about?"

"I've been working," I said. "Talking to the manticore in Arcadia, talking to wraiths. Talking to people who know things about things. And I've discovered some stuff that's beyond huge."

"About the revolution?"

"About the reasons for it. It's kind of an everything-you-know-is-wrong situation, and I'm freaking out a little. I thought maybe you could help."

"I'm glad you came to me," he said, and smiled in a way that gave me some much-needed confidence.

"Do you know why the wraiths are rebelling?" I asked.

"Not a clue." He took a bite of his burger. It had avocado on it and looked *really* good. I felt suddenly displeased with my salad but took a few bites anyway before I dropped the bomb.

"The *sidhe* have been doing a really bad thing, Alvin. For a really long time. So have we."

"What kind of bad thing?"

"Casting spells."

Alvin set down his burger. "Come again?"

"Arcane energy is *alive*. It's spirits. People."

"I know the commoners believe that, but—"

"I've talked to the spirits, Alvin. A wraith told me about this, a wraith that used to be a *ward on the soundstage*. I went back to Caryl, and she let Elliott go, and he voluntarily came back to corroborate."

"What the actual fuck, Millie?" I'd been expecting shock, but he looked more wary than anything.

"Apparently most of them aren't quite as . . . clearheaded as the ones who have been exposed to human thought patterns. Vivian let some of them into her brain and imprinted them, made the wraiths."

"Just stop a second," said Alvin. "Forgive my skepticism, but you seem to spend a lot of time explaining things to people who have worked at the Arcadia Project most of their lives. Why is that?"

"I don't know," I said. "Maybe because I'm the only one confused enough to still be asking questions. Or because Caryl hired me right when the shit was about to hit the fan, and threw me directly into the splatter. Does it really matter who delivers this message?"

"It does. I want to trust you, but try to see this from my point of view. Every time I hear your name it's because there's trouble. Do you have evidence? Are there others who can vouch for what you're telling me?"

"Caryl could, but you wouldn't believe her. Elliott could, but you think he's just a spell she's casting. Then there's the manticore, Throebrand."

"Yeah, I'm not keen on chatting with terrorists even if they're not likely to eat me."

"As terrorists go, he's pretty helpful."

"Want to confer with Baroness Foxfeather on that? I spent about three hours last night trying to convince Duke Skyhollow to give her and her people asylum."

"I get it. Brand's done terrible things. But he also knows the true name of every wraith that worked with Vivian. The wraith

I just mentioned? He turned it back into a ward. That's what spell casting is. It's knowing the name of a spirit and forcing it to do your bidding."

Alvin pushed his plate away and rested his elbows on the table. "Even if this is true," he said, "what could we possibly do about it that won't dismantle the entire Arcadia Project?"

"Maybe the Project needs dismantling."

"The fact that you'd even say that shows how badly equipped you are to make these kinds of decisions. Human progress is dependent on the fey, and their progress is dependent on us. But it's a dangerous relationship. We're playing with fire, and the rules are there to keep people safe."

"It's the definition of 'people' that's starting to concern me. In what way does the manticore, for example, not qualify?"

"Even people can sign away their own rights. Those who endanger the Project lose the Project's protection. That's not classism; that's your standard social contract."

"But the manticore has only ever given back what we dish out. When we started negotiating instead of hunting him, he started cooperating."

"But make him mad and he starts *eating* people."

"He's a carnivore. Are you evil for eating a cow?" I gestured to the burger on the table, and resisted the urge to ask him if he was going to finish it. Instead I grabbed another French fry.

"It's turkey, and I didn't eat it to get revenge on it. Some would call it murder anyway, but that's beside the point. My point is, I am basically the commander in chief of the United States of Supernatural. My job is to protect American citizens, not monsters or spirits from another world. I take my job very seriously."

"Does that mean blindly following rules?"

"Why do you assume 'blind'? The rules of the Arcadia Project are centuries in the making, honed by the trial and error of thousands of people. They work, but only if no one decides they're a special snowflake. It's a constant state of emergency martial law, because we're staffed by people even less stable than average, and iron discipline is all that keeps us from war against creatures who can *melt our brains*."

"Fine then. We don't have to break rules. If the rules are meant to be reasonable, let's revisit them. Let's adjust them to allow for, you know, *not* trapping the entirety of a *species* in a big dark room indefinitely."

Some of the tension in Alvin's face eased. "So that's where you're going with this," he said. He ruffled a hand through his hair, his eyes fixed on a random spot on the wall.

"Now it's your turn to try to see things from my point of view."

"I am," he said. "I can see why you'd be concerned. Given enough time, we could probably find a better way. But if we wait any longer, the wraiths are going to go ahead and perforate Arcadia."

"I *have* another plan. Throebrand. He can punish them *specifically*. Summon them one at a time by name, bind them into spells."

Alvin scoffed and pulled his plate back toward him. "Even if what you say about spells is true, that sounds like an impossible project for a fey, especially a fey who isn't *sidhe*. In the wild, even *sidhe* don't have much in the way of declarative memory, and names are exactly the sort of—"

"He has an Echo."

34

For a moment, Alvin seemed taken aback, but then he just exhaled and picked up his burger again. "He wouldn't be the first commoner to say that," he said, turning the thing in his hands to find the best angle of attack. "Around fifteen years ago we let an ifrit through on that pretext, but apparently he just wanted to burn down a nightclub in Scotland." He took another bite.

"It's no trick, Alvin. I've introduced them."

The burger landed on Alvin's plate with enough force to fall completely apart.

"It's Parisa Naderi."

Alvin pushed abruptly back from the table and strode to the other side of the room, putting his back to me.

"You brought *another* uninitiated human to Arcadia?" he said to the wall.

"No, I didn't."

Alvin turned around, eyes blazing. "You are not about to tell me that you brought that monster *here*."

"You saw him, actually. The dog I brought to Residence Four, remember? Take it up with Winterglass, who had his son make the facade."

"I knew it!" Alvin exploded. "I knew that dog was suspicious, and I knew there was something going on with Winterglass. He's been a basket case, and Belinda has no idea why."

"We followed procedure as much as we could," I protested. "Brand got a little training, and he's always been supervised. But we couldn't go through the proper channels, because like you keep saying, there wasn't *time*. It would take months for his entry forms to get approved, if ever."

"It's like a waiting period for a gun. If you can't wait, it's for the wrong reasons."

"Not this time! You have to understand what's happening! Caryl didn't kill Tamika, and you're not going to catch the real murderer unless you let Brand work!"

Alvin's eyes went dead for a moment, and he stood still, taking audibly deep breaths. When he spoke again, his voice was too calm.

"I'll bite," he said. "Who killed Tamika?"

"She was killed by a wraith."

"Who can't possibly be caught, tried, or punished without giving a terrorist free rein. How convenient."

"We *have* the wraith. It's possessing Stevie right now."

"*What?*"

"It doesn't know we know. For once, we have the advantage."

"If no one can see wraiths, how can you possibly know where it is?"

"Spirits are as distinguishable to each other as people are to us. Elliott recognized the wraith in Stevie as the same one Tamika brought to Los Angeles."

"You're trying to say that Tamika was *possessed*?" He ran both hands through his hair, violently, making it stand on end. "*Before* all this?"

"I'm sorry."

"No. Just stop." His face reddened. "I'll listen while you tell me that energy has feelings and man-eating monsters are reasonable, but you do *not* get to tell me that I failed to notice my best friend was possessed by an evil spirit. That I sat beside her on a plane for five hours without knowing it wasn't even her."

"Wraiths have the ability to lie dormant in the—"

"No. Shut your mouth." His hands were shaking now, and he balled them into fists. "Your desperation is showing, Roper; you wouldn't stoop to slandering a dead woman if you had a leg to stand on."

On any other day, his choice of words might have struck me as hilarious. On any other day, I might have been sure it was an accident. But I'll be the first to admit that the last several days had begun to take their toll on my mental health.

There's an interesting phase in dialectical behavior therapy where you've learned to pinpoint the moments where your Reason Mind takes a vacation, but you still haven't quite mastered the art of stopping it. This was one of those moments: like stomping on the brakes as you crest a long steep hill and finding that the lines have been cut.

It wasn't anger this time. I would have given a great deal for anger.

No leg to stand on, he'd said. Because it was understood shorthand for impotence. And that was me; he'd hit the nail square. Without my prosthetics, I couldn't stand. Without my DBT, I couldn't think. Without this tyrannical supernatural cult I'd joined, I couldn't eat. Toss me in the water with everyone else in the real world, and I'd sink like a stone. Good of him to remind me, because for a few days—thanks to Claybriar and a few small victories at Valiant—I'd started to think I was worth something.

I saw him realize what he'd said, too late. I saw a spasm of sickened regret cross his face, but he was too angry for apologies.

"I'm done babysitting you," he said. "Deal with your baggage and your mistrust of authority on your own time, but *deal with it*. Don't bring it to me when I'm trying to keep the world from ending. *This is not about you.* Bigger things are at stake, and this is when all of us need to be falling into line. So *get the fuck in line*, or get out."

I nodded at the floor.

"This is your last chance," he said. "The next time you so much as bruise a rule, the next time you make this situation even slightly more complicated, I'm handing you over to Dame Belinda. And if you think I'm a heartless bastard, just you wait. Just you try to make her feel sorry for a terrorist and a handful of ghosts."

"Understood," I said. My voice sounded strange, even to me. Carefully I levered myself up off the seat. He turned his back on me again as I walked past him to the door.

I'd skipped therapy for this.

As I was walking down the hotel hallway toward the elevators, more aware of my prosthetic legs than I'd been in months, I heard him say my name from his doorway. But I didn't turn around, because I was crying now, and I was damned if I was going to let him see.

"I wish I had a scuba suit," said Claybriar later that night as he lay on the floor next to my air mattress in the darkness of room 6. "Then I could spoon you at least."

I gave a shaky laugh, blew my nose again, and tossed the

tissue in the trash on the other side of the mattress. I had my clothes on tonight; it wasn't warm enough to sleep in the nude even if I'd wanted to.

"I know it's hard to tell," I said, "but just having you here helps. If you really want to be hands-on, though, a scalp massage would be awesome."

Almost before I'd finished the sentence, I felt latex fingers easing through the roots of my hair from behind, careful not to catch or pull. My hair was still damp from my evening shower, which had calmed me a little but done nothing to ease the heavy feeling of dread that had settled in. Claybriar explored the slight irregularities of my skull, the long scar on the left side where they'd put in the steel plate.

"Want to hear something ironic?" I said. My voice was hoarse from crying.

"Sure."

"Nobody really uses steel for surgery anymore."

"What?" He moved his fingertips in gentle circles over my scalp. "How'd you end up full of it, then?"

"Luck." I managed another laugh. "Nah, it was more—they had no idea if I was going to be able to pay. They used scraps and leftovers that did the job at minimal loss. Obsolete stuff they wouldn't have used on anyone who'd filled out insurance forms."

"What the fuck," said Claybriar with gentle indignation.

"The irony is, I had shitloads of money socked away; my dad's inheritance. Most of it's gone now, but paying the bill wasn't a problem at the time, once I was conscious."

"That sucks," he said. "Ever think about having it replaced?"

"That'd make me a much easier lay, wouldn't it."

"That's not what I—"

"I know," I said bitterly. "But I blew all my money on DBT. Plus, there's just so much they'd have to yank out. So many little bolts and pins and—I'm doing okay, you know? Scars fading, a lot less pain. Better to leave well enough alone."

We lay in silence for a while. Claybriar laid the gentlest of kisses at the edge of my ear, turning my bones to jelly.

"You stopped crying," he said. "Doing better?"

"I don't know," I said. "I feel okay right now, but I also don't feel much like getting out of bed in the morning. Or ever."

"There's still time to stop them," said Claybriar, "but not much. They're doing the ritual tomorrow afternoon at one o' clock."

"Ugh."

"I know Alvin hurt you, Millie, but we need your devious brain."

"No," I said. "My devious brain is the problem. I've been reckless and arrogant and stupid. I can't bluff my way through a war; if we're going to stop the wraiths, we need to do it by the rules."

"Since when have you cared about rules?"

"I can't get fired, Clay, I can't. They'll wipe my brain. And I can't get by in the real world anyway; I'm not strong enough."

I waited for him to be a sap about it, to tell me I was the strongest person he knew. That was the boyfriend's role, right? But he just kept massaging my head and said, "By the rules then. Let's find a way."

"My options are basically, what? Talk them out of it? Tried that."

"You've only tried Alvin."

"And Winterglass, but I'm pretty sure we broke him. Going over Alvin's head to Belinda seems like a terrible idea, so who does that leave? The Seelie Queen, and we're basically insects to her."

"Well . . ."

I turned to face him, pushed myself up on my elbow. "You have an idea?"

"She can't be thrilled about having the harp taken off-world. Maybe I could play on that, get her to consider using Brand to trap them."

"You think? From what you told me, she's a crazy tyrannical slave mistress. She's going to trust an Unseelie commoner?"

"She might trust me. I have a kind of—influence with her. I don't use it, because it's not right, but I maybe could, if I have to."

"Have you got dirt on her or something?"

Claybriar looked away. "Not exactly. I just know some of her—vulnerabilities."

"Like what? She have the hots for you?"

I watched his ears turn slowly red, and I was a little too distracted to appreciate the meticulous detail of his facade.

"Clay, have you—is she one of your nymphs back home?"

It sounded ridiculous even as I said it. I almost laughed, but his expression stopped me.

"You've fucked her," I said.

"Millie, don't."

I grabbed his arm, forgetting, startled by his sharp intake of breath and the way the air shuddered as his real body snapped back into being. I released him as roughly as I'd grabbed him.

"You slept with the *queen*?"

He wouldn't meet my eyes. "It's—not exactly—a past-tense thing," he said.

I sat up completely, wrapping the sheet around myself as though I were naked. "You're the queen's *fuck toy*?"

"If you want to put it that way."

"How long has this been going on?"

"A while, Millie. How do you think I got her to listen to me when my sister disappeared? Why do you think she even bothered about it?"

It took me a minute to work through why my hands were shaking. I'd already known that he slept around. But this . . . even before I'd met the queen, we'd talked about her. He'd had a thousand chances to mention that they were fuck buddies, and he hadn't brought it up once. Not until he was cornered. He had *deliberately withheld the truth*, which was the closest fey could come to a lie. Why would he try to mislead his own Echo, unless it mattered?

It hit me like an ocean wave to the face, cold and stinging. And then I couldn't get warm again; all the blood seemed to seep out of my body.

"Well," I said. "It's not like you'd have any choice."

"Millie," he said gently. "Seelie don't—"

"Don't tell me you wanted to!"

He was silent for a moment. "All right," he said.

Of course he'd wanted to. She was the most beautiful and powerful creature in existence; she'd *allowed* it, that was all. And apparently she liked it enough to stick her neck out for his sister. Enough to make him her champion.

And her lover. He was the Seelie Queen's lover. And here I'd thought I was doing him such a huge favor by showing him what remained of my tits.

I came perilously close to throwing up in front of my Echo for the second time in as many weeks. But with effort, I forced my French fries and my feelings down. I found a lockbox somewhere deep in my viscera and crammed everything into it, cauterized the wound with rage, then steeped the smoking brand in ice water.

"Millie, are you okay?" His voice was soft in the darkness. "I thought—I mean we both—neither of us—"

"It's fine," I said. "I just didn't realize—the goddamned *queen*. Okay then."

"You're still—"

"Don't." I flopped back down on the bed, curled onto my side, my back to him. "Please just shut the fuck up immediately. Thank you for your honesty, not that you could help it, but we are not going to discuss this anymore."

I couldn't look at him. Everything I would otherwise have been feeling was so impossibly, lethally vast that its absence left an echoing void. Everything around me, even the sheet clutched in my hand, felt distant. I knew there was a name Dr. Davis would have given to what was happening, but I couldn't remember it, didn't want to think about it, because that would mean thinking about what had caused it.

"Should I—go downstairs? Sleep on the couch?" he said.

"Yeah. I think maybe you should."

35

Claybriar wasn't at the Residence when I woke up just after dawn. I tried to tell myself that I intended to talk Queen Dawnrowan into calling a halt to the ritual, but that wasn't the urgency that drove me, the engine that got me dressed and forced a few bites of breakfast down my throat. It wasn't the reason that David Berenbaum's old house pulled me as relentlessly as an arcane summons, driving out other thoughts. Before leaving, I nabbed a pair of surgical gloves from the box Claybriar had left in my room, feeling as dirty at the sight of them as I would an ex-boyfriend's condoms.

In the cab on the way I texted Inaya to tell her that due to an emergency I wouldn't be in until after lunch. What was she going to do, fire me? I put my phone on silent after that, because I really didn't want to hear her reply.

I wasn't sure what, exactly, I intended. I hadn't thought it through particularly well. Whatever demon was riding me dug in its spurs until the very moment Queen Dawnrowan answered the door, looking almost comically human. Her hair was intricately braided, and I recognized her long knit dress from the Anthropologie website. Cocking her head like a bird, she backed away from the door, leaving it open.

"Where's your translator?" I said. "Still upstairs in bed?"

She looked bewildered and tense, clearly picking up on my mood even as my words sailed right over her head.

"Upstairs," I said, pointing. "Is he there? Is he in your bedroom?"

A light of understanding went on in her eyes, and she murmured something in the Seelie tongue, turning to climb the illusory slope. She paused and glanced over her shoulder; she wanted me to follow. I made my way carefully up the hidden steps behind her, my eyes raking over the elegant curve of her lower back and ass, trying not to imagine Claybriar's hands doing the same. We reached the second story and ducked through the space between the two close-growing trees into the room I'd ruined on my last visit. Claybriar wasn't there.

The remains of what must have been breakfast were spread out on a blanket on the floor: the green ends of strawberries, grape stems, and a bowl half full of sugar cubes. Blesskin was on the unmade bed, burrowing around under the quilt and singing tunelessly to herself. Queen Dawnrowan gestured to her eloquently.

Oh crap. I'd promised to babysit.

"That's—not what I came for," I said. "I need to talk to you. Can you—get inside my head or whatever? So we can understand each other?"

But of course she didn't know what I was asking. Maybe didn't want to know, since it had to be obvious I was balking at fulfilling my promise. Blithely ignorant, Dawnrowan went to the closet and started putting on shoes. Blesskin tumbled out of bed and crawled giggling over toward the blanket on the floor, hair shredded loose from her pigtails.

"You're going for a walk right now?" I said to the queen. "You're going to *leave me here alone* with the rug rat who's supposed to play the harp? You realize, under the circumstances, how strongly tempted I am to stuff her in a box and mail her to Hong Kong?"

Queen Dawnrowan smiled vaguely at me, then barked a single quelling syllable at Blesskin, who was licking the discarded end of a strawberry. The queen spotted the half-full bowl of sugar cubes still sitting on the floor nearby and snatched it up out of Blesskin's reach, placing it on top of the dresser. She said something imperious to me in the Seelie tongue, accompanied by an easily-understood gesture: *Stay here. I'll be back.* And then she waltzed out of the room.

Crap, crap, crap. I pulled out my phone, tried hard not to read the all-caps text message that I knew was from Inaya, and glanced at the time: just after eight. I had five hours to stop the ritual. I stuffed the phone back in my pocket, looked at Blesskin, and ignored the urge to just grab her and flee, lock her in a closet somewhere. It was tempting, but it wasn't as though I had a snowball's chance in L.A. of getting away with it.

"I don't suppose *you* would listen to reason?" I said.

As though in answer, she lifted one of her chubby feet to her mouth and began licking her own toes. Apparently it tickled, judging by her cascade of impish giggles. Yeah, no help there.

The queen had left a few of her possessions in the room, so I kept anxiety at bay by going through them, pretending I was conducting some sort of helpful investigation and not just snooping. Her closet was somehow full of clothes and shoes in her facade's size; how she'd acquired them in the scant hours she'd been here was a baffling-enough mystery to occupy me for a few minutes, but then I was distracted by Blesskin's attempts to climb the heavy curtain at the side of the bedroom window.

"Quit it," I said, and my tone must have conveyed authority even if she couldn't understand the words. She skipped clumsily back to the blanket to examine some grape stems.

The drawers in the bureau were empty, but I found a small bag about the size of a laptop case leaning against it. Inside it was some expensive makeup, a ridiculous amount of candy, and . . . a bunch of Claybriar's drawings.

My stomach flipped when I saw them. The queen carried them around with her? I was at the same time ravenously curious and terrified of what I might find. Some ugly sketch of me, to reassure her? The queen herself, wearing only a fancy necklace?

My thoughts were interrupted as Blesskin quite suddenly grabbed me around the legs, nearly toppling me over. I looked down and saw a knee-high, genderless little brown manikin with vacant, slitted eyes.

"Stop that!" I said. "Let go!"

She did, turning back into a pigtailed preschooler, but now that she had my attention she pointed to the out-of-reach bowl of sugar cubes with one fat little finger.

"I think you've had enough of those," I said.

She read my refusal in my body language and expression, and gave me what I'm sure she hoped was a ferocious mad face, spoiled by her impossibly long lashes.

"All right, what do I care about your health?" I said. "If you will *sit down* on that blanket I will give you one. *Sit.*" I pointed emphatically to a spot on the corner of the blanket and repeated the word several times until she got my gist and tried it, clearly curious to see what would happen. What happened is that I gave her a sugar cube, then slipped on the gloves I'd brought and pulled out Claybriar's drawings, finally getting up the courage to look at them.

Mostly it was sketch after sketch of Los Angeles. A few were scenic, but most were details of everyday things: crosswalks, cars, escalators. Keep-away warnings, laced with his genuine affection for the city and its wonders. This should have comforted me, but I actually felt sicker and sicker as I paged through them. I'd been afraid of finding pornography, but somehow these artifacts of his protective instinct were worse. It was a glimpse into a relationship that predated not only his relationship with me, but my very existence.

Blesskin grabbed me around the legs again, her facade dropping.

"Goddamn it, kid," I said. "Doesn't that hurt?"

The creature only laughed, a chittering, spiderlike sound that made the hair on my neck stand on end.

"Go sit," I said. "Sit, and I'll give you more sugar."

She just looked at me blankly with eyes like chisel scars. I physically pried her hands off me, and once it was only my gloved hands touching her, she was a three-year-old human again. I picked her up under the arms, grunting as my back protested, and placed her on the blanket. "Sit," I repeated firmly, pointing downward. When she complied, I gave her another sugar cube. The distraction served to remind me, though, that I wasn't likely to stop the ritual by mooning over Claybriar.

Blesskin turned out to be relatively trainable; I was able to finish my search of the room just by periodically saying *sit* and gradually stretching out the time she had to remain still before I'd reward her with a sugar cube. But even after I'd combed every inch of the room, there was nothing there that gave me any ideas about how to get Dawnrowan on my side, and I couldn't leave the little lackey-monster unsupervised, for the sake of the house if nothing else.

Eventually I realized I was trapped, practiced some radical acceptance, and went back to the drawings. I thought I'd steeled myself against the feeling of grief that looking through them gave me, but when I came across the one of Winterglass, the one I'd watched Claybriar making, I lost it. I remembered his hair falling over his eyes as he bent over the table. I remembered the way he hadn't even noticed me standing there.

I stared at the picture through tear-misted eyes and tried not to think about the artist. Turn the mind, as Dr. Davis would say, but it was like trying to make a U-turn with a semi. Focusing on the subject of the drawing made me sad in a different way, which was as close as I could come to relief. I tried to reconcile the horrible creature Claybriar had drawn with the tormented man who had tried to save the tsar, who had loved a novelist, who had carried a human child in his arms from Saint Petersburg to Helsinki.

And as though touched by my Echo, I was suddenly bowled over by an inspiration. I laughed out loud.

"Hey, Blesskin," I said. "Do you want to learn a new trick?"

The queen returned in about half an hour, which was good, because aside from the one I'd smuggled into my pocket for later, we'd long since run out of sugar cubes. I left the house to avoid further royal commands and called Tjuan, begging him sweetly to come and pick me up. He sounded icier than I'd heard in months but said he'd do it.

After I'd spent nearly an hour leaning against a palm tree admiring the city below me, he finally showed up in his gray Camry with Brand in the backseat. The dog's presence didn't surprise me; what surprised me was that Naderi was there too. She had a hectic, sleepless look, but her eyes were bright with joy.

"Shouldn't you be working?" I asked her as I got into the passenger's seat.

"Tjuan said he had to take Brand with him," she said. "I'm not letting that dog out of my sight."

"I keep telling you," said Brand, "I'm not a dog."

"Anyway," Naderi went on, "I deserve a break. I've finished scripts through the second season, and it's too soon to write a third."

"She never went home last night," said Tjuan as he drove cautiously down the sloping road. "Normally sleep dep doesn't make for great writing. But I looked at some of it, and *damn*."

Naderi jerked a thumb enthusiastically at Tjuan, addressing me. "Did you know that's T. J. Miller? What the hell is he doing chauffeuring dogs around?"

"A question I often ask myself," said Tjuan.

"Still not a dog," said Brand.

"I know who Tjuan is," I said. "And if he says your writing's brilliant I believe him. So now if you want a place to make all the episodes you just wrote, you've got to help us get your soundstage back."

"What do you need me to do?" she said. "I have to warn you, at some point I will probably pass out."

"Mostly we need Brand," I said. "We need him to summon as many wraiths as he can, and bind them in the soundstage in a form we can show the others when they arrive. But I think your being there will help him remember the names."

"I hate to rain on your picnic," said Tjuan, "but I just talked to Alvin. Brand and I spent half the night making up English names for all of Vivian's wraiths so I could make a list for us to check off, and I'm pretty sure they're planning on doing the ritual anyway."

"No they're not," I said smugly.

"Do I even want to ask?"

"What you don't know can't get you in trouble."

"You're not wrong," he said. "But do not get yourself fired, Roper. I'm not here to lose another partner."

"I promise I'm not planning to break any rules," I said. "I'm probably going to piss some people off, yeah. I'll get disciplined, maybe. But almost certainly not fired."

"Kind of wish you could shave off that 'almost,' but I'll take what I can get. Am I right in assuming you want me to turn right back around and drive to the studio I just got done sleeping at?"

"You *slept* there?"

"I'd like to have seen you pry Naderi off that tablet of hers, or get the dog away from her. Eventually I got tired of her yelling at me and just sacked out in her office."

"I love this man," said Naderi. "He's got a heart of solid concrete."

"So hire him," I said. "Get him the hell out of that loony bin."

"I don't need a writer. I do all the scripts myself, and he refuses to stoop to any other kind of work. I asked if he wanted Javier's job."

Tjuan scoffed. "After I'd just finished hearing him vent about you for ten solid minutes. Unlikely."

"Arrogant bastard," Naderi said. "You won't get a better offer."

"Get a room, you two," I said, then raised a brow at Brand. "Or you three."

"The dog's got better chances," said Tjuan.

"I'm not a dog!"

The whole ride was pretty much like that, but once we got to the soundstage and forced ourselves through Brand's surprisingly potent keep-away ward, we got startled back to business.

Someone had already delivered the harp.

36

I recoiled at the very sight of it. The harp sat on a small wooden platform in the center of the soundstage, not far from the well. What looked like the remains of a large wooden crate lay nearby, as though the sides had been dismantled and the harp left sitting on the bottom.

Its name made sense now; the thing looked as though it had been crafted from some poor creature's spinal cord. Something about it spoke of an arrested moment of violence, as though the victim it was made from had been alive at the time and left an echo of its suffering. It was difficult to imagine the instrument producing actual music, much less sitting around somewhere at the Seelie Court.

"Jesus," I said into the silence.

We all stood and stared at it for a moment.

"Makes sense they'd deliver it during the night," said Tjuan. "Fewer people to get curious about what's in the box."

"Now that I'm looking at that thing," I said, "I can see why it takes some empty-headed critter like Blesskin to play it. Pretty sure any rational being would drop dead or go crazy if they touched it." I turned to study Brand. I wasn't great at deciphering dogs' facial expressions, but his fixed gaze suggested curiosity at the very least.

"Do you remember the harp," I asked him, "now that Parisa cleared your head?"

"I've never seen it before," he said. "I was never close to Court; that was a whole other part of the world. Besides, I was nobody; my mane was hardly grown in. So this is . . . weird. To look at that thing and know *she* touched it—maybe even *made* it—it makes my fur stand on end a little."

Naderi moved to stand next to him, stroking him sympathetically, even though there was no way she could understand what we were discussing. Claybriar had always known what I felt too, often when it made no sense even to me.

Not now, Millie. Don't fall apart.

"That whole legend that Dame Belinda told me," I said. "About the last queen, the war, her suicide. Is all that true?"

"I don't know what your dame told you, but I remember the war. I remember hearing when the queen died. She was a celebrity, you know? Shiverlash—that's probably the best translation of her name. The most powerful siren who ever lived, arguably the most powerful fey. I never saw her, but everyone *knew* of her."

"Was she really a beast? Or is that just propaganda?"

"I only knew her by her politics, and my feelings were . . . mixed. Don't get me wrong; I find the Seelie as frivolous and useless as the next guy, but something felt off about trying to exterminate them just because they were stupid. So when she took herself out of the picture . . . it wasn't entirely a bad thing for Arcadia. But the Accord—the *sidhe* taking advantage of everyone's fear to stage a coup—that was horrible. End-of-days horrible. Unseelie followed their queen's example and killed themselves in *droves*."

"Oh my God. Why?"

"I can't even describe the upheaval. It happened so quickly you barely needed a memory to watch the world change. Somehow in what must have been a couple of days, we went from being on the verge of wiping out the Seelie to being ruled by them. People couldn't cope."

"Wait, ruled by the Seelie? I didn't hear that part."

"The *sidhe*, I mean," said Brand. "All *sidhe* were Seelie back then. They sent us their princess as part of the treaty, and everything went to hell."

"A princess? This part I definitely didn't hear."

"Really? She's what started the whole thing. The Seelie King and Queen were *sidhe*, right?"

"If you say so."

"They were. And our king, you'd probably call him an ogre or something. He fell in love with the Seelie princess, courted her on the sly. Shiverlash found out and went totally batshit, escalated the war to all-out genocide. So ogre-king begged the Seelie princess to murder his wife. That way, by the old rules, she'd be queen instead, right?"

"This actually happened? This sounds more like a fairy tale than Dame Belinda's version."

"I was there. This little Seelie princess, she was going to do it. Kill Shiverlash. Not sure if she had a thing for ogres, or was leaping at the chance to destroy Public Enemy Number One, or just wanted to be a queen without killing her own mom. But her dad got wind of the plan and wasn't cool with giving his daughter away to an ogre, so he tattled to the siren queen, and well, you know what happened next."

"I'm not really sure I do, at this point, aside from Shiverlash killing herself. Did the princess marry the ogre?"

"Yeah, as part of the treaty. Became princess-consort of the Unseelie, turned every bit as ugly and mean as her husband. The first Unseelie *sidhe*. Because all the bigwigs got together and made these rules with the scepters, and about how the thrones can only pass to *sidhe*. Your Accord. Now the ogre-king was a lame duck, the *sidhe* consort got herself knocked up by some Seelie duke, and their *sidhe* son was next in line. Not only was Shiverlash the last Unseelie Queen, but the guy who betrayed her ended up being the last *real* Unseelie King."

"Winterglass isn't Unseelie?"

"Oh I *suppose* he is, technically. He uses Unseelie magic, and so did his parents and his grandparents. But not all fey races are designed to go either way, no matter how many generations deep their allegiances go."

"I thought all you had to do was kneel a certain way."

"Look, if manticores swore themselves Seelie, they would still suck at it, right? And so would their cubs, and their cubs' cubs. Make us as pretty and feathery as you want on the outside; poison and terror are buried deep in our bones. And the *sidhe* . . . they're addicted to beauty, so of course Winterglass can't help but hate the people he rules."

"Sounds like things in Arcadia kind of suck for everyone."

"Everyone but the Seelie *sidhe*," said Brand. "They're the ones who really won that war."

I stared at the harp and felt a strange moment of empathy for the lost Unseelie Queen. Back at UCLA I'd watched my lover-turned-nemesis use his power to undermine me, and it had driven me off a roof. But there my similarities to Shiverlash ended; I hadn't been trying to wipe out an entire population.

I looked around the soundstage as though its contents might

inspire me. There really wasn't much else there, except for a long table and some folding chairs off to the side. They must have brought them in during the night in anticipation of a meeting.

"Brand," I said, "how fast can you go down that list you and Tjuan made and turn those wraiths into wards?

"Charms would work better," he said. "Charms are quicker, and plus, wards are huge spells. I'm no expert on your world, but I suspect if we layer too many wards on top of one another, especially Unseelie ones, really unpleasant things will happen. Get me about four hundred of some kind of small object, though, and I should be able to lock down the whole list in a couple of hours."

"That's about all we have. The ritual is scheduled for one o' clock. But I don't have four hundred of anything."

Naderi moved to the long table and plunked her bag down on it, rifling through. "I've got . . . a deck of cards?" she said.

"That's only fifty-two," said Tjuan.

"Do pages of a book count as separate?" She pulled out a battered paperback: *A Game of Thrones*. "I'm never going to finish the damned thing anyway."

"Hey!" said Brand, perking up excitedly. "That's perfect. Because there's a *sequence* to the names, so a sequenced object . . . yes! Not sure I can hold them on paper for more than a couple weeks, but that should be enough for a demonstration, right? Tjuan, you can even write the page numbers down next to the names on your list! Then we can spend the next few days calling them out one by one and finding better places for them."

Naderi handed Tjuan the book; he flipped through its pages with a wry smile. "Congratulations, Brand; you finally found a way to make this thing grimmer."

"Good idea for a charm, actually," said Brand. "I'll make each page *extra* depressing." He gave a vicious doggy grin.

At first I was excited to see the process of binding the wraiths into the book, but as it turned out, it was every bit as entertaining as secretarial work, and a lot stinkier. It consisted of nearly two hours of droning Unseelie spells by Brand and careful note taking by Tjuan. I couldn't really help with either, so I parked myself at the table with Naderi to play an interminable game of double solitaire. Every so often, when Brand would start to tire, Naderi got up to give him a few pats, and he'd start into the project with renewed vigor. He managed to bind the last wraith into the book about twenty minutes before one o'clock, then immediately collapsed for a nap.

"Are we sure that's all of them?" I asked Tjuan in a half whisper when he drifted near the table, as if anything short of an air horn to the face would wake the dog now.

"He said he's sure," Tjuan said. "Vivian told him about the ritual she did back when she made the wraiths. One represented each day of the Arcadian year, and their names have to do with the days—he tried to explain it to me but it was very . . . fey. Short version—he's sure."

"So now all we have to—"

I'd hardly started my sentence before the cavalry arrived. I'm not sure literal horses would have made it any more intimidating. They came in a pack: king and queen and dame and Alvin, Claybriar carrying Blesskin, everyone talking over one another about the harp in that tense, loud, overly agreeable way that's just a veiled argument waiting to get naked.

I met Claybriar's eyes for just a moment, and my insides went liquid, so I forced myself to look away.

"Hey, everyone!" I said in a sharp enough voice to poke a hole in their conversation. "Great news! We don't have to use the harp after all!"

Tjuan presented the book to Dame Belinda. "Our friend Brand here has bound all three hundred sixty-five wraiths into this book."

Belinda gave Tjuan a long, unnecessarily cold look that reminded me how deeply racist many old white people are, then took a pair of reading glasses from her handbag and opened the book to peer inside.

"Very clever," she said, turning a page forward, then back. Either those were fey glasses she was wearing, or the pages were altered to plain sight in some way I hadn't noticed before wandering off. She closed the book then and tuck it in her handbag, making a muscle in Tjuan's jaw twitch. "And the dog, I am led to understand, is our manticore?"

Naderi, the only person in the room who didn't seem intimidated by Dame Belinda, nudged Brand with her foot, waking him. "This is Brand," she said. "My Echo. He did all the work, spent two hours at it."

"A pleasure to meet you," said Dame Belinda with remarkable aplomb as Brand clambered drowsily to his feet. "Mr. Lamb has told me of you."

"That's all of them," Brand said with a huge, fanged yawn. "Every spirit that was serving Vivian."

"Very well done, all of you." Dame Belinda turned to me, slipping her glasses back into her bag. "Miss Roper, as controversial as your actions have been, it seems that I was correct in assuring Alvin that there must be sound reasoning behind them. We will need to work on enticing you to trust your superiors and proper procedure, but one cannot argue with your results."

Blindsided once again by unexpected support, I glanced at Claybriar. A sad smile tilted his mouth. He was proud of me, even now. I felt giddy with gratitude, and dangerously close to hugging them both.

"I . . ."

"Just thank her," Tjuan whispered between clenched teeth.

"Thank you," I said dutifully.

"Now," said Belinda, turning to Alvin. "Let us have our harpist do her work, and then we can begin the meeting."

"Wait, what?" I said.

"Millie . . ." Tjuan said warningly.

I ignored him. "Why are we still playing the harp? The reason Brand did all this is so that you wouldn't have to."

"It was an excellent plan, and he has done well, but unfortunately as head of the Arcadia Project I have access to information I cannot share, information that suggests more extreme measures are necessary at least for now." She smiled a little, softening her words, but they still carried a discussion-over sort of vibe.

Time for the Hail Mary pass. I sidled my way over to Winterglass, and as soon as Alvin set Blesskin down on the floor, I grabbed the king by the wrist.

His blowtorch eyes turned to me in shock, but after a brief, gentle effort to withdraw from my iron grip he seemed to decide that further physical struggle was beneath his dignity.

"Is there some reason for—" he began in a chill whisper, but Blesskin had already spotted him. Recognizing the man from the drawing, she instantly ran to prostrate herself at his feet.

37

Queen Dawnrowan shrieked. Claybriar reached to catch the queen as her knees went out, and I let go of Winterglass so that the king could rush over to the lady's aid as well. Now everyone was thoroughly distracted by the swooning damsel.

Except for Blesskin of course: the king's newest little Unseelie subject. She was intently focused on me, waiting eagerly, so I slipped my hand into my pocket and retrieved the single sugar cube I'd smuggled out of the Berenbaums' house. It disappeared so fast I'm not sure anyone could have spotted it in my hand even if they'd been looking at me.

"Blesskin!" Alvin of all people finally barked. "What are you thinking? Swear fealty to your queen immediately!"

But of course, Blesskin didn't understand. Queen Dawnrowan snapped something at her too, but, apparently, without arcane compulsion or sugar cubes, there was nothing in the world that could make Blesskin do anything that she didn't damn well feel like doing. Right now she seemed to feel mostly like dancing in a circle and singing a creepy little song to herself.

"This complicates matters," said Dame Belinda dryly. She was no idiot; she was looking directly at me. And I think she'd gotten over being pleased by my initiative. "She's now a member of the Unseelie Court; she cannot touch the harp. Millie, would you care to explain why you have—somehow—sabotaged these proceedings? The why is what concerns me; you needn't explain *how* unless it pleases you."

"We can't play the harp here," I said. "I was worried I couldn't convince you of that, so I did what I had to do. I'm sorry. I haven't broken any rules."

"I will allow this much:" said Dame Belinda, "this is certainly the *least* destructive way you might have interrupted these proceedings. But I do not think you realize how catastrophic the results will be if there is even one wraith still free."

"Did Alvin tell you what arcane energy actually is?"

"The commoners have always believed in spirits," said Belinda. "And while I have no intention of interfering with their religion, I do not adhere to it."

"Can I say something?" said Claybriar.

Dame Belinda turned to him, and for a moment I saw the same sort of distaste flicker over her expression that she had shown when she looked at Tjuan. "Do you feel it would add substantively to the discussion?"

"Since I'm the only person I know of who has converted from the commoner beliefs to the *sidhe* ones, and then converted back? Yeah, I think it would add."

At last Belinda was able to master her sense of outraged superiority and inclined her head to him in patient acquiescence.

"I've been sick about this plan, ever since I heard of it," Claybriar said quietly, his voice almost swallowed up by the great empty soundstage. "I know it's hard for you to understand, because the only spirits you've ever spoken to are wraiths, and they're not great poster kids for a race. But I've spent my whole life in the most . . . beautiful relationship with the best of the spirits. Even when I was 'taught better,' those lessons never quite stuck. I know what I experienced."

"Tell us the truth, then," said Belinda evenly, "as you see it."

"Half of the spirits you're about to trap here . . . they're the ones who least deserve it. The innocents, the very essence of beauty, of desire, of laughter. They're everything that has ever made life worth living, joy given life and purpose. And when you bring them here, they won't know what's happening. They'll forget what it was to move, to flow, to *breathe*. Imagine if you couldn't speak or even blink, trapped somewhere in the dark. Imagine that going on so long you forgot anything else. What would be left of you? And you're about to do that to the most beautiful beings in our world. You can't."

"Well, we most certainly cannot *now*," said Dame Belinda, "as our harpist is currently unable to touch the instrument. But I'll confess that your words are moving, and there are certainly portions of your argument that—"

Queen Dawnrowan didn't let her finish. Possibly the first living being to dare interrupt Dame Belinda, the queen suddenly cried out something unmistakably commanding in the Seelie tongue.

And Claybriar, like an automaton, started toward the harp.

"Don't!" I cried, on my way to him almost before she finished speaking, because I knew what she had commanded. Intercepting him, I locked my arms around him and planted my prosthetic feet in a wide stance that I hoped was more stable than it felt. "Don't!" I said again, but to the queen this time, even though I knew she didn't understand me. "Why would you do this to him? How could you make *him* be the one to destroy his own gods! He won't ever, *ever forget!*"

"Millie," said Claybriar hoarsely. "You're going to have to let go of me."

"No!" I said, looking up at him. The real him, horns and all. "Not a chance."

"She ordered me," he choked out, his strong hands digging into my arms, prying them away. "I can't help but fight you. You'll get hurt."

"Better me than your gods," I said. "I'll understand. I'll get over it. No matter what you do to me, it won't make you not my Echo anymore."

"Let go!" he said, and then shoved me away with a sound as though he were wrenching his leg out of a bear trap. I staggered back a few steps, but managed to stay between him and the harp. As he advanced, I tried to stop him again, but he was too strong, too heavy; all I succeeded in doing was getting myself waltzed backward toward it.

Both Tjuan and Alvin started toward us at a sprint, but it was too late. Clay tried to push me to the side, reach past me to the harp, but I got there first. Wrapped my hand right around its spine.

Which obviously, in hindsight, was a really bad move. But I don't think anyone could have predicted how bad.

I don't know what I was expecting, but being blown back twenty feet by a blast of greenish-purple light and coming damn close to breaking my neck in a near back somersault on the soundstage floor was definitely not it.

There were about two and a half seconds of shock and almost deafening silence; then I groaned and tried to move through the pain and adrenaline that turned my muscles to water. I felt Claybriar's hands on me, but shrank away from them. I squinted, my eyes swimming with spots from the flash, and that was when I saw her, weakly pushing herself up onto her elbows where the harp had been standing moments before.

Her parchment-yellow face suggested a human woman's only vaguely; instead of eyes there were shallow indentations, and beneath a sharp nose and hollow cheekbones an impossibly large, toothless mouth gaped in a silent scream. Black-feathered wings shimmered sickly, like gasoline on water, as they feebly unfolded; each stretched twice the length of her body. Instead of hands and feet, her limbs ended in rubbery talons.

This creature, this siren, this stomach-turning abomination, turned her head from side to side like a snake scenting the air. The awful *wrongness* of her poured over our senses, icy and howling.

I didn't need to ask who she was; none of us did.

"What have you done?" said Winterglass in a strained half whisper.

"Well," I said breathlessly, "I guess we all just found out where the Beast Queen's been hiding."

"She'll kill us all!" Winterglass cried.

"How?" I watched as the siren's taloned arms buckled, sending her collapsing onto her chest. "She can't even sit up!"

But then Shiverlash pushed herself weakly onto her arms again, and she began to sing.

It was barely audible, a broken, breathless hum like a fleeing mother trying to soothe her child. But as soon as I heard the song I fell still, listening—my world narrowed to a pinpoint. There was the song, and nothing else.

We all waited, watching her, except for Winterglass, who paced helplessly, pulling at his hair. I was too busy idling in a soothing mental limbo to even try to work out why he was free, or why he was doing nothing more than pace.

To all appearances, the siren was occupied with trying to remember how her limbs worked. She was figuring it out with a rapidity that would probably have alarmed me if I'd had room in my brain for anything but song.

With a great cry of frustration, Winterglass crossed the room to her and seized her head between his hands.

"My queen!" he said, and then something in the Unseelie tongue.

She stopped singing, her alien face almost seeming to register shock. For a long moment she looked at Winterglass, and then began to make a strange, chittering, coughing sound that was almost certainly a laugh.

The pause in the song returned me enough brain cells to realize that we were in serious trouble, but I was too terrified, disoriented, and sore from my fall to do much more than panic.

Shiverlash said something I didn't even need to translate to hear its contempt, then gave the utterly unprepared Winterglass a shove that sent him toppling onto his ass.

"God*damn* it, Millie!" It was Tjuan's voice. I looked at him; his eyes were wild with panic and rage. "What did you do?"

"How was I supposed to know that harp *was* the goddamned Beast Queen?"

Beside me I heard Brand growl. He started to advance on Shiverlash; I felt a jolt of fear for him and tried to snag his collar as he went by. I missed, but my flailing hand brushed his flank, reverting him for just a moment to his true form.

The Beast Queen's eyeless head snapped up, nostrils flaring. She let out a raptorish cry, and Brand, back in dog form now, stopped in his tracks. Then he hung his head and padded to her side.

"Brand!" Naderi cried. She was crouched on the floor not far away; I'd never seen her look so helpless.

"I'm sorry," said Brand. His tail drooped. "She recognized me as Unseelie. She's old, Parisa, older than I am. I have to—"

The queen let out another cry, and Brand fell silent. He kept his sad brown eyes on Naderi, a caricature of canine apology.

"Shit," I said.

Shiverlash ran her talons over the dog's fur, learning him by touch. Apparently she was as blind as she appeared. They seemed to be in some form of silent communication, judging by the intense focus they had on each other. Something in her posture shifted, as though she had just shouldered a new weight, and Brand slowly turned his head to look all around the room. The siren's head echoed his movements. When Brand turned to face the door, the siren smiled.

"She's going to leave," I said. Then, again, desperately trying to get to my feet, "She's going to *leave!*"

But then she started singing again, and whatever I'd been thinking of trying didn't seem relevant anymore. I relaxed into the ecstatic simplicity of single-mindedness, a kind of Zen peace I hadn't known since the last time I'd worked on a film. I hardly noticed the grotesque, stiff, zombielike shuffling of her gait, or the way she blundered through the side door, shedding feathers. Her voice was all that mattered; everything else was excess weight, and I let it all go.

Until the door shut behind her and I couldn't hear her anymore.

Her magic lingered like a bad smell; it was hard to shake off completely. Even when I remembered that we needed to stop her, I couldn't quite recapture my sense of urgency. My limbs felt sluggish, and without Alvin's help I probably wouldn't have gotten to my feet at all. I turned to thank him, but his euphoria must have worn off faster than mine; he looked like he wanted to *murder* me.

Oh, right. Escaped siren, totally my fault.

38

"No one open that door yet," I said. "Here, at least, we have our wits about us."

I whipped my phone from my pocket and used voice recognition to send a text to Inaya: *evil zombie bird woman loose near stage 13 make sure studio gate locked down before she gets there don't approach she will hypnotize you.* And then I called security. I may have left out some of the details, but I said the word "emergency" enough times that I think I got through.

"Even if we trap her here, so what?" said Tjuan. "What are we supposed to do? When she stopped singing the first time, I told myself I'd fight if she tried again, but fighting it is the first thing you forget."

"I don't have a plan right this second," I said. "But I've bought us some time to think of one. Even if Brand manages to lead her to the gate now, it should be locked down."

"Can't she just hypnotize someone into opening it?" said Alvin. "And what about the people inside the studio lot? We have a massive containment crisis here; there's a wild fey wandering around in plain sight."

"We'll come up with an explanation later," I said. "Special-effects prank? I don't know. Inaya will back up whatever lie we come up with. Right now we just have to keep that thing from getting loose in the city."

"I am the only one who can stop her," said Winterglass. "I am the Unseelie King; she can neither destroy nor command me."

"Are you certain?" spoke up Dame Belinda. "Every version of the story I ever heard says that she could silence even the king."

"She will not try her song of silence," said Winterglass. "Not here. The brief glimpse I had into her mind assures me of this."

"Please explain," said Dame Belinda.

"Quickly?" I added, earning a glare from every royal in the room.

"She cannot see the physical world, only hear it—but she can sense the spirit realm just as the spirits themselves do. The first thing she 'saw' was the book, and the ward on the sound-stage door. She knows that she is in another world, where spirits are prisoners. She would not call them to her and trap them where they are helpless."

"What the hell did she just do to *us*?" I asked.

"Anything with ears, she can render inert," said Winterglass, "but unless you are an Unseelie fey, she cannot command you specifically. So no, Mr. Lamb, she could not order a guard to open the studio's gate."

"And Brand doesn't have opposable thumbs," I said.

"Brand," said Naderi miserably. She hadn't moved.

"Our priority," said Dame Belinda, "must be to contain the situation. King Winterglass, might I make a suggestion, so that we might accompany you and aid you as you attempt to communicate with this creature?"

"Of course," said Winterglass with a slight bow.

"You will have to—temporarily—deafen everyone in this room except yourself."

"Excellent idea," said Winterglass. "If you cannot hear her song, she cannot ensorcel you."

I opened my mouth to object—had we not just finished talking about how spell casting was slavery?—but somehow the words didn't materialize. I tried to convince myself that it was because I knew it was futile, that I had no power to effect that radical a change. I tried to ignore the part of me that was simply desperate enough not to care whether it was right or wrong.

"I consent," said Dame Belinda, "so long as the spell can be reversed once the danger is past."

"I'm cool with it," said Tjuan.

Claybriar stared at the floor and said nothing.

"Just us," said Alvin. "It won't hurt the bystanders to be hypnotized, right? So I'm not down with making people deaf without their consent, even temporarily."

"As you will," said Winterglass. Dame Belinda's gaze on Alvin was decidedly chilly, but he ignored it.

Winterglass directed us all to stand close together, then murmured the words of a spell that made me wish I were deaf already. Bile rose in my throat, and from the expressions on the faces of those around me, I wasn't alone.

"I really hate Unseelie magic," I said. But no one seemed to hear me.

"I THINK IT'S WORKING," Alvin bellowed. "OH WOW, THAT'S WEIRD."

I was still a little rattled from my last hypnosis, so it took me a moment to figure out what was wrong with the picture.

"Uh . . . Morozov?" I said. "Slight problem."

Winterglass turned to give me a look of profound disgust. "Oh, of *course*," he said. "Well I suppose you'd best stay in the soundstage."

"Not a damned chance," I said. "Just find me some earplugs or something."

"Even if there were such a thing lying about, there is not a chance it would create deafness profound enough to protect you from her song."

"I DON'T THINK THE SPELL WILL WORK ON MILLIE," Alvin shouted helpfully. "WE SHOULD LEAVE HER HERE."

"I'm Ironbones!" I said. "If she needs killing, I might be the best person to do it."

"You cannot inherit her throne," said Winterglass, "and therefore you have no power to slay her. She is subject only to the old laws."

"What happens if I decapitate her or something?"

"Your blade would not reach her. This is an ancient, powerful magic."

I took a moment to recover from that dismaying bit of information. "Still," I said. "I'd rather risk getting hypnotized than stay in here with no clue what's going on."

"We waste time," said Winterglass. "Come with us, if you are so foolish, but do not get in the way."

Shiverlash had already managed to stagger a good distance across the studio lot, but finding her was going to be easy enough. A couple dozen nearby crows seemed to have become curious about her and were flapping about like a mobile signal flare as she made her way between the soundstages.

I was unlikely to make good time on foot, and the fey were leery of the golf carts, so without much need for conversation (thankfully) we split into two groups. Tjuan loaded me, Alvin, Naderi, and Belinda onto a cart, while the king and queen followed us on foot, Claybriar right behind them with Blesskin making wild shrieks and whoops on his back, apparently fascinated that she could no longer hear herself. I gave Tjuan directions by pointing, as the shortest way around the buildings wasn't always obvious.

We caught up to Shiverlash just as she'd spotted the studio gate. Thanks to Inaya's swift understanding of the nature of the emergency, the gate was already locked down, and Shiverlash was studying it, one taloned hand resting on Brand's head. All that iron must have been making her bones ache.

At our approach, she turned and began to sing.

Winterglass said something to her in the Unseelie tongue, or maybe even in English, for all I was paying attention with that song shivering through my soul. But he must have been telling her he'd deafened us all, because she stopped singing and let out a hiss of frustration. Tjuan hopped out of the golf cart and beckoned to us. Without a word we advanced on the siren. She started to back toward the gate, but it was as though the iron pushed against her like the wrong pole of a magnet. She found herself trapped and reacted accordingly.

With another hiss, she spread her oily black wings.

"Hey, guys?" I said, futilely. "Do you suppose she can fly?"

Not very well, it seemed. Her wings expanded beyond all physical logic and beat the air until it turned cold and foul, but she couldn't seem to find the right rhythm to gain momentum. A thousand years as a harp and you forget a few things, I guess.

All she could manage to do was wobble around a couple feet in the air and crash back down.

Tjuan, Alvin, Claybriar, and—to my shock—Naderi closed in on her, grabbing at whatever limbs they could reach. Shiverlash hissed and lashed out, knocking Tjuan to the ground, slicing open Naderi's cheek with her talons.

"SHIT!" Naderi cried, putting a hand to her face and then pulling it away in horror as she felt the blood pouring. It was ugly, stomach-turning ugly. Even if she got to an ER right now, she was going to wear that wound for the rest of her life.

"Go!" I shouted at Naderi, waving my arms dramatically to catch her attention, then pointing sharply *away* from the scene, toward the golf cart. "Get out of here! This is not your fight!"

Naderi couldn't hear me but seemed to understand. I saw real fear in her eyes for the first time since I'd known her.

"I'M SORRY, BRAND," she shouted, backing away. "I'LL BE BACK!" She hopped into the driver's seat of the golf cart and turned the key.

Tjuan was already back on his feet, but it was no use. Shiverlash had figured out her rhythm. She launched herself into the air, wobbly but gaining altitude. Still on the ground, in her shadow, Brand let out a bone-chilling howl. Whether because he was being abandoned by his Echo or his queen, it was hard to say.

Shiverlash hesitated, then landed again. Wrapping all four of her grotesque limbs around him, she heaved him into the air and carried him over the studio wall.

"God*damn* it!" I shouted to Winterglass, since he was the only one who could hear me. He was holding Blesskin now; her head was nestled on his shoulder. "What do we do now?" I asked him. "How are we supposed to follow a *flying fey* through the streets of Los Angeles?"

"We don't have to follow her," said Tjuan, apparently free of the king's spell. "There's only one place she can be going; we just have to get there before she does."

I caught up with his line of thought immediately. "Residence Four," I said.

"Why would she be going there?" said Alvin, twisting a finger in one ear as though to clear out lingering traces of magic.

"It's the only route home that Brand knows about," I said. "She's digging around in his mind, right? And Earth is no place for her; she knows it. She just wants to go home."

"To her *throne*," added Winterglass in a dark voice. "I will stop her. Miss Roper's iron may be useful; she must come with me. Viscount Miller as well, since he is familiar with the property. The rest of you, stay here."

"I need to call Phil and warn him," said Tjuan.

"Have him let Caryl out of the basement and give her back her phone. I need to talk to her."

I had never been so happy to hear anything as I was to hear Caryl's voice, even if it did sound a little panicked. No more Elliott; not unless he volunteered.

"Please tell me there has been a misunderstanding somewhere in translation," Caryl said.

"Turn on the news," I said. "I imagine pretty soon there will be coverage of the rampaging winged monster in the streets."

"We must stop her. There may be no choice but to slay her before she gets too far."

"For that we'll need someone willing to replace her. The Beast

Queen is subject to the old laws of succession and, PS, basically invincible."

There was a long pause.

"I need you to accept, Millie, that we may be looking at the end of the Arcadia Project. And by extension, of human progress."

"Yes, thanks, I've started the next Dark Age, it's all going to be so fashionably dystopian. Can we move past that part and start figuring out how to fix it? The Beast Queen is headed your way and is going to try to get home through Gate LA4."

"The best course of action would be not to stand in her way."

"What?"

"If she is in Arcadia, Millie, she is not *here*. Not on CNN."

"But that means we lose Brand. We've got no harp and no Brand. He never got a chance to tell anyone the wraiths' true names; we only have Tjuan's translations. That means every wraith that has ever possessed anyone is free to carry on the plan as soon as Brand's charm wears off. We'll lose the Arcadia Project."

"Now you understand."

"No, I *don't* understand!" I said. "Just—stay there. I'm not having a conversation about the apocalypse over the phone. We're coming to you."

39

Clouds gathered ominously as Tjuan raced down the 10.

"Glad to see you have it in you to drive like this," I said. "Normally you're like somebody's grandma."

"Black men don't get to cry their way out of speeding tickets," Tjuan said. "But I don't put high odds on living through today anyway, so I may as well try to get to the house on time."

The police must have been occupied with reports of a flying monster, because thanks to the relatively unclogged midday freeways we managed to get all the way to Residence Four in just over twenty minutes.

Caryl was waiting for us as Tjuan pulled into the driveway, sitting bent over with her head in her hands on the disgusting wreck of a love seat that rotted there on the front porch. Tjuan opened the car door for Winterglass, then lent me his arm as I struggled my way through the mess of the front yard, which now contained entire tree branches thanks to the recent storm. It was hard not to cling to Tjuan, but I didn't want to press my luck, so I confined myself to a steadying touch on his forearm.

Tjuan helped me up onto the porch, and the two of us remained standing as Winterglass sat next to Caryl. She looked up at him, face patchy from tears. Her lips parted as though she intended to speak, but before she could, he drew her fiercely into his arms. She didn't resist, leaning her cheek against his chest and starting to sob.

"It's going to be okay, Caryl," I said, since Winterglass couldn't lie.

"Please do not wait for me to calm myself before we discuss strategy," she said brokenly as Winterglass stroked her short dark hair. "I doubt I will find calm at any point today."

"We'll get through this," I said. "We've got the king. She can't command him, and he speaks her language. There's still hope."

"By the time she arrives, she may have access to English, as well," said Winterglass.

"From rifling through Brand's mind. God, Unseelie are such jerks."

"Millie!" said Caryl into the king's shirt.

"I shall temporarily deafen Caryl and Tjuan so that the siren has no power over them," Winterglass said.

"Other than to, you know, rip them apart with her razor-sharp talons."

Winterglass gave me a frigid glare. "I suggest we all maintain a respectful distance from said talons."

"Look," I said. "Is there any way we could get a friendly Unseelie successor to Residence Four in time to murder this bitch?"

"The only two Unseelie visiting Los Angeles at the moment are male," said Caryl.

"There's Blesskin," I said. "She defected to the dark side at the meeting. Long story."

"No," said Winterglass. "Even if she somehow managed to kill a creature many times her size, she would be doomed to a grisly death by the next fey with any ambition. She has done nothing to deserve that."

Caryl slowly sat back and looked Winterglass in the eyes. "I will slay the Beast Queen," she said.

Even the wind seemed to hold its breath for a moment.

"Caryl," I said. "Have you lost your mind?"

"Possibly," she said. "But I am, by arcane law, an Unseelie female. The census ward counts me as such. I have killed when necessary to defend myself. I have refrained from killing on many occasions, when I might have. That is, in fact, why the Project fears me."

"Caryl, you're talking about becoming the *Unseelie Queen*."

Caryl looked down at her gloved hands. "If the king does not object," she said quietly.

I wouldn't have thought Winterglass's facade had room to go any paler, but I was wrong. He said nothing, simply staring at Caryl.

"He would have made you a princess, when you were little," I said. "Of course he'll say yes. But this is no fairy tale. You're talking about going back to the *Unseelie Court*, the place you said you'd kill yourself rather than let Alvin and Tamika send you."

"That was before I knew that I could save us," she said. "It is interesting, having access to all of one's most irrational impulses. At times, passion for others, or for an ideal, is a source of strength."

"Forget it," I said. "You don't get to leave me."

"Think of it as having friends in higher places."

As sick as it made me, as much as I hated to admit it, her idea made a kind of sense. I didn't want to see, through my cloud of panic and loneliness and grief, that having Caryl ruling the Unseelie fey would be the best thing that had ever happened to the Arcadia Project. I didn't want my Reason Mind to speak up and tell me that Caryl was right. My throat closed off and refused to let me agree. But it wasn't my decision. And the one person who could have refused, the one person who could have stopped her, was apparently even more besotted with her than I was.

"If it is truly what you wish," said Winterglass, "I would be honored to share my rule with you."

"Fantastic," said Tjuan. "So how exactly are you planning on killing her?"

Caryl hesitated. "I . . . cannot bring myself to use spellwork, now that I know what it is."

I exhaled in frustration. "Well we're fresh out of rocket launchers, Caryl."

Her eyes went out of focus for a moment, and then a look of profound sadness came over her face. "Ah," she said.

"What is it?"

"Elliott says I may use him as a weapon."

"Will he be hurt?"

Caryl shook her head slowly. "Spirits are indestructible. Immortal. But—binding him into a spell of such violence could change him. I . . ."

"Not sure how much time's left," said Tjuan. "Make up your mind, Vallo."

"Even with magic," said Caryl, "I doubt it could be so simple as casting a lethal spell. Surely someone thought of slaying her in this way during her rule."

"How could they?" said Winterglass. "She could call every spirit to her, render any spell caster helpless. Here, though, she dares not use that power. In this realm she is vulnerable, especially if we take her off guard."

"And how do we do that?" I said.

"We must trick her into believing she is in control," said Winterglass. "When her guard is down, Caryl can reach inside her and tear out her heart."

"Elliott can, you mean," said Caryl, her eyes dull.

"How do we get her guard down?" I persisted.

"I will deafen all of you, but you will feign hypnosis if she should begin to sing. That part should be easy enough for Miss Roper . . ."

"You'll cast another spell?" said Caryl. "By whose consent?"

"I do not require consent from my subjects," said Winterglass coldly. "The spirits will serve their king as do the rest of the fey."

Caryl's eyes burned, but she stayed quiet. How cute, their first marital spat.

"I shall begin a negotiation with the siren," said Winterglass. "Wait until she seems appropriately distracted, and then begin your incantation. Quietly, if you please. Her hearing is superb."

"I'm really uneasy about this plan," I said, "on a number of levels."

"Do let us know," said Winterglass contemptuously, "if you conceive of a superior one."

Before I could even think of an appropriately snarky rebuttal, I noticed a strange shift in the light. I eased my way carefully down the porch steps to the lawn and looked up at the sky; what I saw made my skin prickle all over.

The sky was filling with what must have been every crow in Los Angeles.

"Now," said Tjuan. "Stop our ears. She's coming."

The crows didn't wheel or flock neatly like other birds, but swarmed like cinders in a volcanic updraft, blackening the sky.

As they reached us, they made a fearful racket that Tjuan and Caryl were lucky enough not to hear; the lawn under my feet seemed to seethe with their collective shadow.

Then they were on us. Some of them swooped so low that I felt the air displaced by their wings. Backing toward the porch, I glanced behind me and saw that Tjuan and Winterglass had both risen to their feet. I could see the whites of Tjuan's eyes, but Winterglass strode calmly forward. His long black hair stirred in the chill breeze, and his coat flared open, dancing a little. He lifted his arms as though embracing the oncoming disaster. Caryl advanced cautiously at his left hand, standing literally in his shadow.

The Unseelie Queen was approaching from the southwest, in flight just above the treetops. Her faithful hound loped just ahead of her on the ground, cutting across lawn and street and sidewalk as he did so, doing his best to approximate the path of her flight. His coat shone so red, even with the sunlight mitigated by clouds and masses of crows, that I half expected the grass to catch fire as he crossed it. He slowed as he reached the sidewalk that marked the edge of Residence Four, and the liquid, leonine roll of his shoulders as he paced that boundary looked wrong, almost grotesque in a dog. His eyes were dark pools of apology.

Behind him, the siren descended, her great wings sending buffets of frigid air at us as she stretched out her taloned feet to find purchase on the lawn. Then her wings folded, blatantly defying physics as they compressed and tucked against her back.

"Let them hear me," the siren said to Winterglass, in a voice like poisoned honey. "I will not sing. I only need to speak with the iron child."

Winterglass stopped short, looking equal parts baffled and unsettled. "If it will prevent further violence against my allies," he said after a moment, "you may say whatever you wish to her."

Shiverlash turned her eyeless face toward me. "You are the one who freed me," she said.

"Uh, yes." I figured this would be a bad time to mention that it was a deeply undesired accident.

"And you are the one who has been carrying on the work of my champion, Countess Feverwax."

"I— What?"

"Fighting to free the spirits, to end the tyranny of the *sidhe*. You serve the revolution."

It was probably for the best that she couldn't see my look of slack-jawed idiocy. Vivian's voice returned to haunt me again. *I'm the hero of this story. I know I don't look the part.*

Oh my God. At what point had Vivian and I ended up on the same side? Was I completely deluding myself that I was the good guy here? Or had I been deluding myself that she was the bad guy?

In my mind, I heard Vivian's shrieks as Tjuan shoved her onto holy ground, felt the grit that was left of her when I'd finished draining away her essence. Panic rose in my throat, and my nails dug into my suddenly sweaty palms. I could feel myself slipping from sanity, losing my sense of self, of what was real. This was really not the time.

"We need your help, Millie," said the Unseelie Queen, and reached out to me with a taloned hand.

Caryl, of course, couldn't hear what she was saying; she only saw the siren reach for me. In her panic, her caution slipped; even I heard it when she begin to murmur the words of her terrible spell.

The siren snapped a command at her faithful hound.

I had just enough time to see the look of savage fear that pulled Brand's lips back from his fangs as he propelled himself across the grass toward Caryl. She was so wrapped up in her casting that she didn't see him coming. But then he was on her, and her arm flew up to protect her throat as he lunged for it, knocking her down. His jaws closed on her forearm instead, and I saw her body arch with agony; the red of her spurting blood was louder than her scream.

Without thinking I lurched across the lawn and seized Brand, tried to pull him off her, but the moment I grabbed his hindquarters I only made the situation worse; suddenly I was clutching the rear leg of a winged leonine monster. I let him go, and he was a dog again, his head turned briefly over his own shoulder to look at me with an expression of open-mouthed canine astonishment that might have been meme worthy if his teeth hadn't been red with Caryl's blood.

Caryl seized the opportunity to try to commando-crawl toward the porch despite her mutilated forearm; Tjuan was already on his way to intercept her; but I knew that even in dog form Brand was perfectly capable of killing the both of them.

He lunged toward Caryl's jugular and then—for lack of a better word—exploded.

40

I tasted blood, felt a soft hot chunk of *something* slap me in the face. I blinked, eyes tearing from the sting, and saw bits of Brand decorating everything: the tree trunks, the porch, the grass. I can only assume it was Brand, because everyone but him was still where they'd been a moment ago, and everywhere I looked I saw fragments of bone and flesh, fur and organs.

I turned to gape at Winterglass. His face was misted with gore, his eyes wild with malice. I did not have to ask if he was responsible for the carnage.

"Brand," I said, my voice almost lost in the racket the crows made. We'd come here to *save* him.

The mess that was left of Brand was so abstract, so like something from a horror movie, that it might not have even upset me if not for the smell: raw meat and copper with a hint of sewage where the dog's guts had been vaporized.

I leaned over and got sick in the grass, trying to aim away from my shoes. When I'd recovered, I was treated to the surreal sight of Tjuan standing bare chested over Winterglass and Caryl, holding a pocketknife. I wondered if he was possessed, then realized that he'd whipped off his shirt and cut it into strips while I'd been tossing my cookies. Winterglass was wrapping Caryl's arm, trying to slow the bleeding, but we were going to have to get her to an ER soon.

I turned and looked at Shiverlash. She seemed, for the first time since she'd emerged from her enchantment, completely at a loss.

But why? She couldn't harm Winterglass, but why wasn't she shredding the rest of us? Why was she standing there letting Tjuan and Winterglass help the woman who'd just tried to murder her?

And then I realized. Not only had Brand been her seeing eye dog, but he'd been the only one she'd trusted to get her back to Arcadia. She was stranded now in a world where her spirit allies could not help her. She couldn't afford to eliminate anyone she might be able to cajole or command.

"She couldn't hear you," I told Shiverlash. "She thought you were trying to hurt me. That's why she attacked."

Shiverlash turned toward me again. "And because she is bound to the *sidhe*. You understand, don't you, why the *sidhe* must fall."

"I don't understand anything right now," I said.

"But you feel for the spirits. Brand let me see the time you spent with him, learning the truth."

"He—" I choked up a little. Felt queasy again.

"The *sidhe* have no power over you," said Shiverlash, "not unless you allow it. You can lead me home, and I will wreak a vengeance upon these tyrants that will shatter their world. And you . . . your reward will be beyond imagining."

"Oh wow," I said. "Seriously? Okay, just stop." I held up my splayed hands in frustration, not that she could see them. "I am not cut out for the role of Christ on the mountain here. Can both sides just *stop* exploding people and wreaking vengeance upon vengeance for a second? You, especially. You have *no* idea where and when you are, even." I whipped my phone out of my pocket. "What's this thing I'm holding?" I demanded. "What's it do?"

Her nostrils flared; if she could pick up its scent, or see it through my eyes, nothing on her face gave me any indication.

"No? Okay, who's president of the country you're in right now?"

Again, that blank, eyeless stare.

"Yeah, I thought as much. You may be three thousand years old and scary as shit, but when it comes to right here and now, you're a fucking *noob*. So why don't you sit the fuck down and *listen* to the people who know. As a personal favor to me. In return? I promise, you have my *word*, that if you'll do this much for me, I will not rest until I find a way to help your spirit friends. Because Brand was right about that: there's no way in hell I'm okay with carrying on the way we have been."

For a long moment Shiverlash was silent, and I thought maybe I'd gone too far. But this was no Seelie cream puff I was dealing with, and I guess she appreciated tough love.

"The manticore told me," she said, "that you could be trusted. For the sake of one who died in my service, and because I owe you my freedom, I will make this bargain with you. But if you throw in with the *sidhe*, the bargain is over, and I will find my own way to my desires."

Though I strongly suspected we were beyond this sort of damage control, we ushered Queen Shiverlash inside Residence Four and insisted that she stay there until we'd all reached a satisfactory enough agreement that we could return her to Arcadia. In the meantime the house was a beacon, though; the small nation of crows that congregated on the roof was a dead giveaway as to the siren's hiding place. Sooner or later, authorities were going to come looking—police? Animal control? Who exactly was supposed to respond to reports of a flying monster?—and by then we needed there to be no evidence that we'd ever had anything to do with her.

During the agonizing half hour we had to wait for Dame Belinda and the rest to arrive, an Arcadia-friendly paramedic came to stitch up Caryl's arm while Tjuan filled Phil and Stevie in on the current catastrophe. A few gentle questions from Phil—one of the few people Stevie would actually respond to— revealed to us that she'd never had the slightest inkling that she'd been possessed. The wraith inside her—Tjuan translated its name as Qualm—had apparently been in stealth mode until Brand's summons had yanked it to the soundstage, and now it was hanging out on page 201 of *A Game of Thrones*. Tjuan had made a point of remembering the page number, since he suspected that Alvin would want to have a word with Qualm later on.

When Belinda and company finally arrived, Alvin directed them to make themselves comfortable on the couches while the rest of us stood awkwardly nearby, divided into Seelie and Unseelie factions. Absurd that I had ended up on the Unseelie side of the room, but there Tjuan and Caryl and I were, facing down the Seelie Queen's lackeys: Claybriar, Alvin, and of course, Dame Belinda.

You'd think that bringing Shiverlash into such mundane surroundings would have reduced the horror of her presence, and I suppose there was something theoretically comical about it. But in the reality of the moment, the effect was reversed; instead of the IKEA furnishings bringing her down to earth, she seemed to infect them, lending them the quality of an innocuous dream about to warp into nightmare.

"Queen Dawnrowan will need assistance in order to communicate in our common tongue," said Dame Belinda, as though she negotiated with doom-creatures on a daily basis.

"I can translate," said Claybriar.

"No," said Belinda. "For something of this magnitude, and dare I say time pressure, we need her direct words. Her thoughts will need to be brought to order."

Alvin flinched. "You don't mean . . ."

"You have been through enough," said Dame Belinda. "I shall not require you to open a vein. If anyone has earned that unpleasant duty, it is the young woman who placed us in this position to begin with."

"Am I losing my mind here," I said, "or are we all casually discussing letting the Seelie Queen drink my blood?"

"You did swear yourself to her service," Belinda said wryly.

"Surely there's somewhere else you can get blood. Hell, there's a gallon or two of it splattered across the front yard."

"Queen Dawnrowan is of the Seelie Court," said Dame Belinda icily. "The gift must be given consensually."

"Christ," I said. "Fine, I've had worse. Let's get this over with before the cops show up."

It might have been the same syringe they used when I signed the contract, or maybe they had piles of them lying around somewhere. Just a few drops in a glass of water, and apparently that was enough to let Dawnrowan borrow the words from

Claybriar's head and arrange them herself. More importantly, it allowed her to settle down and focus.

Unfortunately, Shiverlash was the one who insisted upon opening negotiations, and she opened them with a demand that all *sidhe* be removed from their thrones and that no further spirits be enslaved in spellwork against their wills. Naturally that didn't go over well.

"That flies against everything in the Accord," said Dame Belinda. "I know you are not familiar with the treaty, but if we break it, there will be open war not only between the Courts, but between worlds. None of us can afford that."

Shiverlash smiled coldly. "None of us?"

"Let's not forget," said Alvin, "that we're your only chance of ever seeing your world again. So yeah, right now? You've got the least resources of anyone here."

"May I speak, before this escalates?" said Caryl. She cradled her newly bandaged forearm against herself, as though all the talk of blood had made her protective of hers. "My experience living in both worlds lends me a bit of perspective."

"By all means," said the ninety-year-old to the nineteen-year-old with all the dry irony one might expect. "Please share your wisdom with us."

Caryl ignored her tone. "Arcadia's reality exists by consensus. The scepters work because at the time of the Accord, all fey were weary enough from war that they agreed upon the way that sovereignty would function. It is entirely possible to *rewrite* the Accord to suit all parties, but we would have to arrive at a similar level of unanimity. That, I suspect, is why the Accord is so seldom rewritten."

"Interesting but irrelevant," said Belinda. "I cannot imagine a compromise that would please all parties in this *room*, much less in all of Arcadia."

"We're going to have to find one," I said. "Remember, all that's keeping our siren friend from trying to end us all is that she thinks she still has a chance of getting what she wants. Peace is not a motivator for her."

"She wants the extermination of the *sidhe*," said Queen Dawnrowan, her eyes sad and magnificent. "Do you expect us to bend to that?"

"The *why* is the key here, don't you think?" I said. "Maybe it's not so much a knee-jerk prejudice as your people's intractable habit of enslaving her friends. And maybe a little bit because her husband cheated with one of you, but I think mostly the slave thing."

"Let us test that," said Winterglass. "If this is truly a matter of principle and not blind hatred, let us bend on the principle without surrendering to malice."

Shiverlash turned to him, nostrils flaring as though trying to scent his ruse. "What do you mean?"

"Instead of removing all *sidhe* from the throne," said Winterglass, "what if we rewrite the portion of the Accord that bars other breeds of fey from inheriting? I am already forced into sharing my power with a monster, after all," he said with a gesture to his charming queen, "so why not install a monster-king in the Seelie Court as well? If we give power to 'the people' on both sides, will that not, eventually, lead to fairer treatment of the spirits?"

"It may," said Shiverlash, looking at the clearly appalled Dawnrowan with a cruel smile. "It may indeed."

"What it would do," said Queen Dawnrowan coolly, her eyes steady on Winterglass, "is saddle me with an unwanted equal, cripple my rule in the way that yours is already crippled. That is your real interest in making this 'compromise.' You will not suffer your rival to enjoy a secure rule that is lost to you."

"You have no way of knowing my thoughts, Seelie, unless I offer them to you. And I have no intention of doing so."

"There is no use in arguing anyhow," said Dawnrowan airily. "Even if I agreed, the Seelie people would never come to a consensus on *who* ought to be king, particularly if you take every eligible *sidhe* duke out of the running."

"Is it not obvious?" said Winterglass. "Your commoners' most beloved hero is already standing directly behind you."

There was a horrible silence. Then everyone seemed to start shouting except me, and notably, Claybriar. I looked at him for the first time since the meeting started, only to find him watching me with a look of fatalistic despair.

"Silence, please," said Dame Belinda. "This is nothing more than a cruel joke."

"It is no such thing!" protested Winterglass, looking mortally offended enough that Dame Belinda fell silent.

"In order for this decision to have any hope of being binding," Caryl said, "we would need consent from Queen Dawnrowan, and of course, from Claybriar himself."

Dawnrowan turned around for a moment to gaze up at Claybriar behind her. Then she turned back to face her opposition. "If I must share my rule to ensure that the Unseelie Court leave us in peace," she said, "then I would be honored to share it with one who has served me so faithfully." The flush on her cheeks spoke volumes, however, about her real reasons, and I felt my hands curl into fists.

Another round of silence.

"Yes," murmured Shiverlash to herself after a moment, smug as a cat. "I *adore* this idea. Let us see how the pet behaves when off his leash."

Alvin looked poleaxed. "Uh . . . did we just get all three monarchs to agree?"

"For markedly different reasons," Dame Belinda pointed out warningly.

"Still," said Alvin. "What was that, thirty seconds?"

"We have heard only from three of *four* monarchs," said Winterglass.

Everyone turned to look at Claybriar.

"Please don't," he said. "Don't make me a pawn in this."

Wrong chess piece, bro, I wanted to say, but couldn't. My throat felt clogged.

"You demean yourself," Caryl said gently. "You are an intelligent man, and a courageous one. The commoners all but worship you."

"I can't," he said.

"Please think carefully before you refuse," said Caryl. "While a strong enough consensus could conceivably overrule even your objection, your agreement weighs heavily. You could make this a reality, Claybriar. Here and now, you could effectively usher in the Third Accord."

Claybriar turned again to look at me.

"What?" I said, and immediately figured out why speaking was a bad idea. When the word came loose, it unplugged whatever had been keeping my tears at bay.

"I won't do this if you don't want me to," he said.

"So you'll, what, let Arcadia fall apart?" Tears streamed down my face; I couldn't stop them and felt like an idiot. "You'll throw your entire world and probably mine under the bus because you don't want to make me cry?"

"Yes," he said softly.

"What kind of a king thinks that way?" I snapped.

"My point exactly."

"Do it," I said. "Go be the Beast King of Arcadia. It's not like you're much use as my Echo."

"*Millie*," said Caryl.

"No, stop it!" I said. "Stop acting like I have a choice. We've stumbled on the one thing in the world that everyone important can agree on, and I'd have to be the fucking Beast Queen myself to stop it from happening. So do it, Clay. Marry your queen. Let these ignorant, elitist assholes try and use you. Just don't tell me not to fucking cry about it."

"Millie." Claybriar this time, gentle.

"Fuck you!" I snapped at him. "Anyone who's not blind or crazy can see why this needs to happen. But most of me is blind *and* crazy right now—so I can't be at this meeting."

I headed for the stairs. As I passed by Claybriar, he reached for my arm, but I shrugged him off almost violently. No one else tried to stop me from leaving, because the truth was, with the scale of everything that was happening right now, I really didn't matter at all.

41

I don't know how long I lay on my air mattress, too weary even to take off my prosthetics. I must have dozed off at some point, because when I heard a gentle knock on my door and opened my sore, gritty eyes, it was dark outside the windows.

I didn't get up.

After a few more knocks, I heard the jangling of keys, and then the door opened. Caryl came in and sat by the mattress, on the side I was facing. Elliott was with her, or my assisted hallucination of him, I guess; he landed on the floor right in my eye line and folded his wings neatly, blinking at me.

"Are you all right?" Caryl said.

"Peachy," I said, not even looking at her. "Where is everybody?"

She probably knew who I meant by "everybody" but chose to answer the question generally. "Arcadia, mostly," she said. "There is much to be done to rally the population to a consensus."

"So he's going to do it."

"He agrees that peace is the most important thing right now."

"How long will that last? I mean, once Shiverlash sits her butt back on the throne, it all comes apart. The only penalty for breaking the Accord is war, right? And for her that's not exactly a deterrent."

"Then we must work on building the power of the Seelie Court and the Arcadia Project so that war with us both *is* a deterrent. We must also do our best to establish more cordial relations with her. And we must not be slow about it."

"I picked a really bad time to sign that employment contract."

Caryl laid a hand on my arm, just above the elbow. I barely had the time to process that she wasn't wearing gloves before she withdrew the gesture.

"What happens now?" I said.

"If possible," said Caryl, "I would like for you to attend my sentencing in the morning."

"They can't still think you're guilty!"

"Shiverlash can ransack the spirits' minds as easily as they could ransack ours. She has removed all doubt as to the identity of Tamika's murderer. For now she proves herself quite useful."

"Then why a sentence?"

"My fate has always been undecided," said Caryl. "Recent events have brought that question to the fore."

"I can't lose both of you to this mess," I said. "I can't."

"You may," she said. "You must stop telling yourself what will be the end of you. You do not know what you can survive until it is done."

"Would you fight harder if I said we could be together?"

"No," said Caryl. "You were right about that. Sometimes I am not even certain that we should be friends. We are both far too vulnerable, and we are both too good at manipulating others. In my case, arcanely, if necessary. And without Elliott, I can no longer trust my—what does Dr. Davis call it? My rational mind?—to pilot the majority of my decisions."

"For what it's worth, I believe in you," I said.

"So do I," spoke up Elliott, giving me a hell of a turn. I'd sort of forgotten that he could *do* that. "And I will always help you, Caryl, if you need it. Just—*ask* first."

Caryl gave him a faint smile. Her practiced smile, the one moved by the strings of her face and not by her feelings. But then the smile flickered. "Do you hear that?" she said.

"Hear what?" I listened and heard it too: the faint sound of footsteps descending the spiral staircase that led down from the room directly above me.

"Phil?" I wondered aloud.

"It isn't time for a shift change," Caryl said. "And the only people who can travel without prior approval . . ." She trailed off, and we both looked toward the open door.

When Claybriar's silhouette appeared, tall and slouching uncertainly in the hallway, Caryl rose without a word and gestured for him to enter, leaving the two of us alone.

"I can't stay long," he said, hesitating just inside the doorway. "But I didn't want to leave for the High Court without—"

"It's all right," I said. "You don't have to—"

"I do."

I sat awkwardly on my air mattress, hugging myself. "Can I ask . . . do you love her?"

He didn't need to ask who I meant. "Not the way I love you," he said.

"Well, that's nice and vague."

"What is it you need to hear from me?"

"Just . . . I don't know. Do you love her more than me? I mean, I'd understand. You've known her so long, and she's—"

"Millie. Do you know why I finally decided to go ahead and be king?"

"So you can boss her around?"

"No. So I don't have to keep living every second of my life afraid that she'll find out how much you mean to me, that she'll go into a jealous rage and order me never to see you again."

"Oh, Clay." I was glad I hadn't taken off my legs, because I had to stand up, to go to him, to put my arms around him and hear his heartbeat, even though I knew it hurt. I kept it brief, to be merciful.

"I won't tell you she means nothing to me," he said when I'd withdrawn, "but you're my Echo, my first and my last thought in everything, always."

I looked up at him, bewildered and teary. "I've never been anybody's first anything," I said. "I was second place to my mom, for God's sake, and she was dead. So . . . it's going to take me a while to believe you."

"Well, hopefully," he said, "we'll all live through this mess long enough for you to take it for granted, maybe cheat on me a few times."

My face burned. "Clay . . ."

"I'm messing with you," he said. "I'm probably not going to be around enough to justify planting a flag on you, even if you didn't have iron bones. When you do decide to whore it up, though, as your king I'm going to demand details."

"You're an asshole," I said.

"You're an asshole, *Your Majesty*," he corrected me, then caught my wrists with his bare hands before I could pummel him. He held them to his heart, pulse against pulse, and kissed me good-bye.

• • •

The next morning I got to the studio a little early, so I could check on Naderi and make sure she wasn't planning to run off and join David Berenbaum at Dead Echo Ranch.

When Javier cleared me to go into her office, I was surprised to find Inaya there. Naderi looked like shit; the whole right side of her face was all bandaged up from where she'd been mauled by the siren the day before. With baffling cheerfulness, she informed me that she'd had fifty-eight stitches.

"This can only add to my legend," she said.

"Have they not . . . do you not know about Brand?" I said.

She waved it away. "They tell me he's dead, but that can't be right. I'm still writing like a madwoman."

I opened my mouth to explain to her that it took a while for the Echo effect to wear off, but I stopped. There was no point in forcing the truth on her here and now while she was badly injured and still trying to work. Eventually she'd come down from the high, figure it out for herself. And when she did, I'd be there. I owed her that much.

"Right now," Naderi went on, "I'm just trying to get as much of the show planned out as I can."

"Then what?"

She looked at Inaya and reached out a hand, palm up. Inaya reached back, gave the hand a strong clasp, and smiled at her old friend.

"Then Inaya won't be trying to run this place on her own anymore."

"You're going to be a partner in the studio?"

"She is," said Inaya. "This gets you off the hook for finding me a new assistant, by the way. I won't be alone here with all these big secrets anymore, so I can replace you with anyone I want."

"What about *Maneaters*?"

"I'll still be executive producer," said Naderi, "and I'll still approve all the scripts, but T. J. is going to help me put together a writing team."

"Tjuan?" I couldn't help but break out in a huge grin. "You put him on your writing staff?"

"I made him supervising producer."

"So . . . does that mean he's no longer an agent of the Arcadia Project?"

"Well, that's the thing," said Inaya. "We're waiting to find out who's going to be in charge here in L.A. We have some ideas about Valiant's relationship with the Project going forward, so whoever it is, we'll need to talk. We've already got the makings of a Gate here—put in some basic housing and we've got ourselves a whole new kind of Residence."

"This sounds cool as hell," I said, "and I've got a ton of ideas that have been rattling around in my head ever since Vivian told me David's dumb idea last summer. Right now, though, I've got to go make sure my best friend doesn't get sent to the guillotine."

"Go save Caryl," said Inaya. "We're not going anywhere."

The meeting took place in stage 13, of course; it was beginning to feel like the Arcadia Project's home away from home. It was a more intimate affair than I had expected: the only people assembled at the long table were Dame Belinda, Tjuan, Alvin, Caryl, and a swarthy man I didn't recognize. His wrists, disturbingly, were bound in heavy iron shackles.

"Thank you all for coming," said Dame Belinda once I'd found my seat. "Now that the imminent danger of Arcadia's physical destruction has passed, our most urgent priority is dealing with the aftermath of yesterday's—exposure."

"Apologies for interrupting," I said, "but who is this?" I gestured to the shackled man.

"Ah," said Dame Belinda. "That is an unlinked facade, in temporary use by the wraith who slew Tamika Durand."

"Qualm," said Alvin, low and icy, his eyes on the facade. "That's what it's calling itself."

"As a wraith cannot be executed," said Belinda, "Qualm's cooperation or lack thereof during this meeting will help determine the precise nature of its punishment. May I continue?"

"Of course, I'm sorry."

"Yesterday, there were far too many witnesses to the appearance of Queen Shiverlash in her true form. We are lucky in that any would-be journalists were too . . . indisposed to make use of cameras. However, there are innumerable eyewitnesses in the city."

"Yeah," said Alvin grimly. "I think the jig is up."

"Containment failure is not an option, as you know," said Belinda.

"May I be permitted to respectfully disagree, ma'am?" said Alvin. "Shiverlash won't be making a return appearance, at least not in that form, and eventually it will just become another urban legend."

"People will investigate," said Dame Belinda. "Combined with other smaller containment failures, it could potentially form a pattern that outsiders could begin to piece together."

"May I weigh in?" I asked.

Dame Belinda turned to me, her piercing eyes scanning me for a moment. "I have mixed feelings about allowing your opinions into consideration," she said. "But you have proven yourself intelligent, if unreliable. Speak, if you will, *briefly*."

"I just wanted to say, maybe this whole secrecy thing could be more harmful than helpful, now that things are so unstable. I don't exactly trust Shiverlash to meekly submit to the Third Accord for another millennium. Doesn't it seem fair that if there's a potential threat to our world's safety, people ought to know about it?"

"Absolutely not," said Dame Belinda. "You speak beyond your understanding and experience."

Alvin spoke up with an air of reluctance. "Proper containment may not be possible anyhow," he said. "As you said already, we have no way of even knowing who all saw Queen Shiverlash without her facade."

"I have been giving this matter a great deal of thought," said Belinda. "I believe that there is a solution. If a significant reward is offered to anyone who can give eyewitness accounts of the incident, we can process those who come forward."

"Process them how?"

"Evaluate them for invitation to the Arcadia Project."

"And if they don't pass muster?"

"Then we alter the problematic portions of their memory."

I couldn't stop myself from protesting, and Tjuan and Caryl spluttered objections as well, but it was Alvin who wrestled himself to the center of attention.

"Absolutely not!" he said. "You have to realize this is going too far. There could be *thousands* of eyewitnesses. Given the chance of side effects from that kind of tampering—most of these people probably have jobs, families who depend on them."

"It is tragic," said Dame Belinda, "but necessary, if we are to keep order."

"No," said Alvin. "I'm sorry, but no. My job is to keep the citizens of this country safe, not willingly mess with their minds to keep my secrets from getting out. What if Millie's right? What if the people are safer if they know? What if this is a sign that secrecy isn't going to work in the Internet age, and that we need to find a new way of keeping people safe?"

"The safety of the people *is* important," said Dame Belinda, "but you may need to take into consideration that sometimes the safety of an informed minority—of the only people capable of making the necessary policy—takes priority."

"We're only an informed minority because we've barred information from everyone else!" said Alvin, rising from his chair. "For their sake, supposedly. Or so I thought."

"Your concerns have been noted, Mr. Lamb, and will be entered into the record," said Dame Belinda. "Please sit down."

"No, I won't. Not until you promise me that there will be no *brain wiping* of thousands of American citizens."

"You have lost control, Mr. Lamb. Please be seated, or leave the meeting. Your input is appreciated, but not necessary."

Slowly Alvin sat down, his jaw working.

"Let us know when you have regained control," said Dame Belinda, "and I shall proceed to our next point of order."

"Go ahead," said Alvin.

"After a great deal of deliberation, I have decided to grant Caryl Vallo a new position as liaison to the Unseelie Court. King Winterglass has arranged for her to be elevated to the rank of duchess and granted a small estate near the palace."

"You're exiling her?" I blurted.

Belinda turned to face me, looking as though the effort to twist her neck in that direction was particularly stiff and painful.

"This is not a punitive measure," she said. "Ms. Vallo has distinguished herself and has received a promotion."

"Have you asked her if she wants this promotion?"

"Millie," said Caryl quietly. "Don't."

"Mr. Lamb," Belinda continued, "will take over for her here as regional manager, provided he can settle himself about the question of containment."

"And if I can't?" said Alvin, sounding suddenly weary.

"Then you will be dismissed from the Project, and I shall send someone from London to take the post."

42

"I would prefer," said Dame Belinda, "to disrupt existing working relationships as little as possible. You have served the Arcadia Project long and well, Mr. Lamb. Please do not let the unpleasant necessities of war sour your outlook on the importance of what you have accomplished. Caryl, your task will be to help keep order in the Unseelie Court and assist in the binding of the Third Accord."

"I do have an idea about that," said Caryl. "I believe the most effective way to ensure security would be to reestablish the Project's presence in Saint Petersburg."

"Let me worry about Saint Petersburg," said Belinda. "Your duties will require you to remain at Court."

"Ah," said Caryl, her face going blank. "So it *is* an exile."

"You have always known, Ms. Vallo, that your time here would one day come to an end. Do not consider me blind to the injustice, and do not consider it a punishment, any more than the citizens of Los Angeles are being punished for seeing a siren limping up Lincoln Boulevard. Our work requires sacrifices, and sometimes it requires the sacrifice of the innocent. In the long run, all that matters is the continued existence of peace and progress. Magic cannot be allowed to go unregulated on this side of the border, and the truth is—has always been—that we have no means of regulating yours."

"I understand," said Caryl.

My fists clenched under the table. I wanted her to fight. I wanted to fight *for* her, but I knew she wouldn't let me. So I guess I was just supposed to sit there and watch everyone I cared about piss off to Arcadia.

"I think I'm going to head home," I said. "Caryl asked me to come for her sentencing, but it's clear I have nothing else to offer to this meeting."

"On the contrary," said Dame Belinda. "I was just about to allow the wraith to speak, and your insights here could be most valuable. Qualm, consider your mandate of silence lifted."

The shackled man at the end of the table looked up at us through his hair and smiled a slow, hungry smile. "Oh," he said quietly. "This should be fun."

"You will confine your remarks to what is pertinent to the proceedings," said Dame Belinda. "You will not torment Mr. Lamb unnecessarily; he has suffered enough."

"What would you have me say, oh Queen of Earth?" said Qualm mockingly. "I can't decide if letting me speak here, in front of so many witnesses, is a sign of courage, or of ignorance. I can't wait to find out."

"Tell us, if you will, why you slew Tamika Durand. Was it on your own initiative? Or were you following the orders of another?"

"Oh, generally we work as a team, but that was mostly my idea, I assure you," said Qualm. Again I was struck by the way all the wraiths' speech carried echoes of Vivian's cadence. It made more sense now, but it still unsettled me.

"And to what purpose did you commit this senseless act of violence upon an innocent?"

"It had nothing to do with her, at all," said the wraith. "That shackled spirit of Caryl's posed a danger to our plans, so we had to get *her* out of the way. Surely that's something you understand, Dame Belinda? In your heart of hearts, don't you want Caryl out of the way too?"

"Rubbish," said Dame Belinda. But her voice lacked its usual force.

"It must be such a relief," Qualm persisted, "to know she'll be tucked safely away at the Unseelie Court now. How terrible it must have been to have her resurface at seven years old, like a drowned body rising when you were so sure you'd tied it down."

The room went quiet as a graveyard. Everyone turned to look at Caryl.

For a moment Caryl was still, the only movement the slow widening of her eyes. Then she began to shake visibly, her ungloved hands curling slowly into fists.

"What is that creature talking about?" she said in a voice like salted ice.

"I haven't the faintest idea," said Belinda sharply. "And I think we've heard enough."

"No, not at all," I said.

"I'm with Roper," said Tjuan. "I think I'd like to hear a little more."

"She has no idea," Qualm said to us in a faux-conspiratorial whisper. "She still doesn't know what wraiths are. How could a woman her age understand that Vivian uploaded everything she was to the cloud, that it will never die?" Qualm turned to Dame Belinda then, eyes bright with malice. "Tell us, Queen of

Earth, to what purpose did you commit this senseless act of violence upon an innocent?"

"Stop!" cried Belinda, losing her composure for the first time since I had seen her.

"*She* abducted me?" said Caryl to the wraith, bewildered and wet-eyed.

"Of course she didn't," said Qualm. "She would never get *her* hands dirty. But she was so afraid of losing her broken king, and she knew people who *would* dirty their hands for her, oh yes."

"Is this true, Belinda?" said Alvin, his voice barely audible even in the heavy silence. "No, don't answer that. Of course it's true; we're talking to a goddamned fey."

"Someone has to make the difficult decisions," said Dame Belinda, her face taking on unhealthy blotches of red. "You have seen what the Unseelie become when they are not bound to the laws of the Accord."

"You had Vivian's ex-lover steal a *baby*?" said Alvin. His eyes were still full of denial, as though he hoped she would say, any minute, that somehow fey had learned to lie.

"One child!" she said. "One child's suffering to save all of us! Would you rather the vultures had circled, taken the scepter from the king's slack hands, and plunged the Unseelie Court into chaos? Hundreds of Unseelie had already been initiated into our world's secrets, and they were held in check *only by the will of King Winterglass* to uphold the Accord. If he fell, any or all of them could have led armies of their brethren through dozens of Gates in the most civilized places of the world!"

"*Civilized*," said Alvin in a strange tone.

"Can you honestly tell me," she persisted, "that it was not

worth the suffering of *one* child, to keep civilization from falling to pieces?"

"Perhaps," said Caryl with deadly calm, "that question would be best addressed to the child."

Belinda placed her hands palm down on the table as though she intended to stand. She did not, though; she merely took a deep, slow breath.

"It is no wonder," said Caryl, "that you can hardly bear the sight of me. How many years have you carried that guilt, all alone?"

"All alone, she *thought*," said the wraith tauntingly. "She had Vivian dispose of everyone who knew, including the last poor soul in charge in this city."

Suddenly Caryl was nine years old again. She spoke in a hoarse whisper. *"Martin knew?"*

"And then, just when it seemed your dame would never get Vivian completely under her control, Ironbones tied off *that* unfortunate loose end. No wonder the dame's so terribly *fond* of Millie's plucky spirit."

"Silence!" Belinda hissed. And the wraith, either because of some prearranged arcane rules, or because it had already done what it came for, obeyed.

Alvin looked at Belinda for a long moment, and I saw the same steel in his eyes that I'd seen when he'd first put Caryl in the basement. I chewed my lower lip, feeling the air in the room tighten like a pulled rubber band.

Reaching into his pocket, Alvin kept his eyes on Belinda and pulled out his phone. He lowered his gaze to it just long enough to find and touch the right number, then put the phone to his ear.

"This is Alvin Lamb," he said when someone answered. "I need to speak with Adam Park."

"Who is Adam Park?" Belinda asked him in the ensuing silence, rigid in her chair.

"My contact at the DHS," Alvin said.

Somehow Belinda forced another half inch of height out of her spine but said nothing, watching Alvin with her wrinkled lips pressed tightly together.

"Adam," said Alvin coolly into the phone. "It's Alvin Lamb with the Arcadia Project. We'll be initiating the Philadelphia Protocol."

Belinda's face blanched. I had never heard of the Philadelphia Protocol, but I had a theory, and my palms went clammy.

"Three Alpha nine Tango seven one," said Alvin. "This is not a drill. I'll send over the paperwork in the morning." With that, he ended the call.

Dame Belinda's voice came out in a pressurized hiss, as though she were in the midst of a painful asthma attack. "Have you completely—taken leave of your senses?"

Alvin remained frosty calm. "As of this moment, the United States Arcadia Project no longer recognizes London's authority. This is not intended as an act of war, but if you fight us, we will fight back. I strongly suggest that you see to protecting your nation and leave us to protecting ours."

Belinda stood with such force that her chair stuttered backward over the soundstage floor. "You've *destroyed* the Arcadia Project," she said. "Whatever happens now is on your head."

"That's a difference of opinion, ma'am," said Alvin, back to his usual easy manner of speech. This time, though, it rang hollow. "As far as I'm concerned, it was on yours the moment you forgot that your job was to keep people safe, even if that meant giving up control."

"I shall call myself a car before you further incriminate yourself," said Belinda. "Our conversation is finished." With that, she swept from the meeting and out the soundstage door with the alacrity of a woman half her age.

As soon as the sharp report of the door stopped echoing through the cavernous room, Alvin seemed to collapse in on himself, leaning his eyes on the heels of his hands.

I answered his unspoken question, approaching him to rest my fingertips on his arm. "You made the right call," I said.

He shook his head gently without taking it out of his hands. "Part of me can't process it. That she'd reach her gnarly little fingers all the way across the pond to steal one of *our* children. But when she said the word 'civilized' . . . somehow that was it. I was an idiot not to see what she was before now."

I wrapped my hand around his arm. "You're no idiot, Alvin. But neither is she. She's had everyone dancing to her tune as surely as that siren. You're just the first one to fight back."

"Unfortunately, I spoke for everyone else in the country," he said, finally looking up. His eyes were blank and frightened as he looked around the room at its shell-shocked inhabitants. "I can only hope that the people under me trust me enough to fall in line. Otherwise we're fucked."

"At the very least, I'm with you."

"As am I," said Caryl.

"Fuck London," said Tjuan.

The wraith sat silently at the end of the table, the expression on its borrowed face impossible to read.

"Caryl," said Alvin, "you're back in command here in Los

Angeles. Tjuan, I'm promoting you to senior agent; you're free to move into your own residence and work without a partner."

"I'm fine how I am," he said.

Alvin looked at Tjuan as though he might be possessed again.

"Let me be clear," said Tjuan. "I'm not turning down the promotion or the apartment. But I'm fine with the partner I've got."

I wanted to slide under the table. "I'm fine with it too," I managed.

On an impulse, I leaned forward and slammed my hand down on the table's surface. It was a cheesy move, but somehow it worked; Caryl was up out of her chair even before Alvin put his hand on top of mine, and soon we'd all joined the pile, united in purpose like some kind of goddamned superheroes.

It was a good moment, the kind I'd learned enough from Dr. Davis to frame and hold on to with all my heart, especially when I knew things were going to get weird soon enough.

The seasons don't turn in Los Angeles the way they do in other places, but there's something about autumn even here, a kind of transparency in the air that's like a tunnel all back through your past. Every fresh year of school, every holiday with your family, crisp as a new apple. I talked about it to Dr. Davis on Tuesday. I talked about Professor Scott, about what I'd say to my dad if I could, about how heavily guilt always weighed on me this time of year.

Because what was I supposed to do, talk about work?

What we did at soundstage 13 didn't take long to ricochet through the Arcadia Project. New York panicked and refused to let go of Belinda's skirts, so the official story was that the New Orleans office had gone rogue and taken Los Angeles with it. Officially we were just a little two-city hiccup in the chain of command that London would attend to when it had the time. But the fey Courts were divided in half now, with half of each Court in our corner, and New York was already playing footsie with us under the table.

Once the United States stood together, and once we teamed up with the DHS to start gently breaking the American public into the idea that there was More Out There than had been dreamt of, we knew for pretty damned sure that every other nation in the world was going to have a choice to make.

Belinda thought all she had to do was cut us off and we'd wither, but London wasn't the only city with deep pockets, and we'd taken one of the richest. Valiant Studios alone was going to make us a mint. And if Arcadia's old guard thought the new king of the Seelie Court would quietly submit the way he had when he was a servant, they were in for a huge surprise on that side of the border, too.

I'd gone into this thing hoping to put down a revolution, and somewhere along the way I'd ended up starting a whole new one. But that was all right. I'd spent most of my life fighting; at least now I was trying to tear down something other than myself. And this time, everyone who mattered was fighting right there with me.

ACKNOWLEDGMENTS

So many people deserve thanks, but I'd like to focus on the ones who didn't get mentioned at the end of *Borderline*.

My first readers for this book: Tori, Brandy Jensen, Charlie Byrd, Stephanie Gunn, and Kristie Matheson. The first four deserve extra credit for reading an unfinished version of the novel—I had not yet written the ending. Talk about a long cliffhanger.

I also owe gratitude to my second round of readers. Autumn Ashbough is responsible for anything I got right about working as an assistant in the entertainment industry, Nicole Lee helped me arrive at a compromise between what a teenager from Hong Kong would really sound like and what would work for an American ear, and Sarah Gailey helped me tune up everything overall (her commentary may have been more entertaining than the actual story).

Thanks to Victor at the Borders in Torrance all those years ago. I still have the angel bear; my daughters take turns sleeping with it. If this book has somehow found its way into your hands, you know why I'm thanking you. Also, write me a letter sometime and let me know how you are.

Gratitude as always to my agent, Russell Galen, who still leaves me a little awestruck, and to Navah Wolfe, who gets this book's dedication not only for her superb editing but for the radiant kindness and strength of her spirit.

Last but not least: thanks, crows, for creeping me out. It was more than five years ago, seeing a flock of you in a gloomy October sky, that made me decide I'd make the next one a ghost story.